# Nebuchadnezzar
# a novel

## Mimi MacFarland

Number 226 Productions

Number 226 Productions

For information, address

Number 226 Productions, a division of Mimi MacFarland LLC

Library of Congress Cataloging-in-Publication Data has been applied for.

ISBN 978-1-7324261-0-8
ISBN 978-0-692-50228-0 (ebook)

# DEDICATION

With gratitude to eleven generations of my family who
have kept their promise to our ancestors, those rebels who
dared to dream of, to sail to, and to settle the New World,
to fight for, and often die for, a republic that would
become known as the United States of America and the
ideals for which it stands. Without their love and sacrifice,
neither I nor this novel would be possible.


And in loving memory of my Darling brother, James

"Then an herald cried aloud, 'To you it is commanded,
O people, nations, and languages.
That at what time ye hear the sound of the cornet,
Flute, harp, sackbut, psaltery, dulcimer, and all kinds
Of musick, ye fall down and worship the golden image
That Nebuchadnezzar the king hath set up:
And whoso falleth not down and worshippeth
Shall the same hour be cast into the midst of a
Burning fiery furnace'"

— The Book of Daniel

# CONTENTS

# ACKNOWLEDGMENTS

Cover: *After the Battle* by Stephen H. Sheldon, U.S. Army Combat Art Program, 1967, Courtesy of the National Museum of the U.S. Army.

Poetry: "Malcolm I remember" and "Now you see the mottled sky" by Craig Kenneth Duncan, 1987, appear with the poet's permission.

*Nebuchadnezzar* was originally titled and copyrighted many years ago as Time Trials, with the alternative title of Nebuchadnezzar. Many other stories and artifacts were written and published while Nebuchadnezzar festered in its persistence. Yet, there have been more people who assisted along the way than there are pages in this novel. This author is grateful to each and every one. I especially wish to thank the Admissions Committee at Long Island University-Southampton (now Stony Brook) for its Fellowship, a literary leg-up for an already aged author, and for its luminaries with their guidance and tough love, in particular: Distinguished Professor of English and Writing at Stony Brook, Roger Rosenblatt, who simultaneously challenged and defended, a man wise beyond words; Vietnam Veteran, Chicago Native Son, and National Book Award Winner, Larry Heinemann, whose masterpiece, *Paco's Story*, intimidated me beyond any hope of completing *Nebuchadnezzar*, until he sat beside me in the sunshine with its pages in rolled between his hands to say, "You have to do this"; Creator of unforgettable contemporary American poetry, William Hathaway, who took the time to review the thing and to provide his amazingly astute insights; and Harvard scholar and critic, Alan Weinblatt whose courageous and gentle editorial hand guided and whose unstinting friendship and support over the years have made all the difference. Author, editor, and publisher Bill Henderson's Bridgehampton perspective put an end to further heartache and debilitating expense with his much-needed dose of *Pushcart* pragmatism. Finally, to the dedicated conservators at the U.S. National Archives and Records Administration, the John F. Kennedy Presidential Library and Museum, and the University of Oklahoma Bizzell Memorial Library all of whom remained enthusiastic and cooperative during the time this book was being researched and written. I thank each of you for ensuring the accuracy of the historical record, and for being kind.

# PART I

# CHAPTER 1

That period of time would become known to history as the nineteen-sixties. We must go back to the beginning, to a time when Bruce Springsteen was just another aspiring musician in New Jersey. We must return to a time when a charismatic president died in our arms. A phenomenon called The Beatles was sweeping the twelve and thirteen-year-olds off their pretty little American feet with songs like, *I Want to Hold Your Hand*, and there was a band that did a lot of Uncle Chuck Berry's numbers; they were rumored in whispers as The Rolling Stones.

At dawn on Monday mornings all summer long, when foreboding mists lifted from the cranberry bogs of the nine hundred thousand-acre tract beloved as The Pines, New Jersey State Troopers could always find several stretches of fresh rubber glistening in the dew on Highway 9. The cops would grow frustrated as the summer months passed because they could only rarely catch a dragster in the act. When they finally caught Randy Pepper, they beat him up good, cuffed him, and made him watch as they went after his prize-winning Hot Rod with their nightsticks. Randy had the misfortune of paying the price for every street racer who had not yet been caught.

By lunchtime, Randy was in jail on criminal charges of resisting arrest and assaulting an officer as well as many misdemeanors claiming that Randy's Hot Rod was out of legal specifications. The whole idea of Hot Rod racing is to modify the cars as severely as possible in order to extract every erg of energy from them without violating the legal limits. That is the cardinal rule of the game. That is what differentiates NHRA Hot Rods from NASCAR cars and FORMULA cars. Hot Rods are street-legal; stock cars are not.

Randy's machine was impounded and towed away by a toothless Piney with a sloppy hook-drag wrecker. The State Troopers had exacted a small amount of revenge for the headaches that seemed infinite in the 1960s when muscle cars were in their heyday. Most street racers had tremendous respect for the Staties. After all, it was the State Troopers who were going to come along one day and find your machine wrapped around a utility pole and your body lying in some unnatural position many yards away. They had to clean up your mess. Who could blame the cops for being pissed?

"Die young and leave a good-looking corpse. Right. Son of a bitch is unrecognizable."


Teenage funerals were gaudy affairs. A limousine conveying grieving confused parents to the cemetery followed the hearse. The limousine was followed by the most beautiful street stock imaginable. There were always at least a hundred cars that turned out for a funeral cortege. The party colors and gleaming finishes of the racing machines resembled a stream of ribbon candy melded in colors of candy apple red, lemon yellow, British racing green, metal fleck violet, and morning glory blue.

In the meantime, the State Troopers would have the toothless Piney drag the dead car off and place it in the center island of a traffic circle near Packim Pond called Four-Mile Circle. Then, in the wee hours of that night after the funeral, the Hot Rods would follow one another, parading slowly like Indians at a Gourd Dance, around and around Four-Mile Circle in a ritual that released a lot more than energy. Most of the energy was spent in curiosity. "Did you *see* that? Bent the frame right in half. Looks like he shot right through the windshield." The young dragsters also expressed gratitude that the dead driver had died on his home turf, doing what he loved, instead of being killed in Vietnam.

# CHAPTER 2

When a given Hot Rod was deemed ready for the track, its driver and his sidekick who rode shotgun made their way along a double parallelogram of narrow one-and-a-half-car-wide macadam stretches that could barely be called roads. Those roads were all that remained of the old wagon routes that led from New Jersey's gleaming beaches through The Pines to Mount Holly, Burlington, and Philadelphia. Pirates and privateers ran molasses for rum before the Revolution, then guns and ammunition for the Patriots. Local folk were called Pineys and they were born, lived out their lives, and died in these woods never having known or cared that any other part of the world existed.

Each Hot Rod could travel alone for miles in the dark pine woods, now and then seeing a white-tailed deer or several. When the racing season was going, there could be more than fifteen hundred cars headed for the same place at the same time. Cars stood aligned at the gates of the racetrack complex for two miles. Which way had *they* come? This was also Jersey Devil country, Mother Leeds' Thirteenth Child, a sore place to be out of gas or lost all alone in the night. The street racers came from all over New Jersey, and from New York, Philadelphia, Delaware and Maryland. They came to compete at Atco Dragway in the Pines.

At the Dragway, drivers would gladly fork over the five-dollar entry fee for the pleasure of racing the quarter mile. In these contests one's fate rested with a slipped shift or a blown gasket. Five-feet-eleven inches tall, sandy-haired, blue-eyed, muscular and angry, David Campbell Adams, three-time Mid-Atlantic States Champion of the National Hot Rod Association, was returning to the pits. He was not at all satisfied with the evening's first run.

Racecar drivers must have pits. They are temporary working places where a sidekick or a pit crew can quickly change a tire or adjust a carburetor, and are maintained at a slight angle to the racetrack for easy access by the drivers. Observing the drivers and pit workers with their cars was entertainment for the thousand or so people occupying an invariably packed grandstand. Wagering, though illegal, was fierce. If one dragster asks another dragster, "How's it hangin'?" And the reply is, "The pits, man," that means that the driver in the pits is pulled over for some kind of maintenance or breakdown and is not on the road. For a dragster, being on the road is the ideal place to be and that is usually expressed as, "Boss."

As he approached his slot along the row of pits, David was thinking about his absent sidekick, Dieter, and he was thinking again about giving up the metallic blue Chevy for a Dodge. But, as David pulled into his slot, he was distracted from the smells of gas and oil and burnt rubber, the cheers of the crowd, the squeal of oversized tires, and the constant revving of hugely powerful engines. He was momentarily distracted from the thrill of the spectacle that is Hot Rod racing. The setting sun was casting its final orange glow against the gloomier darkening forests of The New Jersey Pine Barrens. David took comfort in a different kind of thrill, the thrill of all that orange light refracted thousands of times by highly polished mirrors and chrome and gleaming lacquer finishes in a psychedelic rainbow of color. And the boom and twang of Duane Eddy's *Rebel Rouser* crackled over the loud speakers between races.

Women were not entirely unknown at the track, but they were rarely taken seriously. It was a certainty that, aside from the famous NHRA National Champion, Cha-Cha Muldowney, any woman at the track was not the least bit feminine, or even good-looking. David had to admit that the woman who was working in the pit next to him really had a cute butt. But the rest of her was hanging over the fender working with a sparkplug gauge deep inside the hood of cherry red 1953 Mercury. David would never have suspected that the little woman was not the sidekick, she was the driver.

David brought his slender body madly flying out the Chevy door and slammed the chocks beneath the wheels, preparing to raise the hood to investigate. He looked for the blown seal which was the culprit he suspected, the cause of the sudden loss of compression that had just proved so disastrous in his most recent run. The Chevy was quickly making its way to the elephant's graveyard. David lay on the ground beneath the Chevy. He was trying to hold his light and follow a drop of oil back to its forbidden source. He kept banging his elbow every time he tried to move the light, which kept him thinking Dieter is useless, he's never around when I really need him.

The magnificent roar of the crowd and the scream of the engines and the loud mumble coming from the loud speakers meant that it was time for the next run. Racers in the pits and viewers in the grandstands stopped whatever they were doing to pay their undivided attention (hands over ears) to the two drivers whose vehicles were throwing flames, burning rubber in place, and just roaring and chomping like two huge animals for their freedom to chase one another straight to the finish line. The green light. Thick black smoke of burnt rubber wafted past the nostrils, sometimes burned the eyes.

Ah, bad luck! The driver of the white Ford banged third gear and missed the crucial timing for the shift into fourth. The black Ford opposing ran away with the race and would be meeting all comers in the final heat for 240s. The next two cars were already situated for their run.

David let out a deep sigh and returned to tracking the telltale spewed oil that would lead him back to where the seal blew. He was thinking that it had been a bad day at the track. So many little twisters had come along in this day's racing. The yellow '48 MGB Roadster had already caught fire under the hood; that took several minutes with extinguishers to put out and would cost its owner a fortune and the rest of the racing season. Another driver's gearshift came off in his hand leaving the car to the quarter mile in second gear, the driver getting laughs from the crowd and whiplash trying to stop the car. About the time David was getting a little greasy again and thinking that it might not all be coincidence, thinking that perhaps they were all beginning to get a little sloppy, and wondering where it all might end, and knowing that it might all end with a bad crack-up like the one they had six years ago there came again the screaming of the crowds, the screaming of the engines, the bellowing from the tower. David stopped working and turned his attention to the track. He was standing in front of the hood of his Chevy with a torque wrench dangling loosely in his hand. But David never saw the race.

David's attention was diverted to the lovely tomboy who was cheering loudly and jumping up and down a few feet from where he stood. Her breasts were bouncing, smallish and taut beneath a baggy yellow sweatshirt with the sleeves ripped off. Her pretty heart-shaped rear end didn't jiggle at all in faded Levi's. She was flashing a big smile with straight white teeth and burgundy lips, deep set sparkling gray-blue eyes, a slightly snobbish nose and a face full of freckles. The last of the sun glinted on her bright gold hair, not quite red enough to be a real strawberry blonde and definitely not yellow. The curls in that ponytail must have been three feet long, fat, bouncy curls like Al Capp's sweetheart, Daisy Mae.

David's Adam's apple wanted to bob a little up and down, but was somehow stuck. He tried to pull his attention back to the race, or even back to his Chevy, but he could not. What was she? Where had she come from? Then a tall golden man, a little taller than David, a little heavier than he stepped into David's line of sight. What on Earth, David wondered, is she doing with *him*? Paul, the other man, was Darling's older brother and he pretended not to notice dumbstruck David.

David asked himself, "Shall we say hello?" Himself replied, "What if that's her old man?" David's penis interjected, "Go on, did you ever see such a lay in your life?" David said to himself, "All we want to do is say hello." David's penis replied, "Wanna bet?"

Paul replaced the Mercury's last two spark plug wires and slammed the hood down with a quick swipe of his fingerprints with his hand-rag saying, "All set Darling, let's try her out now."

Darling jumped into the driver's seat. Her brother stood at their pit-gate and watched as she backed the Merc out of its pit and rumbled away down the access lane to get a place in one of the two lines that were forming for the Friday evening round robin.

David worked on his car and pretended to pay no more attention to the round robin than he ever did. But he was peeking, first under his left arm and then under his right, watching the cherry red '53 Mercury blow the doors off a bright orange '57 Chevy sedan. David was certain the little mystery driver would be smiling. He smiled for her success then returned to arguing with himself. This is going to have to be it. Dieter is fired. *Fired!* Dieter doesn't even get paid; you can never get rid of him.

Paul stepped into David's view; he began bluntly enough, "So you like my little sister."

David's mind shattered for an instant with, just my fucking luck! But he calmly extended his right hand and said, "How do you do? My name is Dave Adams."

"Paul Randolph."

The two men shook hands. The hands were rag clean, a custom familiar to them, and both hands were very strong.

# CHAPTER 3

With full headlights, Darling pulled the Mercury onto the narrow strip of rough macadam that would lead them to a main road toward home. Darling did not like this time of growing evening in The Pines. She tried hard not to think about the foolish fears that faithfully descended with the night in these parts. People, not uncommonly, disappeared in these woods never to be seen or heard from again. Darling's fears would grow worse even later when the fogs settled in. She did not want to think about it. She drove on. She wanted to get to a main, a lighted, road. Darling chose a subject to distract herself, so shoved Paul in the shoulder and giggled, "Well?"

"Well what?"

"Well, who is he? What's his name?"

"Oh, you saw him."

"Of course I saw him. Come on Paul, what's his name?"

"Dave."

"Dave What?"

"Dave Adams."

"He likes me, doesn't he? Come on Paul, he likes me, doesn't he?"

"Seems like it."

"Neat!"

"What's so neat about it?"

"Well you like him, don't you Paul? He's a *champion* driver."

"Now hold on there. I only shook the man's hand. He *was* a champion driver."

"Yeah, but you wouldn't even have said hello to him if you didn't think you were going to like him. I think he's nice. He wasn't looking at me like other guys do."

"And how is that?"

"Like they're trying to undress me."

7

"Shows you what a great judge of character you are. Besides, you don't even know the guy. Neither do I." Paul sometimes wondered why Darling, with so much going for her, could be such a screwball. "Watch it! Try and keep this damned thing on the road will ya?"

"Sorry." Darling tugged at the steering wheel of the little red car, which she had gradually allowed to wander until the right front tire was almost entirely onto the shoulder of the road. The shoulder of this particular road was a three-inch drop-off from the tarmac and consisted of a narrow strip of fine marled charcoal gray and pure white sand cramped by large and very solid conifers. Darling did not want to "kiss a tree" as they say in racing. "Well, you do like him don't you, I mean, you do think he's all right."

"Maybe I didn't like the way he was looking at you. Maybe I just wanted him to know I was around."

Darling's eyes emitted a helpless light, "Oh, Paul! You didn't tell him to stay away did you?" Paul and Darling were in mourning; she hadn't had a date in months.

Paul said, "No. I didn't," but he was thinking it's too soon. He gave an exasperated sigh and rested one of his big bony elbows against one of his big bony knees and watched where the little driver was taking the little red car. She did not know that money was beginning to dry up. He knew it had not occurred to Darling that without their parents there was only so long the two of them could live in the house in reasonable comfort. Paul had already given up his plans for law school, completely and in secret. Now he was thinking that unless more money came from somewhere soon the first thing that was going to have to go was the little red car. All Paul could think of doing was to survive for two more months until the fall when Darling would be going off to college, to live in the dorms, to have a meal card, to be safe.

It was now the first week of July 1967, two days after the celebrations of The Fourth, and Darling had only two weeks ago turned eighteen. She would not have to know any of the details of the estate. At least not much more for a while. Paul just wanted to get through to September, but how? At least they'd had this evening together. It had been their special evening. Paul thought of Aunt Maggie and of how confident she was of Paul and Darling's ability to handle their new situation, of his assurances to her. He thought of Mark Cymrot and wondered how he was doing with the estate papers. Business.

Darling worried over who would look after her brother while she was away. Washington was only a three-hour drive from home, but she doubted her studies would permit her the freedom of coming home very often. Then there was the money. Paul is worried, she thought. If I just could have earned a bigger scholarship things wouldn't have to trouble him so, or maybe I should get married. Maybe not. Surely there must be something I can do. Oh, Mom, sometimes I really miss you. "Paul, do you think he'll find me?"

"He might."

The two rode along in a comfortable understanding of one another, a quiet union of concentration, as Darling negotiated a particular series of hairpin turns and snakelike curves in the Grand Prix style, clutching and down-shifting, accelerating on the straight-aways. And it was very dark.

"Paul."

"What."

"Do you think he's out there?"

"Who? Dave?"

"No, him. *It!*"

"Oh, you mean the Jersey Devil."

"Yeah, him. He's out there, isn't he."

"Yeah, he's out there. But I don't think he's close by. I think he probably stays mostly up by the point when the season's going here."

"You've seen him?"

"No. But there's good men who swear to God they've seen him, just watching. Like he wanted to be seen, and then he'd disappear. I only know I can smell him, sometimes, when the breeze catches just right, especially down at Sweetwater, down there where the creek joins up with the Mullica River, it's rich heathen down there."

Darling turned the car radio on for distraction. Paul reached past Darling's arm and turned the radio off. Darling returned her hand to the steering wheel. "What'd you do that for? That was *Maybellene!*"

"'Cause."

Darling was quiet for a minute or two.

"Paul."

"What."

"Can we roll the windows up?"

"Christ, no, we'd suffocate!"

"Well, then, will you at least lock your door?"

"Wouldn't do any good. If the Jersey Devil wanted to get in this car there's no locked door that's going to stop him. Why, he could just fly over and land on the roof of the car and lean over and scare the shit out of you and you'd die, or he could decide to rip the roof off the car and eat you. I've never heard of him dragging any women off to rape."

"Just lock the door will ya? Aren't we coming to a mainer road?"

"No, the last turn was the last turn. This does come right up on 206 though. Then you'll know where you are."

Darling drove along rather mumbling to herself about the dangers of driving around here at night, she just hated it. You never knew when some Piney was going to come four-wheeling out of the woods and stop you and kill you for your Lucky Strikes, and to top it off New Jersey had its very own resident demon. What a place. Now she was getting the kinds of feelings she had when she made decisions like going away to school, and traveling, and meeting all kinds of new people, not just Pineys and hicks. Darling's memory was stirred by thoughts of Alain, so perfect, the Seine, so alluring. Her mother's first concert tour in years, her last. Back to London, back to New York. She remembered Washington and warm sunny days at the zoo, Sonny Terry and Brownie McGhee at The Cellar Door in Georgetown; she wondered who her roommate would be at school.

Paul barked, "Fucking wake up and drive, or pull over!"

Darling woke up and drove on. Home could not be all that far away now. It was getting late. Then Darling came upon a street light, a lone street light, but where there was one more would follow and they did so the lights became more and closer together as they gradually emerged from The Pines and stumbled upon traffic.

# CHAPTER 4

It was six a.m. when Dieter entered Dave's Hilltop Garage in Bordentown. The radio was blaring, *(I Can't Get No) Satisfaction*. David had not slept at all during the night. After bringing the metallic blue Chevy coupe home from that disastrous evening at the races, David had begun to mindlessly walk around and around the Chevy, then the garage. He had rubbed a lot at the back of his neck. He was actually sick. He was in love, although he had not yet diagnosed this for himself.

He wanted her. He wanted her so much he simply did not know what to do. The energy created by thoughts of Darling made David tremble. David's mind was awash with how and where to have a place to keep her and how in the world he would ever go about getting her there. The muscles in his groin were so tense he was afraid to sit down. One trip to his room had proven that he dared not go anywhere near the bed. So it was back down to the garage for an all-nighter. The fresh air would do him good.

David emptied oilcans that had been waiting to be emptied for months. He went over all the shelves with a rag and solvent, and wiped clean every can and bottle, belt, hose, and instrument, replacing each item to its proper place, thinking, what the fuck has happened to you David? When you started all this, everything had a place and you wanted everything in it; it was the only way you could work. Now you've become sloppy. Your machine was obviously a failure tonight, last night. How do you expect to be able to take yourself to her brother's garage if your own racer doesn't even run? Damn.

Dieter was surprised to find so much had been made neat and tidy. He wondered out loud, "What broke loose around here?" David immediately began to swear at Dieter's presence, more to the point of just exactly *where* Dieter's presence had been on the night before, the night he had blown a seal in the Chevy, the night he had been forced to scratch in the second heat, and consequently forced to scratch for the rest of the night, only in small part because Dieter was not there to help, for the most part because David simply could not run this car any more, it was run out as they say. Dieter was skinny and quite humble but he ignored David's tirade. He asked, "Hey Davie, like what's with the cleaning kick, going domestic on us?"

"Leave me alone. I've got a lot on my mind. I've got a lot to think about."

Dieter thought, oh, all of a sudden Mr. Big has a lot to think about, but said, "Like what's a lot?"

"Like the Army for one thing. Like I'm scratching the season. Like I'm scrapping this fucking chevro-shit and I'm scratching the whole damned rest of the season."

Dieter squeezed around to the other side of the Chevy, "Yeah, that's a lot. Well if it'll help you any Davie, I'll take the Chevy." Dieter smiled his big goofy smile. "How come you're acting like this? Wouldn't happen to be something else, like, maybe a female, would it?"

"Shut up."

The tension. The tension. Dieter chewed his cuticles. He said, "Hey Davie, like I hate to spoil your party and all, but don't you think you ought to just go and get yourself a little shuteye? You do have to be to work in two hours, and you've got school tonight, don'tcha?"

"Yeah."

"Well you'd better get goin' then. You just tell old Dieter here whatcha want done and I'll take care of everything. You just get yourself on upstairs and get forty winks or so. Go on. Git."

David knew that there was never any sense in arguing with Dieter, such activity only frustrated David until he would work himself into a blind rage, and that the best thing to do really would be to get some rest, if David could only rest. As David climbed the stairs he looked back at Dieter who had turned the radio off in the middle of something by the Beach Boys and was dusting the grease and oil stains of the garage floor with fragrant absorbent cedar shavings and said, "You're fired Dieter." Without looking up, Dieter replied, "Okay Davie, night."

"Night."

His room was excruciating, the sight of his bed even worse. Red curls, no golden curls, billowed around the ghost of lovely shoulders, the shoulders broad and smooth and buttery soft, the curls here hiding a round pink nipple, there exposing one, tickling at the not-so-tiny waist and tearing David's heart out.

Time, time is what I need, he thought. I can make her mine if I can just have the time to do something, build something, something to offer her, some way to make her love me. David's self asked him, yeah man, that's cool, but what about everything else you've worked for so far, isn't that enough? No. I wonder if she even noticed me last night. That sure is a pretty little red car her brother's put her in. I'll bet she's got everything. I'll bet she'd never give me a second thought. But, then, why did her brother invite you to come over some time, well not exactly over, but to his place, that's pretty darned close to home for a grease monkey. I wonder if she hangs around the garage much, seemed like she knew what she was doing at the track.

David removed the card from his breast pocket, fondled it, and then tossed it onto the dresser.

---

# STREET STOCK

## Restoration and High Performance Road Machines

1st Avenue at High Street
Littleton, New Jersey 08068
Telephone: Twin Oaks-4-0407

---

He quietly spoke to himself, "Well, David, like man, after all this fucking time you finally discover what your parents were talking about when they kept going on about 'the right girl.' They'd love her too." At first this thought made him smile, but then came, "Ah, piss on it." The smile and the thought were dismissed.

David was trying to chase away the horns. Nothing seemed to work. He thought about his art class coming up the next evening, an event he looked forward to every Saturday night; his four-hour seminar. Nudes. Oh, no, they would be working again on that study, number seventeen. Jeez! Is this how love is? Am I to see this woman in every woman I see? How in the hell am I supposed to sleep? Nothing is ever fair and in a little while human nature took over completely and left him slipping into the warm security of REM time.

# CHAPTER 5

That night had not been spent easily by Darling either. She had balked at Paul's idea of stopping for a shake and a burger at the familiar White Dot, and opted to make scrambled eggs on toast for the two of them for dinner. After a shower, Darling said her goodnight to Paul and lay quietly in her room.

She did not even look at the half-finished *Dr. No* that waited by the bedside. She did not notice Balzac, the dark tabby Persian cat who looked up sleepily from his position on the cushions of the window seat; he yawned, he stretched, he walked around in a circle and then curled up again in the very same spot. Now, with candle lit, Darling ran her hands along the thighs of her naked body. Her hands wandered up to embrace the ruched nipples of her insignificant breasts. She wondered why she wanted to be touched in such a way, and who, if anyone, besides Paul might ever love her. A frown consumed Darling's pretty face and she became angry at the slipperiness between her legs.

That was all Buzz had ever wanted. It seemed like that was all anybody ever wanted, boys and girls alike, just to get their fingers or their dicks inside the slipperiness. Darling Randolph was eighteen years old. She had been fondled when she was very young, an incident that her memory refused to allow. But she did remember that a girlfriend had molested her at her private school, which Darling could not admit she had enjoyed and from which Darling promptly ran away. She had gone through an illegal abortion because of what Buzz had done to her when she was fifteen and had suffered all its attendant fury, shame, pain, and punishment until the day her mother died. All these experiences and Paul was still the only person who ever put his arms around her, held her, rocked her, and cuddled her, just because he loved her, unconditionally. So much for free love.

Darling Randolph had a room of her own and $3,000 a year as Virginia Woolf had prescribed, but she didn't know what to do with it. Mrs. Woolf had never given instructions on how a young woman might overcome the trap of teenage sexuality. Darling rolled onto her side and curled up with both hands tucked between her thighs.

Something is happening, she thought, something Paul won't tell me about. Paul is worried. Mom hasn't been dead long and Dad not much longer. Sometimes it hurts a lot. And Paul never says anything much about how he feels.

Paul sat downstairs on the arm of the leather sofa in his father's study. He thought about going to the garage for a while but was too exhausted. As always, he resented energies spent solely in paperwork and he would get stuck up to his ears in waiting paperwork if he went to the garage right now. Law school was already out. And Paul was well on his way to thinking the Army might be in. What would it do to change things? He should at least speak with a recruiter. 1967 was closing too fast for them and the war was continually stepping up, he may be called to go anyway simply because of need. Paul was also forfeiting his 2-S deferment, he expected to be reclassified 1-A as soon as the bureaucrats found out he would not be going to graduate school after all.

Paul knew he should be thinking more about the house, the Will, his sister, even his parents. This new burden was not unwelcome, inasmuch as such a situation can be welcome or not, it was okay. But Paul's ideas encompassed a greater measure of security than the survival of his person and that of his sister; he wanted somehow to save the family property itself, in perpetuity as had been intended. And he couldn't help thinking they could have given us another ten years for Christ's sake. Well, this whole shooting match never would have been willed to you and Darling directly if it had not been believed that the two of you would be of reasonably sound mind. As it happened, neither Paul nor Darling had quite become of age at the time of their parents' death, but they did both reach majority during final probation of the estate.

It was late. He should retire. Paul was beginning to dread his sleeps simply because of the guilt. For the past few mornings he had been waking to find Darling beside him in the big old bed, and he had loved it and it frightened him. But in the morning light he could look down upon her sleeping face and it gave him such a sense of responsibility and, yes, of power. Now he was beginning to want her there. And it must stop.

Now Paul was faced with a dilemma he had not faced since the pair were small children, children at all for that matter, for after that time neither of them would ever really be children again, or perhaps, because of that time, both of them would always be children forever. It had happened when Paul was about eleven; that would have made Darling about seven or eight. Paul could only remember that it had been a summer's day. The two had napped together in Paul's big old bed and when Paul awakened he discovered himself with an erection, uncomfortable and confusing. Paul got out of bed and wandered around the quiet house, no sound but for the mockingbird in the tall pines along the drive, no one in the house, no one except the sleeping Darling. Paul scratched his thigh and stared into the refrigerator. He poured himself a glass of milk and drank it down in one breath. Then he went back to bed and began the slow molestation of his sleeping sister. He did not really penetrate her, and for that he had always been grateful, and when Darling woke up she had behaved as if nothing had ever happened. She put her arms around his neck and rested gently in his. But Paul remembered.

Paul had vowed from that day that he would never do anything like that again and that he would never give anyone else the chance. He felt he had betrayed his parents' trust. He was certain he had betrayed his sister's trust. Now things really were his responsibility. This time his parents had placed in him their ultimate trust. They had died. So this night Paul would lock his bedroom door. Darling might cry. Don't make her cry. The creases and folds of her secret little places, you can still feel how soft.

What about this new guy? Wonder what he's up to. Wonder what he does for a living. You'd better get to bed or you won't be doing much for your own living after tomorrow. And you'd better get in early so you can cut out for a while and talk to that recruiter, what's his name? That guy who called you last month. Watson, that was it, Staff Sergeant Watson, T.E. He left himself a note. Why does Darling come and get into my bed? She can't know how it hurts me.

The following morning Paul awoke to find Darling laying right by his side, she even snored pretty. He silently ran his hand along the length of a warm firm thigh; then he smacked the rear end once very hard and yelled, "Get up! Go on get up! Get me some orange juice! How the hell did you get in here? I thought I locked that door!" He jumped out of bed and into his pants.

Startled awake and straight into consciousness, Darling said, "You did! I've known how to slip that lock for years, Paul. Ah, man. What's the matter with you?" Darling pulled the cotton eyelet ruffles of her nightshirt back down around her knees. She rubbed at the red-hot handprint on her bottom and pulled masses of curls away from her face. She rose and tiptoed into the kitchen, hanging from the cupboard door handles while getting out the glasses and pouring the orange juice into the milk jug as well, and thinking through a morning haze, what the fuck's the matter with him?

# CHAPTER 6

"Will you do something with this house while I'm out today?"

"No, I can't. I'm showing Bobby Brooks in Cherry Hill."

"What time is that?"

"Four o'clock."

"Are we gonna have scrambled eggs on toast again tonight?"

"Maybe I'll make spaghetti, but yeah, it'll be sort of late."

Paul recollected the first time he ever learned that anyone could actually burn spaghetti. "How 'bout if I get some Chinese."

"Sounds great!" Darling perused the *New York Times*, as usual back to front of Section A. Elizabeth Taylor and Richard Burton in *The Taming of the Shrew*, a Burton-Zeffirelli production. "Thousands attend love-in at Los Angeles' Elysian Park." Balzac was rubbing up against her legs, purring and calling for his breakfast. "Hey, Paul, it says here that Westmoreland is asking McNamara for more troops."

"Yeah? Fuck. How many this time?"

"Mmm, 100,000 to 200,000."

"Jeez-us Christ!"

"And, McNamara doesn't like it. He says there're already more than 466,000 as it is now."

"Yeah, but I'll bet that old motherfucker gets 'em. What's the kill?"

"Uhm. Yesterday's numbers. Here it is. 19 Army and 22 Marines: 1st Lt. Anthony J. Borrego, West Patterson, N.J.; Spec. 4 Robert A. Woodrow, Ocean City, N.J.; Sgt. Andrew P. Stein, Jr., Syracuse, N.Y.; and Marines, Cpl. Alan L. Deidrickson of Darien, Conn.; Cpl. Frank Divila, Manhattan; Lance Cpl. William H. Tooms of Buffalo..."

"Okay, that's enough."

"Well, that's all from around here. And a Cpl. Hicks of Yardville."

"God, this really sucks."

"I'm glad you've got a deferment. Maybe it'll all be over by the time you finish law school."

Paul did not take this opportunity to tell Darling that he was about to lose his deferment. "Not as long as Johnson's in office. He's got it in his head that this is some kind of a pissing contest."

"But these dead guys were people, they were people our age."

"Yeah. They were. Listen, I gotta get a move on, but I need to speak to you though. We need to talk, about a couple-a things."

"Okay. Sure. I'll be here, but I gotta run too. Come on, don't be such an old prune-face. It's a beautiful day. They're gonna pay me forty dollars and a cashmere sweater! We had a good time last night didn't we?" She opened a can of cat food and began spooning the shredded tuna onto a clean china plate. Balzac purred.

"God, that stuff stinks!"

"Oh, go on silly. The cat has to eat. You know, it's the very first time we've had any real fun since Mom died."

"Let's make sure it's not the last, okay kid?"

The two put their arms around one another and smacked a kiss goodbye then broke away and fled in opposite directions. Paul was thinking, this whole summer brat thing with the cars is really ridiculous, this shit has to stop. There's a war on, my parents are dead, my sister is shameless and I've got every extra cent I could possibly spend tied up in nine pieces of junk.

Paul's attorney would later encourage him a bit more than that by reminding Paul that he had made a good return on his investment in the value of the Street Stock property, prime, quiet, center of town property where his highest prize was that his prime, quiet neighbors never complained about the noise. Paul's response to this information was, "Then let's sell it."

Paul had dreamt the night before that he was drowning in automobiles. Bumpers and headlights smashed into one another as hundreds of wrecked cars tossed upon dark violent foaming waves stinking of grease, oil, and gasoline. Paul struggled to get a foothold, to save himself, but he could not. He kept slipping, and drowning, and he woke up in a fright. In the morning he asked Darling to leave the keys to the Mercury, leave them on the piano bench so that Ernest could pick the car up around lunchtime. Darling would be taking the Valiant to Cherry Hill; Paul was going to take his father's '55 Mercedes Benz to the garage where he would be faced with four bay doors and eight more cars; and his mother had died in the Buick. The Valiant was the shit car for all-purpose running around and Darling hated it, but it had wheels and it went so she didn't say a word of complaint.

Mark Cymrot, attorney for the estate, answered his ringing telephone with only a hello. In a short-sleeved polo shirt, faded Madras Bermuda shorts, and sandals, Mark had only come into the office to look something up and should never have stopped for a glance at his mail. His wife would be furious. Paul Randolph said, "Hi Mark, glad I caught you. Do you think you could find some time for me today?"

Cymrot was a good-looking thirty-two-year-old man, clever, successful, and not emotionally very sensitive. He knew from the file and from his briefing with Mr. Proboscis, the senior partner, that Paul and Darling's parents had been very old established clients of the firm and personal friends of the boss. Now Mark had the young people's properties and problems entrusted to his care. Mark wondered when it might be time to consult the old man. He had no wish to break a good client relationship and so far, they had done nothing too unusual. But Mark knew there was a huge extended family, all equally independent. He tucked the thought away.

A week ago, Mark had explained to Paul and Darling that although probation would take several months, in the end the proceeds from the estate would have paid just a little more than in full the debts of the estate. The place was free and clear and there were even a few dollars left to spend. But three hundred dollars a month would not go far. It would pay the utilities on the place, of that Paul was fairly certain, until winter came. In winter much fuel oil would be burned to heat the water to pass through the old copper pipes and run all the way up and around three floors and back down, and three showers, well, two that were still in use anyway, and the washer in the basement. The water always came out of the taps at 212 degrees Fahrenheit and scalded you if you were not awake and when you emerged from the shower your nakedness was secreted, as if anyone would be out there, by the covering of frost and ice inside the window. Paul knew it took a lot of money just to keep that old barn from freezing solid. There were a pair of trusts which would only yield them interest until they reached the age of thirty when they each could have the modest principal, and some royalties from their mother's music. In the meantime, the matter of taxes was paramount; quarterlies were due in September.

Paul thought he had the answer. He wanted Mark to begin with liquidation of the vehicles; Paul's instructions were to get rid of everything. Darling could keep the Valiant for her own and Paul would buy a new car, a straight stock showroom variety six-cylinder automobile with payments. Mark Cymrot asked, "Are you planning to get out of the restoration and high-performance business altogether?"

"I meant what I said when I said sell it."

Cymrot okayed the move and said he would make the arrangements. "I'll be in touch on Tuesday or Wednesday with a detailed assessment of the fair market value of all eleven vehicles plus the two trailers."

"And the shop."

"And the shop. Have I got it?"

"You got it."

The cars had been a hobby, a hobby that had paid for itself, but one with which Paul and Darling could easily live without and any profits better spent these days.

Paul asked, "By-the-way, Mark. Do you have any idea where a pre-law student with a baccalaureate in political science and international law, who isn't going to law school, might begin to find a job?"

Mark, who was sure Paul would clear at least a hundred thousand dollars on the sale, asked, "Why aren't you going to law school?" Paul replied flatly, "Because I don't wanna be a lawyer anymore."

# CHAPTER 7

Darling braided her damp hair parted down the middle then she wrapped the braids in fat circles around the crown of her head and anchored the whole business with four huge tortoise shell hairpins that had been her grandmother's. Darling wanted her hair to be kinked by the afternoon, and this would be a carefree way to accomplish that and cooler for the day. July was really beginning to swelter, good summer days for Surf City but not the best for trying to keep a cool head about modeling this fall's fashions for smart women.

In dusting powder and cotton bra and panties Darling stepped into a pale-yellow cotton garden dress and rummaged in the shoeboxes in the bottom of the closet, disturbing Balzac and finally throwing a pair of platform espadrilles into the middle of the room. After some stretching, she found her floppy straw hat with the orange grosgrain ribbon and that landed on the bed. Darling packed her bag for the day's charade and wondered if she should ask Rita for more hours on the boards, but decided to hold out a little longer. Darling was being cautious because she did not want to make Rita angry. She was hoping to be able to count on Rita for an occasional job during the coming school term.

Although Darling did not know just exactly how serious the situation was, she did not feel she needed much more of an explanation from Paul. She was sure that finance was what Paul had been alluding to with the having to have a talk routine. The situation must be serious, and it must be about money and she knew Paul was very worried. She did not need to know the dollars and cents to be able to take what she did know and extrapolate, no money. No, not no money. Just not enough money, so Darling wondered what she could do. For a few moments it all seemed hopeless, what could she really do? There seemed no option but to simply forget about college altogether and work for Rita full time. That might not work either because Rita liked to talk about her girls during the shows and she especially liked to brag about her students. But it would save money. Darling was not sure just how much money such a move would save but she knew a year at George Washington University came to upwards of twelve thousand dollars plus board and expenses, and that twenty thousand dollars would go a long way toward maintenance of the property. Her scholarship only accounted for three thousand a year.

Then, while puttering down the highway, it occurred to Darling that she really could do something. Rutgers, the State University would be fully paid by her state scholarship with a little left over to throw into the kitty, that could probably help keep her car on the road so that she could commute. And she could drop the insurance on the Merc; park it for a while. Then she would be able to live at home and keep an eye on what was going on around the homestead. Maybe she could even get Hannah back to help, or someone. There could be little argument; Darling had entirely made up her mind. With her hair pulled back from her face in tight barrettes and the kinks lying rippled to her waist, Darling smiled a somewhat self-conscious smile for everyone at Town and Country while she walked the boards at tea time dressed first in satin loungees and two-inch mules and then in Oxford shirts and straight wool skirts and sweaters dyed to match.

# CHAPTER 8

You can never find a recruiter on a Saturday afternoon, not one. At four o'clock Paul toured the garage in town and eyed the riches of his youth not a little too coldly. He would keep the BSA. The old motorcycle had been taken in trade for work. The work had been done for a South Philadelphia Warlock who was now too feeble and banged up to ride bikes any more. Paul had modified the Warlock's brand-new Chevrolet Camaro. Now the Warlock placed well in the races by the Delaware River, on Front Street just under the Walt Whitman Bridge approach. The Warlock was a happy man.

Paul prized the BSA as much for its secret history as he did for its engineering. Today he would leave behind his father's '55 Mercedes; a 240 SL the professor had had since the odometer was all goose eggs. Paul would miss the whine of its fuel injection, the soft worn leather seats, and his father and his pipe and his eyeglasses that he had never worn often enough. He brought down the bay doors and locked the garage, kick-started the bike and headed for Arrowhead.

He threw the saddlebags from the BSA into the corner of the sofa in his father's study; his bike jacket, his leather, landed on top and he left the room. First, he washed and dried all the dirty dishes. He sang along with the Eric Burden and the Animals cranked up on his amplifier, *The House of the Rising Sun*. Paul's gravelly tenor-to-bass range nearly matched Eric Burdon's but Paul often wobbled on the high notes.

Paul sang as he wiped the countertops being sure to get all the spilled sugar. He hummed as he swept the kitchen floor, and was silent when he went to the linen cupboard, haunted by a blast of his mother's memory as soon as he opened the cupboard doors. He was smiling and thinking of her as he removed a fresh tablecloth from its stack.

With the dining room ready, Paul began to feel more set in his plan, Dee-dee, dee-dah, dee-dah-dah, dee, dee, dah, dah, da-ah-dah… He went to the linen closet in his bathroom and removed the last two huge clean cotton terry towels then began his usual shower routine. But showering while knowing he was going to have fresh linen when he dried was giving Paul great pleasure.

Once showered Paul made his rounds of the house, taking all the stairs in sets of two. Still in the all-together Paul went about gathering towels, sheets and pillowcases and any odd laundry that got in his way and shoved it into either the upstairs or the downstairs clothes chute in huge balls that hardly made it down the tube. Paul was overjoyed to know he was creating a gigantic pile of laundry, which waited for no one on a table in the basement.

Paul made a lumbering trip down to the basement and made himself feel as if he had magic in his fingertips because he managed to get the washing machine running and pumping and making lots of suds and he knew when he finished he was going to have a drawer full of clean underwear again. Ah, simple happinesses.

Paul poured himself a glass of milk, which always made him think of Darling, and put two big handfuls of pretzels onto the tray then he went to his father's study. This room, venerated by the lad now belonged to the young man. Half a glass of milk and a handful of pretzels witnessed the unpacking of the saddlebags. The contents were record books and significant files to what had until this day been his first experience with business and with building things.

Paul carefully placed his files and notebooks in two stacks at the center of the green blotter. He sat in his father's chair. After several minutes of sitting in the chair he was sitting in *his* chair, at *his* desk. Paul pulled the chain of a brass desk lamp. He performed a cursory opening of the usual desk drawers then removed a four-inch-high stack of files from the file drawers, briefly skimming across the headings of the remaining files. Paul called in an order for Chinese food, to be delivered at eight. Then he began the task of reviewing the files and placing them in what became several different stacks around the edges of the desk, the categories based on what little he knew of each piece.

By eight p.m. Paul was so engrossed that it took several tries at the door before the Chinese food could be delivered. Paul put all the food into the oven and set the thermostat for two hundred degrees, he lit candles and put napkins, silver and china on the table, he boiled the water and made the tea, Darling would be home at any moment. Now Paul remembered he had a washer full of underwear and made a quick trip to the basement to throw everything into the dryer and set the timer for the max.

Darling was a little late. No matter, she could make more tea. Paul returned to his stacks of files; there was a stack of action items, utilities, tax files; there was a stack of files to ask Mark Cymrot about, he thought Mark probably had all that information; and there was a tremendous amount of information which for the moment Paul could only classify as DAD-Personal.

Darling arrived, exhausted and carrying her shoes. She plopped onto the sofa in the study. "Did you do all this for me?"

"I'm doing it for both of us. Food's in the oven."

Darling's curiosity pulled her up from the sofa. She asked, "Chinese?" Paul never looked up from his business. "Yup." Darling meandered over to the desk and sat her left rump down on the edge, she snatched a pretzel from Paul's tray and stuffed it into her mouth saying, "Mmm, terrific, everything copacetic?" Paul responded almost absentmindedly, "I don't know, I really don't quite know for sure. Yet."

"Watcha doin' in here?"

"Tryin' to get set up. Tryin' to figure out what the fuck's goin' on around here. It's for certain somethin' is. But, anyway. Don't worry about it for now. Listen, I'll be working from here from now on." Paul was determined to pull no punches this time.

"So who's gonna run the office at the shop?" Darling's eyes lit up, "Me?"

"Nobody. The shop goes."

"Goes? Like Whaddya mean 'goes'? Paul?"

"Which word didn't you understand? We need the money, Darling. Look, there's just lotsa shit we need to talk about. So, like, let's not get started about it right this minute. Why don't you run along and freshen up and then we can have some cold tea and some warmed-over Chinese. Okay? Tired?"

"Not too bad," she lied.

Paul leaned way back in his chair with his hands clasped behind his head and his huge elbows poking at the air around him, he heaved an immense sigh. "Ah, man." He rolled his head around on his shoulders and listened to the tiny crackles of cartilage and bone. "So how'd it go today? Lemme see your sweater."

Darling smiled proudly and pulled a rusty-colored cashmere pullover from her bag and fluffed it out into the air.

"Looks too big."

"Nuh-uh. It just fits nice, I like 'em baggy."

"Yeah," he grinned, "I know."

Tired and confused and excited all at the same time, she floated over and pushed Paul deeper into his chair so that his elbows came down and his arms enclosed her as she sat down on his lap and rested her head against his chest and cuddled the sweater and Paul. Ordinarily this was perfectly normal behavior for them, but this time Paul froze. After a moment of no reaction, Darling pushed out her lower lip and pushed herself out of the chair and headed up to her room.

The house was quiet again for almost half an hour while Darling showered and became if not more rested then at least refreshed after a long hot day. Now she wished for a good swim, but part of their mourning had been to forego the pool for at least the first summer. Their mother had at age thirteen set an AAU record for the five hundred-meter freestyle. Though the mark was never made official, Gracie Littleton's record would not be broken until the Mexico Olympics in 1968; it would be broken by a seventeen-year-old boy. The pool *was* their mother, the pool and the piano.

Darling lay on the bed, her naked body shimmering in dusting powder and tingling from splashes of witch-hazel. Coolness, peace, then thought, and Darling began to hold her feet up in the air and to examine and then rub gently at her swollen ankles. I wonder how much of this-type shit there's gonna be. Paul thinks he's so damned tough. I guess it really doesn't matter to Paul whether I change schools or not, or maybe it does and he's just engrossed in his new project. Then Darling thought, you haven't even told him about it yet. I'm too tired to do that. We'd have to go round and round. Maybe I'll just go ahead and look into it by myself. Deep in her own thoughts, Darling wandered into her mother's bedroom then through to the pink bath beyond. The Seconals. Darling counted them. There were only thirty left. Darling took two.

When Darling returned to the study she was far more comfortable in her peacock blue paisley caftan. She had her wet hair pulled back into a long tight braid and she was smoking a cigarette and carrying the cat over her shoulder like a baby. Darling put Balzac down on the floor in the study but he immediately wandered from the room. Darling padded back and forth between the study and the kitchen, in the study first, sitting, smoking, looking at Paul with curiosity, then into the kitchen to see if the cartons of Chinese food had caught fire yet, no, but they were browning nicely. Paul's concentration was finally disturbed by his sister's announcement of dinner.

Paul began immediately as Darling poured the tea. Darling was pleasantly remembering old Mrs. Simms and the first time she had ever been offered the privilege and honor of pouring when Paul burst forth with, "God-all-fucking-Mighty. I feel like I've been living with my head in cement."

"That's a little drastic, don't you think? Even though you *are* a blockhead."

"Honestly. I'm just glancing through those files of Dad's and there's all kindsa shit in there I've never known anything about."

"For instance?"

"Did Mom ever mention anything to you about Dad having a lover?"

"No. But it wouldn't surprise me. She certainly had her share."

"Yeah?"

"Oh, yeah. Like, just last year when she was on tour. Now that I think about it, I think that whole tour thing was cooked up so she could get together with Brod. We did spend an awfully long time in Paris before we finished in London. It was nice for me because Alain was responsible for keeping me happy during the days."

"You were in love with him?"

"I was in *like* with him. Alain was the first guy I'd ever met who wasn't always trying to get his hand down my pants. We were friends. We are friends."

"And his father?"

"Oh, Brod and Mom were definitely lovers. Brod made Mom's eyes twinkle the brightest green I've ever seen. He made her complexion rosy. Jeez, he even made her hair curl! I had never seen her so happy, even when she was seeing the redhead."

"The redhead? Who was that?"

"Dunno. She just called him the redhead. It went on for a good ten years."

"And then?"

"And then he went to Vietnam as an advisor or something. Uhm, '63 I believe it was. Came back in a box. That's when Mom really started hitting the Seconal."

"Did Dad know?"

"He knew something was going on. There were arguments; a couple of real humdingers."

"Where was I?"

"At Princeton, *El stupido*."

"Mmm. But you never heard about Dad and another woman?"

"I think I would remember that. Why?"

"There's an awful lot of stuff in Dad's desk that I can't make heads or tails of yet. I'll have another shot at it after we eat. But it sure as hell looks to me like he's been paying somebody what adds up to quite a little bit of money, and it's been going on for twenty years or so. It's either an affair, you know, some woman he's been keeping, or it's blackmail, or both."

"Juicy! But Dad was a pretty old man. He was drunk at eleven o'clock every night for as far back as I can remember. Who'd want him?"

"He wasn't always an old man. Besides some women really dig older men. It doesn't matter if they're fish as long as they're flush."

"Dad wasn't flush."

"But Mom was. How's some sweet young thing going to know who paid for the Mercedes?"

"I thought you said this was twenty years ago. If there ever was a sweet young thing it's a lead-pipe cinch she's not young anymore. And if she was blackmailing Dad, I doubt she was ever sweet."

"Point. But men can be really kind of dumb sometimes."

"Tell me about it. You've been acting pretty weird yourself lately. Like tonight. When I walked into the house it almost felt like home, as if maybe Hannah were here and Mom. Why'd you do that to me?"

"Why'd I do that to you? I told you I'm trying to get it together, for us! What is it you've been doing to me? Didn't I hear you ohm-ing out upstairs last night? Christ, Darling, you've just gotta stop conjuring the past. There's nothing wrong with loving Mom and Dad or their memory but please, quit trying to summon their spirits from, like, THE GREAT BEYOND, man." Paul ceased the sarcastic bobbing of his head and said, "They're dead."

Darling cried, suddenly, silently, unnoticeably at first. Now she was insulted on top of all her other nervous frustrations and it all began to tumble forth in the candlelight. Tears dripped into her hot and sour soup. Then she began blubbering almost uncontrollably, "I'm not trying to conjure our dead parents, you big creep! You just don't understand the principles of Kundalini yoga. Jesus H. Christ on a crutch!" Darling rose from her chair and threw her napkin down onto the table as if it were a gauntlet. Balzac shot out from under the table and up the staircase in a blinding flash. Darling paraded back and forth at her side of the table. "Dammit, Paul, why do you have to talk about yoga as if it were among the Black Arts? Besides, their spirits are still here, at least Mom's is, somewhere, I'm sure of it, and shit-man-fuck you can't tell me they're not. I wanna go to Rutgers Paul. I don't wanna go away from home. I can't leave Arrowhead here all alone, and there's nobody here and there's nobody there and it's going to cost so much money, and it's just so much more than I deserve." The tears began to dribble again. "I'll take the education I earned Paul. Rutgers is a good school."

Paul sat watching his sister whom he thought remained rather well composed under the circumstances except for the fact that her eyes were often mere water spigots. Occasional deep heaving sobs lasted well after her outburst. Paul gave Darling his hanky. He tried to tease, to cheer her, "Okay, okay, so I stepped on it. I forgot. The Yoga of Light. But it sounds to me like you've been thinking again. How many times have I warned you about that? You'll give yourself a headache. Come on, tidy up your face."

Darling smiled weakly and blew her nose and nodded in agreement. At least he was trying, she thought. Then she thought, yes, very trying. Paul backed off a little, "Why don't you tell me about the school part first," but he was interrupted by a knocking at the door. When Paul returned to the dining room he was carrying one of those long white cardboard boxes that announce the arrival of roses. Darling had received twenty-four long stemmed American Beauty roses with a plain white card that simply read: DAVE.

Paul, whose attempt to intimidate David had apparently backfired, mumbled beneath his breath, "I'll be a cock-sucking-mother-fucking-goddamn-son-of-a-bitch." As Darling impatiently opened the box and stuffed her face right into the very center of the whole bunch of moist red intoxicating fragrance, Paul reconsidered only slightly, "The guy's got balls, I'll say that much for 'im."

# CHAPTER 9

Darling threw her long braid over her shoulder in triumphant posturing. As she rose from the chair she reeled a tiny bit, the Seconal. That night in her dreams she would park the Mercury, somewhat miraculously, without tire tracks or skid marks, almost fifty yards off the road in the middle of a cornfield. For the moment, Darling removed a Waterford vase from the piano. She dallied with the flowers, snipping the stems and feeding them a ground half an aspirin then placed the vase at the center of the dining room table. Paul appreciated Darling's pretty smile as she returned to her dinner. Her nose and eyes were very pink.

"Well Paul, now what've you got to say?"

"I say, he can afford roses she thinks, but I'll bet they cost him two days' pay."

"You're shitting me!" The thought of David spending two days' pay on her only served to prove him even more endearing in eyes. "Oh, Paul, do you really think so? They're just gorgeous."

"Darling, are you falling for this guy?'

Darling smiled and took a little bite of shrimp toast, "Well, so far, I sure do like him a lot. But nobody ever falls in love at first sight, do they Paul?"

"I'm pretty sure he has."

"Terrific! Oh, I just knew I was right! I knew you'd say that! He's just the greatest, isn't he!"

"Oh, come on Darling. Frankly, no, he isn't. Anyway, it's only been twenty-four hours."

Darling sighed, "I know. I told you. I like that he doesn't look at me the way other guys do. I kinda think he might be my type, you know?"

"Bullshit Darling, your type had better be an attorney. What would everyone think if you married some dumb cluck?"

"Oh, Paul, jeez, I never said I was going to marry the guy, besides, you're just jealous. You just want me to wait for you."

Paul exploded. "No! No, I don't. And you've got to stop saying things like that! And, Darling, you've got to stop coming in and getting in my bed. It isn't right. And it's making me very nervous."

Darling was furious. So *that* was it. "Paul! I didn't think you'd mind. I didn't mean anything by it. I just don't know what else to do. You think you're nervous! Well what about me! I'm so lonely. And I don't want to work for Rita any more. And who's going to take care of this big old empty house? Me, that's who."

"Oh? And how the hell do you propose to do that?"

"I'm not exactly sure yet, but I'm going to be staying in New Jersey."

"With the Pineys and the hicks?"

Darling suddenly calmed, she stroked the soft rose petals, "You know that's only petulance."

"Yes, and you're famous for it, you do it so beautifully. Why stay here? *I'm* staying here, and if we sell the garage and all those cars out there, we can live pretty comfortably while we both have a chance to get our shit together."

A pout, no words. Darling stared into her folded hands, "I--told--you--Paul. I am not going to George Washington. I'm going to go to Rutgers and I'm going to commute to Camden. So, while you're off to Virginia or Marysville or wherever it was that finally decided to take you, you'll know everything is okay here at home. I think I could almost get to like living here alone."

Paul laughed. "Well, I've got news for you little sister. I'm not going to Virginia. I'm staying here, and I'm taking over the place, and you're going away to school."

"Oh no I'm not."

"Oh yes you are."

"Oh no I'm not and you can't make me! Dad's dead, Paul. And there's nothing in this world that's ever gonna make you into Dad and that's all there is to it. So quit trying. Damn Paul, I can think for myself, I can be independent."

"I see. Okay. What about everything you wanted to do? What about Washington, and politics? I thought you wanted to be a radical, work for Rap Brown, SNCC, shit like that."

"Things have changed for us Paul. I know they've changed for me. Oh, shit, Paul. I've been doing a lot of thinking about who I am, what I can accomplish right here. I want to get serious, more serious than I thought I could ever be, I mean, like, since yesterday even. Mom was the one that wanted me to model, always adorable. Dad was the one who wanted me at GW, and he only wanted me there so that you and Aunt Maggie could spy on me. 'Meet someone and marry well.' Hah! Besides, The Movement just doesn't need me the way you do, the way this place does. I can be a Student for a Democratic Society right here."

Paul's face flushed scarlet, his thick blue jugular veins stood out firmly. "Fucking all right then, go ahead, be a stubborn jackass, but you just tell me how we're both going to live in this house without sleeping together!" Darling found it hard to believe Paul could be serious about what he was saying, but she was capable of giving as good as she got so she let him have it. "Well, fuckin'-A big brother, we'll both just have to find somebody else to sleep with, won't we?"

"Darling!" Paul looked shocked but then broke into laughter. Darling arched an eyebrow and stood her ground, "Well?"

"You're being childish. I would say that's rather an over simplification of things, wouldn't you?"

"I don't think Einstein would ever have admitted that matters can be oversimplified. And besides, you're the one with the big goddamn problem. Don't worry, Paul, I'll never come and get into your stupid bed again. As a matter of fact, I will never even touch you again."

"What the hell has Einstein got to do with any of this?"

"You wouldn't know, would you? You're so set on being a backward ape!"

"Darling! What's got into you?"

"Well, Paul, what did you expect of me?" She began to cry a little, sniffling and breaking into her fortune cookie, it read:

## LIFE IS A JOKE SO YOU MIGHT AS WELL LAUGH

Paul continued, "It's not that I expect anything, but I do want something. Having a female that close to any male, well, it's just too much to hope for without something happening."

"A female? I'm impressed."

"Well. One like you anyway."

"One like me. Well, Paul, maybe something should happen."

"Darling! You have no idea what you're suggesting." Paul's expression could not remain stern and he smiled in a boasting kind of a way. He knew immediately he'd made another mistake.

"Fu-u-uck you!" Darling flipped him the bird with her middle finger straight up in the air. "I know very well what it is that I'm suggesting, and if that's your big goddamn problem, then why don't you just get over it. It's no big deal."

"No big deal! I'm sorry Darling, but sex to me is a big deal."

"That's just because you're a guy."

Paul was embarrassed both by and for his sister. He was genuinely alarmed to hear his precious speaking in this way. He was most alarmed by what her arguments implied. Paul was, in fact, frightened, although he would never have admitted this to himself. Darling's voice brought him back into her presence when she said, slyly, "Yes Paul." Paul looked at Darling pleadingly. She looked right back into his eyes and said only, "Yes Paul." Paul's eyes grew large in their sockets, "Who?" Darling turned her head away slightly, folded her arms across her chest and tipped up her nose. "Only Mim knows that."

Darling rose and put the fortune in her pocket. She began quietly removing dishes and scorched little white cardboard boxes from the table. Paul was in shock. Paul wanted to get up right that minute and drag his sister off to bed; it was the worst feeling he had ever experienced except for that summer's day. But, for some reason, a veil had fallen to the floor. Paul's major deterrent had simply vanished. Now he thought of Darling as warm and slippery and dangerous. He wondered, can she know?

But Darling wasn't thinking any more about it. She had been overdosed with fretting over Paul that day. She thought him a fake and a blowhard. Her exhaustion and the Seconal were depleting her insane anger. Darling chose to wonder instead how the roses had made it to her doorstep without even an introduction to herself. She wondered how David had found her and this mystery was far more enticing than trying to analyze all the implications of whatever it was that Paul was trying to say.

She said, "By the way, she's picking me up in the morning. We're going to church."

"Why bother?"

"Shit, Paul, I haven't seen Mim in weeks. Besides, maybe I just want to make sure I'm not struck by lightning or something."

"Ha, ha."

"Ha-ha-ha. You and me. Little brown jug, don't I love thee!" And so Darling chided and sang and disappeared at the top of the stairs. Paul remained at the head of the table, cross-eyed.

# CHAPTER 10

Dieter's cigarette smoke was hanging around beneath the streetlight as David left the Rembrandt Studios in Trenton. It was eleven-thirty or so. Dieter removed a flask from the pocket of his Wrangler jacket, "How 'bout a drink?" David had to laugh and agree to this, Dieter-the-fired's suggestion, "Don't mind if I do."

On the way back to the hilltop in Bordentown and Dave's Hilltop Garage, the two stopped at a place called Mastori's Diner. Now this diner would have satisfied even the skeptical wife in James Thurber's *A Couple of Hamburgers*, a fine dining establishment in disguise. Frank Sinatra stopped at Mastori's whenever he was in the neighborhood. Everything that is served at Mastori's is prepared from scratch behind the doors of their kitchen as if by magic. David and Dieter sat at the counter devouring complimentary cinnamon yeast rolls and drinking coffee while they waited for a table. David kept winking at the waitress whose name was Sheila. She only had to look at them once and the young men began to get serious again.

Dieter stirred his coffee incessantly. He was wishing he knew more words so he could say them now. "This is real nice Davie. I'd really like an omelet."

"Breakfast? It's only midnight."

"But Davie, I wanna buy you a nice meal but I can't afford a big dinner."

"Dieter? Dieter, what the fuck's the matter with you? We'll split dinner, man. Just like always. You want a steak? We'll split a frigging steak. You want, I'll buy you a steak."

"I want an omelet."

David wondered why Dieter was behaving so strangely. But, David thought, you did fire him this morning. Dieter must know I'll get over it. I always get over it. "Okay, okay, we'll split an omelet. But, Jesus, man! What's this all about, anyway?"

"I kinda wanted to wait until we got a table."

David looked around. "Wanna just sit in a booth?"

"Yeah."

Sheila took their orders for omelets. No one in Mastori's knew the two young men. Of this she was now sure, although she did think she might have seen the winking one before.

"Okay, so we're in a booth, so, like, what's the deal?"

"Well, like, I, I joined the Army today Davie. And, and, I was like wonderin', if you're really going to ditch the Chevy and all, if..." Dieter had to break it off. He sipped his coffee. He lit a Marlboro. David said, "Now wait just a minute Dieter..."

"Not this time. You wait a minute Dave."

"Shit, Dieter. What's got into you, man? I've never seen you like this before."

"Well. I never did nothin', anything, like this before. It's a done deal Davie, and I'm going."

"But why?"

"Got my reasons Davie." His mother haranguing him to get out of the house ran through his mind. "But I can't really talk about 'em right this minute. You know what I mean. But they are gonna help me get a diploma Davie."

"That's great Dieter." David felt like a heel. He couldn't help thinking, stole my fuckin' thunder. The Army had been a mere flicker in David's mind during the past twenty-four hours, one thought, no more. The Army thing was probably why Dieter had disappeared from the track last night. That was probably what Dieter had come to talk to him about this morning at the garage. But no, Mr. Shit had to be so self-involved, now Dieter had made up his mind, and now it was too late. Except that Dieter seemed to feel so good about it. David kept having a quiet urge to be happy for him. David asked, "Is it the money?"

No reply.

"It is."

"Nah. Well, maybe, partly. You know. You ain't been winnin' a lotta prizes lately, and you ain't been handin' much cash around lately, but I coulda gone somewheres else. But it's partly this stinking war too, Davie. My little brother, Nathan, you know, he's in Vietnam." David had not remembered. "Well, I think my mom, she hates me for it. You know, he's the baby and all and he's over there gettin' shot at and I'm not. Even when I was makin' money old Mom, she still called me a bum. No, it's not the money. Not really."

David reached across the table and clapped Dieter against the arm. "You blow me away, Dieter McKenzie. Jeez man. What can I do to help? You want my car? You can have my car. It's yours. Insurance is paid up 'til February."

David felt a little more satisfied with himself as heavenly green salads arrived with a beautiful smile from Sheila. And Dieter was greatly relieved that he had managed to spit it all out. There, you see, he thought, you knew you could be brave.

But David's satisfaction, generosity, pomposity, only lasted until the omelets arrived plump on their heated china platters, garnished with charcoal broiled scallops, slices of tomato and green pepper, three quarters of an orange and sugared grapes. He looked at Dieter who was now a triumph of composure and obviously enjoying his meal. Dieter said, "I'm headed for Basic in three weeks. Take the physical on Monday, day after tomorrow."

David's face grew pale and deadly serious. Unconsciously, David glanced at his watch, quarter-to-one. It was now Sunday. Dieter smiled and ate. He said, "I'm gonna be learnin' a lot Davie. Be happy for me, will ya?"

David forced himself to recover, saying, "I am. I'm glad pal," knowing he was lying, then he said, "I'm proud of you," and he was.

"Thanks Davie. But I treat tonight, okay? I don't think we'll be gettin' another chance. I'll be tellin' Mom tomorrow and then I s'pose I'll have to be stayin' close to home and takin' tests and fillin' out forms." Dieter was really beginning to enjoy his new sense of purpose.

"It's all right, I'm tellin' ya, it's all right goddammit. You don't have to lay all that on me, really. But, yeah, I guess you're right. Just let's split the tab at least. Come on. Let me. Come on, Dieter, you know, the guy who works buys, remember?"

Dieter grinned widely, "Well I'm workin' Davie!"

David was crushed, he was thinking, oh Christ, but said only, "Okay, okay thanks," and went about attempting to eat and be pleasant.

# CHAPTER 11

Later, after a five-inch-high wedge of fresh strawberry shortcake, David stared into a tank full of live Maine lobsters with their wide red rubber bands around the claws while Dieter paid the nine-dollar check and left a three-dollar tip for Sheila. David thought, whoa, man, and whispered to himself, "The last of the big-time spenders." He's really gone. He's like really gone. He can't afford this; he's probably going to be earning seventy-nine dollars a month.

David tossed the keys to the Chevy to Dieter as they walked across Mastori's parking lot, saying, "Hey, Private, catch!" Dieter grinned as he caught the keys and nodded, "Thanks!" David smiled widely and said, "No sweat. But I gotta warn ya, don't try layin' on it, you'll lose compression instantly at exactly sixty-one miles an hour, look out for it, that could kill you on the highway, you oughtta bring it around the garage later and we'll get that seal replaced properly." Then he singled out the red key, "This one's to my place."

"Yeah Davie, I've got a key to the garage."

"Yeah, but that's a green one. Everybody's got a green one. This is the red one, mine, and it's to the upstairs."

"Wow, man."

"Yeah. Wow. How 'bout dropping me off on your way home."

Dieter was so happy he did not know what to say. He grinned so widely as he drove along that the streetlights gleamed in his eyeglasses and sparkled from his teeth. The two sidekicks headed for the hilltop.

David asked Dieter to let him out at the corner, almost a block from Dave's Hilltop Garage.

"But how'll you get in?"

"Don't worry about me pal. Just be careful and have yourself a good time. Okay?"

"Okay, Davie. Will do. And thanks, thanks again."

"Yeah, you said that. Just be careful will ya? Night."

"Night Davie."

David enjoyed the walk, the moon, the faint stars, the neon here and there, the humidity of a summer's night, and the company of the wee hours. He was upset that his friend was leaving. He felt emasculated. With a troubled brow, David wrapped his sketches in his Wrangler jacket and laid them on the ground by the bay doors of the garage. Then he walked over to Ed's Egg, the breakfast shop that was his neighboring business, and borrowed one of the cafe chairs, a minor midnight requisition.

With the assisting boost of the chair, David climbed onto the roof of the garage where he nonchalantly walked over to the skylight cover and removed a tight-fitting black magnetic key case, replaced the cover, then slithered back down the side of the roof, let himself drop down onto the ground and walked back to Ed's Egg and replaced the cafe chair. By the time Bobo passed by on his two-thirty-five round, David had just entered the empty garage. It was not unusual to see the lights glowing from Dave's Hilltop Garage at two-thirty in the morning so the Bordentown Township cruiser carried on about his rounds as David climbed the stairs to his lofty garage apartment.

David gave no thought to the roses or to Darling until after he had been some time in his room. He assembled a new key ring and threw it on the dresser. He placed his sketches between their pieces of cardboard; this required some time in the examination. Bodies; he could never get the knees right, and faces, they were the universe.

As he placed the contents of his pants pockets on a little walnut tray, David counted his money. Twelve dollars and fifty cents. "What the fuck?" He counted the money again. Twelve dollars and fifty cents. "Oh, yeah. Thirty-seven fifty for the roses."

Atop the garage, the apartment was quiet but for the hiss of traffic on the highway and the soft drone of David's tiny air conditioning unit. The moon was getting lower in the sky. David lay in all his clothes on the unmade bed, smoking, gazing through the skylight at his personal map of the heavens. He grumbled, "No work tomorrow. Sunday. Today. No car either."

Across town Dieter was sitting peacefully in the dark on the back step of his mother's house smoking a cigarette, taking an occasional hit from his flask, and gazing affectionately upon the Chevy parked in the narrow drive. He was pleased. He had known a lot would change once he had signed on the dotted line but he never expected it would happen quite this fast. By the cover of waning darkness, Dieter imagined himself straight and tall in starched fatigues snapping a smart salute. "Next thing is t'tell Mom." He flicked his cigarette into the street as he rose to open the screen door.

In Littleton, Paul Littleton Randolph was walking the BSA to the end of the lane so that the noise of the engine would not awaken his sleeping sister. At the end of the lane, Paul gave the motorcycle a single kick-start and swung the rumbling bike hard to the right and onto the road up the mount, headed north for Trenton.

Darling had not yet awakened in a cold sweat from her dream, the nightmare she was having of the chase. Someone was chasing her. She could see only headlights at full beam in the rear-view mirror of the Mercury. She had just made the corner of the conical intersection, the Mercury screaming and balancing on its two left wheels, and was headed straight for home. She was passing fast the misty fields on either side of the road, pushing, pushing the little red car harder than she ever had and still the headlights remained only two car lengths behind her, one hundred and ten, one hundred and twenty, the speedometer needle was buried. Then she saw the rabbit, just a little brown cotton-tailed bunny, sitting in the middle of the road and staring straight at Darling. Darling swerved slightly to avoid the rabbit and that was all it took. The Mercury was airborne. It seemed like the longest time, and Darling felt the knowing. It seemed like the longest time, knowing this time she was not going to make it, this time she would die, no banged knee this time, no bump on the chin, no bruised ribs, but Death. She could see his scraggy figure waiting for her silently, his arm open welcomingly, he was standing near the base of the ancient oak tree that survived alone at the center of this particular corn field. He was standing near the edge of a little natural depression in the terrain, the depression that often filled with water in the late autumn rains and made such an excellent skating pond in winter. There he waited, and it seemed like it took the longest time getting there and the Merc made the longest arc, missing the telephone pole by a hair then up and over the shoulder of the road and up and up, over the drainage canal, over the farmer's fence, over the summer green cornstalks and into the night. The headlights were gone now, there were only the stars to be seen, and the wide spreading crown of that oak tree and Death standing there as if waving her into her slot in the pits. Then the tremendous thud of impact. Then hurrying, hurrying to get out of the car before Death could catch her. Then running, running across the field toward home, looking back just once through the cornstalks only to see the Mercury buried axle deep in the dirt amid the cornstalks, running, running, then waking, sitting bolt upright panting and breathless, cold and sweating.

Darling jumped out of bed and began to run down the staircase to Paul. On the second stair Darling remembered. No. You cannot go to Paul any more. Go back to bed. No. Yes. You can do it. You can. It will be daylight soon. Go on. Go back to bed. Let it go, you know how. And it seemed that the stairs were so high and the climb was such a long one, just a couple of stairs. Her room. In the moonlight and the already pearly gray hours. The Merc. It was out there, wasn't it? Right there where she left it, parked in her favorite spot beside the poplar trees. No. It isn't there. Oh, yes. Took it away. Ernest came and took it to the garage today. That's right. It isn't in the cornfield? No. Okay. I guess it's all right. Let it go. It's all right. Yes. Lie down now. Just rest. That's it. Okay. You're fine now, you're fine, it's all right, it's all right, then sleep.

# CHAPTER 12

Sunday morning rise and shine. Miriam honked the meep-meep horn of her Volkswagen. Darling went in stockinged feet to the south window of her room and although she was unable to see Miriam's car in the drive she knew her voice would carry and gave a holler that she was on her way down, "Come on in!" Morning mist was rising from the summer fields; it was being chased away by the fast-rising July sun.

The two young women bumped into one another in the kitchen. Miriam, so tall and slender, was sipping quickly at half a cup of coffee. Darling hugged her friend. Fuzzy old Balzac purred lovingly trying to get attention for his breakfast and meandered in and out of four pretty legs. Miriam's deep green eyes were animated by the moist morning and by her curiosity. "Whose car is that parked in the drive?" Darling's eyebrows raised, "Car?" She cranked open the casement window above the sink and craned her neck to see. Miriam said, "Yeah. A Mustang."

"I'll say. A yellow ragtop! And it's brand spanking new. What a pretty little thing. Well, Paul did say he was gonna buy a new car, but how did he manage to do that overnight? Shall I wake him?"

"Yeah. Go ahead, we've got time. Maybe he'll let us take it to church."

Darling tiptoed down the hall toward her brother's room. The door was locked, she rapped lightly. "Paul. Paul? Are you in there?"

No answer.

Darling thought, of course he's in there.

She went softly up the stairs to her room and came back down with two different sizes of bobby pins; this time the little one didn't work but one prong of the big one did. The room was nearly dark and quite aromatic; a votive burned very low. Darling was pretty sure she could distinguish two lumps in the bedcovers. She quickly turned the lock button and heard a little moany exhalation as she quietly closed the door. She tiptoed hurriedly back down the hallway and with eyes the size of saucers she exclaimed to Miriam, "There's somebody in there with him!" She dropped the bobby pins into her shoulder bag.

"She's got a nice car."

"Well I'll be damned."

"Come on, let's go. You ready?"

"Yeah. Son of a gun, right in our own house. Well! Oh, shit, Mim, wait. I forgot to feed the cat!"

All the way into town Darling ranted and raved about the "intruder," even though it was already a hot muggy day, too hot to waste much energy in angry display. Miriam drove along, her nose always close to the windshield so she could see, and tried to reason with her friend. "He's a grown man, Darling. I guess he can do what he wants," then asking, "But who do you think it could be? I thought you and Paul weren't doing any of those kinds of things for a while."

"Yeah. I mean, no, you're right, we're not. But we had a real blowout last night. We said some really rotten things."

"Oh, no. Darling. You didn't. Why do you two have to carry on like that?"

"I don't know. We've just always been fighters I guess. We get over it. You know that. And sometimes it clears the air. But sometimes I wish it wasn't that way."

"Darling. What would your mother say?"

"Oh, she'd either side with one of us and then things would really get good. Or she'd just tell us to knock it off. Once in a while she'd get Dad into it and then she and he would go at it for days, long after Paul and I had forgotten about the whole thing."

"It's so sad."

"No it isn't sad Mim. We never really mean any harm."

"No. I mean like I just love you both, you know. And I just hate to see it happening, especially now. You know?"

"Can we drop it? He's obviously doing this to get even with me. And I'm sure we'll have another fight about that! Anyway, I don't wanna fight about it now. How's it been going with you?"

"Oh, eh, it's okay. I'm really pretty bored though, you know? I'm thinking about getting another job. You know, like, now that I finally have my degree."

"What's wrong with being a buyer for Wanamaker's?"

"Nothing, textiles is a very exciting business. But, you know, I mean, I dunno. It's just not me I guess. I mean it's not what I've been going to school for. I think I should be looking for a teaching job, I liked student teaching at Rider. Do you think I'd make an okay teacher?"

"Are you shitting me? I've always thought you were perfect for it! God, yes, you'd make an excellent teacher. What do you think? Kindergarten or third grade?"

"Oh, I dunno, something like that, or maybe a Freshman Spanish class, high school, you know. It's gonna take me about a year to find something and get situated. Maybe by next fall, you know, '68. I'd love to get my own place. I'm twenty-one now you know." Darling was slightly jealous of Miriam's unexercised freedom. "Yeah. But, shit man, what would your mother say? She is not going to like that idea."

"We'll just have to wait and see."

Miriam pulled the Volkswagen up to the curb beneath a maple tree on Main Street. The two chattered as they passed along the shady street with its eighteenth-century homes, every house with a porch and spindles, some had gingerbread trimmings, all were painted somber grays or rust browns or bright white clapboards with contrasting louvered shutters at the tall four-over-four windows with their pale green wavering panes. Darling watched Miriam's eyes glisten and flash in the sunny shade and watched Miriam's shoulder length platinum blonde hair turn golden in the dappled morning light. Miriam was a good two inches taller than Darling's five-feet-six-and-a-half, and all of it was legs; a whole lot closer to the Twiggy look. Darling had long thought that it was Miriam who should be modeling and often tried to coax her older friend to take her eyeglasses off more often to reveal those bottle-green eyes surrounded by heavily thick and lustrous sable lashes and brows. But the lenses of the glasses were three-eighths of an inch thick and Darling knew Miriam was nearly blind without her spectacles. Contact lenses were still very experimental and expensive in those days.

The atmosphere was oppressively close inside the big white Baptist church, and people were fanning themselves with their programs and singing *Rock of Ages* not very enthusiastically. Darling squirmed quite a lot, wondering what her brother was up to now. Oh, well. She knew she would corner him and grill him next chance she got.

After church and before Sunday dinner at Miriam's house, Miriam played with her new hot curlers, the latest rage, and Darling floundered around on Miriam's bed with a *Cosmopolitan* (which was always tucked beneath the mattress) and watched. "What do you make of that brother o' mine?"

"Oh. Please don't ask me that Darling. You know I have a horrific crush on him. Maybe he's just lonely."

"For heaven's sake, Mim, we're all lonely, aren't we? What do you suppose he'd do if he came into my room and found somebody besides me in my bed?"

"Maybe he wouldn't just come sneaking into your room."

"Come on, Mim, the damned car was parked right outside the kitchen door. If it'd been my turn to drive I would've had to drive the Valiant across the front lawn the way that idiot parked!"

"Green-eyed monnnssstter."

"Think so?"

"Really, Darling, you should hear yourself. Why don't you just get yourself a new boyfriend? I sometimes think I'd like one. And you would certainly have your choice. I really don't think your mother would want you to punish yourself so badly. She did love you."

Darling let the magazine slip to the floor. "Oh, Mim. I guess you're right. But, like, it's not just about Mom any more, you know? I'm just, like, not very inclined to, like, drop everything I'm interested in and become involved with something somebody else is interested in, just so that somebody else will be interested in me. Know what I mean?" Miriam was seated at the little white dressing table, brushing out long soft pale curls, "Think that's really how it is?"

"Seems like it." Darling rolled over on the bed and stretched like a cat. She let her head dangle over the side of the bed, she laid looking upside-down at the trim white panel door and feeling the rush of her own blood making tiny pools inside her head. Her long gold hair lay puddled on the floor. She sighed, exasperated. "Why can't men and women just be friends? Why does it always have to be so complicated?"

Miriam re-assembled her hot curler kit. "You would definitely know more than me on that score. But I do think I'd like to have a date now and then. Of course, I think I might drop everything for Paul. But, he never even sees me. They can't all be bad, can they?"

"Maybe not Mim. I'm sure I've still got a lot to learn. Especially after that fiasco with that vulture Buzz. I'm not so sure I know very much about anything anymore. So. You really are in love with Paul, aren't you? I can't blame you. Me too. But he's not Mr. Perfect either, Mim. He's been a real son-of-a-bitch the last couple of days." Miriam started, "Oh, shshsh, she'll hear you!" Then she giggled. "Ugh." Darling made one of her best ugly faces at the door. "Maybe it's just me, I don't know," continuing in barely more than a whisper, "I did meet a real nice guy at the track Friday night, the Merc did real well too."

"Yeah? How was it?'

"Oh, it was boss! We blew the doors off a '57 Chevy, didn't set any records, but we won!"

"Oh. Well that's great and everything, but, I mean, with the guy, you know?"

They laughed, then quickly covered their mouths, trying not to be too loud. "Oh, with the guy. Well, I didn't exactly meet him. But I did see him. And, oh, Mim, he's just sooo cool. He's got a fifty-six."

"Well that's not going to bring you much closer is it?"

"Maybe, maybe not. I got roses from him last night."

Miriam draped her long self across the bed and lay face to face with Darling. Their mouths were only inches apart. In an excited whisper she said, "You're shitting me! Neat! How? What?"

"That's what has me, like, really puzzled. I don't know how he found me. But he did. He could have looked up the registration on the Merc I guess. But the Merc is registered to Street Stock. But. The insurance is in my name, maybe that was it? No. How'd he find out about our house? And on a weekend!" Darling would never know that the little driver of the flower shop truck, Keithy Head, had simply assumed that since the garage was closed, he should deliver the flowers to the Randolph home. Small towns.

"If you ask me, he sounds pretty yummy so far. I imagine he is good looking."

"Mmm. He kind of looks just like Paul, only a little shorter."

"Mmm. At the track you say. You mean to tell me this one might actually be interested in something you're interested in?"

"Yeah."

"Ooh, Darling, this sounds like it might be a good one."

"Just may be."

"You're not scared are you?"

"A little. Besides, Paul doesn't like the idea much."

"Oh, Paul. You've always been able to wrap him around your little finger."

"Not any more. Something's happened to him, Mim. He's been getting weirder and weirder. What about this morning? Who was that? And, Mim, he says he's getting rid of the garage." Miriam rose when she heard the motions of dinner being served. She bit her lip, "The garage? Wow. Then that means you won't be coming into town so often, will you? We'd better go in now. Well, uhm. Oh, shit."


Mr. Bolton never even looked up from the Sunday paper until everything was served and the girls were seated and Mrs. Bolton had removed the apron from her squat girth. The short hairless deacon of the church never mentioned that the great Vivien Leigh had died, or that two B-52 Stratofortresses had collided on a bombing run killing six crewmembers, he just stood at the head of the table to say grace. At this Darling always bowed her head and peeped through sparse fawn colored eyebrows at Miriam who, sitting directly across from Darling, seemed intent on solemnity but reached her long leg over to give Darling a jesting tap on the foot while her father prayed for the food but not for the dead.

When they finally set to, Mrs. Bolton began the instant she passed the green beans with her never-ending criticism. This time in particular, it was why the girls were not wearing their hair pinned up, especially since they were supposed to be young ladies, and besides it would be more practical in all this heat. Darling, who took every available opportunity to aggravate Mrs. Bolton, claimed it would be an even better idea to take a drive down to the shore on a day like today, which was true enough but caused the immediate knitting of stern eyebrows. Miriam attempted, as always, to repair the damage by saying, "Oh, Darling. You are so right. But, jeez, we'd never be able to make it down and back and shower and be ready for evening services. Why we'd never even have a chance to get our feet wet."

Mrs. Bolton nodded in definite agreement, and holding her food in the side of her mouth heartily agreed and went on and on, "I'm glad you're finally beginning to think with your head, Miriam. And the flies are always so detestable, and the traffic in this sweltering heat, and the sand is so hot, and the water is always too cold, or else it's so warm that it's filled with jellyfish..."

"Yes, Mother."

"Mrs. Bolton, now that we all know how much you love the ocean, did you enjoy the service today?"

Mrs. Bolton launched into her tirade about the overuse of *John 3:16*, and why she didn't think Reverend Pitman would last long and so on and so on. Mr. Bolton, true to his character as well, shoveled his dinner into his mouth without a word more than "pass me," placed his knife and fork at four o'clock and left the table without so much as a by-your-leave and returned to his Sunday paper, picking up at, "Hanoi losses put at 505 in two days."

As usual, by the time Mrs. Bolton had complained her way through the meal, no one cared for dessert. Miriam and Darling had the dishes washed and dried and were out the door in twenty minutes, laughing their way to the Volkswagen and enjoying the hot sunshine and the humid fresh air. In the safe haven of the VW, Darling threw herself back as if exhausted and said, "God. I still don't know how you can stand it!" Then she sat up just as quickly. Miriam said, "At least she's consistent. I'm working on it. Wonder what Paul's up to now." And they were off for the trip to the Randolph's.

# CHAPTER 13

David hitchhiked from Bordentown to the Littleton address shown on Paul's card. The garage was deserted. There was, however, a card posted in the office window that directed all inquiries to the telephone number of their home in the country. David wrote the number on the back of Paul's card.

He walked about a mile back through town and found Kaelin's Flying-A Station just about to close. There he inquired about the Randolph place and how he could get there. David was in luck so far; he had at least been headed in the right direction. So, he followed Vernon Kaelin's long skinny finger for two and a half miles west by northwest, "up the mount," as Kaelin had said, and he stumbled upon a narrow lane marked by a rural route mailbox, Prof. P.M. Randolph, and immediately set to walking the meandering half mile tunnel of trees. David was thinking, hmm, a professor. Dad would like this all right. Jesus, they really live all the way out here? David felt strange as he walked the lane, like he did during the long walks of hunting season. He saw rabbits scurrying from his path and heard the quail teasing him from the cover of the blackberry bushes. David's heart nearly stopped in his chest when he spied a magnificent golden pheasant cock bird and two hens making their way as bold as could be across an open field, the sunshine glinting brilliantly in all directions from the cock's iridescent neck rings.

Even with a Frequency Modulation (FM) converter (which Miriam did not have anyway), you could only get church music on Sunday mornings in those days. But now it was afternoon and a group called The Box Tops was performing *The Letter*, which was quickly making its way to the top of the charts and would leave The Box Tops as a band with something of a reputation as a one-hit-wonder. Miriam and Darling were groovin' with the tune and trying to learn the words.

Miriam and Darling puttered up the lane in the little blue Volkswagen. The music was blasting heavy on the bass, they had the windows rolled all the way down, their hair was flying everywhere and the VW was trailing a matched pair of rolling dust clouds.

The two ladies pulled up just short of a young man who stood aside as they approached and was smiling at them from the canal side of the sandy lane. As soon as David and Darling recognized one another they both began to laugh. And for a moment Miriam wondered what was going on, but then she heard Darling exclaim, "It's him!"

"Who him? Oh, *him* him!"

"Shit, yeah! It's Dave! Remember the guy I told you about from the track? Well that's him!"

"Looks like he's found you. Better ask him if he wants to ride the rest of the way." Darling smiled happily, bussed her friend on the cheek and said, "Thanks, Mim." And through the open window David heard the two pretty girls beckoning him to get into their car. His fantasies were suddenly the order of the day. David jumped onto the running board and hung on to the frame of the door on Darling's side of the car. The VW jumped into gear and the Yardbirds were going gulng, gulng, gulng, gulng, *For Your Love*, as they passed through the gate to a place denoted by a brass plaque on an old oak tree: ARROWHEAD.

When the three arrived at the house, the yellow Mustang was gone and so was Paul. The house felt oddly vacant, like a museum after hours. Miriam quietly made up her mind to stick around for a while. It would not be proper for her friend to be left alone like this, and this situation might just prove to have some interesting results.

David's self said, "Whoa, man. Be careful." David said, "I kind of assumed your parents, or, like, Paul, or somebody would be around."

Darling resisted the urge to tell David that to assume is to make an ass out of 'u' and 'me.' She did not tell him that her parents were dead. She did not know what to say about Paul. Best to let him think what he wants, he will anyway. She gaily chortled, "Mim and I are somebodies."

Miriam could find nothing inexcusable about David's manners. In fact, he seemed like he might be pretty close to a gentleman for a twentieth century man. Miriam did not know many twentieth century men. Her three older brothers were much older, Miriam being a late life surprise to her parents. Miriam's parents were in their late sixties now; her three brothers were all grown and gone and all missionaries. It was expected that Miriam would become the wife of a missionary one day in the not too distant future, there to serve for the remainder of her life. For this reason, young Miriam lived a rather cloistered existence, forbidden the company of any but the few eligible men of the church who had not already been drafted; there were three who seemed to be bound for missionary service. Miriam found them all homely and profoundly boring. Square. (That's expressed with the two index fingers drawing a box in mid-air.)

Miriam always depended on Darling to be her alter ego, and devoured any news that Darling could provide of the outside, "the greater world," as Miriam called it. But this was really something else. This guy had just come from out of nowhere it seemed and a long way from nowhere at that, just to see her friend.

Miriam took her place at the piano. She could not stay too much longer, she would be missed, but she did enjoy playing a medley of old hymns on Mrs. Randolph's Cunningham; and although Mrs. Randolph had always accused Miriam of having only an "upright touch," it was the first time anyone had touched its ivories since the day she died.

David was busy admiring a portrait of Darling. Pastels. Really quite a good likeness, and such an emotional touch. Very nice. He thought he recognized the noise in his ears as *Onward Christian Soldiers* and for a moment he thought, oh my God, don't tell me my princess is a Holy Roller! But he did not complain out loud. His self told him she would be worth whatever trouble he was getting himself into. And his penis would have to wait. The young women were reading one another's thoughts. Miriam was thinking, I've got to get home, but I don't want to leave Darling here all alone with this guy and I don't know when I'll get to see her again. It's so hard to get her to church anymore. Darling was thinking, this is all very nice and everything, but where in the hell is Paul? How did David ever find us? How long does he expect to stay?

So Darling neglected to offer anyone refreshment and Miriam moved into a short and light-hearted rendition of Chopin's *Polonaise (in A-Flat Minor, Opus 53)*, and without verbal communication it was agreed that after this last number, the two women would offer to give David a lift to wherever it was he was going. That turned out to be Bordentown. No one had noticed the note left by Paul.

Now, here's where Miriam always got into trouble for being friendly with, "that troublesome, pig-headed little monster," of whom Miriam's mother spoke often and warned against repeatedly. Miriam phoned her mother and told her that she would be gone a bit longer than expected because she and Darling had an errand to run before Miriam could come home. Although it was agreed that Miriam could indeed run the errand with Darling, Miriam knew in her heart that the Inquisition awaited her whenever she did get home again. And Miriam hoped she would make it back in time to attend evening services. That would help greatly to ease the situation. Maybe her mother would even forget. There must always be hope.

# CHAPTER 14

The three drove the twelve miles to Dave's Hilltop Garage in Bordentown. Trophies and ribbons adorned the shop. Loving cups and engraved hubcaps and racing colors turned up even in the pristine tile bath. A wall-length poster announced: I LOVE MY HOOKER HEADERS

David had started out at age thirteen changing tires for "Big Daddy" Don Garlits. David lived the track. And a stint at Bordentown Military Academy had not stopped him. His parents had given up on him shortly after that, when he made "some silly little girl" pregnant and she had refused to have an abortion, no matter how much they were willing to pay. David opted for a job instead of pre-med school and his parents simply threw their hands up and banished him.

Darling wandered about the garage in amazement. "Dave, this is really far out! I mean, like, Paul and I, we fool around, we like our Rods but damn! You're a *champion* David, the real thing."

David no longer blushed when he heard remarks like the one Darling just made. He was not really listening to her at all. He was busy wrestling with his own mind and body, trying to keep himself from pulling Darling right straight into his arms. If she had been any other girl he would have, but this one was not just any other girl. David was disappointed with the sound of his own voice but the words were out before he knew what was happening. "Please. Don't make me want you any more than I already do. It's just wrecking my fucking life, or I'm wrecking it, or something is. I'm only sure it's falling apart."

"Say what?"

Is this what he walked all the way to Littleton to tell me? Darling was either flattered or insulted, she wasn't sure which. She did not even know David, although now she had an admiration for him that was not inconsistent with what she had observed of his behavior at the track last

Friday night. But this guy was being very straightforward, out front as they say. Was he like this all the time? Darling wondered. She thought, I'll bet he never has a minute to waste. But, if he hasn't got a minute to waste, he's not ever gonna have the time for me. Darling knew she needed a great deal of attention. David was at the very least well accomplished, especially for his age and apparent circumstances. Darling changed the subject quickly. She could be very bold herself. But when she was on the receiving end of bold, unless it was from her brother, Darling was still not quite sure how to react, or where it might lead. Mistakes she had made in the past reared up to haunt her, and besides, she had left her friend to the hundreds of autographed photographs too long ago now. As Darling had so recently discovered, even Miriam could get bored. "We mustn't leave Mim alone for so long." Darling slid along the fender of the Chevy, away from David's adoring gaze.

"Oh, I doubt if she's alone. She's prob'ly upstairs, it's a lot cooler up there." And David smiled his very best bad boy smile.

"Upstairs?"

"Yeah. Dieter's upstairs, haven't you heard him walking around?" Darling looked up in disbelief, asking herself, how in the living hell could you possibly let this happen? Saying, "And just, like, who might this Dieter be?"

"Oh, Dieter's my sidekick, we're buddies. He's going in the Army in a couple-a weeks. I gave him my key. And my car. I have a studio upstairs, it's where I sleep."

Darling's left eyebrow arched radically. As the two made their ways back into the office she caught David nearly drooling over the backs of her legs. She ignored David's gaze and went back to looking around for Miriam. "Do you really think she's found her way up there?" She looked up at the ceiling again, praying not. "Maybe she's gone out to the car." She peeked at the Volkswagen. No.

Darling did not like this at all. Although Miriam was the older, Darling took her responsibility very seriously. And if anything ever happened, like that, Mrs. Bolton would no doubt never let them see each other again. It was definitely time to find a way to make as hasty a departure as could peacefully be managed.

At the top of the stairs, Darling saw Miriam seated on David's bed better than elbow to elbow with this person she presumed was Dieter. Both Dieter and Miriam were intently examining David's drawings and sketches. On the floor beside them lay a yellowed surrealistic watercolor heavy with lacquer, even then the morning glories remained bright and most excellent, it was titled *The Innocent Garden*. A calmness and a peace dominated the atmosphere surrounding the couple on David's bed; the two themselves were radiant. Darling knew right away she had trouble.

Darling carefully approached the couple and quietly she said, "Mim. Mim, we'd better be going." She lightly touched Miriam's hand. Darling's voice became a bit more, then a great deal more, insistent, "Mim, come along dear. Mim. Mim, please. Your mother is going to flay me alive for this."

Miriam looked at Darling and did move to go along, but Dieter did not easily give up her hand. When Darling saw them trying to part and gazing deep into one another's eyes, she looked furiously at David and, leading Miriam down the steps by her shoulders, announced, "I'll drive."

# CHAPTER 15

That summer of 1967 would be remembered in some circles as the Summer of Love. In truth, our nation was in the throes of becoming so sorry it elected Lyndon Johnson it could die. Industrial perfection was nearly achieved and there was money for everyone in the making of tanks, planes, bombs, smaller ammunition, helicopters, submarines, and the further development of napalm. Unemployment was low and taxes skyrocketed under The Great Society, and as long as there was a war on it would work. Darling had just discovered that David was employed in the making of ammunitions, bombs, and rocket boosters at the Burlington Ammunition Plant.

A late afternoon thunderstorm was gathering as Darling and Miriam drove home. Darling was on a tirade to Miriam about how she could not possibly have any further sentiments toward this guy for he had suddenly become a representative of everything that was presently driving her crazy. "Come on, Mim, snap out of it, at least a little, will ya? That guy, that Dieter? You know, like, man, he's going in three weeks?"

"Yeah."

"He told you about it?"

"Uh-huh."

Miriam was deep within the reverie of her own experiences. She had finally met someone whose person was genuine, honest, decent, and very pleasing to her. In fact, even in appearance, Miriam and Dieter resembled one another (except that Dieter had carrot red hair). Dieter was tall and lanky too and he even wore glasses, coke bottles. He had been wearing a neatly pressed pink Oxford cloth shirt with only a few freckles exposed at the open collar, no hairs showing, and the cuffs on each sleeve turned up neatly, twice. His blue jeans were old and faded and soft and so were his blue eyes. Although not formally well educated, Dieter seemed to have an appreciation for art and the good things in life. In a way, he reminded Miriam of Paul. Dieter was quiet and simple, humble with an underlying warmth that suggested ability far deeper than the eye could see. Miriam was sure he would make a fine soldier. And Miriam was grateful.

Darling drove along, for a time putting up with the silence. She was driving very carefully, for Miriam's sake, and besides, the Volkswagen just would not go very fast. Darling tried to be patient, but patience is an art, it cannot be taught, it can only be learned. And Darling had not learned very well; she had never learned very well at all about patience. Miriam was more than unusually quiet it seemed to her. Something was bad wrong. Darling wanted to know just exactly what was going on. She could not believe the whole thing could be this serious right off the bat. She nudged at Miriam's elbow. "Mim."

"Hmm?"

"What happened up there?"

"I dunno, for certain. We just kind of fused together; it only took a few minutes. God was there. He smiled on us."

"Fused together. Whadderya Bonzo-Dog-Band?"

"Guess so. I only know we're staying together. For all time."

"He told you that?"

"We both just knew it."

"But Mim, he's leaving. Dieter's going into the Army."

Miriam looked quite naturally into Darling's eyes. She said, "Yes, Darling. He is. And he's probably going to go straight to Vietnam. He knows that; he's already been told that. But I am going to wait for him."

Darling was dumbfounded and before she knew it she had blurted out, "God, Mim, forty-one guys died just yesterday. How many are dying right this minute?" She slammed the heel of her hand against the steering wheel, frustrated. What the hell was she going to do now? Mrs. Bolton would murder them both for this.

Miriam's mind wasn't listening, it was thinking quickly now, like computer digits flicking over faster and faster. She knew her parents would not approve. But if she could get that teaching job and be out on her own, doing her own thing, then by the time Dieter came home from Over There, there could be nothing to stop them from being together. And she was thinking, if it is meant to be, the way will be made. She finally said, "We mustn't tell Mother. Not yet. Promise me."

"No shit! Oh, fuck, man, no, Mim, I can promise you that. Cross my heart and hope to *die*. You're right about that one." Darling could not give up without one last ditch effort to dissuade her friend, all she could see was heartache ahead, but then again, Darling had never felt the way Miriam apparently felt about Dieter about anyone. "I'm just going to drive you on home. You're late enough already. I can walk on down to Street Stock. I wanna have a look at the Merc anyway." Miriam hesitantly agreed. "Listen, Mim, how can you possibly be in love with this guy?"

"It's a higher love Darling. You see, Dieter liked me right away, he accepted me for what I am, and I he. He has no one to wait for him, so I will wait for him. It's that simple."

"It is? Well, hell, Mim. I've just found out that the person I thought might be good for me is a lecher and a warmonger. He makes brass casings for one hundred fifty-five-millimeter howitzer shells! Believe me, I just went through this yesterday and it isn't worth it. He can have all the NHRA championships he wants. He's still a creep. First impressions don't mean a goddamn thing! You don't even know who Dieter is or where he came from."

"I'm tellin' ya, it doesn't matter. Can't you see? It was a religious experience. Does Dave really make those shells you said?"

Darling's mind flashed blind with disbelief. A religious experience. Holy shit. "That's what he says, eight to five, five days a week, plus a lot of overtime when somebody needs something right away. He says it's been a pretty good living since he dropped out of his first semester of college. Can you fucking believe it? Until lately he's had his winnings to make getting by into luxury, and now something's happened and he thinks he's lost his touch."

With a wry smile, Miriam said, "Heavy. If he's working in an ammunition factory, it's no wonder his car fell apart and he isn't breaking any records lately."

"So, you *are* in there!" Darling grinned widely and Miriam laughed. Darling pouted, "It isn't funny, Mim, my little black heart's just broken over it."

"Oh, come on, of course it isn't. You fall in love at least once or twice a year."

"But, you saw his work, he's an artist! Like, how can a goddamn artist exist in peace inside the rest of that person?"

"Maybe he doesn't exist in peace."

"God, I love you so much."

"With Dieter and me it doesn't matter what happens when he gets back. I'm not expecting anything. It's just that if he knows there's someone here, waiting for him, well, that might just help him to get back safely."

"You, Mim, are just the purest heart I have ever known."

On the hilltop in Bordentown a similar conversation was taking place. David was not feeling good about himself, not good at all. He knew something had gone very wrong. He just wasn't really sure of what that something was. Perhaps he should have taken both Miriam and Darling upstairs to meet Dieter as soon as they arrived, or perhaps he should have called Dieter downstairs. It was just that this had been his first opportunity to be alone with Darling; he just couldn't let such an opportunity go by without taking advantage of it and now he had. Now whatever had happened had happened. David was not too sure just what that was, but he was pretty sure he had blown it.

Dieter came bounding down the steps shortly after the girls left. He stood at the windows of the bay doors, wearing a smile David thought was going to break his face as he watched the little blue Volkswagen disappear at the highway bridge. "I knew she'd have a Bug."

"Oh, you *are* conscious. Man, you were like in a fucking trance. What happened up there?"

Dieter, in one telling motion, stuffed his hands deep into his pockets, shrugged his shoulders and said, "Oh, nothin'," but his face and particularly his slightly protruding ears were rapidly becoming a bright crimson. For a moment David thought he saw Dieter positively glowing, he said, "Well, it sure as hell seems like you made out a damned sight better than I did." Dieter said nothing, he simply walked over to the workbench and began choosing and fondling a few tools.

David noticed the sudden spring in Dieter's movements, the new lightness of his touch. Dieter stripped from his shirt to his T-shirt saying, "We'd better get to work on this old Chevy. There's not a whole lot of time." David agreed, but as he began to raise the hood he decided to give it one more try. "Dieter."

"Yeah Davie."

"Are you like for certain you don't want to tell me anything?"

"Yeah, I'm fine."

"Okay. Well. Then. What did you think of *my* girl, Darling?"

Dieter smiled a bit self-consciously and looked down at the floor for a moment, "*Is* she? Your girl?"

Now David began to get busy removing the manifold cover. "Oh, yeah. She may not know it yet. But she is."

"She's fine, Davie, real fine." Dieter joined again in the work, adding, "So's Mim."

"Mim." David and Dieter both chuckled and went to the serious business of replacing the seal on the Chevy. It would give them problems and they would be working far into the night to get it right; take it out and run it, bring it back and fix it, over and over. The two friends tried to allay their innermost thoughts and fears by keeping their hands and minds busy. But in their hearts, each knew what the other was thinking and that thought was, then let's get these wheels on the road so we can at least take those two pretty girls out.

Darling left Miriam and the little blue Volkswagen in the drive. She waved goodbye and blew a kiss to Miriam's mother who was waiting at the front door, and Darling knew she was probably fuming. Without a word Darling headed on her way back through town.

Miriam would stand up well against Mrs. Bolton's severe looks; she was used to them. She just said, "I'm hurrying Mother, I'll be ready for services. Just give me a minute to freshen up and we'll all be on our way, okay?" This Mrs. Bolton could only complain about but did allow. And so, Miriam escaped the great maelstrom of difficulties Mr. Bolton had had to suffer right up until the very moment Miriam's car pulled into the drive.

Miriam stared into the glass at her dressing table and knew this was not the time to mention anything to her mother about wanting to teach, or to move away. She wondered as she dressed when would be a good time, but was confident that the right time would eventually be made clear to her. Miriam could see the storm breaking in heavy droplets, "Oh, Darling's going to get soaked!" For a moment Miriam thought about chasing Darling down in the Volkswagen and giving her a ride home, but she shot a glance at her closed door and knew she'd better get a move on. Reality was waiting, just on the other side.

# CHAPTER 16

Darling approached the garages. It was so quiet in town on Sundays. There were still Blue laws in those days; all the shops were closed up tight. All she could hear was the steady shshsh of the rain falling, the thunder rolling down, and the clopping of her wet yellow patent leather flats hitting the driveway at the shop; looking up to anticipate the crackle of lightning, discharging ions, the flash, smelling the air so clean.

Street Stock was quiet, almost stark, Paul had really closed everything, shutting down. A brief tidbit of their conversation popped into her head, "The garage goes."

"Whaddya mean goes?"

"Which word didn't you understand?" Or something like that anyway.

Behind the darkened windows of the first bay rested the cherry red 1953 Mercury. It looked as if it had been freshly washed and waxed. Ernest always took such care when he did things; it always had to be just right. She guessed he must be looking for work again now. Darling thought about letting herself into the garage, just for a little while, just to see the Merc one more time, but she knew she would not be able to settle for just a look, she would want to drive it. That thought quickly took her mind back to the way she had parked it in that cornfield. She shivered.

Darling set out for home. What was now a heavy downpour soaked her hair flat against her bare arms, making the goose bumps rise, the water rolling down her forehead and dripping from her eyelashes, her nose, her chin. Her lips were almost purple and she was wondering why in the hell she had wanted to walk in the first place. Darling chastised herself half-heartedly for some of the stupid things she did, wondered what she had gotten herself into this time, first with David, now, and more importantly, this thing with Mim and Dieter. This was bad. But, Darling had never seen Miriam look so beautiful as she had on that ride home. Miriam's eyes always became so exotically rounded and deep whenever the humidity was high, even more so on very hot thunderstormy days like today, and it was for certain she was in love with Dieter. I guess he's not so bad, she thought, he's just as shy as Mim is.

She walked beneath the dripping maple trees on Main Street, past the happy old homes. She tried the door of the Post Office but it was locked. NO BOX HOLDERS AFTER 2PM ON SUNDAYS. She carried on toward the news agency where you could still get a fountain Coke with a shot of cherry syrup in it, and where one went to thumb through the new magazines and play a little pinball, hang around, meet people, or to pick up the *New York Times*. It was closed now too. The nice green and white striped awning was cranked shut, but the porch that it was attached to was good cover. Faint strains of the Byrds' *Hey, Mr. Tambourine Man* filtered down from the tiny apartment above the shop.

Darling rubbed her arms and wrung her hair and threw it back over her shoulder. She sat down on the red brick steps under the porch-roof and rested. She emptied the water from her shoes and waited for the rain to let up at least a little bit. It was really coming down hard now, pitchforks and hammer handles as they say in New Jersey. The news agency made her think about its crowd, it would be a new crowd now, but the crowd of her young teen days. She thought about Al Williams, he was nice, and so tall and good looking too. His father owned the big dairy farm on Fostertown Road. Al was probably going to be finishing at Texas A&M this year. There was Carl Paetzel whose parents had a whole pack of new money to spend on Carl, so he was probably still doing nothing. There was Karen Irons, three years ahead of Darling, and the captain of the cheerleading squad who had married Billy Doyle, the captain of the football team. They were in Florida where Billy was training to be a fighter pilot. They had gone together all through high school and college. And then there was Toby Fenton, the shy chubby boy who had grown up to be a shy chubby man with the biggest darkest brownest eyes anyone had ever seen. He worked his father's small farm now and spent the rest of his time as a hook-and-ladder man for the Volunteer Fire Department, which was right next door to the news agency. Hillman Chambers had wrecked his brand-new Harley Davidson about a month after he returned from Vietnam and died. The dragsters and bikers from three counties lined up like silver-studded ribbon candy the day they buried Hillman. Darling wondered what the rest of them were up to these days.

Across the street and over just a few houses, was the big white Baptist church, its white stucco front now gray in the rain. Its original Georgian lines had been enhanced about sixty years before with a columned facade and broad marble steps. That made it a nice wedding church, much prettier for grand entrances and recessions than the dark red brick and steeply gabled slate roof of the old Methodist church just a little farther down and on this side of the street, where Darling was a member. No fun though so Darling went to church with Miriam. The Methodist church did boast some of the most beautiful stained-glass windows in the colonial states and a very fine pipe organ. There was a big old Buttonwood tree out front that gave such a lovely shade to the chattering emergent congregation on hot summer days. But then there was the graveyard coming right up to it, and all the way up to the sidewalk. Uncle Hank Littleton was listed on that War Memorial among many others. Uncle Hank, a fighter jock had survived World War II only to be killed in Korea, which was another war that had never been called a war.

Darling stood up and fluffed her thin cotton blouse out until it began to respond and lift away from her skin. Not one car had passed by during the whole time she'd sat on the news agency step. Upstairs, Ray Charles was crooning *You Don't Know Me* but the rain was letting up and would soon cease. It did, at least to a tumbling mist, and Darling carried on toward home.

The sun began to peek through now and then just enough to encourage a lot of steam to rise in little jets from the Earth, making the pavement seethe and the growing things appear lush, dense and heavily laden. Darling walked along in silence and listened carefully, certain she could hear the photosynthesis, and she was having in her heart a strong urge to flee. She walked. Her mind soon followed after a place in her heart and she was gone, into a peaceful place, that full-blooming rose, taking comfort in knowing that both feet were striking the Earth one right after the other.

Past Kaelin's, across the conical corners, and up toward the mount and Littleton Lane. Soon she was passing the very cornfield of her nightmare. The bright green stalks stood tall and glistened from the rain; they were standing still now for there would be no breeze after a storm like that, just the heavy-clear air and the late bright sun; perfect conditions for a rainbow. She stared at the oak tree, its crown barely visible in the distance above the cornstalks from this point of view, with both feet on the ground. She dreaded its feeling as she had never done before and her mind became shrouded in that vision of Death. She cried out loud, "LET HIM WAIT!" and made a dash for the end of the lane, the lane that meandered along deep into a mystical place of safety.

When at last she arrived at Arrowhead, the house was empty again. Darling ran up the stairs to her room, threw her wet clothes across the foot of her four-poster bed, pulled the peacock blue paisley caftan over her head and dried her hair roughly with a towel. Curiosity overcame her as she did so. It seemed as if the harder she rubbed her head the stronger that sense of curiosity became. She went barefoot down the stairs to look for Paul. There was still no Paul, but this time she found the note: **I'm still in love with "Effie," tra la -**

The roses caught her eye and she touched them by cupping her hand under just one bud and letting her fingers find its tenderness as if it were a breast. She left the note on the dining room table, "Dammit." She lit a cigarette and wandered down the darkened hall and into her father's study. She sat in the leather swivel chair behind the desk and gave a tug on the lamp chain. Balzac jumped into her lap. He purred and pushed and she stroked him mindlessly. Beneath the concentrated spot of light there was a file lying open. There were two or three rumpled pieces of paper and some doodles in red ink done by Paul. Paul had spent quite some time with this one and he had left it lying there. "For me to find."

The open file contained a few papers, crinkled and yellowed, and each seemed to be a ripped off section of some larger document, each amounting to an expense of some kind. The rest of the worn old file contained ancient ledger pages. The ledger pages dated back to the year Paul had been born, to the very month Paul had been born, "Oh, Jesus. This is within three days of the day Paul had been born!" Page after page documented disbursements from their father's personal account for expenses beginning with obstetrical care and hospitalization to living expenses and gifts for the past twenty-two years. "A child."

Darling was nearly beside herself with a feeling not unlike the grief she felt for her belated parents, she unrumpled the nearest of the waste papers and found a half-written note from Paul; it began: **I don't know how to tell you this** then ended. The second note began: **Darling - I think we've been missing out on something** then ended. The third began: **I don't think I can go on this way** then ended.

"Oh, God, he's flipped his lid!" Darling stood up in alarm. Balzac hit the floor with a thud. He stretched then calmly walked over and jumped up onto the sofa in one precise leap. Darling was busy digging further into the file. There was no name mentioned anywhere. "Who the hell is this? Who was this for? There was definitely another woman in Dad's life and he has paid her bills to have this child and has continuously given the woman not all that much money toward its support, but was it a boy or a girl? And where are they?" Darling felt the butterflies. To think there must be another one of them somewhere, she and Paul were not really alone, but where?

What was it Paul had said? "I feel like my head has been in cement!" At least that's what I think he said. "Why couldn't I have just listened to what he had to say? Selfish, selfish. Stupid." Now Darling was beginning to think she knew how Paul had felt. At least to a point she could be genuinely sympathetic, but all this had happened before Darling had even been thought of. Paul had always taken his responsibility as the oldest very seriously, and now he knows he's not really the oldest. There is another who arrived just three days before Paul. Darling wondered where Paul was and why he had not stayed home at least long enough to introduce his Effie. She was feeling strangely dizzy. She was suddenly very tired.

Darling went blindly to Paul's room, the door stood half-open. She went to each of the windows and threw back the heavy draperies, something that was rarely done in her brother's room. There did not seem to be much that was missing. Paul's bath was mostly together. But his grooming articles were gone. The suitcases were still in the closet, maybe a duffel bag was gone, and his leather. She shouted, "WHO THE HELL IS EFFIE?" She listened to the question as it rang from the rafters and reverberated from the piano strings. "I WANT MY BROTHER!"

Darling collapsed and snuggled up to one of Paul's pillows, right in the middle of Paul's big old bed and sobbed away what was left of her anger. Balzac wandered into the room with his fluffy striped brush of a tail standing up as straight as a feather. He jumped up onto the bed and curled up to purr beside Darling's knees. Darling never took notice of the cat, or that most of the bedclothes were missing.


It was very dark when she finally woke up. The house was cool and breezy with the evening. The crickets were chirping loudly and the fireflies hovered near the creek at the edge of the woods. Darling latched the screen-doors and wandered up the stairs to her most familiar places.

She showered in a daze as depression began to take a firm hold on her head. She rinsed oceans of bubbles from her hair. Then, sitting on the edge of her bed, and beginning at the bottom then working slowly to the top she began to remove the tangles from her hair. She thought, Paul and I can't even talk about this, it's just not working out at all. There isn't even a soul around here for me to talk to. My dog's dead, my parents are dead and my brother's run off with someone named Effie of all goddamned things. She asked the cat, "What do you think we should do?" Balzac purred. Darling went on combing her hair and talking to herself. "Maybe I should go to George Washington, get out of here. But September isn't soon enough. I've got to get out of here now. It's downright spooky. I've never been here all alone at night before. I'm eating these pills. I just live for these pills. My little reward is always the Seconal. Maybe you're just not giving it enough time. Your father was a stone-cold bastard and an alcoholic, what will it do for you?"

Professor Randolph, always secretive, always pontificating, had drunk himself unconscious every evening for as long as Darling could remember. It was kind of the family joke that he continued teaching at all, embalmed, at least until his heart seized up suddenly and violently and fatally.

Entombed. He had given them books and good looks, strong jaw lines and plenty of criticism.

"Will the Seconals make you like Mother?" Darling's mother had been a woman who had in her own mind given up several potentially brilliant futures just to be the professor's wife, and to give birth to his beautiful and talented children. When the cord was cut, however, her obligation had been fulfilled.

The Randolph children would always be reminded of their sturdy pioneer stock, their birthrights, and their advantages, all of which they were given freely and none of which provided any excuse for failure. Their mother had given them music, the arts, and athletic posture. Although immensely talented, Mrs. Randolph remained weak-spirited and hypochondriacal, no matter how often she tried to make a comeback, until the day she died.

Darling took two more of the Seconals and lay down between crisp sheets thrown over an unmade bed. She was wet haired and naked and she knew there would be a little red trickle before morning but she did not care.

# CHAPTER 17

On that Sunday morning, shortly after Darling had intruded on Paul and Bernadette and then left with Miriam for Sunday services, Paul Randolph knew he had at least an hour to get Bernadette out of the house.

It sure had been a long night of drunken revelry mixed in with a little help from Bernadette's "beans." The morning light laid bare the perversity of it all. Bernadette was a morning nightmare, a ghoulish pallor drizzled with ruined eye makeup and a pair of eyelashes lost somewhere in Paul's sweaty pungent sheets. She really looked her age. Paul was embarrassed for Bernadette Carlani. But he persisted in treating her well until the right time arrived for them to part without him actually having to dump her.

Paul brought Bernadette a tall glass of orange juice and said, "You rest up, I'll bathe first." Bernadette had gladly wallowed among the feather pillows while Paul picked his way along, black fishnets here, strangest looking things, a miniskirt there, and his own underwear, toward the bathroom door and the redemption of a hot shower. And at that moment he couldn't remember very well why he brought her here, to Arrowhead. This was the last place he wanted to be. He had intended to stay gone until Monday afternoon, to shake Darling up a little bit, to make her realize she couldn't stay here all alone, not for long. But. Oh yeah, they'd swung by the house to drop off the BSA. "Guess I was too beat to take her all the way back to Trenton. Ah, well, ahhh." The steaming streaming water of life took it all away, at least for a good ten minutes.

Bernadette Carlani drank a few sips of juice, just enough to help wash down a couple of black beauties. Pennwalt Biphetamine 20s (amphetamine = 10mg-Dextroamphetamine = 10mg) were prescribed liberally in bottles of 100 throughout the 1960s. She threw her bluish ankles over the side of Paul's big old bed and stared at her dimpled thighs. She peeked through a crack in the curtains. Her pupils immediately constricted against the sliver of bright daylight that was cast upon dense greenery.

Bernadette had fallen for Paul Randolph right away. Who wouldn't? She had wanted to take him home and keep him, at least for a night. She had given the anxious young man a fair deal on a 1967 Mustang convertible, $2,465.00, which he had promptly christened Effie. Ef for the 'F' in Ford. Paul had said he was buying the car as a present for his sister and that he planned to join the Army on Monday. Bernadette just thought Paul Randolph was corny to the point of the adorable. And she wondered, how could such a beautiful thing be this accomplished and so naive? Well, that was her department. She knew he would be good in bed. She would make him good in bed.

Being good in bed was one of Bernadette's goals in life. She had developed her talents over twenty-five years of "doing it." She'd had boy scouts and rich old geezers, bikers and a mad scientist or two; in fact, more men than she could possibly recall, but it was only a hobby, men were not something she was serious enough about to devote any of her life to a particular one.

She'd had a baby once, gave it up for adoption. No big deal. It really was for the best. Her mother had always hated Bernadette and Bernadette thought it was because her mother was jealous.

Bernadette and her mother knew that Bernadette's father's one and only love was Bernadette. So, he had helped her out of her jam and loved her anyway. She was packed off to the Florence Crittenton Home for Unwed Mothers in Atlantic City for six months where she kept going to school and the adoption was arranged, and when she came back nobody knew. People always suspected, but who cares? Yet, privately, she would be torn apart inside whenever she had to hear about someone else's situation.

She had met lots of interesting people at Carlani's Ford Showroom. Bernadette's daddy had a lot of friends; important friends who wore a lot of heavy gold jewelry. When she was eighteen he had given her a secretarial job at the showroom where she got on well with Gino, the manager (very well hung), and eventually she was making more sales than any salesman on the floor. Then her father gave her a real job as a salesman so she could get the commissions. And Bernadette had made a lot of money. She'd had a lot of fun. But, in the last few years, she had begun to notice the time bomb of age suddenly ticking louder, another line here, there, a creaky knee joint. She had found that no trip to the Riviera, no visit to any spa, no Egyptian tomb, and no amount of money-spending seemed to be able to change it.

In her efforts to reinforce her faith in herself, Bernadette started hitting on younger and younger men. By the time she was thirty-five she had done everything from smoke pot to shoot heroin and had been pissed on or fist-fucked by numerous strangers in sleazy motel rooms to the point she had once come just a little too close to being strangled to death with her own stockings. She'd had trichomoniasis and so many abortions that her gynecologist finally tossed his hands up in despair and refused to see her any more. She thought that one in particular was unfair since he had enjoyed fucking her twice a year for a good 10 years from the end of an examining table with her feet up in stirrups and he standing on a stepping stool and how the hell else was a four-foot-eleven-inch Filipino gynecologist going to boff a beautiful woman like herself? And *she* paid *him* for the "office visit". Anyway, after he chased her out she saw another gynecologist, NOT a Catholic this time (she knew her father would not approve), and the new guy had put her on this new thing called the birth control pill and that was the end of that. She thought it was great and it hadn't taken long before she figured out that if she just kept on taking the Norlestrin and skipped the placebos she never had to have a period at all and she just loved it, no inconvenience, no embarrassment, and no hassle.

When Paul returned from the bathroom shaved and wrapped in a towel, he was surprised to find Bernadette dressed and ready to go. The eyelashes were back where they belonged and the makeup and hair were perfect again. Everything was just the way it had been when Paul first encountered Bernadette at Carlani's Ford Showroom in Trenton. Paul was internally horrified that she had not had a bath but caught himself before he blurted out anything of the kind and concluded that the big black leather shoulder bag must contain a little of everything. There she stood, sleek again from head to toe. Her perfectly teased and coifed jet-black hair flipped up at the shoulders. Her heavy straight bangs peek-a-booed those dark black eyelash-enhanced eyes. The kohl eyeliner, top and bottom, was perfect, as were the brown tinted cheekbones and the white lipstick. Inside the black fishnets she concealed the cellulite thighs to a slender effect beneath the black and white checked Celanese Fortrel miniskirt topped with the sleeveless black turtleneck. Her still small waist was draped in chains adorned with the images of Roman Emperors. Her shoes had the squared toes and low wedge heels of the Mod look she flattered herself with very nicely. Still not a bad looking woman, just a cold contrast to the glowing health and bronze musculature of the tall golden man who turned his smooth firm buttocks to her as he dressed. Bernadette pretended not to watch the rippling muscles of his broad back or the tight narrow waist or the way he put his shirt on, both sleeves at once, shooting his fists in the air as if punching out power.

What a night they had shared. Paul had come all over her, between her tiny breasts which he'd squeezed so hard around himself as she doubled her chin to hold her tongue out to every stroke, then up from behind and that old bed was just the right height. Oh, the essences that surrounded them and sent Paul's head into an eerie twilight kind of a place. And, Paul was thinking, no bath. But, she smelled okay now. Oh, well. He was dressed. He said, "Let's get something to eat. I'm starved."

At the last minute, before they left the house, while Paul was making a check to see that all the switches were turned off, Paul noticed a distinct odor that wafted toward the hallway and it was coming from his bedroom and was found to be coming from his bed. The sheets and pillow-cases were rumpled and stained, and there was no time to start another wash, Darling could be home very shortly if she didn't go to Miriam's house for Sunday dinner and Paul wasn't certain if she had said she would or not. Anyway, there was nothing to do but to rip the sheets from the bed and the coverlet and most of the pillows. Paul gathered everything into the bottom sheet and tied it and tossed the whole lump into the trunk of the Mustang thinking he would take care of it when he got home.

As Paul headed toward Trenton with Bernadette, he took no notice of a Chevy half-ton pickup headed in the opposite direction. In the passenger side of the pickup was the hitchhiker, Dave Adams, who was on his way to Street Stock in Littleton where he hoped to find Paul or Darling or both.

By the time Paul and Bernadette had reached the red light at the hilltop in Bordentown, Paul had talked Bernadette into having their Sunday brunch at Allison's Clown Alley at New Hope. They would divert at the White Horse Circle and take the River Road along the Delaware, passing Washington's Crossing and exquisite vistas all along the way, over to Pennsylvania from Lambertville via the New Hope Free Bridge. This was easy enough to decide and by the time the green arrow went out and the straight arrow went green the two were already laughing again. Paul only caught a half-interested glance at what he was sure was Dave Adams's metallic blue '56 Chevy making a left turn on the same green arrow, but it didn't seem to be Dave at the wheel.

Dieter McKenzie was making that left at the hilltop. He was on his way to Dave's Garage. A huge blowout with his mother had driven Dieter out of the little house on Orchard Street and straight toward the haven of Dave's apartment where, within the next few hours, Dieter would have his first encounter with Miriam Anna Bolton. But Dieter's mind was unaware of the little miracle that would occur in his life that day. He was still shaking and trying to get the Chevy safely to Dave's. Dieter never expected his mother to react anything but proud of him for joining the service. Instead she had launched into hysteria and shouted ugly names at him. He'd suffered her fit at least until she started throwing things at him, a few dishes, then the coffee pot (full of freshly perked coffee), then reaching for anything she thought she could hurt him with. Dieter fled his mother's house with a broken heart and was still shattered as he entered Dave's

Hilltop Garage and climbed the stairs to lay down for a while. Dieter had hoped his friend would be there so he could find some comfort, but Dave had already left for Littleton. Dieter could wait. Wherever Davie was he would be back, and there was no place else to go now, at least not for the next three weeks.

# CHAPTER 18

New Hope, Pennsylvania is a cliquishly small Colonial town whose limits go right up to the Delaware River. It is separated from New Jersey by a narrow stretch of river with heavy rapids. In 1776, General Washington had taken one look at the rapids and turned his troops back. They went further down river to where they would make an only slightly less deadly crossing in his Christmas Night trek toward the Battle of Trenton.

Allison's Clown Alley is a long narrow building whose two-story frontage exposes to view the churning rapids and swift waters of the Delaware. There is a fine restaurant at the lower end with its cantilevered balcony overhanging the river. At the higher end there is a series of little rooms where artists often gather and farther on there is a separate bar with a bandstand, a control room for the week-night disc jockey, and a dance floor in front of a massive sandstone fireplace.

Next door to Allison's Clown Alley and sharing the same parking lot is the nearly three-hundred-year-old gristmill, which long ago was converted into the Bucks County Playhouse. Many of the fine old manor houses of the Village of New Hope have also been converted, into museums or dining establishments. The smaller old homes are now antique and curiosity shops, coffeehouses, and craft shops of every variety. Every summer there is the Antique and Classic Car Show and Auction which draws the best crowds of the antique car and horsey set and is held in the midst of a field of wildflowers which grow in spite of the show in that field just opposite the Old Friend's Meeting House.

The Village of New Hope abounds in stone bridges, little canals, cool summer days, and is a sanctuary for many of America's best artists, artisans and musicians even as is Provincetown or Carmel-by-the-sea; it is also the haven for a thousand or so homosexual couples and many aging hippies. But hippies were not yet truly the fashion of the day except when one came much closer to Columbia or Berkeley, or UCLA. The dissident groups of 1967 were still evolving from the beatnik to the hipster to the hippie and in truth the young people who were actually making the changes had not yet identified themselves as hippies, only with The Movement. They left it to outsiders to give them a name. They only thought of themselves as Brothers and Sisters. They recognized one another not by their long hair, nor by their bell-bottomed blue jeans, nor by their colorful braided belts, Indian cotton gauze shirts, or their African dashikis. They knew a Brother or a Sister by the look in the eyes and a certain tone of voice, and by their irreverent common language of the four-letter word.

In New Hope, one could flock with or just stroll along Mill Street among others of one's kind. You could wear your very best grubbies and the puka beads that would be ripped from your neck if you tried to wear them at home. In New Hope, being called a freak was not an unkind reference, but just another way of identification with one's Brothers and Sisters.

Bernadette Carlani was entirely out of place. Her crowd was a different crowd, an expensive and somewhat tasteless crowd whose premise was snobbism in the form of anything that was expensive was therefore good regardless of taste or aesthetic value, a material girl in an ethereal world. So, Bernadette drank. And she ate a few more beans. She waited for it to be night when she would feel more comfortable.

Bernadette did not want to stroll the sunny sidewalks and examine handmade laces or woodworks or antique crockery, and she did not want to mingle with all those very young and dirty looking people. She just waited around while Paul ate and drank and mingled with a few very strange looking people who wandered in and out of the bar, and she waited while he carried on a lively banter with someone who was apparently his friend, the bartender, Joey McNellis. Bernadette was growing very tired of hearing Paul tell every person he met that he was going to join the Army tomorrow. She was bored with hearing about how Paul's father had been a Navy man, but Paul didn't want to be in the Navy, and about how his grandfather, his uncles, his cousins, were all Army and about the ones who were West Point and the aunt who worked at the Pentagon and so on and so forth and none of which interested her in the least. And there wasn't one good-looking man in sight. Bernadette was growing extremely bored with the boy, and fast.

At nine o'clock the late bar opened and Paul took Bernadette in to hear the DJ's music and to watch the party lights bob along the balcony and the nighttime river-rafters being beaten up by the outcroppings of boulders. That was all right, at least it was darker in there. And, after two or three more of those Jack Daniel's-and-Cokes that Paul had convinced her to try, the place didn't seem so bad at all.

Bernadette took to the dance floor, always with a stranger. Paul had said he wasn't in the mood to dance. Bernadette began knocking back shots with the younger men and positively knocking herself out doing the Bristol Stomp, The Stroll, the Frug, the Hully Gully, the Twist, and the Loco-Motion when Little Eva's 1962 hit brought a whole lot of people to the dance floor.

But when the DJs broke to change shifts, Bernadette did not return to the bar. Paul stood at the bar peering around the heads of the crowd and trying to find Bernadette's hairdo. It was a long moment before Paul noticed the little wonder who had appeared at his side. She asked, "Looking for someone?" Paul found himself looking down onto a very pretty girl with many red highlights dancing in glossy dark brown hair that reached to her waist and big brown eyes and long dark eyelashes and a pleasing inquisitive expression on her sweet rounded face. He said, "Well, kind of, I did bring somebody with me."

She was a little bit too short and very busty but somehow perfect with a sweet face and a sweet voice. She said, "I'm pretty sure she went upstairs. Black bouffant?"

Paul smiled widely in a spontaneously natural enchanting grin; he couldn't help himself, "Yeah, that's her. Upstairs?"

"Yeah. With Fred, you know, Fred."

"Ah. Fred still the pusher man?"

"Yeah. He's got some new really pure shit. Your friend's gone up that stairway to heaven."

"Mmm. Guess she won't be back for a while."

"Yeah, well, the old bastard promised he'd buy me dinner."

"Well, now. How 'bout if *I* buy you dinner."

"Groovy."

"What's that you're drinking?"

"Coke."

"Want another?"

"Nah. I wanna eat. Fred's been promisin' me for two fuckin' hours now that we'd get somethin' t'eat."

"Well, whadda we waitin' for? Where ya wanna go, The Willows?"

"Nah, we can go down to the River Walk."

"Sure. Let's blow."

As the two stepped out into the heavy breath of the night air, Paul said, "So, listen, my name's Paul, Randolph."

"Alice."

Late into the night Paul told Alice about his going into the Army and about why. He told her about his sister and of his love for her. And about

71

the brother or sister they'd never known they had until yesterday. Paul told Alice everything, she was just one of those nice people you could talk to. And Alice was so soft. They made an odd entanglement, those two, when they finally reached Alice's little crash pad atop the Open Mouth, he so tall and she so small. But Alice solved the problem and she listened long into the wee hours alternately moving slowly astride Paul's hips or resting her head against his chest but never letting him leave her body even for a moment. At one point Alice said, "You know, this sister-a yours sounds like a spoiled little bitch to me."

"Yeah, she is, kinda. But she's pretty special to me. I'm just leavin' her alone for a day or so, shake her up. I'll go home, tomorrow, you know, sorta late. Bought her a new car too. With me joinin' the Army and all, it's gonna be pretty hard for her on her own. I really want her to go away to school like she's s'posed to, and, with me away, she'll have to spend her breaks with our aunt or something."

Slowly grinding, "You've got it all figured out, don'tcha."

"Mmm." He pulled her face toward him. "It isn't gonna be easy, little one, but, just doesn't seem like it was meant to be easy, not in this life."

Alice sat up. She threw her right leg behind her and dismounted from Paul's penis as if it were a bicycle seat. The long dark hair disguised much of her nakedness as she pranced across the room and took a joint from a shesham-wood box and lit the joint and then a candle, which was the next of many to have been plugged into the top of that Chianti bottle.

Alice smoked; she passed the joint to Paul. She said, "You know. You don't have to go."

Paul inhaled and held, exhaled, "Eh, they're gonna get me anyway. Looks to me like by the end of the year they're gonna be taking guys that are dead and still warm. At least if I join up I'll have some choice of branch, training, *modus operandi*, MO they call it. I mean, if I can get into OCS and then, like, go on to jump school or something like that, maybe, you know, all that'll take a goddamn year. Darling thinks maybe this stinking war'll be, like, over in another year."

"Doubt it." She smoked.

"Alls I know is I gotta go."

Alice attached a pair of hemostats to the roach. She held the tip to Paul's lips. He sucked in hard. She said, "No, you don't."

"I wish I didn't. I really like you."

"Like? That the best you can do?"

He pulled her head to him in that way she would always remember and he kissed the bridge of her little turned-up nose. "No. But, I'm not gonna be around long."

"None of us are gonna be around long, Paul. But I'm tellin' ya, you don't fuckin' have to go in the goddamn Army."

Alice crawled in beside Paul and Paul pulled the sheet up to cover them while she snuggled down deep within Paul's strong arms. Like a little child she lay in his big arms, curled up as she was in a nearly fetal position and resting her head against Paul's broad solid chest. She kissed his moist chest and toyed with the little line of golden blonde hair that grew in an intoxicating pattern across his chest and tapered down in a narrowing rivulet to his navel. Paul lifted long strands of Alice's dark fine soft mane and let them fall gently from his fingertips at the full length of his long arm. Paul's eyes opened just a little wider. Daylight was on its way. In a strong quiet voice, he said, "You're an angel, aren't you." And he could feel her sweet head nodding against his chest. He said, "I love you, Alice Angel." She never lifted her head, she just said, "And I love you, Paul Randolph. And I do not want you to die."

"Will you be coming with me?"

"For part of the way."

"Why not for all of the way? Why not forever?"

"Because there will be others."

"How many others?"

"You will be Number Seven."

"Number Seven. Sounds so personal. But, you're my very first angel."

"There will be others."

"How many?"

"Two."

"Will they be as beautiful and as wonderful as you are?"

Paul could feel her sweet face smiling against his chest. "Yes, they will. But they're guys."

Paul frowned into the candlelit lavender morning upon his newfound loss. "Oh."

"I'll get you to the next one and he'll send you to the next one and then you'll be on your own."

"Alone."

"I'm afraid so."

"Can't you come? Shit, Alice, I know we could be happy if we were together. There's just something about you that makes me want it to be that way."

"No, Paul. I can't. And I do love you. But, we have to save as many as we can. It's our job."

"Your job. Do I pay you? For this?"

"Nope. You don't pay me for a thing."

"Do you do this with each of us?"

"No. Not this way."

"But you sleep with them."

"A few."

"A few. Was it like this with them?"

"No. Not just like this."

"But you did love them?"

"Mmm-hmm."

"Like you love me?"

"Not just like I love you, but yes, I do."

"Do? You mean you still love them?"

"Yeah. I love them all. And all the ones who're Over There, too."

"That's a lotta love. And I know you've got it to give. But that's one hell of a big commitment."

"So's going to Vietnam. So's going to Canada."

"Canada."

# PART II

# CHAPTER 19

Dieter McKenzie was scheduled to depart for Basic Training on Sunday, July 30th. Another 415 American men had died in Vietnam during the three weeks since Dieter enlisted. There were also 4,307 American men who had been wounded. Average casualties.

U.S. Secretary of State, Robert S. McNamara, expressed dismay after returning from his most recent Saigon conference with General Westmoreland. America had Allies. Australia, The Philippines, and South Korea had joined the fight to help save South Vietnam from communism. The trouble, as McNamara saw it, was that comparatively few South Vietnamese were actually involved in the battles. The toll of human sacrifice for the cause of South Vietnam's independence seemed pointlessly disproportionate. Secretary McNamara had seen what he thought were too many South Vietnamese men of fighting age roaming the streets of Saigon, leisurely and free. McNamara, a holdover from President Kennedy's administration, returned to the States determined to hold the number of U.S. troops sent to Vietnam to a minimum, but President Johnson had already promised Westmoreland he would have at least 85,000 new troops by October.

During those three weeks of scheming to get Dieter and Miriam together before Dieter had to leave, David and Darling became not friends, but partners in conspiracy. They dreamed up all sorts of possibilities. They thought of a ride up to Seaside Heights for an afternoon on the boardwalk and a go-round on one of the few remaining calliope carousels left in the world. They thought of arranging for Miriam to sleep over with Darling so that they could all go down to Atlantic City for a concert on the Steel Pier. They even dared to think that maybe they could all stay overnight in one of those palatial and decrepit fine old hotels, some architectural wonder like The Traymore, The Claremont, or the Chalfont-Haddon Hall. But they decided that idea was so far out that is wasn't even worth mentioning. Besides, The Byrds had played the Steel Pier on the Fourth of July, too soon, and The Rolling Stones would not be coming until Labor Day, too late. Oh, well. Darling and David were certain they could work something out. Maybe an afternoon at Atco, you know, the drags.

But the odds were against them. There was just a whole lot of shit going down in America during those long hot midsummer days of 1967. Not one American knew where violence was going to break out next, so Miriam's parents became more protective of her than usual. Getting her away from home, even for a few hours, suddenly became an impossible task.

The Reverend Dr. Martin Luther King, Jr. had targeted Operation Breadbasket for the Southern Christian Leadership Conference's Summer 1967 campaign with the intention of coercing inner-city businesses into hiring more American Negroes (who would soon succeed, not without struggle, in being referred to as Afro-Americans or as Blacks). Dr. King had hoped Operation Breadbasket would be a more peaceful action than the Fair Housing Marches of the summer of '66 which had resulted in white violence against Negroes but did finally end with pledges of support from white churches, realtors and business groups. And *nobody* wanted things to get as bad as they had in the summer of '65, committed to memory as the summer of the Watts riots. The riots in Los Angeles' Watts community were not the only riots that were ignited by the spark of life that was assassinated with Malcolm X. But they were by far the most violent and certainly the most destructive.

In spite of Dr. King's efforts at peaceful demonstration, the 13th of July 1967 marked the beginning of what was to become two full months of hellish racial violence. Newark erupted first, and New Jersey's Governor Richard C. Hughes called the National Guard into action against its own citizens. Newark was soon followed by riots in Cambridge, Maryland and a fiery revolt in Detroit where within two days Michigan National Guard tanks were roaming the streets.

And so it was that in the dead heat of the summer of '67 the fires of our cities raged out of control and many hundreds of people died, black and white, and thousands were wounded and thousands more were jailed. The war in Vietnam had taken yet another insane, diabolical, and deadly turn for the worse while the battle for civil rights at home mushroomed into lethal clouds of smoke and dust and hatred. Together, those conflicts created a firestorm whose winds would forever blow change.

Hanging ominously above the burned-out hulks of what had been our black neighborhoods were the cries of the central issues. Blacks wanted equality of life. Women wanted equality in the work place. Young people wanted the voting age lowered from 21 to 18 and were chanting, **"If you're** old enough to carry a gun, you're old enough to vote;" and all Americans wanted out of Vietnam.

H. Rap Brown, National Chairman of the Student Nonviolent (believe it or not) Coordinating Committee, had been hauled in by the FBI on charges of Inciting to Riot. The next day, after his release on bail, Rap was introduced to a huge crowd of followers at a meeting in Washington. Brown was still bandaged from a head wound he sustained in the Cambridge riots. He advised everybody to get guns. He announced, **"Violence is as American as cherry pie."** Norman Mailer agreed.

Our country was more and more with each passing day becoming a place where no one over 30 could be trusted. It was a place where young people routinely fasted and recited their mantra and followed the teachings of Gandhi or Christ or Moses or Muhammad or Lao-Tzu or their navel. Many were carefully studying Thoreau's *Walden and Civil Disobedience* or becoming Hesse's *Siddhartha*, or losing themselves in *Sometimes a Great Notion* which Ken Kesey titled after a few famous lines from *Good Night, Irene* attributed to Huddie Ledbetter (Leadbelly) and John Lomax.

It was a time when editors anxiously awaited Kesey's new novel *One Flew Over the Cuckoo's Nest*. It was a time when a young journalist named Tom Wolfe was living among Kesey's Merry Pranksters for long enough to come out with *The Electric Kool Aid Acid Test* which would provide for the world the definitive spelling of Day-Glo and would quickly become the bible of LSD (lysergic acid diethylamide).

We lived in a world where Allen Ginsberg was free to go from talk show interviews to poetry readings at love-ins. He was even seen in London's Hyde Park helping out at a smoke-in amidst the tinkling of Tibetan bells and the gentle smiles of flower-giving youths. And it was a time when the world's premier ballet dancers, Rudolph Nureyev and Dame Margot Fonteyn (in a full-length mink coat), were arrested in San Francisco on charges (later dropped) of "visiting a place where marijuana is kept."

The image of the Hippie (as in Long-haired-Hippie-Commie-Pinko-Faggot) was about to become galvanized as the national uniform of The Movement. The Movement even had its own anthem because of a young Army veteran who showed up at the Monterrey International Pop Festival in June of '67. Jimi Hendrix died a few years later of complications brought about by an overdose of barbiturates, but he left us with his unorthodox rendition of *The Star-Spangled Banner*; later, he threw in a little number called *Purple Haze* for good measure. And the Doves were shouting, **"Make Love Not War!"** And the Hawks were shouting, **"Up Against the Wall Motherfucker!"**

THEN, on Saturday, July 29th, 1967, a nation at war within itself and largely burning out of control, seemingly inured to the day after day, year after year killing of its young people in a country few Americans had ever heard of prior to '62 and still fewer could locate on a map and whose primary export was averaging 21.43 dead American Servicemen per day, The United States of America was finally stunned to silence, momentarily brought to its knees.

The *U.S.S. Forrestal* took direct hits from a pair of North Vietnam's Russian MIG fighters. The destruction of the bombing together with exploding ordnance on deck made it clear by the still burning early morning of Sunday, July 30th that there were already 129 known dead and another 29 sailors still Missing-at-Sea, with more than 700 severely wounded, mostly burns.

North Vietnam will never know how close it came to being nuked out of existence on that day, for in their hearts that's just exactly what all Americans thought about, Hawk or Dove. But Ho Chi Minh's troops were backed by the Red Chinese and they were supplied by the Soviet Union. God only knows what might have happened if President Johnson had let it all go to hell. But, in one of his few known instances of restraint, the President bowed his head and knew that for once somebody else had *his* balls in *their* pocket.


That same day, Sunday, July 30th 1967, Dieter McKenzie boarded the 4:27 a.m. Greyhound Charter at the New Jersey Transit Authority's Central Terminal at Trenton. That Greyhound carried a full busload of bright young not-quite-civilians, many of whom were hanging out the windows, a few of whom had tears in their eyes, and all of whom were waving goodbye to a very special someone.

Darling stood back from the milling crowd as Miriam alternately waved and blew kisses and blew her nose. Her eyeglasses, for once, were held in one hand as the tears rolled down her long face. Miriam was trying to be brave, she really was, but she had only held Dieter in her arms for one precious hour before it was time for him to go. There had been no way, as hard as Darling and David had tried to find a way, for Miriam and Dieter to get together before he left for Basic.

As the lumbering omnibus rocked and rolled away from the terminal, Miriam waved with her hanky until Dieter and the bus disappeared from sight. The crowd of lone souls waved helplessly, David and Darling too. Most of them had only one thing in common: that bus. They all had great lumps in their throats. The mothers invariably let the tears flow freely once the bus was gone. No need to put on a good face now.

Dieter settled back into his seat with the warmth of his farewell engraved upon his memory. He sat clutching, as if his life depended on it, a box of plain white stationary with fifty 5-cent stamps inside all tied up with half a yard of lavender ribbon. After a while, Dieter settled in to the companionship of the rest of the boys on the bus. They would all awaken at 05:00 the next morning in time for Monday reveille at Fort Leonard Wood, Missouri.

Darling had to step from the curb and take Miriam by the shoulders and guide her back to Dieter's Chevy so that David could take them home. Although Darling was concerned for Miriam's feelings, Darling's mind had already turned to the next matter at hand, which was the stealth of getting Miriam back through her bedroom window before daybreak. It would be a forty-five-minute ride back to Littleton but Darling was confident David could easily cut it to 37 minutes or better.

Darling gave Miriam a foot-up and a boost through the bedroom window, and left her safely inside. Miriam changed back into her pink cotton baby-dolls and went straight to writing the first of what would someday be 201 letters to Dieter. Darling ran back up Second Avenue and around the corner to meet David on High Street. So long as no one noticed the footprints through the dew-covered lawn at the Bolton's, they were home free.

> My dear Dieter,
>
> I know you're not allowed to have mail for the first two weeks but I just had to let you know I got home safe.
>
> Your friend Dave is just the best. I really don't understand why Darling doesn't like him more than she does. Well, they are both our friends and I'm so grateful that they took me along this morning. I will never forget your smile, or you.
>
> I'm going to get a Post Office Box this week. As soon as I do that I'll let you know where to write. I can hardly stand it until I know that you're all right and how they're treating you. Remember. I'll be waiting.
>
> With much love, your Miriam

It was going to be three long months until Dieter's first leave came, not until almost Halloween. That was a long time away. First, Dieter would have to sweat it out through the crevices and the scorching heat of the Missouri Ozarks enduring Basic Training for six weeks. Then he would have to low crawl through the barbed wire of Advanced Infantry Training, only hoping he might also get the training he had asked for to become a maintenance specialist. Dieter wanted the maintenance specialist job and he wanted it bad. As a Specialist Fourth Class Dieter would draw much better pay and he would be able to keep up his skills as a mechanic by working on the trucks, cars, jeeps and vans of the Motor Pool.

How does the Army prepare young men for war? It's all about mental and physical discipline and conditioning. The first object of Basic Training is to break each individual down until that person is willing to become a part of a team. Recruits are subdivided into companies, batteries, platoons, and squads. Beginning at the squad level, one recruit is selected to be squad leader. Selection is usually based on level of education or some other demonstrated leadership skill. Before the abolishment of military conscription (the draft), the Army filled its ranks first with potential criminals and high school dropouts. By those standards, a high school diploma might be all it took to be a leader of men. Before long, Dieter was a squad leader. Two squads form a platoon of 32 men. It is the duty of the Platoon Sergeant to ensure that recruits are drilled, demoralized, humiliated, chastised, and otherwise disciplined until they are properly reformed as stuff from which the Army intends to make soldiers. Once a recruit enlists or is drafted, there are only two ways to get out of Basic Training, either on a medical or psychological discharge; it is called washing out. Such a discharge does not entitle an individual to any veteran's benefits, but such a discharge does remain as a black mark on the individual's government record for the rest of his or her life.

Advanced Infantry Training continues the mental and physical conditioning. Additionally, it is in AIT that certain recruits who have applied for and shown themselves worthy of specialized training will receive such training. The difference between a Private First Class and a Specialist Fourth Class is not in the number of weeks of Advanced Infantry Training but in the demonstrated ability for and the amount of training the recruit has received. A Private First Class (PFC), at some point in the future of his or her military career, may be promoted to a Specialist Fourth Class (Spec4). A Spec4, if he or she has the requisite college degree, may go on to officer training and have a shot at becoming a commissioned officer. Alternatively, a soldier may remain a Specialist Fourth Class until such time as he or she may be promoted to Specialist Fifth class (Spec5), which is the lowest rank of non-commissioned officer. Whether a recruit finishes AIT as a PFC or as a Spec4, he or she is not considered a soldier until each person has successfully completed those first twelve weeks of training, Basic and AIT.

Private Dieter McKenzie may have thought it was hot and dry in the Missouri Ozarks, but he still had no idea yet where the Army was going to send him for AIT. Nor did he think about it much. Dieter was busy surviving from day to day: up, shit, shine, shower and shave, police the barracks and be on the parade grounds at 06:00; calisthenics before morning mess; dress-right-dress, single file to the mess hall. Next it might be the obstacle courses or a forced march with a full backpack weighing between 30 and 50 pounds. After noon mess, it was back to the parade ground for weapons drill, to the training ground for man-to-man combat with pugil sticks followed by more calisthenics. Police the barracks again before evening mess. Evening parade drill. Police the body and personal effects including spit-shine boots. Inspection. Lights out.

Dieter was taking it one day at a time. He popped blisters and got more blisters on top of those. Eventually the requisite calluses did form on his hands and feet. He peeled the loose and continuously peeling skin from his burned over and over nose and lips until his fair young skin became tough and leathery. He made a bit of chat with other squad members whenever possible. "Name's McKenzie. Bordentown NJ."

"Rocky. Queens."

But little talk was possible. Disciplinary actions were distributed liberally and all those who wanted to survive Basic had best get with the program ASAP. Next to a Leave of Absence, or a Weekend Pass, both forbidden during Basic Training, having one's name called out at Mail Call, which was forbidden during the first two weeks of Basic, was the best thing that could happen to a buck private. There were also rules for mail: Absolutely no foodstuffs allowed, in fact, no parcels of any kind. All life's necessities would be provided for recruits by Uncle Sam.

Dieter's box of stationary was confiscated on the day his body was stripped for inspection, which was the same day his head was shaved, day one. The stationary and its length of lavender ribbon (which drew several wisecracks) was boxed up along with the civilian clothes Dieter had on his back when he arrived at Fort Leonard Wood. The small parcel was shipped back East to Mrs. McKenzie's house, Dieter's Home of Record.


What became evident during that ride back to Arrowhead was that Darling didn't really want to see David again, at least not until late October when Dieter returned and whatever their new plan turned out to be could be implemented. Darling left the Chevy saying, "Gimme a call," as she slammed the car door and charged toward the porch steps. David said, "Right," and was furious. He churned up plenty of river rock as he peeled out of the Randolph drive. From the safety of the living room windows, Darling could see the rising clouds of yellowish-gray dust that David left behind as he barreled down the lane.

Darling did not know nor would she have cared that David spent the remainder of that day putting Dieter's Chevy up on blocks inside the

Hilltop Garage, and figuring out how much he would have to spend for the new Dodge Dart he'd been shopping for lately. Darling only knew that she was stretched out emotionally, stretched out as far as she thought she could get. Although there had been phone calls, none of them had been from Paul, and although there had been mail, there had not been one single letter from her brother. Darling fed the cat, made herself a pot of coffee and quite clinically went about the business of laying out all 21 of the remaining orange 30-milligram Seconal capsules. Then she settled in for what would turn out to be a three-day Seconal funk.

*Barefootin'*. Drifting about the grounds as if she were a graceful bird, soaring on a high draft of heated nothingness. Darling let herself forget about the real world. She only wanted to wander uninhibited through this one, floating, or walking on marshmallows, just being, humming, singing, gliding across the lawns, twirling and watching that peacock blue paisley caftan float like a butterfly on the breeze. How carefully she gazed upon each thing that surrounded her, every blossom and every leaf presented its own kind of wonderment. Her view of the world was uninhibited and particularly childlike. She stood at the edge of the creek and gazed into the deep red veins of infinite grains of sand, every grain a slightly different shade of reddish-brown. She gazed at the creek's clear swift-running waters sparkling and making great art for her in the tiny alluvial ripples that traveled ever so slowly, undulating their way across the bottom where she could almost touch. A vivid cardinal, watch my friend, as he makes a bold dive from the very topmost branch of that draping fir. There he is, sweeping down on his crimson, down, fluttering, down into the lower fronds of that oh-so-delicate low-spreading mimosa, and there, he's gone and left such a long trail of his phosphorescence, his life stuff, a bleeding scarlet trail through the moist haze of an otherwise true-blue sky, as blue as the eyes of Paul.

Darling collapsed on the lawn in a heap where she listened to the grass whispering as it grew and she could smell how deep and rich the dirt was, and she could feel the Earth moving and she thought it felt just like Hemingway said it would. But, then, Darling Randolph didn't have the slightest clue of what an orgasm might be. Dazed and confused no longer, only comforted by a peace that knows no boundaries, no limitations, by a place where one can live comfortably alongside the River of Death. Watch. There goes the Ferryman. Who does he take across? A soldier? A doctor? Lawyer? Indian Chief? But, no, it's a baby, that tiny little face. He will be back again for the rest. That's all he does, all the time long, he ferries the souls across the River of Death, to THE OTHER SIDE. "Me too? Please. I've always wanted to be there."

"Not now. Don't bother me. You may go as high as you like, *that* way, and as far out as you like in any other way but this."

"But why? Please, don't go. Tell me."

"Because. It -- is -- not -- your -- turn."

Sad. It's so exquisitely beautiful here, peaceful, safe. Mother's ashes. The Earth is trembling in my ear. A pair of sensibly shod feet stand before my eyes. My eyes are squinting against the light. "Why, Darling Littleton Randolph! What in Heaven's name are you doing lying out here on the ground? Just look at you all covered in mud. Goodness-deary-me. You've got grass all stuck to your face, all tangled in your hair. Whatever's come over you? Come on. Let's get you up. It's in the shower with you. I swear what you don't get up to. I'll fetch you a nice tall glass of ice water with a little twist of lemon. That'll fix you right up. You get yourself clean and into that bed in there." Hannah. Son of a bitch. What the hell is she doing here?

"There now. You're looking much better already. You just lie there. Darling, this place is an absolute tip."

Darling was unresponsive. She was thinking, wondering, I know I saw my own likeness hovering just above me, my gown, my hair, my self, floating, weightless, transparent. And I was looking down on me, feeling pity for that thing, that broken empty shell. Gone. Girl, you are really gone.

"I only stopped by to see how you two were getting on. By the looks of things, you could both use a little help. Why, that grass must be a foot high!"

"Yeah."

"I've got to be running along but I'll straighten up the kitchen before I go. If you need me, well, just a few hours a week I mean, all you have to do is pick up the phone. Darling? Can you hear me?"

"Yeah."

"You'll be all right then?"

"Yeah."

"You go ahead and sleep then."

"Yeah."

# CHAPTER 20

Darling Randolph clopped around the grounds of Arrowhead in her red Dr. Scholl's exercise sandals and white hot-pants with a red bandanna tied around her breasts and her long bright ponytail gleaming in the sunshine. She was weeding here and there among the sandstone boulders of her mother's rock garden, catching some rays.

It was mid-August now, definitely, hot, humid and oppressive. Today was the first day she had been out of the house since Hannah found her lying face down in the grass about two weeks ago. Darling couldn't remember. "Oooh. Think I've had enough sun for now. Prob'ly all freckles. Guess I oughtta get in touch with Mark Cymrot. Hannah. Did she say she'd come back? Hafta find out, gotta do something. Gotta get my head together. Gotta try. What's the use? Don't care, gotta do it."

Telephones had dials in the 1960s. There were no answering machines or wireless handsets, nor were there any cell-phones. Don Adams, star of the hit science fiction and comedy television series *Get Smart* was the only man of his times to have use of a shoe-phone. Special Agent Maxwell Smart's shoe-phone was thirty years ahead of its time. Naturally it was based on a comic book series. And so it was that while Darling was weeding outside the house at Arrowhead, inside the house at Arrowhead the telephone was ringing and ringing and ringing.

Paul Randolph slammed the receiver back onto its hook, hailing curses at its inability to reach his sister. Then he walked across the street to the Edison Hotel and asked for a pen, paper and an envelope from the clerk behind the counter in the lobby. A few minutes later Paul returned the pen and thanked the clerk and gave him a dollar to post the envelope.

Paul experienced heart-sinking guilt as he passed along to take a seat in the carriage, for every third person or so in that train was dressed in either crisp summer khakis or immaculate whites. Most were holding their hats in their hands and staring into them, seeing a mother, or a lover, a wife or a friend. Some were staring out the windows. Paul knew they would be seeing Princeton, then New Brunswick before the train submerged for the final traverse of the Hudson River and the last screeching rolling-in at Pennsylvania Station. He knew they would also be seeing the same things that Paul was seeing – passing scenes of home and the shining image of someone left behind. Peace Brothers. When will there ever be Peace?

When Paul emerged into the bright light of the City streets in front of Madison Square Garden, he stepped into a cab and told the driver, "Lower East Side please. 10th Street and Avenue A."

Clean. That was what was really hurting him; got the stares, the hoots, the cat calls. He stood above the crowd by nature but what brought the house down on Manhattan's Lower East Side was Paul's obvious cleanliness. The golden-ash blonde hair had grown to a thick shaggy mop in just a few weeks. The beard had ceased to make his face itch. The turquoise and silver beaded choker had been a gift he'd bought for Alice, but she had kissed it and placed it around his neck. The pale blue Oxford shirt was properly rumpled. The worn old English saddle-leather belt was okay, its simple brass buckle badly beaten. But the Levi's were straight-legs. The loafers must once have been gorgeous. In the Hippie Kingdom, Paul Randolph was definitely just passing through.

The filth would grow soon enough, just a little street grime, just a little shading-in that would cause his existence to blend into the shadows. Paul loitered at the corner for a minute or two, looking up at the rows of five-story walk-ups that crowded close to the streets, up into a gray summer haze; then he stepped into a store displaying a sign that proclaimed it a psychadelicatessan. The East Village Other was the first head shop Paul had ever seen; in fact, it just may have been the first head shop in the country. There he waited to be contacted.

"You must be Alice's Number Seven," the voice said.

"Sixty-nine to you too, you stupid bastard." Paul stuffed his hands deep into his pockets and continued to examine a vast selection of handmade bongs.

"Come on. Let's go see The Digger."

Out on the streets again, Paul noticed that there seemed to be cops everywhere as the two turned the corner of St. Mark's Place and Second Avenue. Are there really that many, he wondered, or am I just being paranoid?

Paul had expected The Digger to be something of a guru, which he was, and surrounded by loads of fringed and tasseled cushions, which he often was, but there the imagery ceased. It was for the likes of Timothy Leary and Richard Alpert (later known as Baba Ram Dass) to project those more romantic images. The man Paul was meant to see was the "politico," the organizer, the instigator, the one who would get Paul through the last leg of the pipeline.

There was no harem of devotees, no incense wafting through the air, only the vague sensuous aroma of good reefer. What Paul saw in The Digger's digs was a bunch of young men and women stacking leaflets and others preparing to get the leaflets to the street for distribution. There were many bare feet protruding only slightly from Navy-surplus bell-bottomed trousers, not quite jeans. The bell-bottoms were tattered at the back from being dragged around on the concrete of the local street corners, which were swept and kept spotlessly clean by local residents while the rest of the City was immersed in drifting garbage and inconsiderate piles of dog-do.

Back out on the street, now holding a pile of leaflets in the crotch of his left arm, Paul alternately tried to read the poem, hand out leaflets to anyone passing him as he moved along beside his escort, and tried to pick up as much of his surroundings as he could. There were an awful lot of kids, sixteen, seventeen, not much younger than Darling, smoking, panhandling, newcomers, practically asking to be arrested. One took a leaflet from Paul.

The man who would be Paul's escort, and who called himself Sweet Acidophilus, took Paul down to the Free Store. As they walked through the mountains of donated junk, Paul noticed a couple of signs that read: GOODS FOR GOOD LOOKS, NO STEALING; YOU ARE THE FREE STORE. At the Free Store, Sweet Acidophilus piled Paul with a few things he would need for his trip: a bright Mexican blanket for a bedroll; a Swiss Army knife; toothpaste; toothbrush; tin cup; face towel; pocket notebook (edible, Acidophilus explained) with pencil (not edible); a battered black Kangaroo hat; two six foot lengths of leather thong (not meant to hang oneself with); and an Army-surplus jacket that was two inches too long in the sleeves. This last made Paul wish he could vomit, but the feeling passed.

"There's a big difference between sitting around in a room bullshitting with your friends and making things happen," one of the men who was making it happen said. He called himself A. Digger. He was a good ten years older than Paul and looked it. He gave Paul, still called Alice's Number Seven, a firm handshake and a big welcoming grin of gleaming white teeth that was somehow complimented by a long bulbous nose and a plethora of curly dark brown hair, all of which belied a certain gentility of voice and character. It would be another year or so before the name of Abbie Hoffman would truly become a household word, not until the 1968 Democratic Convention at Chicago.

Two days later, Paul tossed his bedroll into the back of the cab of a double-parked sixteen-wheeler and climbed aboard. Sweet Acidophilus gave a nod to the sympathetic truck driver and slammed the door shut tight. Paul reached a long arm down to shake hands with Acidophilus, saying, "Bye. And thanks." Acidophilus smiled up at Paul and said, "Don't worry. We'll get that message through if the call comes in. But remember, Alice's Number Four didn't make it. We just got word that he's headed for the hoosegow at Leavenworth. So watch your pecker." Paul and Acidophilus made Peace signs at one another with their fingers held up in a **V** as the fresh load of New Jersey tomatoes with the laughing Tomato King on the side pulled smoothly away.

The truckload of Jersey tomatoes pulled into the final weigh station on the U.S. side just after Rochester on the New York State Thruway (I-90); the next stop would be the safety check at Grand Island just before they crossed over into Canada at Niagara Falls. The trucker said, "Ya got everythin' there? Bread? ID, all that?"

"Sure do. They fixed me up good." Paul didn't mention, no bread though.

"Cherry. Jus' remember, they haul you outta this rig for anything, I mean anything, and I ain't never seen your ugly mug before. Picked y'up thumbin'. Get it?"

"Got it."

"Cherry. And kid, just in case anything does happen. Thanks. For the help back there with that tire, ya know."

"Forget it man, it's cool. Felt good gettin' my hands dirty again. Besides, that was nuthin' compared to what you're riskin' here."

"Fuck. I planted all three o' my boys. All three. First it was young Tom, that was in '64. Then it was Robbie in '66. And then my little short-shit, my little Harper. He didn't even have to go 'cause he was the last one, ya know, the only survivor, but Harper, man, just another chip off the ole block, he figured he'd rather go the way his brothers went than sit on his ass in Sapporo. And he did. Bastards. Just last January. Three of them flag-draped coffins. Old lady's a fuckin' basket case. Motherfuckers. Goddamn good-fer-nuthin' gooks, anyhow. What the fuck are they anyhow? We been fightin' this fuckin' war for seems like ten thousand years. And our kids, they just keep gettin' blown away Over There and those gooks, they just keep fuckin' and makin' more gooks and there's fuckin' twelve-year-old kids over there throwin' Molotov cocktails at our boys. Kids that wasn't even fuckin' born yet when this whole goddamn thing got started. They wiped out my whole fuckin' family, all of 'em, all the way from Over There. Piss on it. Anyway. Now I run for the pipeline, and I dare the motherfuckers to haul me in for it. I fought for this fuckin' country in the big one, WWII, and I was goddamned proud o' my boys, and my Uncle Sam went and killed 'em, every single one of 'em. You bet your ass I'm haulin' bodies, live ones, and that's the only way it's gonna be 'til this whole fuckin' mess is over, whenever the hell that'll be. Goddamn Democrats man, fuck 'em, givin' the whole friggin' United States to the niggers and sending every goddamn white boy who can't afford to go to fuckin' college like all the rich kids right straight over to that hell-hole so they can wind up hangin' upside down with their dicks cut off and stuck in their mouths. Jesus."

Paul remained absolutely silent. He didn't say that it had been a Republican, President Eisenhower, who had committed the first U.S. troops to South Vietnam in October of 1954, almost 13 years ago. Nor did Paul say there were a lot of Democrats as well as Republicans these days who were becoming openly critical of President Johnson's Vietnam policy, namely Fulbright and Kennedy and Javits. The man deserved this private chance to spout his hatred; it was all he had left. Paul didn't say he was one of those kids who could've gotten out of it. Paul didn't say how sorry he was for the man's grief, or how a lot of Negroes and Indians were dying Over There too. Paul didn't say any more about anything.


It was four o'clock in the morning, maybe a little past, when Paul jumped down from the cab of the Jersey tomato truck and the old boss tossed Paul's bedroll down to him saying, "Peace, motherfucker. Maybe you'll catch up to me someday. Say hello."

"You got a date," said Paul as he pulled up the collar of his jacket and headed toward the sidewalks of East Toronto. He turned again and waved, calling, "Peace! And God bless you!" and made the **V** sign as the trucker pulled away headed for market. Paul had another three hours to wait before he could call at the window, General Delivery-Royal Mail, where he would receive his envelope from a man named Ploughman. Then Paul would have his own identity again, his own New Jersey driver's license, and five thousand Canadian dollars. At the moment all he had was about enough for a cup of coffee, the equivalent of 27 cents in the Queen's money.

# CHAPTER 21

Darling Randolph was experimenting with combining her separates into an evolving eclectic style. Today, for her meeting with Mark Cymrot, she paired an above-the-knee Madras A-line skirt with one of her brother's white cotton undershirts. It smelled so good, so Paul. At first she didn't like the look, but after pulling the shirt off and the bra off and pulling the shirt back over her head and leaving its long tail tucked but blousy, she liked it better. She chose flat leather sandals and wore no stockings at all now that she'd had a little new sun. She wore no makeup, which always made those gray-blue eyes into bullets peering out from a pink and bronze haze, and her hair was kinked by the humidity like Maureen O'Sullivan's Jane of the Apes. Darling liked it. It was the look she wanted; it was an attitude. She paraded before the mirror, checking herself at proper angles, hanging her hands in the skirt pockets in The Slouch, tucking and untucking the shirt again, rolling up the waistband of the skirt to show a little more leg. Then she started thinking of what was behind the broad mahogany double doors on Mercer Street in Trenton. "This is not going to get you what you want."

She stripped down to nothing again and started all over. This time she pinned her hair up tightly in a huge French knot, carefully pulling down a few curly tendrils around her face and at the nape of her neck. Then she donned a fresh bra and a panty girdle and stockings, Hanes' Barely There. While studying the reflection of her closet, she pulled a tube of Revlon's Cherries-in-the-Snow and dabbed a little of the red lipstick at the top of her cheekbones and at the orbits of her eyes, blended carefully, curled her blonde eyelashes and brushed both the lashes and brows with the oldest mascara wand in the drawer, leaving just the barest hint of Lancôme's Black and a little distraction from her freakishly fair and freckled countenance. As she did this she decided on the embossed white cotton sleeveless dress with its very short A-line skirt and Empire waist. She clamped her mother's oversized turquoise and silver bracelet at the mid-point between her wrist and her elbow. Good, it stayed put. She transferred the bare essentials from her shoulder bag to a white leather handbag with a Chanel clasp. She left the house tiptoeing across the river rock so as not to ruin the heels of her little white sling-backed pumps. "Be a good Balzac. I'll be home soon."

By the time she got to Trenton, Darling was very glad she had changed. The back of her neck caught a slight breeze now and then and she became more comfortable as she sat like a lady in the reception area of Foreman, Proboscis, Matthews, Cymrot and Bean. The dampness between her legs had nearly dried when she was received by Mark Cymrot who led Darling to a brand-new leather armchair in his office.

Darling gazed beyond Mark Cymrot and fixed her eyes upon the early morning bustle along the cobblestones of Mercer Street. She worked to exercise complete control. It wasn't easy. Her hands were not delicate hands. They were strong hands, the hands of an athlete, an artist or an auto mechanic. But they were clean and converted well to pleasant gentle hands with just a little length to the nails, all precisely even, enhanced by a French white stick and covered with a coat of Max Factor's translucent matte finish. At the moment, they were cold sweating hands, hands that fumbled with a huge pair of heart-shaped sunglasses.

Mark Cymrot was a very attractive man who sported an Ivy League look complete with Princeton haircut and black-framed Buddy Holly glasses. Mark had only met Darling once before. That had been last April when Mr. Proboscis had read Mrs. Randolph's Will and had assigned to Mark the responsibilities of ersatz-trustee for the two young Randolphs. It was left to Mark Cymrot to address the Randolphs' more immediate day-to-day needs while Mr. Proboscis remained available for consultation on the more important matters.

Darling thought the entire wall of reference works that created a backdrop for Mark looked too new and unused. But Mark was quite capable of exercising his duties for the Randolphs. He had recently been working with their file, trying to get a couple of the more exotic cars (one 1955 Mercedes Benz and one 1953 Mercury) from their collection into the autumn auto show at New Hope where he knew they would bring the fairest price. He had a buyer lined up for the garage, a very good deal for Paul Randolph. He had contacted selected speed shops in the tri-state area regarding disposition of Street Stock's other assets, mainly the tools, easily worth thirty-five thousand, and the miscellaneous trailers, vehicles and professional accoutrements. Mark had discussed the details with Paul Randolph only ten days ago and had cut Paul a check for an advance of $7,500.00 which Paul had picked up that very same day when he popped in to sign the Agreements of Sale, review the Titles, and to authorize Jim

Mariner to distribute the remainder between their trust accounts, raise their income, and so on.

It was Paul's sister, Darling Randolph, who made Mark Cymrot so uneasy. Here he was, a married man, a happily married man, with two young children, a beautiful home, a junior partnership in one of the most prestigious law firms in the state of New Jersey, and still only 32 years old. Now, for the second time, the same goddamn thing was happening. His proximity to Darling Randolph was making him uneasy with his whole situation, making him wonder if there might just be more to life than what he could see on the face of it. There was just something about her, something that was exuded through her skin or something, some aura of a different world. And not knowing what that something was caused a kind of sexual frustration for Mark. He'd thought about it, hard. Was it the nonchalant way she crossed those long shapely legs, with one foot almost always slightly bouncing, or the foot on its ankle going round and round then the re-crossing in the opposite direction? Was it the shape of the ankle, or the shape of the knee? Was it the elegant arch of the neck, or the way the large skull was positioned on it, or the broad clear forehead or the broad straight shoulders? Or was it just those damned Lolita sunglasses with the big red hearts for the eyes? Mark thought it was more than likely the energy that she emitted, a strobing pulsing energy that could give a man a headache if he'd only let it.

Mark Cymrot removed a document and a check from the file and closed the folder. He said, "Well now. Seems like everything is in order here. We were going to mail this to you, but since you're here you may as well take it with you. Would you please sign here, just so we have a record you've received it." He turned the document to face Darling and laid his Waterman fountain pen beside it.

Darling looked the document over. Something about an advance against the proceeds from the sale of Street Stock; Paul gets this, she gets that; the rest goes to Jim Mariner who handles their accounts. According to the balance sheets, Darling and Paul Randolph would each receive a check in the amount of $3,250 every three months with the first payment beginning in December. Darling had a warm rush when she understood that Paul, even though he was gone, was doing his best to take care of her. She looked at the check for $7,500.00. This would go a long way toward solving some of her more immediate problems. She said, "What about the seventy-five hundred for Paul?"

"Oh, Paul picked his check up a week or so ago."

Darling's eyes grew wide. She quickly brought this under control, but not before a small note of helplessness escaped her lips. "He did?"

"Why yes." Again, Mark went to the Randolph file, removed a document and closed the folder. "Here's the signature. The date. Anything wrong?"

"No. No. I guess not." All of a sudden Darling didn't think she should tell Mark that Paul had been gone for a month now or that she didn't know where he was, or that she hadn't heard a word from him. But he was here just a few days ago! Where the fuck is he? Her mind was racing now, adrenalized. Her thoughts immediately flagged that topic and skipped over it then whizzed on to how she needed Hannah back to help around the house and someone to look after the lawns. She could do the gardens herself, but general maintenance, that sort of thing, the stuff Paul usually took care of in the summers. But how could she manage to discuss even that without telling Mark that Paul was gone? The check she had not expected and which she now held in her hands would allow her to make her own arrangements for those things, at least for a while. So she skipped over that topic too.

Mark Cymrot cocked his head to one side in the manner of a curious puppy. He asked, "Is there something else, Darling? Something you wanted to discuss?"

The other kid. What about that other one, Dad's secret. No. She couldn't dare mention that. Not right now. Darling needed an answer fast. What to say? Go on. Quickly now. "No, Mark. No. I think this should take care of everything. Thank you very much. I won't keep you then. You must be very busy." Darling rose to leave. Mark rose to escort Darling as far as reception. Darling paused. "There was just one thing more. I was thinking about a job, Mark. Do you think you can help me out there?"

"What kind of a job, Darling? I thought you were modeling. School starts in another month."

"I'm not going to be modeling much anymore. It was only for pocket money anyway. And I'm not going down to Washington in September. I've decided to go to Rutgers. Camden, that is, if they'll accept me on such short notice. I'd really like to stay home at Arrowhead, and work, go to school part-time, something like that if I can arrange it."

"I see. I don't know, Darling. Have you discussed any of this with your family?"

"What family?"

"Well, Paul, for one thing. And don't you have an aunt, down in Maryland, a Mrs., Mrs...."

"Mrs. DeLamar. Aunt Maggie. Yes. Well, Aunt Maggie doesn't need to know any of this right now. She's a very busy lady. She's with the Pentagon, you know?" Whenever Darling thought about the Pentagon, she was always reminded of her childhood visits there, of shaking hands with lots of gold-braided men, and of what a great place it would be to roller-skate.

"Ah, yes. Mrs. DeLamar. A very handsome woman as I recall. Yes. All right, then. But what does your brother say about it?"

"My brother." Think fast ding-dong. "Well, he didn't go for the idea at first, but he's kind of come around to it. Lately, he hasn't said anything about it at all. Besides, somebody has to stick around and keep the place running."

A slip? Maybe not. Cymrot said, "But, you do know that Paul intends to stand out for at least the first semester. He'll be there. In fact, I think he's been looking for a job himself. Although I did advise him against it, the draft and all. It's very risky."

"Do you think you might know of anyone? I can spell and I can type. And I'm pretty good at math. Maybe an office job somewhere?"

"Wish we could offer you something here, but we just brought in a new typist about a month ago. Do you know stenography?"

"No. I only ever took college prep courses. And typing of course. Uhm, and piano lessons. Oh, and guitar. Latin. A little French, better at Spanish though."

"What is it you're going to study at Rutgers?"

"I don't know, yet. I guess I'll have to wait and see what's still open, it's so late and everything."

"Yes. Well, good luck. You could try the Sunday paper, classified ads." Darling knew that meant that Mark was going to be no help at all.

"Thanks, Mark. I'll be in touch." As she left his office and entered the reception area, Darling turned to Mark Cymrot one last time. She quietly asked, "By-the-way, Mark. Paul didn't happen to tell you what he was going to do with his money, did he?" Cymrot rubbed his chin, trying half-heartedly to remember. "No. No, I don't believe he did. Why? What are you going to do with yours?" He smiled. Definitely patronizing thought Darling. But Darling had already started prancing toward the big mahogany double doors. She reached her arm up waving goodbye while waving the check in the air and said, in her very best dumb broad impersonation, "Oh, I dunno. Maybe I'll get my hair done. Bye Mark, and thanks again."

The new typist looked up as the door closed and asked Mark Cymrot, "What was *that*?"

"Just a client, Ruth. Just another client." Mark returned to his office not revealing a little blush and quietly closed the door behind him. Ruth went back to her quintuplicate pleading, saying, "Hmmph."


Miriam Anna Bolton walked out of the Post Office in Hightstown while carefully tearing the edge from the envelope of her very first letter from Dieter. She unfolded the paper and began to devour Dieter's words and in so doing stepped off the curb she had not noticed and landed hard enough that all her teeth slammed together. Not a good idea, Mim. You don't need to get run over just yet.

Darling Miriam,

I was the only one from our platoon who had letters waiting at Mail Call. All the guys were jealous and every one of them wanted to read <u>mine</u>. Nothing doing!

What a miserable place this is. Ft. Lnrd. Wd. must be the rock quarry of the nation. Here I am, just an old boy from NJ but I'm no more lost than the rest of these guys. They're all just as sick of looking at the place as I am. We're all sunburned, blistered and peeling, bruised and dog tired all the time.

We get to go to church on Sundays. That's our only hour off every week and we all snore through the whole thing.

Please send me a picture. I'd just love to have a picture to show off. All the guys here love you 'cause you wrote so many letters. But they know that you're for me. Still it would be real nice to have a picture. Then they'd really be jealous!

Gotta run. These GED classes aren't hard but they take up a lot of time. So I'm always in a hurry to get everything else done. Think of me will ya? I think of you every minute of every day.

Yours till the sun don't shine, Dieter

# CHAPTER 22

By the last week in August, Rap Brown had finally been released from jail and was in the process of lying very low, awaiting trial. Thirteen U.S. jets had been shot down over North Vietnam that week. One of the pilots turned out to be Billy Doyle, the former captain of the football team, husband of Karen, the former cheerleader. Word had it that in spite of the fact that the U.S. was offering a troy ounce of gold to any North Vietnamese who helped a downed American pilot escape to the South, there had been no reported sighting of Billy. Air Force Captain Billy Doyle was officially listed as Missing in Action, the baby was due in about a month, and Karen was just about to lose her mind.

The United States Senate confirmed President Johnson's appointment of Thurgood Marshall as the 96th Justice of the Supreme Court, the first black person in history to receive such an appointment. But that did not curtail the riots in New Haven or curb the growing criticism of President Johnson and his Vietnam policy. Jimmy Howard received the Congressional Medal of Honor. Miriam Anna Bolton told her first lie.

Miriam had secured permission from her parents to pick Darling Randolph up on Sunday after church so that they could go to see Sandy Dennis in *Up the Down Staircase*. That would have been a nice thing to do. Where Miriam really took Darling Randolph was to Trenton, to the train station, to pick up the yellow '67 Mustang convertible that waited there accumulating parking fees. The key to the Mustang had arrived in the mail with a note from Paul.

> I've got to do this sugar plum - just
> didn't occur to me before - I know you
> can handle things at home, you could
> always handle anything -

forgive me, little Darling.
you just don't know


With the lot number, the parking stub, and the key, Darling and Miriam walked along the high chain link-fence. The August sun was punishing them. The yellow Mustang wasn't hard to find. A note inside would tell them more, they knew.

Behind the wheel of the Mustang, Darling let herself absorb the static jolt of Paul's leftover energy. Miriam sat in the passenger seat. "I'll bet he bought it for you all along. Sure does have a lot of neat stuff. It's like an oven in here though. See if you can figure out how to get the top to go down. Try this one. Oh, cool! Check it out!"

Miriam opened the glove compartment to find the trunk key in an envelope along with the owner's manual and the bill of sale, and there was a note. She laid the envelope on the console of the three-speed automatic. Strong hands with high blue veins carefully unfolded the bit of paper.

> Drive careful, you hear me?
> No more road show shenanigans. It had to end
> somewhere.
> Who could have known it would be like this?
> I'll always love you. Remember me -
> Your big brother, Paul


Miriam's eyes grew wide behind her spectacles as she read along with Darling. She waited for a moment as Darling read the message again and again, turning over the painful little slip of paper, examining it in disbelief. That really was all it said. Then Miriam said, "Doesn't sound like he's coming back."

"No, it doesn't." With tears welling, trying to overflow, Darling looked to Miriam for an answer. "But where's he gone?" Miriam pushed Darling's matted hair away from her face, "I dunno, Darling, I dunno."

Darling let her head fall forward so that her forehead banged against the steering wheel. After a little time, she said, "This sucks, Mim, it really does."

"I know," said Miriam, "I don't know what I can say, or do. Seems like Paul's lost it somehow."

"Somehow." And Darling began to cry. "I don't want to cry anymore, Mim. I'm so tired of crying. What is he doing? Maybe he's in trouble? Maybe he really needs me and he just doesn't know how to ask? I'm so frightened for him and I'm so mad at him and I just miss him so much. Oh, God, Mim. How can he not know that? How can he tell me he loves me and go and do something like this? Where the hell is it he's going? When's he ever gonna come home?"

"Well, maybe he's joined the Peace Corps or something."

"He can't join the Peace Corps, Mim. They won't take you if you're eligible for the draft."

"I forgot about that."

"Well, I haven't."

Miriam was strong for Darling. She had no further comment, only comfort. She held Darling in her arms and waited until Darling had cried it all out, and then she followed her all the way home.


By the time Miriam felt comfortable leaving Darling alone, it was already dark late hot humid with stars that shone like pinholes in a density that clung to the skin like atmospheric sludge. Paul, whom Miriam had idolized for as long as she could remember, had done this, caused her best friend, his own sister, so much grief. But, why? And it was grief. Almost as if Paul had died. Almost. All that remained was the hope that he hadn't died, that he was well somewhere, confused maybe, but alive. And if he was alive, then he just might come home. Not the shock of a sudden death, but the mournful heartache of an unexplained departure, an empty space that no one else could ever fill, a loneliness that showed in tiny lines about that burgundy mouth of Darling's, an age that grew all at once and pushed her once-intelligent expression far deeper, into intensity, into a contemplation that took her gaze far away and far beyond her years.

Miriam went home. She took a deep breath and walked into the house on Second Avenue. "Hello, Mother."

"Oh, hello, Miriam, I didn't hear your car. Late, aren't you? Did you and Darling have a pleasant evening?"

"Oh, yes, Mother, very pleasant."

"And how was the movie?"

"Oh, it was wonderful. The first show was sold out. That's why it's so late. Sorry about that." Miriam had done her homework; she had read a review of *Up the Down Staircase* in the Sunday paper.

"You know your father and I don't approve of movies and those kinds of things, but we're willing to make an exception every now and then. So long as it doesn't become a habit, and so long as it doesn't influence you. Isn't that right, Miriam?"

"Yes, Mother. Oh, I'm certain it won't influence me, not in the least. Just an entertainment, that's all. My eyes are tired though. I'll say goodnight."

"Good night, Miriam. Don't forget to pick up your father's sports jacket at the cleaners on your way home tomorrow."

"I won't, Mother."

The door to the little white bedroom was closed now. Miriam lay across her bed and let her narrow skimmers drop to the floor. She watched in the darkness as the faintest of breezes rustled the lilac bushes outside her window making a gentle brushing at the screen. She'd have to hurry into town on her lunch hour to pick up the damned jacket. She had an appointment right after work; an interview with the Superintendent of Schools in Hightstown.

Later, by the glow of the street light (candles were forbidden), Miriam dutifully dashed off her letter to Dieter. She reminded herself that Dieter would be finishing up Basic Training in just a few days. "Where was it I was supposed to start sending letters? Where is it he's going to now? Oh, here it is. Advanced Infantry Training (AIT) at the United States Army Field Artillery Training School at Fort Sill, Oklahoma. Then he's there for six more weeks." A deep sigh. "Six more weeks." A toss of the head. "Six more weeks and he'll be home on leave, for a month! Remember that, Miriam. There. Isn't that better?"

> My dearest Dieter,
>
> I've just returned from taking Darling to Trenton.
>
> There was a whole awful scene with another one of Paul's stupid notes.
>
> This time he sent her a key and an address and when we got to the address she's got this brand new yellow Mustang convertible waiting for her. It was pitiful. All she really wants is her brother back. Naturally, he left her another one of his cryptic messages. Honestly, I don't know what's holding that poor girl together. She must be made of stronger stuff than any of us ever suspected. Well, it seems like Paul's done a runner.
>
> Poof! He's disappeared.
>
> It didn't seem from the note like Paul intended to kill himself or anything like that. Besides, why would anyone go to all that trouble to do that? Darling says he's got money. I just don't know what she's going to do now, poor creature, all alone out there in the country. Wish I could be of more help.

I'm so glad to hear that you've finished your last run for this session. Still, I'll bet you look great with a tan, even if it is just your face and hands. And I know how disappointed you must be that you didn't get the Motor Pool assignment. But I'll bet you'll make a great gunner, and a very handsome Spec4.

I've got my first interview coming up tomorrow.

Wish me luck. It's in Hightstown. There are lots of nice apartments around Hightstown. I'll say goodnight for now.

I know you'll be busy with your transfer to Ft. Sill, but drop me a line if you can. I took the P.O. Box for two years so don't worry. Love always, Mim.

The following weekend, shortly after posting a notice on the bulletin board at Littleton Township High, Darling received a telephone call from a girl named Deannie Ruiz. Deannie and her father found their way to the Randolph place and they both liked the Valiant. It was a very clean '62 with low mileage. Darling mentioned that the Valiant had been her car for running around but mostly Darling listened. She soon began to like young Deannie Ruiz who was explaining that she needed a decent car to get back and forth to her after-school job. Deannie's father explained that he wanted Deannie to get home safely at night, and that the old clunker she had was not reliable transportation.

Deannie Ruiz wanted to go to college and, although she was an honor student and was certain she would be getting a full scholarship to somewhere, Deannie was realistic about all the expenses, and she would need some clothes. Darling handed Deannie the keys to the Valiant and the file on the Valiant, which contained the owner's manual, the bill of sale, the title, and all the maintenance records. "Good luck. You can send me thirty-five bucks when you can afford it."

Deannie's father asked, "What's wrong with it?" Darling smiled softly and said, "Nothing."

Deannie and her father left the Randolph place in separate cars. Deannie followed her dad in the Valiant, very high-headed, being careful and proud. Darling waved goodbye to them from the back-porch door. "I might get to like calling my own shots."

After much discussion with herself, Darling made her next move, which was to quit her modeling job. There was no one left at home who could argue with her. She fully understood that she was acting in open rebellion against her mother's wishes. It did not matter that her mother was dead.

Darling didn't care that she had been ticketed for speeding on her way to Cherry Hill. She went straight to the back of the shop and through the hanging glass beads to find Rita fitting Annie Sherwood for next February's Bridal Show. There were several other girls trying on a variety of bikini swimsuits, fur coats, and brightly colored Caribbean print sundresses. Darling knew they were preparing for the Thanksgiving weekend showing of South Seas Travel Wear. Darling smiled and greeted a few of the girls. She was nervously waiting to catch Rita's attention. The small radio that always sat on one or the other of the dressing tables was playing *Time Won't Let Me* by the Outsiders.

When Darling finally caught Rita's eye, Rita immediately swept over with a big hug and a mouthful of straight pins. A measuring tape dangled around Rita's neck and she wore it as if it were a silk scarf, or the latest rage in fashion. Rita removed the straight pins from her mouth. "I just love those plum colored stockings!" Darling gave a brief leg show. "Those are the most adorable suede shoes I've ever seen, Darling, they're pumpkin!"

Darling tried to keep her trembling hands out of sight. She was terrified even though the conversation had begun rather well. Rita was kind, generous, even maternally interested and protective of her girls, but she was not to be crossed. Rita's word on anything was always the last word, be it sportswear or boyfriends.

Darling approached the subject with caution. Rita herself provided an opening as she took Darling's cold hands and held Darling's arms out to her sides and turned her to and fro, "You're losing weight!" Then Rita immediately checked Darling's eyes for any signs of dark circles, not too bad. "You look great! Just be sure to get your rest, and don't get too flat-chested. You're my sweater girl you know! Oh, and by the way. Would you like to wear the black Jantzen and the blue fox jacket? I've been keeping them back for you."

Darling hesitated only for an instant then she blurted, "Rita, I'm quitting." Rita laughed. "Oh, no, not to go with that damned Alfredo. Darling! He's such a fraud. Didn't you know his real name is Ralph!"

"I'm not going to be in rags anymore, Rita."

The smile disappeared from Rita's face; the charming lilt disappeared from her voice. "You're for real about this, aren't you."

"Yes, I am. I came by because I just had to tell you in person. I can't work anymore shows." Rita grew huffy and brooded.

"Oh, please, Rita, don't be mad. I have to quit. Honest."

Rita paused. She thought. She went to a long red lacquered sideboard and poured herself a cup of Earl Grey tea and plunked two sugars into the Noritake teacup. "Is this what you really want?"

Darling laid her shoulder bag on the red lacquered sideboard. She did not take tea. She said, "Nothing's what I really want right now, not now, but it will be. I just have to get through this somehow. I think this may be the means to an end that I think I want."

"You *think* you want." Rita sipped her tea. She did not ask what *this* was. Darling leaned her rear end against the sideboard. Just as if she were ON, she ignored the faces in the room, her eyes seeing only the inside, the glimmer of what was most important to her. "Well, damn, Rita, I don't know. I just don't think I get to have what I really want. It just doesn't seem to be in the cards."

"What about school?"

"I've enrolled at Rutgers South Jersey. It's just one course, four credits, but it's a beginning."

"Won't you lose your scholarship?"

"No. I've got a year before I have to forfeit. They don't pay for the part-time hours though. You have to be a full-time student to qualify."

"And next year?"

"God, Rita. I don't know." Darling fumbled in the silver box on the sideboard for a cigarette. Blindly she lit the filter end, removed it from her mouth, looked at it in disgust, threw it into a Baccarat crystal ashtray that weighed ten or eleven pounds and tried again, exhaling long and hard. "You have no idea how far away next year is to me right now. Please. Don't grill me."

"I'm only trying to help you, Darling. You know I don't want you to go." Rita put the teacup down and leaned against the sideboard right next to and in the same manner as Darling. Darling stubbed the cigarette out after two or three drags, "I know. But I have to."

"Your mind's made up?"

"Oh, yes. Absolutely."

"Well, that's it, then."

"I'm afraid so."

"You don't have to be afraid. You're a natural. The real thing, Darling. You'll be fine, whatever you choose to do. I'm certain of it."

I'm glad you're so sure, Darling thought, I wish I was, then she picked up her things and bussed Rita on the cheek, "Thanks for everything." Rita touched the crown of Darling's head and let her fingers slide down to caress the jaw as if examining a sculpture. "You're very welcome, my Darling." Then she smiled and instantly that professional lilt returned to her voice. "Just don't go getting fat!" Darling smiled a sad upside-down smile and said,

"I won't, I promise. Thanks, Rita, thanks again, for everything." Then she hurried to leave.

Rita clapped her hands twice loudly and commanded, "*Andiamo!* Get on with it! We've got a show to do!" Although the others wondered what had happened, Annie Sherwood, who had been standing on the fitting block and had heard the whole thing, said nothing. She simply fluffed out her train and straightened her shoulders and sucked in her waist and waited for Rita to return so she could continue to be pinned up. And she knew that she would get to wear the black Jantzen with the blue fox jacket and those terrific new black dancing-heels with the skinny little ankle straps. Darling Randolph had prettier ankles, but she was gone now.


On the first Saturday after Labor Day, Darling's first day at Rutgers, she joined the Young Democrats and began attending meetings every Saturday evening after class. Although, at eighteen, Darling was still too young to vote, she could help out by canvassing the neighborhoods around the Rutgers-Camden campus to try to help bring the issue of voter registration to each of the mostly black and largely Democratic households.

As Darling became more confident in her abilities, she began to sleep at night with the help of a half of a quarter-grain tablet of Phenobarbital. The Seconals were gone, but Mrs. Randolph's treasure-trove of downers revealed most of a bottle of two-hundred-and-fifty of the tiny white tablets in its brown glass bottle, the one with the skull-and-crossbones on the label. Darling figured that if she cut each tablet in half with a Gillette Blue-Blade, that bottle of Phenobarb could last her for a year.

# CHAPTER 23

Mom and Pop Richarde had been operating the Woodside Farm since their arrival from Quebec in 1930. In their mid-seventies now, almost all the work on the farm, from planting to harvest to winter chores, was performed by hired hands who labored for meals and a warm bed in the bunkhouse. Hired hands are by nature transients so a 12-gauge shotgun stood at the ready in a corner of the old couple's walk-in bedroom closet.

The Richardes liked Paul Randolph just fine; he worked hard, ate heartily and asked for nothing in exchange for his handsome pleasant smile. The old couple had grown to count on Paul this last month since he had arrived on foot. They cared not that he was a young American male of draft age. He was well mannered, clean and trustworthy and that's all they needed to know. Winter was coming soon now, and their old bones would ache with the cold. It would be nice to have a strong young man to count on, but one never asked how long a hired hand planned to stay on, not, that is, if you wanted an honest answer.

Paul's paranoia, his desperate and unnecessary fear of being identified or captured, picked-up, nabbed, had kept him to the outskirts of civilization. He'd chosen not to go to the cities, or to the campuses, too many people to talk to, too many opportunities to spill the beans about himself, and there were too many private torments for Paul to wrestle with. He did not want anyone else's opinion or influence.

Paul's motives had taken him westward, away from the busy provinces and toward the frontier. At first, he headed north toward James Bay and the high timber country, but it was already so very cold, in August? No. That was definitely not where he wanted to spend the winter. He would certainly freeze to death. No. He did not know enough yet to risk spending all his cash to get set up in someplace warm. What if he was unable to find work? That was when he decided to head west instead.

If Paul had only known that he could relax once he'd made it to Canada. But he didn't know this. Instead, he continued to deprive himself of even the most basic comforts, which he certainly could have afforded. Perhaps it was just a subconscious form of self-loathing; perhaps he knew what he was doing all along.

Paul was so hungry that he was on the verge of desperation by the time he found the notice pinned to the bulletin board of Blue Cloud's Trading Post:

---

**HIRED HAND**

Need one more man for harvest, possible

winter over. Good opportunity for

the right person.

Inquire at Woodside Farm. NO DRUNKS!

---

Paul removed the notice. He followed the aroma of warm rich coffee to the back of the store. He stood there warming himself at the huge black cast-iron wood stove, enjoying its warmth and the company of another human being in silence. Finally, he approached the quiet man who slowly methodically marched a push broom across the wood plank floor. Thinking that the man was more than likely this Blue Cloud, the proprietor of the Trading Post, Paul asked how much it would be for a cup of coffee. Blue Cloud replied, "On the house." Paul's gratitude was expressed in his face as he poured. After a couple of sips on an empty stomach, Paul was hit with a caffeine head-rush and was all of a sudden in a hurry to leave.

With directions from Blue Cloud and the notice folded in his pocket, Paul was on his way to Woodside Farm. As he left the Trading Post he noticed a gold-colored Lincoln Continental Mark II parked alongside the building. "Guess he's got a pretty good thing going here."

Paul walked along the footpaths of late summer Manitoba. A dense fog blanketed the morning fields and the fences; it shrouded the road beyond ten feet in front of him in mystery. Paul walked along, reminded of home, forgetting that it was still technically August, for it might as well have been early October, but then, this was Canada. It would not be until later in the day, on towards one o'clock, that Paul could view the Woodside Farm; it was stretched out for as far as the eye could see.

It was one week to harvest time in the wheat country of Manitoba. In the barnyard, Paul could see the unenthusiastic motions of a couple of men in their late thirties trying to get a combine running. Paul knew he could fix that. The huge old farmhouse was in need of a good painting. Paul knew he could do that. That project would have to include repairing those shutters and getting some new supports under the front porch. What the hell, we can get that barn painted as well, maybe even white-wash the fences, at least around the yard and out to the road. And there's plenty of other machinery lying around that looks like it could do with some attention. Besides whatever harvest chores there are, it looks like there's plenty to do around here to keep me out of trouble. Paul ascended the porch steps. He was standing tall and stork-like when Mrs. Richarde came to the door.

Paul introduced himself, showed the notice to Mrs. Richarde and asked if he had the right place. Mom Richarde said, "Why, yes, young man. Pop's out back."

Out back, behind the chicken coop, Pop Richarde was spreading some feed for Mom's hens. He told Paul that he wanted to make sure Paul understood that there was no money for wages, only good homemade food from Mom's kitchen and a warm bunk at night. Pop Richarde asked Paul when he had last eaten. Paul said, "Couple of days I guess."

"Well, then, why don't we take you to Mom's kitchen first and you can get your fill and then you can stow your gear and get to work. Flynn out there can get you started, he's having a time with that combine." As they headed back toward the kitchen door, Paul was asking about the problem with the combine and Pop went on to explain it as he saw it. Pop was pleased. He could tell from the light in Paul's eyes that Paul already knew what to do about that.

Paul found the bunkhouse more than adequate. There were two rooms on the south end, each with two smaller rooms. The room at the rear of Paul's side had a cot against each of the opposing walls. Each cot had a horsehair mattress, no pillow, but the beds were made up in clean homespun sheets and black wool blankets from the Hudson Bay Company. That room had a window facing onto the fields behind the bunkhouse. The viewer would be protected from the wind and rain by a straw-filled pony shed that leaned-to from the back of the bunkhouse and through which a Shetland pony named Cookie would often poke her nose for a nuzzle. There were rugged shelves along the walls of this back room; good places to stash things; and several old books including a Georges Duhamel, *In*

*Defense of Letters*, and one of Tolstoy's collections *Tales of Courage and Conflict*. There was also a wash stand with fresh towels hanging at its sides. There were no rugs on the rough plank floors, but the floors were raised and tightly fitted. You could stow your bedroll or rucksack and work boots under the bed, hang your clothes on a peg, and read by the kerosene lamp until sleep enveloped you in the soft sweet scent of new hay.

Each of the bunkhouse's bunkrooms had a front room. They were pleasant rooms with two windows in the one Paul was assigned, for he had the far end. Paul's front room contained a wood stove of Norwegian manufacture on top of which sat a blue-spattered-white enameled kettle. Beside the stove, on an upended apple crate, were a can of coffee, a can of tea leaves, sugar cubes in a Mason jar and a pair of cups and saucers, cracked and chipped but still worthy, both in Wedgewood's *Edme*. There were two over-stuffed chairs, old but clean with lace doilies to prevent head and hands from soiling their faded tapestries. Paul's front room was different because it had a Victrola. Beside the Victrola sat another apple crate, this one containing scads of 78-RPM records, still in their brown paper sleeves. Paul was immediately reminded of his mother and her collection of classical 78s, which had its very own atmospherically controlled room at Arrowhead. His mother's piano came clearly into view. He could hear her playing Grieg's *Piano Concerto in A Minor Opus 16*. Paul's uncooperative stomach performed a flip-flop that made him dizzy but he ignored this by forcing himself to carry on flipping through the records. The apple crate did not contain Victor Borge's *Phonetic Punctuation*, or George Gershwin's performance of his own *Rhapsody in Blue*, or anything with Leopold Stokowski conducting, as Paul had thought for the briefest of moments it might. But there were some neat little pieces from the thirties and forties, like the old ditty, *Meirzy Dotes*; crank up the Victrola and let her rip and you could hear the *Winchester Cathedral*-type sound of daguerreotype in music.

# CHAPTER 24

The apples fell to the ground to rot, food for the birds, as September came into its own. The fighting in Vietnam had grown ever more bitter since the *Forrestal* disaster. Men died, 50 or 60 or one at a time, while thousands more came home without legs, or arms, or testicles, or minds.

An envoy of American politicians, including New Jersey's Governor Hughes, traveled to Saigon as observers, while rumors of campaign fraud in the upcoming South Vietnamese supposedly democratic elections ran rampant. Meanwhile, America was already gearing up for the 1968 presidential elections. The Reverend Dr. Martin Luther King, Jr. issued a proclamation advising Americans to "...make the 1967-68 elections a referendum on the war in Vietnam," by choosing leaders who would lead us into a new world rather than... direct us to the brink of a dead world."

"What is a Hippie?" was becoming a popular editorial question even though The Death of the Hippie had recently been ceremoniously enacted at the corner of San Francisco's Haight and Ashbury Streets and was fully covered by the underground newspaper, *Rolling Stone*. On the boardwalk in Atlantic City, the Rolling Stones (the band) played the Steel Pier without Keith Richards who had just pulled down a one-year jail sentence for possession of Indian hemp. But Mick Jagger was there because his 3-month sentence for possession of pep pills had been commuted to probation. Marianne Faithful was there just because. Down the boardwalk from the Steel Pier, at Convention Hall, Debra Dene Barnes of Pittsburg, Kansas won the talent competition with her piano improvisation of Henry Mancini's theme from the movie *Born Free*. She was presented with the traditional rhinestone tiara by outgoing Miss America of 1967, Oklahoma's Jane Anne Jayroe.

The riots in Providence and Milwaukee had just about burned themselves out, and an estimated 4 million Americans were regularly using

Acid. Jack Nicholson's screenplay *The Trip*, starring Peter Fonda and Susan Strasberg, Bruce Dern and Dennis Hopper, opened in theaters across the country. At the New Hope Antique Auto Show and Auction, David Campbell Adams nodded the "SOLD" bid of $3,075.00 for one cherry red 1953 Mercury.

David ordered a rollback to come and pick the car up that same afternoon. Had he gone completely whifto? He could no more spare the money for that car than an extra hole in his ass. But when he'd seen it there, he just knew he had to have it, just like the day he first saw that bitch, Darling Randolph. Bidding-fever took over from there and when the auctioneer's gavel went down on, "Sold American," David had finally won. Now he wondered what the hell he could sell to make up for the depletion of his savings account. The Dart was only a month old and the first payment would be due next week.

The NHRA racing season had ended. Dieter was gone and would soon be headed overseas. David was suddenly stricken by how lonely his life had become. He had already opted not to return to the Rembrandt School. No big deal. He was putting in a lot of overtime at the ammo plant. There just wasn't enough time to do everything he wanted to do. Soon Dieter would be Over There, and if Dieter had to be a gunner then David felt as if he were supplying ammunition for his friend. David heaved a great sigh. "Yeah. But wait until you get a look at Darling's face when she sees her Merc again. Ah, man. This, like, really oughtta do it."


September's late afternoon sun brought with it fat juicy blackberries all along the lane, and hurricane season. *Doris* and *Chloé* were fast chasing one another out of the Bahamas and right into a good slam at the New Jersey coastline. Forty miles inland, Darling Randolph flip-flopped around the house in her coral dream-pajamas, four rows of deeply ruffled nylon tricot at the bodice with little bows that met the ends of spaghetti straps front and back, exposing plenty of arms and chest while the pleated culotte bottoms extended to the floor exposing the fuzzy toes of a pair of bright blue scuffies. Darling gathered candles and matches, and set out the big hurricane lamp that had survived family service for three generations. And Private Ronald Lockman, refusing to go to Vietnam, was sentenced to 11 years hard labor and a dishonorable discharge.

*Observer 5* had just made the first ever soft landing on the moon leading scientists to be encouraged about the genuine possibility of a manned expedition by 1969. President Johnson was still defending himself against congressional charges that in expanding the U.S. presence in Vietnam he had exceeded the authority granted to him by the Gulf of Tonkin Resolution. In a scenario of convoluted logic of which Joseph Heller would have been proud, the Johnson Administration claimed that high troop turnover was to blame for all the high casualty figures. As it was explained, sudden death led to the use of more and more inexperienced soldiers in Vietnam. Inexperienced soldiers were more susceptible to sudden death, which created an even greater troop turnover. High troop turnover was blamed for all the high casualty figures. So more and more green troops were headed for the deadliest place on earth.

The phone rang and, by the beige light of an impending hurricane sky, Darling Randolph spoke to David Adams. "Like, Dave. I'm busy. Not around much."

"Yeah, but Darling. I left three messages with your housekeeper, that Mrs. Sarn lady. You couldn't call me?"

"I didn't feel like calling you, Dave. Like, what can I say?" David lit a cigarette. "You could say you wanna see me."

"I don't."

"*What* is your major malfunction? Dieter's gonna be home in a month. Don't you think we oughtta try to patch things up?"

"That's a month from now, Dave. And, like, there's nothing to patch up."

"Why do you hate me?"

"I don't hate you. I don't hate anybody. I'm just very busy right now."

"What about the two love birds?"

"What about 'em?"

"Are we gonna at least be decent to each other?"

"Dave. We'll see each other, okay?"

Darling dragged the receiver across the kitchen where she opened and seeded the summer's last cantaloupe. She pared one half and put the other half upside-down on a salad plate in the fridge. David offered, "I've got a surprise for you." Darling answered, "I am really getting to hate surprises."

"Oooh-kay... Everything, like, copacetic out there?"

"Sure. Waiting for this storm to hit is all. The sky is getting like really eerie, man. What's it doing up there?"

"Overcast. When's it s'posed to hit?"

"Sometime tonight."

"What're you eating, anyway?"

"Cantaloupe. Good, too. D'y'eat much fruit?"

"Tryin' to quit. You got everything tied down out there?"

"Oh yeah. Just me and 'Zac here. Got the front door open though. It's, like, there's no fucking air anywhere." Then she smiled to herself. "Bet ya don't like clams or smoke-fish either."

"Clams're okay. Don't like 'em raw though. Never tried smoke-fish."

"Smoked Whiting? Ah, man, it's the best. Wanna try it?"

His chance! "Sure! When?"

"I dunno. Mim's been sayin' Dieter says he wants to go downna shore while he's home. We've got a little place on Long Beach Island. Think that piece-a-shit-Chevy'll make it down there an' back?"

"Long..." David's voice cracked for the first time in years. Shit-man-fuck. He cleared his throat. "...'Scuse me. Long as we got a dollar for gas. The shore, huh. I could feature that."

"Mim says they're gonna be making Dieter into a gunnery specialist, Howitzers and stuff like that. Says they call 'em gun-bunnies. She tries to stay kinda cheerful about it, but it sure as hell looks like he's goin'. No orders yet though."

"Yeah, I heard. Well. They'll come. And we'll get down the shore before he goes." He was smiling. "What else's he wanna do?"

"Dunno. Prob'ly the same thing Mim wants t'do."

"Yeah." David almost said me too, but gave it a miss.

"Look, Dave, I really gotta go. There's just like all this stuff I gotta do." She did not mention that one of those things was to urinate.

"Yeah. So, like, what's Paul up to these days?"

"Keepin' pretty busy I guess."

"Mmm. How come he decided t'sell Street Stock?"

"Felt like it I guess. How'd you know?"

"Word gets around."

"I guess. Gimme a call in a coupla weeks."

"Cool."

"See ya."

David looked at the receiver as he listened to the dial tone, "Bye."


That night gradually turned from impending terror to an animistic comforter as a howling wind drove sheets of rain down onto the rooftops of the big empty house in the country. Darling lay awake for a long time, listening, waiting for the violent lashings, the punishment the storm would inevitably exact from all those in its path. She prayed that Paul was safe somewhere, warm and dry, as she was. But the worst of the storm never arrived.

Hurricane *Doris* took a fickle turn in the night as hurricanes are wont to do, which is why they were originally named after women, and smashed into the Carolinas. Then it backlashed right into *Chloé* and the two biggest hurricanes to head for New Jersey in four years had fizzled into tropical storms by morning.

There were no downed trees, limbs or power lines, only a few prematurely fallen maple leaves and a soft consistent drizzle to greet Darling on Sunday morning. She banged around the house in jeans and a sweatshirt and the bright blue fuzzy scuffies. She sat on the floor in a small corner of her room for a while with her little record player, sifting through an aging stack of 45s. She placed a pile on the spindle: Nino Tempo and April Stevens harmonizing *Deep Purple*; The Ventures' *Telstar* and Ray Stevens' *Ahab The Arab*; and The Chiffons' *He's So Fine*. On top of those she added Ferrante and Teicher's rendition of the theme from *Lawrence of Arabia*; Booker T. and the MGs doing *Green Onions*; then Herb Alpert and the Tijuana Brass doing *The Lonely Bull*. Her spirits lifted as she tried to sing the alto of the *Deep Purple* harmony, but the tenor, Paul, was missing so she choked. Her spirits plummeted with a crash. "Time to get moving." While the records played out, Darling wandered down to the kitchen and stared mindlessly into the refrigerator. She opened a bottle of Royal Crown Diet Cola as she started sliding with a little shake-and-finger-pop, then went back upstairs to her room, doing her homework, doing her nails.

# CHAPTER 25

The first week of October brought the first bright clear whiff of autumn to the northeastern seaboard of the United States. Lingering Indian summer afternoons gave way to the chill of early morning mists that would soon become a sharp frost. The *New York Times* published its first-ever front-page photographs of the killing fields; U.S. Marines wounded and dying in the rice paddies during the long siege near Con Thien. There were also confused reports of the death of 39-year-old Cuban heartthrob and hero, the revolutionary leader Ernesto "Che" Guevara. Che was reportedly killed during some guerilla battle deep within the Bolivian jungle where he and a few loyal followers had been hiding from Fidel Castro's bounty hunters.

The Soviet Union, who backed the Chinese, who backed the North Vietnamese, brought out a declaration that peace in Vietnam could only be achieved if the United States withdrew its forces. The Berlin Wall was turning six years old, and the Soviets were preparing to celebrate the 50th Anniversary of the Bolshevik Revolution. France charged that the U.S. was endangering the peace of the world through our involvement in Vietnam. Vice-President Hubert H. Humphrey escaped unscathed when Saigon Palace came under rocket and mortar attack during inaugural festivities for newly elected president of South Vietnam, a creep named Nguyen Van Thieu.

Specialist 5 David C. Dolby was awarded the Medal of Honor, and off-year election criticism of the Johnson Administration's Vietnam policy continued to intensify. In what was becoming an annual pre-holiday effort, President Johnson offered a pledge to halt the bombing of North Vietnam if talks would follow. Hanoi spurned the President's offer and vowed to fight on. More men died. The chilly nights brought a brief respite from the rioting across America, which activity was in the process of pivoting from the inner cities to the new semesters of college campuses, soon to occur not just throughout America, but in France, Germany, England and Czechoslovakia.


By that time, Canada was well on its way into winter-like weather and Paul Randolph had actually become what he thought was, if not happy, then at peace with himself. He had spent every waking moment rebuilding himself and much of Woodside Farm in the process. He had bought three plaid flannel shirts and three plaid wool Pendleton shirts, and long johns and a mackinaw jacket, gloves lined with rabbit fur, and boots lined in lamb's wool. He had buried deep in the woods of Woodside Farm, the bedroll from the Free Store and all its contents as well as the Army-surplus jacket that had made him feel so guilty every time he put it on.

Paul had made a cozy place for himself in the bunkhouse where he went only to sleep, never to think, where he went only at the end of a very long and hard-working day. He had every piece of farm equipment polished bright and running in tip-top order. Pop Richarde let him have the old Ford Woody, which Paul had discovered so broken down out behind the barns, but man, it was a Canadian Windsor engine under the hood. Although it had no seats in the back and the front was just a leather bench, with new tires and a thorough cleaning it made a damned good set of wheels. Paul even ventured farther than the Trading Post once in a while, for a new book or for paint. He scraped and sanded and hammered and shimmed until that old farm house showed its gratitude in a bright white stateliness and dark forest green shutters. He did the same with the barns, which were now barn-red with white sashes. Paul's reward was to collapse into bed every night, to lay without thinking and to sleep without dreams.

Darling went from deep black depressions to anxious high hopes, from applying herself diligently to lazing in bed all day where she seemed to be contesting Balzac's championship in the laying around category, thinking things out sometimes, blotting all thoughts out at others. It was bad enough knowing Paul was not coming back, but what about that other kid? There had been no provision made in her mother's Will, what about her father's? How could she get her hands on a copy of that? Mark Cymrot is blind if he can't tell there's something very un-cool going on out here. "God. Sometimes I really hate it here."

Since Sundays were her worst days, Darling didn't think going to church could possibly make them any more intolerable and it might even make them better because she would be able to sit next to Mim for an hour. So, on the second Sunday in October, Darling Randolph showed up at the First Baptist Church in Littleton dressed in a gray wool straight skirt and pink cashmere V-neck sweater. Miriam, dressed in her usual starched white blouse with a Peter Pan collar, plaid hip-stitched pleated skirt and coordinating cardigan buttoned at the neck, was delighted. She had not the slightest notion that Darling was going to pray like she meant it or be "saved." Miriam knew that Darling had inconvenienced herself so that they could do more than talk on the phone, so that they could be together for a little while.

As on other Sunday mornings, announcements were made by the pastor during the first few cordial minutes before he began his harangue of the week. Darling's attention perked up when she heard that one Mrs. Elizabeth Killian, aged 94, needed a ride from Littleton to Mount Holly twice a week for her physical therapy sessions. Whoever volunteered would have to be available at the designated times and to bring Mrs. Killian back to Littleton safely. The volunteer might also be asked to help Mrs. Killian do some grocery shopping now and then. Darling Randolph volunteered. She loved to drive. She had the time. She was more than happy to be of service.

Elizabeth Killian was a frail old brown lady whose cataracts were so thick that her eyes appeared a milky blue. She was pleased that Darling Randolph was so punctual and drove so carefully, and Darling was always on time to collect her at the physical therapy department, which Mrs. Killian referred to as the torture chamber. Darling Randolph was enamored of Mrs. Killian's warm and generous spirit and she often took tea when they reached Mrs. Killian's ancient house in Littleton. Darling could always count on Mrs. Killian for a good story from the old days. The old lady and the young lady learned to laugh together. "Mrs. Killian, I'll bet you were a pip in your day!"

"Mr. Killian always liked to think so. God rest his soul."

Elizabeth Killian had been born in Vicksburg, Mississippi just after the end of the Civil War. She told stories of her trials growing up in the South during the Era of Reconstruction, and of her bold and secret and dangerous migration North to Chicago. That's where she met Mr. Killian, an itinerate tinker. They were married for nearly forty years and she bore eleven children, nine of whom survived. Mr. Killian had been killed under circumstances Mrs. Killian cared not to reveal when their baby was not quite ten. That was when Mrs. Killian brought the remaining three children who were still at home to live in New Jersey. "Oh, let me see. It must've been the early '30s." One of her older sons had a job working for the railroad back in the days when the cranberry was king in New Jersey. "He had him a white wife you see and mixed couples were against the law in most states, still are. Both dead now. Don't outlive your children, Darling. Don't let it happen." Darling Randolph loved Mrs. Killian and she would be the old lady's companion and driver until the day she died.

Miriam was ecstatic that Darling was reaching out in new directions for places to apply her energies. Miriam still felt rotten that Paul had been such a huge disappointment, but she was developing a new faith that Darling would eventually pull through all right. The more friends Darling had the better off she would be especially since Miriam planned to move to Hightstown next summer. It didn't hurt that Mrs. Bolton was shocked and pleased to find that Darling Randolph, "…had a decent bone in her body." Mrs. Bolton's new impression of Darling would only help when it came to the subject of Miriam's permissions to get together with Darling. Dieter would be home in two weeks.

It was the second Monday of October, Canadian Thanksgiving Day. As Paul Randolph bowed his head and stared into his big bony hands, he wrestled with emotion. Here were these beautiful old people, the Richardes, who reminded him so of his own grandparents and who had brought him to their Thanksgiving table as if he were family. Paul and the four other men who labored on the farm (three of those others would soon be moving on, as there was not enough work in winter to keep all of them occupied), ate well of turkey and venison, creamed peas and pearl onions, corn on the cob, boiled potatoes, and sweet potatoes baked and sweetened with pure maple syrup, and there was rich brown gravy and hot brown bread. All of these things had come from the Woodside Farm.

Paul's appetite was not what it could have been. He, as were a couple of the others, was reminded of Thanksgivings that were gone-by, family days. But Paul Randolph was the only American among them. This feast was for him not a traditional one; *his* Thanksgiving Day did not arrive until late November. Although these skies were the same lead-gray skies of Thanksgiving at home and although this corn-stubble was crunchy with frost, the same as in New Jersey at the Thanksgiving time of year, it was all just somehow out of synch with what Paul had always known before.

These little similarities and differences in themselves did not make Paul unhappy in the least. What made Paul unhappy was the knowledge that many men his own age would be eating C-rations in some rain-forest or seated on a log with a view of some rice-paddy, or in some field hospital when real Thanksgiving arrived. He pondered; many who are alive today will be dead by then. And, Darling. He had gone and left her all alone there, with only her memories and the skeletons of the past for warm company. Flag-draped coffins.

Funny. When he had left, it had been high summer, free and easy. It had never occurred to him then that summer might evolve into autumn, or winter. Paul's mood was too black to remind him that eventually it would also be spring.

How easily Paul remembered Thanksgivings of his childhood when there had always been a nice fire in the fireplace and a fat gobbler roasting slowly in the oven and his dad's old friends stopping by for a morning's gunning, deer season; his mother looking especially breathtaking with a bit of a rosy cheek and flashing green eyes and bouncing short auburn curls in a crazy maze about her head, happy; steaming coffee in big clumsy crockery mugs. But they're dead. And you've gone off and left your sister all alone in that house. Random episodes of their childhood sparkled in and out of Paul's mind, scenes like the time the two of them were experimenting with the making of gunpowder and blew up the oven, giving Hannah fits, but she got a whole new kitchen out of it. Or that time they got caught throwing a pair of kittens into the creek at the count of one-for-the-money, two-for-the-show, three-to-get-ready, now-go-cat-go, and making bets with their allowances as to which kitten would paddle back to shore the fastest, wonder what ever happened to those kittens. Seems like Grandma Littleton must've taken them over to Mr. Oldrey's farm where they would be safe.

How could you have left? You would have gone back, you had intended to, remember? Why did you run? Because you got a break for it. Maybe. Maybe it was the shock setting in, of finding that file of Dad's. For twenty-one years you believed yourself to be the first born. All of a sudden you were not, are not. For almost all of those twenty-one years you were agitated and pushed, demanded into perfection, by two parents who pretended, only pretended, to be perfect examples of upstanding American citizens; bigots, hypocrites. That other one didn't have to suffer the consequences of being a Littleton-Randolph. No. Not the consequences. But, Paul, not the privileges either. Did he go to college? Did he (or she) have the luxury of a fine home and family connections, or Hot Rods, or a two-thousand-dollar sound system, or summers at the ocean, or holidays abroad, or, or...

Mrs. Richarde served up a perfect apple pie still warm from the oven, accompanied by a big pitcher of thick heavy cream, and dark rich coffee which they would all enjoy Boston style with lots of cream and sugar as the grand finale of her fabulous repast. She had prepared the pie especially for her young American friend and she placed it on the table saying in her velvet and still heavily French, voice, "For my American boy. As American as Mom's apple pie, eh?" And Paul simply cracked, right there at the table. The web of pain spread across his face like the crazing in fine old porcelain. He raised his hand to squeeze the bridge of his nose, yet huge hot tears began to roll from beneath the curl of fawn-colored eyelashes and down the sharp, high, almost Native American cheekbones. Paul rose to excuse himself, swallowing hard, almost whispering, "I'm so sorry Madame Richarde."

Paul left the table and went straight out the front door, down the broad steps of the front porch and out into the cold. The leaden sky still threatened to snow. Once the snows began, it would snow at least a little almost every day keeping the rich soil moist and fresh beneath its frozen crust, fertile for the planting in the spring.

The old-folks were counting on him. Those leaving had already packed-up. They would be off at first light with full bellies and Mom Richarde's care packages to see them safely on their way. The tears would not stop. The pain inside only grew deeper, doubling Paul over and sinking him to his knees, holding his belly and wrenching at himself in disgust, letting his proud head fall to the ground in unbearable hatred. He finally let cry that primal scream and then Paul rocked and moaned, pounding and pounding his fist against the frozen Earth, "Can Hell really be any worse than this? Well, can it? Can it? Can it?"


Late that night, Pop Richarde went out to the bunkhouse. He bid farewell to the three men leaving and wished them all luck and God's blessings, reminding them not to forget they could always stop back in the spring. God willing, he and Madame Richarde would live to see another at Woodside Farm. Then he invited Paul Randolph to step outside. The shrinking old man in the buffalo plaid jacket sat on the stoop of the bunkhouse steps toying with his bootlaces, untying them, pulling the laces tighter, tying them again, doubling the bows into another knot. Pop began in the privacy of low tones. "Mom and I never did have any children, came close a couple of times, it just never did finally happen. We were young once, although you wouldn't know it to look at us now. Yes, there was a time when we thought we had all the time in the world. Never die. Young people don't even think about things like that. Unless it's a war on. But we've made it through two World Wars and many smaller ones. Seems like somebody's always at war, somewhere. That old Nasser and King Hussein, they talk a lot about peace, but I don't see it happening over there. You ever think about going home, son?"

Paul nearly chuckled. "Home. Yeah, Pop, I think about it. Think about it just about every minute of every day, no matter how I try and stop it. But you don't know how I got here, Pop. I'm a criminal, Pop. A draft-dodger. A traitor."

"In some people's eyes perhaps. But, we know, son. Mom and I. In our hearts we've known all along. We just didn't want to think about it. And it's such a senseless war, isn't it, meaningless. But I must tell you, the French went through the same kinds of revelations you Americans are having right now, and in the very same place, back in the late forties, early fifties. Only we called it Indo-China back then."

Paul nodded his head as if to say he was listening. He waited. Now and then Paul would pitch a pebble at the big red hand-pump at the well head. Once in a while one would strike dead-on and make a sharp ping that shattered the stillness of the late clear star-spangled night. Pop Richarde found it annoying, but did not complain. He knew Paul Randolph was irritable, nervous, and anxious, in transition, in pain. He went on, "Perhaps I ought not to be telling you this… There are very few things in a man's life that he can un-do. But, son, this is one of them." Pop Richard rose slowly giving his complaining spine plenty of time to bring him fully upright. "Time for me to be in that featherbed up there with Mom. Think about it, son. We'll get by. We always have. Just think about it."


In the morning Paul Randolph was gone. Madame Richarde seemed to be in a huff as she set out large earthenware bowls of porridge, and a big crock of freshly churned butter, and a huge pitcher of maple syrup for the others. Paul Randolph had eaten no breakfast, Paul Randolph had no sack of turkey and cheese and warm brown bread to take along for his journey.

Mom and Pop Richarde did not discuss Paul's absence at breakfast. Never in front of the others. Nor did they discuss it at all during another long busy day at the farm. But late that night, the sweet old lady lay as she had for more than fifty years, in her husband's arms, this night wide awake, wondering if her young American boy would be all right, her husband knowing and pulling her head closer and saying, "Not to worry."

"Do you think he is going back to his home?"

"I think so. I hope so."

She whispered, "I am praying for him." Pop, who had been convinced for years that one of Mom's prayers was worth scores of anybody else's, sighed deeply, "Good."

She turned her face up to her husband and asked, "Did you see, out by the kitchen door? He's laid enough wood to last the whole rest of the winter."

"Yes? Hmm. He must have done that in the night."

"We shall miss him."

"Yes, we shall miss him."

# CHAPTER 26

On Saturday, October 14th, while a strong enemy force was attacking and killing Marines in the buffer zone South of Con Thien, Specialist 4th Class, Dieter McKenzie was making his way home to New Jersey. By Sunday morning at 03:54 hours Dieter and Miriam pranced arm-in-arm across the taxi-island. Dieter walked tall and straight in his Class-As. He wore the insignias of the U.S. and the crossed-cannons of the Field Artillery in gleaming brass on the lapels. His Marksman's medal dangled over his breast pocket. Dieter's airline tickets, a copy of his Leave papers, and his Orders to Report to Cam Ranh Bay were tucked into the inside breast pocket.
Dieter easily wielded his overburdened duffel bag while his free arm was clutched tightly about the waist of Mim Bolton. Miriam appeared even taller and more slender than usual in her bottle-green mohair sweater and black stitched-to-the-hip box-pleated skirt. Their smiles and eyeglasses flashed in the lights of the parking lot.

Miriam had told another lie. It was becoming so much easier. But then, it wasn't really quite a lie. Miriam would be spending the night at Darling's house. It was just the unsaid thing about Dieter spending the night at Darling's house too.

Dave Adams lay uncomfortably in his room atop the Hilltop Garage; the radio was pumping out sounds of The Cookies singing *Chains*. He stubbed out another cigarette and turned the radio off. He was about to go mad suspecting as he did that Miriam was about to lose her cherry. This suspicion was forcing David to fight back an erection that was constantly on the rise. David felt that he should have been balling Darling long before this and he could barely understand why he had not been successful. Tight-ass. David tossed and turned against the night, waiting for it to be time to head for Arrowhead. The plan was that David would drive out to the Randolph place to see Dieter and drop off the Chevy so Dieter would have wheels. That would be just before Miriam and Darling came home from the necessary trip to church.

At least now David knew, or was pretty sure, that Darling only went to church as a front. It was an excuse to get Miriam out to Arrowhead for a visit or maybe just to get herself out of house, but it was for certain that *that* little monkey was no angel. Why, she had brought the Mustang up to the Hilltop Garage three times already. She kept messing up the timing in her constant efforts to bury the speedometer needle. "You're going to ruin this car!"

"It's *my* car!"

"It's not made to do 110!"

"Then why does the speedometer go to 110?"

"Okay, maybe it'll do it. But you're beating the shit out of this car. Not good."

Darling practiced by either going up to or coming down from the top of the mount. She especially liked the straightaway on Juliustown Road where she could go flying over that little hump at exactly 87 miles an hour so that all four wheels left the ground and she could lose her stomach as the car came down into the invisible dip just on the other side. David warned her again and again that she was turning her brand-new baby carriage into a bomb. All Darling had to say was, "So what's it to you?"

Even though Darling helped by holding the timing light and playing step-and-fetch-it in Dieter's absence, she insisted on paying David for the work he did on the 'Stang. Would he ever figure her out? David tried to be patient, to wait for just the right time, the right moment to present Darling with the Mercury. He thought about that moment and about how special it would be, and about how it would probably be his big chance. David flopped over onto his stomach again, turning his back to the stars in the skylight, hugging the hell out of his pillow and ejaculating into the sheets.

There were only a couple of hours until dawn by the time Miriam pulled her Volkswagen into the drive at the Randolph house. She and Dieter whispered as they quietly entered the house. Miriam led Dieter down the hall to Mr. Randolph's study. "I think you'll be comfortable in here. Bathroom's across the hall."

Miriam had made the leather Chesterfield into a nice warm comfy bed. "I put an extra blanket out just in case. I'll be in Paul's room if you need anything." Dieter looked a little put out but said, "Thank you sweetheart." Miriam gave him a long, warm hug, "Pleasant dreams," and then went to Paul's room and closed the door. She was exhausted and exhilarated and she was thinking happy thoughts as she undressed in the darkness, pulled a pretty blue flowered flannel nightie over her head and put her glasses on the nightstand. Then she heard footsteps.

Miriam's heart announced its tachycardia. She did her best to ignore the footsteps, telling herself, "Maybe it's just the bathroom." She slipped into bed and under the covers. She lay in the cold darkness of crisp cotton sheets and shivered and listened and waited. Oh. He was. He was going to do it. Miriam pulled the covers up over her head.

The tie slid through the shirt collar. The Olive Drab wool jacket came off; its brass clanked against the doorknob. She heard the rustle of his stripping, heard the unzipping of his fly. OD dress pants with pocket change and a belt buckle dropped to the floor. She sneaked a peak from under the covers to see Dieter standing in his T-shirt and boxer shorts. He was neatly folding his pants and laying them across the back of the chair. Miriam was shocked. She'd never seen a man dressed only in his underwear in her life. What kind of a man was this man whom she loved?

Miriam slid the covers back over her eyes. Good grief, she thought, not only is he getting into bed but he's getting into MY side of the bed. As Dieter slid into the covers Miriam slid over to the other side.

Miriam had no way of knowing that Dieter's heart was pounding away, just the same as hers. She had no way of knowing that he was asking himself, "What am I doing?" and letting it happen all at the same time, just the same as she was.

He reached out to touch her. She shrank away. He put his long arm around her waist and tried to draw her to him, but she pulled away. She rolled over onto her stomach and pulled her elbows in tight beside her. As she turned her head away from him, she whispered, "I can't."


In the cold and pearly gray hour before dawn, Miriam awoke to Dieter's gentle stroking of her angular face. Her face was only inches from his on the pillow. His fingers lightly traced her jaw, her cheekbones and eye sockets, her forehead, then back along her chin. Over and over again his gentle hand passed along her face. Then, after a long while, Dieter slipped his arm around her body and pulled her to him, oh, the warmth of his body, and oh, how like a stone she was, so frightened, so frozen. Dieter pushed Miriam's head down onto his chest and then he rocked her, he rocked her softly, he rocked her in his arms. There they stayed, there they lay, and there they waited for the pearly gray of cold infinity to justly give way to a warm and pink and just as pearly edge of dawn. Their two bodies entwined, rocking gently before the morning light. No words were spoken as she breathed in the essence of his body. She had never been so loved, so adored in all her life. And she knew it would never happen again.

Sunday morning arrived soon enough and it was time to go to church. Darling knocked at Paul's bedroom door. As she did so she was feeding the end of a narrow black leather belt through the belt-loops of her new gray wool-flannel trousers. Women in trousers, especially at church, was still a very daring idea in 1967 and this was going to be Darling's silent statement about what she thought of conventional morality. "Mim? You just about ready? We gotta go."

Dieter opened the door and smiled his big goofy smile at Darling, "Good morning beautiful!" He padded down the hall toward the kitchen. Darling followed him as she adjusted the collar of her starched white Oxford shirt inside the black wool-cashmere blazer. "I'm sure you can find everything. Dishes. Juice. Cereal's in the pantry." Dieter said, "Thanks, I'm starved." But Darling could hardly take her eyes from Dieter. My how he had changed.

"Mim. We've got to stop and pick up Mrs. Killian!"

"Right there."

Dieter wandered around the kitchen in OD socks, rumpled fatigue pants and a T-shirt. Darling couldn't get over it. Dieter had biceps and triceps and a pectoralis major that bulged against the T-shirt almost as impressively as Paul's did. Jeez. "Looks like the Army agrees with you."

"Nah. They don't seem to like nothin' I do. But the body sure benefits from hard livin'."

"I'll say. Mim nearly ready?"

"Yeah. Just makin' the bed!"

Miriam entered the hallway dragging one skimmer by the toe and sliding it around until it found its way onto her foot, "Ready." Darling grabbed her keys and her shoulder bag and headed for the car. Miriam stopped for a long cuddle with Dieter. Darling called, "Hey! Now, now, now!"

Miriam dashed down the porch steps and jumped into the car. Darling threw the Mustang into reverse saying, "You've got between here and church to wipe that shit-eating grin off your face." Miriam bopped over and kissed Darling on the cheek, "Thanks."

"For what?"

"Everything."

"*De nada.* Besides. I owe you."

"For what?"

"I don't know. I'll think of something." She giggled. "Never thought I'd ever see the day when *I* would have to hurry *you* off to church."

Miriam grabbed the rear-view mirror and turned it to herself. "I look all right?"

"Don't worry. You've got a long way to go before you start to look like a brazen hussy."

"I need to look like a virgin."

"You are a virgin."

"What makes you so sure?"

"Grrrr." Darling grabbed the mirror and adjusted it so she could see what she had already missed while driving, "Brag, brag, brag."

"You sure you're okay with all this?"

"Just jealous, that's all. I've never felt like you look like you feel right now."

"You will. You will someday."

"Let's change the subject."

"Right. We gonna try to go the shore next weekend?"

"Yeah. And Dave called last night. We're having dinner at the Smithville Inn this afternoon. You'll make it home in time for evening services. He should be at the house when we get back. How're you gonna be able to stand knowing Dieter's here and you can't see him 'til next weekend?"

"After twelve weeks, five days doesn't seem like much. 'Sides, we both know we've got to take what we can get. Whatever memories we make now are going to have to last us for a year, maybe for the rest of our lives."

"Oh, Mim. How can you even talk that way?"

"You're the free spirit. I'm the pragmatist."


Paul Randolph's heart thumped and his eyes grew red and swollen as his ride dropped him off at Exit 5 of the New Jersey Turnpike. He forced himself not to head east to Littleton. He made himself face west into the wind and toward the U S. Army Induction Center at Burlington.

Much as he loved her, much as he missed her, and much as he wanted his arms around her, Paul could not bring himself to face his sister. Paul wanted to redeem himself first. It was not for Darling's benefit. It was for his, Paul Randolph's, sense of self that he needed to overcome what he now considered to have been an act of cowardice. It was okay for some, and he had given it his best shot but for Paul Randolph the instinct to fight had gained the upper hand over his original urge to flee. He needed to prove himself to himself before he could confront any more of his personal demons. Life in a barracks could not be all that different from life in a bunkhouse. He would have more company but he doubted the meals would be anywhere near as good.

# PART III

## CHAPTER 27

Holidays are actually harder on the families left behind than they are on combat forces. American forces in Vietnam were enjoying Thanksgiving dinner in the mess if they were at base camp. If they were out in the field on maneuvers then they were too busy trying to keep from getting their asses blown off to think about what particular day it might happen to be. On Thanksgiving Day of 1967, Darling prepared a nice little dinner for Miriam and David and Mrs. Killian and herself. She built a roaring fire in the fireplace and filled the house with the aroma of spices and many pots of yellow chrysanthemums, all in an effort to try to cheer Miriam in Dieter's absence. Darling was also trying to steer her own ship well clear of the doldrums.

Only four years ago, in 1963, Thanksgiving Day had been just one more day in a series of days of National Mourning. President Kennedy had written and spoken many words in his short lifetime that an entire generation of the world's young people would live by; among them, Darling's favorite, from his Pulitzer Prize winning *Profiles in Courage* "…there are few if any issues where all the truth and all the right and all the angels are on one side."

By Thanksgiving of this year, 1967, Dieter had been In Country for more than a month so it was especially rough on Miriam. But she tried to be a good sport about it and showed up at the Randolph place with a new record album; one of its numbers had become famous earlier that year when it was first performed at the Newport Folk Festival. After dinner, which turned out to be not too bad, Miriam and Darling and David played the album over and over again until Mrs. Killian finally sang along too, while Arlo Guthrie picked and strummed his guitar and told the legend of the Thanksgiving Day *Alice's Restaurant Massacree*.

Darling put another log on the fire but Miriam was soon ready to go home. "Black Friday tomorrow, you know? Still the busiest shopping day of the year. Promised I'd help out. I'm so tired. And full! Think I'll go to bed early." Mrs. Killian said that a nap sounded like a good idea and asked Miriam, "Would it be too much trouble to drop me off along the way?"

"Not at all."

An hour later David and Darling were working on the Mustang and arguing over what should be done. David was trying to convince Darling that the Mustang only had six cylinders and that she should stop trying to get 110 out of it. Darling stomped away in frustration and went straight upstairs to her mother's medicine cabinet for the barbiturates. That was the moment when Darling found the Phenobarb bottle quite a bit lower than she thought it should be. Her memory flashed open to a conversation with Miriam earlier in the day, the one when Miriam asked all those questions about Darling's thing with Buzz so long ago, and about the abortion and what it was like.

"I guess I'll never know if it was the right thing to do. But, then, it's okay to say that now because I didn't have to have it. It probably would have been messed up anyway. Mom just, like, tried so many different things before her GYN finally found somebody who would do it. Buzz didn't know anything about it. He wouldn't have cared one way or the other. He was just my Latin tutor and I certainly would never have married the guy. Jeez. I only went out with him 'cause he had this really cool-looking Galaxy 500, a convertible; it was this deep gold-metal-fleck green. It all just kind of happened."

Darling was not about to tell Miriam that Buzz had threatened her with humiliation: If she didn't let him do it then he would tell everyone that she had, and if she would let him do it then he wouldn't tell anyone. "He didn't care a thing about me." Sadly, Darling went on to say, "Love's only free for the guys. I know that now."

Darling stood at the bathroom mirror. She was still holding the Phenobarbital bottle in her hand. "Oh, my God! Oh, oh, you stupid, stupid..."

She raced down the stairs. Her eyes were huge and panic-stricken. David was walking in from outside, wiping his hands with a clean rag. He was beginning to tell Darling that he thought she should bring the Mustang up to the shop for a really good going-over, "Looks like you've started blowing a little oil..." but Darling had herself worked into a state and he didn't know why. He watched as she telephoned Miriam's house with her hands trembling and her fingers fumbling as she tried to dial the number. He could not hear Mrs. Bolton telling Darling that Miriam was in her room or that she wouldn't answer. But he did hear Darling say, "I'm on my way."

David muttered, "What the..." but Darling flew right past him without a word, slammed the hood down on the Mustang and hauled ass out of the drive spewing an awful lot of river rock. David cringed as he heard the gravel dinging the Mustang's wheel-wells, "Jeez-us H. Christ!"

Darling blazed over to the Bolton's cursing herself and slamming the heel of her hand into the steering wheel as she drove. Darling tried Miriam's bedroom door but it was locked. Mrs. Bolton launched into a diatribe about how, "Locking doors in this house is forbidden! This kind of behavior will not be tolerated." Darling hysterically dug around in her handbag until she found a bobby pin with which she easily popped the push-button lock. She knew it. Dammit.

There Miriam lay in her little white bed, dressed in a soft blue flannel nightie, all ready to yield up The Ghost, peacefully and with no expression on her face at all. Mrs. Bolton rubbed her hands together beneath her pendulous breasts, cursing Miriam. "She will surely go straight to Hell for this." Darling hollered at Mrs. Bolton, "Call an ambulance!" But Mrs. Bolton stood firm. "What for?" Darling smacked Miriam's cheeks, lifted Miriam's eyelids, and held her ear to Miriam's breast, and shouted, "Because she's still alive! Hurry, Mrs. Bolton! Get help!" Mrs. Bolton said, "Let her die."

Darling barged past Mrs. Bolton to the telephone. When she returned to Miriam's room she found Mrs. Bolton reading a note:

God has said He will forgive me.
I pray you will as well -

Darling grabbed the note from Mrs. Bolton's hand. Mrs. Bolton turned away as Darling looked at the note, folded it neatly and slipped it into her bra. She kneeled beside Miriam, patting Miriam's hand, stroking Miriam's face, running to the bathroom for a cold wet washcloth, all the time calling to her, "Mim. Mim. Come on, Mim. Come on, baby girl. Come back to us, Mim. You just can't leave us like this. Oh, Mim, not now. Not now! Think, Mim. Don't, Mim. Oh, please, please, don't."

Mrs. Bolton stood at the foot of the bed. "She'll die. She has to die."

"What're you, crazy? How can you say things like that? She's your daughter!"

"No daughter of mine would do this. This one is indeed a sinner, born in shame. I should've known all along. And that note, how she blasphemes! Who is she to think that God might hear her? And that He would answer her! Blasphemy. Let her die."

That ripped it. Darling rose from her knees. She raised her clenched fists firmly, yanking her elbows close at her sides, her rage practically raising her up off the floor. "Why you self-righteous old bitch! Who the fuck are you, anyway? You're not even human! You have no idea in hell what's going on around here! And you don't know because you don't wanna know! You don't care! You never did care! Couldn't you ever have cared about her? Couldn't you ever just have loved her?" Suddenly it occurred to Darling that she was speaking of Miriam in the past tense. "Oh, God. No! Please!" She went back to Miriam's side. She hurried to the front door to check for the ambulance. As she passed Mrs. Bolton, she gave the old woman a glancing blow with her eyes. Then she paused. In a cold measured tone she sneered, "And let me tell ya. If my Miriam says that God spoke to her, then I'm sure He did!"

"And what would you know about it? Everybody knows what you are. Jezebel! Get out! Get out of my house!"

"Make me."

"Well!" Mrs. Bolton waddled off in a huff.

Darling would particularly remember the ambulance ride and how she wished she could have done the driving, how it seemed to take forever to get to the hospital. She would always remember calling David from the pay phone in the hall just outside the Emergency Room. She would always remember seeing David burst through the doors of ER, rushing over to envelop her in his arms, and how she had cried.

# CHAPTER 28

There were so many cups of lousy vending-machine coffee. David and Darling shared so much of themselves, often mumbling mindlessly just to hear their own voices, just to keep one another awake. Darling jumped up with a pounding heart and an anxious inhale whenever a doctor entered the waiting room. Neither of them was allowed to actually be with Miriam because only a member of the immediate family was permitted to enter the glassed-in shrine of the Intensive Care Unit where she lay. And no family called or came to inquire.

Sometimes Darling's head nodded and rolled over onto David's shoulder. David sat so still, so still that his arm would fall asleep, so as not to wake her, just so still, so that he could feel the nearness of her. In sleep she appeared so soft and kind, not at all the fiery hardheaded stinker he was used to.

They talked in low-volume hospital voices, reverent, open, entire conversations in some kind of a convoluted prayer. David told Darling all about how he had left home, and about the fiasco with school and with the girl and all. Tina was her name. She had his son. He told Darling of how he had come to know Dieter McKenzie, both of them buying the same size Fram filter and the same size Gates belt from the same auto parts dealer at the same time and seeing one another's purchases and laughing at the coincidence and striking up a conversation about the cars for which the parts were being purchased. It just snowballed from there into a ridiculous form of everlasting friendship.

David confessed, "We've been able to keep the shop going, and Tina going, and the Chevy going, and we've both been able to better ourselves along the way. We go to school, went to school, you know, I draw. And Dieter was into getting his G.E.D. He really likes poetry, all kinds of poetry, stuff like John Donne and Sylvia Plath. Pretty far out, huh? But, what the hell, it's no weirder than what I do. I think he only wanted to be an ace mechanic so he could help me get us back in the running again. We talked about it anyway. But, really. Unless you're, like, a champion *every* year, they forget about you. They fuckin' forget you fast, man. I would've had to make a big comeback this year, but, man, I couldn't get my shit together if I had a rake."

Darling told David about the death of her parents, not a whole lot about who they were; she didn't seem to want to talk about it much, but she did tell David she was worried about Paul, and about why. That was evidently the foremost subject on her mind, after Miriam's survival. She confessed to David that it had only been a couple of days since some men came to the house, police investigators. They were asking a lot of questions about Paul and about where Paul was, and about Paul's involvement with some woman named Bernadette Carlani. These men said that Bernadette Carlani was a Missing Person. They claimed that Paul was one of the last people she was known to have been with. All the way last summer. This really had Darling worked up because she finally had to lie for Paul. She fed those cops some cock-and-bull story about Paul being away at school, even knowing how easily they would find out that he wasn't at Virginia at all. But it had been such short notice and there was just no way she could tell those investigator guys that her brother was a Missing Person too, or that she hadn't heard from him for months. Since all the way last summer.

It's one thing to tell someone your darkest secrets, yet another to ask someone for an opinion about what to do about it. "Do you think I should let Mark Cymrot in on what's really going on at home?"

"It doesn't sound like there's any way out of doing that."

What Darling didn't know was that if it had not been right before Thanksgiving, a great deal more might have been discovered a whole lot earlier. As it was, David was learning that Darling was alone. He didn't know why he should've been surprised. It all made so much sense after he knew the scoop. It was then and there, in that claustrophobic waiting room with the bile green latex semi-gloss walls and the plastic flower arrangements, that David promised himself that, no matter what, he would behave himself, that way, until the right time came. He cleared his throat. "You think we oughtta get in touch with Dieter somehow?"

"No."

"For why?"

"Let's wait. The news is either gonna be a whole lot better or a whole lot worse. Either way, what's he gonna do about it from Over There?"

"And we don't want him unnecessarily distracted 'cause he could get his head blown off. Right. Okay doll-face."

For three days and three nights they waited for Miriam to live or to die. On the fourth morning, Miriam's right index finger lifted from the gurney. Eight hours later she opened her eyes. Miriam did not know that her face was swollen to the size of a pie, or that the eyes she thought were wide open appeared to observers to be mere slits on the face of the pie. But none of that mattered a damn because Miriam was regaining consciousness; she was coming back to life; she was as resurrected as any mortal can ever hope to be.

David and Darling were both so happy and so relieved that for a time it seemed like all their quiet truths had been forgotten, even imagined. They suddenly became very busy. There were preparations to be made before Miriam could go home. She would be going home to Arrowhead because her parents would not have her in their house again. There was also the matter of this little guy named Tommy, David's son.

Darling had taken a particular interest in Tommy right away. She was adamant that David should know his son and make certain that Tina's child knew who his father was. After all, weren't she and Paul having their lives turned topsy-turvy because of a long-held secret, an indiscretion that had been compounded by lies into hypocrisy? David had never thought of getting to know his son as even the remotest of possibilities. Tina was such a wretch. She just hated David, mostly because her trick had backfired and he had not married her after all. David only wondered whatever made her think he would. He wasn't even sure Tommy was his until after he was born when Tommy looked as if he had been carved right out of David's ass.

By the end of that first week after Thanksgiving, Miriam was recovered enough to be transferred to a regular hospital room. But because she had attempted suicide, the hospital room was located on the sixth floor of the hospital, the psychiatric floor, and it was under lock-down. Miriam was going to have to continue recuperation while receiving twice-daily counseling sessions. Not until the consulting physicians were satisfied that Miriam was no longer a risk to her own life or to the lives of others would she be transferred to one of the general medicine floors.

Miriam was still very weak and she slept a great deal of the time. It was going to take about a month for her liver to process away all the Phenobarbital to which she had subjected it. But she was determined to make it and she was horrified by her own mistake. She insisted that Dieter was to know nothing of what had transpired. She did agree, however, that she should inform him of her pregnancy. Miriam was very concerned about what, if any damage had been done to her fledgling fetus.

Two weeks before Christmas and still in the hospital, Miriam took a long time to write a coherent letter to Dieter telling him that there was a baby on the way. She anticipated that if all went well Dieter would be a father by late July. She assured Dieter that everything was going to be fine and that she was preparing to move in with Darling for the duration because her mother and father would never understand, let alone forgive her. And she begged Dieter not to worry. "Just keep writing me whenever you can, my beloved. I (we) will be here waiting for you to come home."

That Christmas Eve, while Miriam lay sleeping it off in a nice fresh bed in a regular hospital room on a regular floor and Darling had finally been able to touch Miriam and bid her goodnight with a kiss. Darling got David to take her out shopping. Exhausted as they were, she was certain there were stores that stayed open all night on Christmas Eve, it was only a matter of finding them. Until two in the morning they bombed all over Burlington County, a "See-and-Say" here, a big fuzzy Teddy bear at the next stop. Alvin and the Chipmunks were singing their famous *Christmas Song* and, of course, the great Brenda Lee, aged sixteen, was *Rockin' Around the Christmas Tree.*

## ALL WRAPPING PAPER AND
## CURLING RIBBON: HALF PRICE!

There was no snow that Christmas Eve and no moon either so Sirius, the Dog Star, shone uninhibited. David dropped Darling off at Arrowhead with a gentle Merry Christmas kind of kiss then made his way back to Bordentown. Darling had done her bit, now it was up to him. Santa still had to make his rounds that night and all good little children should be nestled in their beds.

That Christmas Eve turned out to be a long cold night for David. For when he reached Tina's townhouse in Bordentown, he found his son's mother so stoned she did not even know that David had entered the house. Twenty-one-month old Tommy was sleeping huddled on the floor beside the darkened Christmas tree with his little hands and knees tucked up under his tummy and his soaking-wet diapered bottom sticking up high in the air.

David carefully climbed the stairs with the sleeping child in his arms. He could hear soft voices on the other side of the party wall. A young woman asking, "Did you get the oranges today?" A young man saying, "I forgot! What do we do now?" And she, "Oh, don't worry about it, honey. Those big navel oranges are always nice but I think we've got enough. Let's see. There are apples and tangerines, hard candies and nuts and look at these cute little chocolate Santas I got at the drug store today." David heard them softly laughing. He knew they were happy, Pete and Angie, and their two kids. Nice family.

David carefully laid Tommy into his crib. He gazed down upon his son's face, just a chubby cherub of a child, as he fitted Tommy's bottom with a dry diaper. Then he returned to the living room. He plugged in the tree lights and buttoned his Wrangler jacket over the black cashmere muffler he had just received from Darling. Warm thoughts. Then he went out to the Dart, opened the trunk and began carrying a small stack of brightly wrapped packages into the house and placing them lovingly beneath the tree. He set the big brown Teddy bear up against the yellow Tonka dump truck and it was done.

David went to the sofa and tried to bring Tina around enough for a bit of conversation. "I'll make some coffee." He picked up Tina's frail arm and let it drop again. "Listen. I want you off the dope." Suddenly Tina was there for him. She lit a cigarette. "You smoke."

"Yeah, but it's not the same, Tina. I can live without it. Besides, you've started sticking needles in your arm. Only scumbags do that shit. Just look at you."

"So?"

"So. What if something happens to Tommy and you're out of it?"

"Just get off my back, okay Davie?"

"It's Christmas Eve, Tina, come on. Straighten out a little bit, will ya? At least try. For Tommy."

"For Tommy. What the fuck would you know about Tommy?"

"Okay, okay. But shshsh. You'll wake him up. Listen Tina, I care. I really do care, and I want to help. And I'm willing to give it a try, honest." David tried to take Tina into his arms. She pulled away. He stood up, rejected. "You just will not cooperate." He stood for a moment looking at the Christmas tree. Then he said, "Fuck it," and he left.

The Hilltop Garage was dark and cold. In the deep glow of the almost abandoned garage sat the metallic-blue '56 Chevy coupe, Dieter's Chevy, and right next to it was parked the cherry red 1953 Mercury. It didn't seem like he'd ever get a chance to see that twinkle in Darling's eye. The heavy metal of the cars gave off the impression of a pair of cold graves, waiting there as they were, in the dim starlight. David did not light the gas heater. He climbed the stairs and wrapped a blanket around his shoulders and sat on his bed looking out from the hilltop, out over the quiet streets of Bordentown. He gazed at the twinkling Christmas lights touched with a dash of neon, and the Christmas red and gold and green of the traffic signal changing over and over as he wondered how he could possibly keep his promise to Darling, to change the way things were.

Darling made sure that Dr. Dovi knew that Miriam had been disowned by her parents and would be going home to live with Darling Randolph. Dr. Dovi said, "I'll only release her to your care if you promise to see to it that she returns for long-term psychological counseling." They both knew that Miriam was well over twenty-one and was responsible for her own welfare, but Darling reassured Dr. Dovi. Miriam would benefit from good counseling as well as healthy diet and a good obstetrician for as long as she wanted to stay at Arrowhead.

Many of the hospital personnel, including Dr. Dovi, were familiar with Darling Randolph and her brother, Paul. For although they had both been born at some special hospital in Trenton, they had been treated at Memorial Hospital both separately and together for all of their lives. Those two were always in and out of the ER for some minor auto accident or another or for a broken toe or a sprained wrist sustained during one of their notorious knock-down-drag-out fights. They had been in and out of admissions a couple of times as well, Darling for an appendectomy and a broken nose, Paul for a compound fractured tibia and also for a broken nose. Indeed, the Randolphs were well known to the staff of that busy county hospital in southern New Jersey.

# CHAPTER 29

Miles and miles of steaming jungle. Razor sharp bamboo slices a man's hands wide open. Inland waterways harbor malaria and leeches. The dirt pathways are swamped, sometimes up to your thighs during the rainy season. DEET (diethyltoluamide) is hardly effective against *swarms* of mosquitoes. Your own body salts make your eyes burn, sweat, tears, you can hardly see. And always an M-16 slung across your chest. Nail one every now and then along the way, pushing and pushing, ever farther north, bogged down again, hauling the big guns. DogFace Smolinsky, the radioman, remains in constant touch with Fire Direction Control. His gruff barking voice heaves coordinates at you and you wheel the turret around, aligning those cross-hairs just right. Pull the lanyard. Plug your fingers in your ears and duck, quick, the shell is off so fast you can hardly see it, then comes the BOOM! Later, you find out the Forward Observer has called the fire in so close that you've blown him to smithereens, right there in the crotch of that gum tree. "Who was it? Lieutenant Hammond?"

"Nah, Hammond bought it the other day. Don't know, wasn't around long enough to really catch his name."

Had the dead man known? Had he wanted that little pocket of VC that bad? God. They die like flies. And then, of course, there is the body count, always have to have the body count.

Thousands of young people marching in front of the White House, chanting, **"Hey, hey, LBJ. How many kids did you kill today?"**

Move out. North. Hurry now, come on. "Move it! Move it! They'll know where the fire's coming from. They'll be here any minute. Where's Trupin?"

"Hey, I dunno, man, he was here just a minute ago. Probably taking a crap."

"Well, find him, tell him to move his ass, we gotta move, hurry, find him and catch up quick."

134

"Ah, sir, never mind about Trupin. He's over there, sir, his guts are all over the ground."

"God damn it! Grab one of his tags. Doggie, call it in. Let's get a move on."

You get used to it.

Bloody hell! If you're a human being you never get used to it. You may become stronger or crazier but it will never be easy.

Dieter McKenzie drifted often now into his vision. Miriam visited him most often in the dense heat of the afternoons. The convoy would be pulled to the side of some small path beside a long row of rice paddies, or just outside an empty village and there she would be. It began when Dieter was so upset because he lost Miriam's photograph. He thought it had been so safe inside his thigh pocket where it always was. But then that time came, when they stopped and he went for the picture and it was gone. He couldn't find it anywhere. And he slumped there, forlorn. That was when she first came to him, her image wavering, just there, at the end of the road, walking toward him it seemed, but never really getting any closer. Her hair was so fine and pale, blowing softly about her, drifting lazily upon some imaginary breeze, and, bless her heart, she was holding out to him a tall frosty glass of lemonade. Her nakedness was so lovely and pale against the burning sunlight. Her breasts and belly were swollen and firm.

Another day of chilly rain and dark brown glossy wet leaves. A new record album, *The Who Sell Out*, was spinning on the turntable and booming from the speakers in Paul's room. All except for this one song, *I Can See For Miles*, the album had been a big letdown for Darling, but after all, they were still the same Who who'd done *My Generation* a year earlier. Darling was following her practice of recording her favorite cuts onto a tape Paul had started for her. The tape was simply called Darling's Selections. Miriam was tucked up on the living room sofa alternately knitting and snoozing. Darling sat before the hearth pasting clippings into her scrapbook: A really good one of "Broadway" Joe Namath, flashing that brilliant smile; Mrs. John F. Kennedy riding in an open car beside Prince Sihanouk in Cambodia; and the telegram announcing the death of Grandma Littleton's cousin, John Nance Garner, aged 98 years. Darling sent flowers from herself and Paul. There was a photograph of the Metropolitan Museum of Art's famous Greek Horse, which had just been proven via a new x-ray technique, to be a fake. And there was a small piece reporting that the complete manuscript of Chopin's *Waltz in G Flat Minor (Opus 70, No. 1)*, was found in a chateau in France, the real thing, written in Chopin's own hand. The phone rang. Darling charged into Paul's room to lift the needle and stop the reel. This got Miriam's attention.

In the United States, *The Holidays* connote a joyful generous, spiritual season that runs from Thanksgiving Day, when Santa arrives at Macy's through Hanukkah, and then on to include Christmas Eve, Christmas Day, Boxing Day, soon followed by New Year's Eve and New Year's Day, and, for the heartiest of partiers, to the Epiphany, on the sixth of January.

Early in the New Year was still technically *The Holidays* and there are no telephones in the jungle. *INTELSAT II* was still the only communications satellite in Earth's orbit. So, from Thanksgiving through mid-January every year that American soldiers were in Vietnam, ham radio operators from Ukiah in Northern California to Vancouver, British Columbia to Juneau, Alaska ran a lottery of servicemen's serial numbers. A few lucky candidates would get to place a static-crackling ham-boosted radio transmission to someone just as lucky stateside. This one was for Miriam.

"The connection's very bad, but it's me. OVER."

"Oh, love, is it really you? Uh. Oh. OVER."

"We've only got a couple minutes, baby, OVER."

"Yes, yes. Are you all right? OVER."

"I'm fine. Miss you. OVER."

"Oh, sweetheart, it's so good to hear your voice. OVER."

"You too. I'm trying to get Leave so we can get married. OVER."

Static. "Did you say married? OVER."

"Huh? Oh. Gotta go now. OVER."

"Oh, no. Oh, I love you so much. OVER."

"Love you too, sweetheart. I'll be home soo..." static-crackle.

Ham operator: "Happy Holidays. OVER."

"Oh, Happy Holidays! And thank you. What's your name?"

"Sorry, can't say. OVER and OUT."

"Oh, well"... buzzing... "Thanks again..." dial tone.

"Oh, I can't believe I actually heard his voice! Oh, and I think he said he's trying to get a Leave! Oh. Oh, Darling, thanks so much."

"*De nada.*" Darling lounged with one leg thrown over the arm of the wing-backed chair; the leg of her black silk Capri pants was riding halfway up the calf. She was smoking a cigarette and gazing off into the distance, through the wide eight-over-eights, out across the winter lawn, at the Persimmon trees along the property line. The bare limbs of sky-high trees were laden with fat tart Persimmons. One more frost and they would be just right. But there was no Paul to shinny up the trees for her and gather the fruit they loved to eat at that time of the year, guess the raccoons could have them all. Darling did not say she wished she would get a phone call like that, and she knew she owed Aunt Maggie a really nice Thank-You note. "So, why the long face? Better get you back on the sofa."

Miriam moved carefully and lay down. "Oh, I just feel so badly that I wasted so much time. I'm such a numbskull. Kept forgetting to say OVER and everything. And the silences, nothing but static, you know? All my fault."

Darling tucked Miriam in beneath the old patchwork quilt; one of Grandma Littleton's many works of art. She sat beside Miriam on the sofa's very edge. "Don't be so hard on yourself, Mim. Jeez."

"I guess. Wonder if he's really gonna be able to get a Leave. Think he got the letter yet?"

"If he's trying to get Compassionate Leave then he's claiming it's an emergency. I think it's safe to say he got the letter. You better rest up. You just might be having to run off to Hawaii or Japan or someplace to get married."

"Don't tease me."

"No lie!" Darling patted Miriam's hand. "Dieter's good for you. Aren't you glad you stuck it out? Look pretty happy right now."

"Yeah. I am. It's okay, isn't it?"

"Of course it's okay. Jeez, Mim. Everybody has a right to exist. And everybody who's bold enough to go for it has a right to be happy."

"Oh, it's just that it's all been so confusing, that's all. Mother and all. I mean, I really hated to hurt her."

Darling started fussing, making herself busy. She tucked Miriam's feet in again. "Oh, quit it. I'll make us some tea." From the kitchen, "She could've been a better sport about it, you know."

Balzac sat like a sphinx on the very edge of the eighth stair of the staircase, just watching, taking it all in. He was eyeing Miriam tucked into one of his favorite quilts, but he was not quite confident that it was time to re-stake his claim. Miriam returned to her knitting, the needles clicking and sliding mysteriously along their way. Knit-1, Purl-1, "Yes. I suppose." Knit-2, Purl-2, Knit-1, Purl-1, Knit-2…

Miriam could remember very little of what had actually taken place. She had an image of the Emergency Room doors banging open, and another of herself sitting bolt upright and vomiting right straight at a wall, and of a pretty face getting splattered in disgust. She could remember seeing four doctors standing at the foot of her bed, and that after a while they only became two doctors and that finally she had asked for her eyeglasses and it had only ever been one doctor all along. They told her they thought they were going to lose her. They told her she had been in a coma for three days. She believed them.

# CHAPTER 30

The passing of yet another broken Christmas cease-fire brought deep resentful criticism, both in the press and in Congress, of President Johnson, the perpetrator of the greatest escalations in the history of the war. Vietnam remained an undeclared war; it was still being referred to as a conflict at that time. The Vietnam Conflict would soon place fourth in casualties in the history of American warfare, worse than Korea but not as bad as World War II, World War I, or the Civil War.

The man on the street was becoming acutely aware that the optimistic reports he had been spoon-fed for the past four-and-a-half years were just so much claptrap. Westmoreland continued to insist we were winning a war of attrition while, in fact, the North Vietnamese and Vietcong forces were only becoming stronger and more sophisticated as they inherited, bribed and captured higher technology weapons. President Johnson committed the United States Armed Forces to having 525,000 troops in a country half the size of the state of New Mexico by June 30th of 1968.

Americans were learning the meaning of bamboo cages and pungi sticks. Billy Doyle's status was amended from Missing in Action to Prisoner of War. Karen was said to be very happy at the news, at least that meant he was still alive.

With the war expenses running at better than $2 Billion per month (in 1968 $s), taxes were going to have to be raised. The method of choice was a hitherto unknown tax called the 10% surcharge. At the same time, war *expenditures* were to be cut in an effort of appeasement to the American Citizens who were squirming under the new tax burden. But most of those citizens did not know that the cuts in "non-essentials" would be made not in munitions expenditures, but in medical supplies, and the refitting and repair of aging ships and equipment. More American servicemen would die.

DUMP JOHNSON was becoming a movement. DRAFT KENNEDY was becoming a movement. Senator Eugene J. McCarthy of Minnesota was running strong for the Democratic nomination against the leader of his own party, the President of the United States. McCarthy's popularity was largely based on his determination to hammer a Peace-plank into the Democratic Party Platform for 1968.

The Republicans had Richard Nixon whose idea of hitting the war in Vietnam with everything we had short of nuclear forces sounded pretty good compared to the alternative Johnson plan of eternal warfare. The Democrats needed a candidate who would get us out of Vietnam. McNamara was right. If the South Vietnamese were not willing to fight and die for their own independence, why should we?


But it was only a brand new 1968. Darling Randolph and her brother, Paul, were the only Democrats, considered radicals, in a traditionally Republican family. Darling was not yet of voting age. (The 18-year-old vote was still just a cause back then.) Although she, along with most of the females in the country, had a crush on Bobby Kennedy, she was actively spending Saturday evenings after class knocking on doors in residential Camden and handing out McCarthy literature. After all, McCarthy had said it would not disturb him if his campaign against President Johnson in the primaries resulted in making New York Senator Robert F. Kennedy the Democratic candidate.

The one thing that was painfully evident was that, nice as President Johnson was, a longstanding Democratic leader, the architect of the Great Society and champion of Civil Rights, his conduct of the Vietnam War was way behind the times. This was not Dwight Eisenhower and General Patton flogging the hell out of Hitler, this was not even another Korea; this war was a different kind of a monster, something we had never come up against before. Che Guevara would have known what Ho Chi Minh was up to and what his tactics were, but we left him there in the jungle where he died.

David started spending many nights and most weekends in Paul's room; Paul's room, with its dark heavy furniture and dark heavy draperies, the reel-to-reel tape recording and sound system, and all the shelves of canisters, live music, and poetry recitals. And that was good, although David was no longer quite the carefree and happy go-lucky kind of a guy he once appeared to be. But he did bring with him a few good records that neither Darling nor Miriam had ever heard, including a very strange one called *Surrealistic Pillow* by The Jefferson Airplane which included a couple of hit singles, *Somebody To Love* and *White Rabbit* that Darling added to her taped selections. It was good, too, to see the black light on in Paul's closet again. Its eerie light illuminated the hallway at night as well as Paul's collection of Peter Max posters and the hot pink (Day-Glo) toilet seat that hung from the ceiling as if it were a hangman's noose.

Miriam was living in Mrs. Randolph's room. Darling had made sure to remove the contents of Mrs. Randolph's medicine cabinet. Those contents now resided in a shoebox among the dozens of shoeboxes in Darling's closet. Balzac was going to take his own sweet time adjusting. He preferred to hang out in Darling's room most of the time, unless it was a Hannah day. On Hannah days he would sit for a while on his lookout eighth stair of the staircase, just far enough down the stairs to view the activity but close enough to Darling's room to make a run for it.

Hanoi's embassy in Paris repeated its offer to talk to the United States, provided the U.S. unconditionally stop the bombing of North Vietnam. *Forget. It.* There were great displays in Paris with much posturing and ruffling of feathers and little or nothing accomplished. The circus that came to be known as the Paris Peace Talks would go on for nearly a decade.

The U.S. Senate voted unanimously in favor of the *Mansfield Resolution* bidding President Johnson to put the issue of Vietnam before the United Nations Security Council. And a lot of American hopes hit the floor when it was revealed that Secretary of State Robert S. McNamara really was leaving the Johnson Administration for a job as president of the World Bank.

# CHAPTER 31

Alice only knew that her Number Seven got through. That's all she would ever know. The pipeline only ran one way. Number Four was in the Federal Penitentiary at Fort Leavenworth. By the first week of January, Alice's Numbers Eight and Nine had made it, and Number Ten was well on his way.

Public resistance to the draft began to sprout in a big way. Although Draft Card burning was not yet fashionable, there were a number of huge demonstrations which began with STOP THE DRAFT WEEK. At the Induction Center on Whitehall Street in New York City, about 60 brave souls turned in their Draft Cards and another 250 pledged in writing to aid and abet anyone who resisted induction into the Armed Services. Among those arrested during that first anti-draft demonstration was Dr. Benjamin Spock on whose book of practical advice *Baby and Child Care* most of the very generation who were in Vietnam had been raised. Now Dr. Spock was watching the cruel death and senseless mutilation of thousands upon thousands of the very babies he had so helped their mothers to bring up healthy in mind, body and spirit, and this knowledge was unconscionable to him.

Darling bought a pair of those terrific new maternity pants for Miriam. They had a Lycra Spandex stretch panel in the front, much warmer and more comfortable than the kind with the hole in the belly and the ties at the top, and these were even styled like blue jeans. Miriam was just getting to the stage where she needed them. Next, Darling commandeered half-a-dozen flannel shirts from Paul's closet. She added a couple of long warm roomy nightgowns from Mrs. Randolph's lingerie chest so Miriam's maternity wardrobe was quite satisfactory for the time being. Darling threw in a pair of white satin bedroom slippers and a new pair of olive green suede Hush Puppies, very practical.

Miriam was flat broke and not all that well yet, and she was out of a job. She had been awarded a teaching position, the one she had worked so hard for, sixth-grade Spanish at Lincoln Middle School in Hightstown. But there was no way that the Hightstown Board of Education was going to let a pregnant woman into the classroom, let alone an unmarried pregnant woman. When Wanamaker's found out she was "in trouble" they fired her. She had no income and no possessions.

Miriam knew she had a handbag that sat beside the night table in her bedroom on Second Avenue and that inside the handbag she had a well-worn savings account passbook with a current balance of $3,209. She needed that money. If she couldn't get the passbook, she would have to go to the bank and explain and hope they would let her have her money. Perhaps, she thought, if she borrowed a stadium coat from Darling, no one would notice her embarrassing predicament.

Miriam had saved that money, five dollars, ten dollars at time since all the way back to her early teens when she had spent her summers stooped over with the other pickers in the blueberry fields. Until recently, she had thought she would use the money to get set up in a certain adorable apartment she had found in Hightstown, very convenient to her new job. But now she had no new job. Unmarried and pregnant she would never be allowed to rent a decent apartment. Miriam was often frightened almost to death and she felt that she was a burden to Darling. Darling was determined not to allow this to happen so she continually reminded Miriam that Arrowhead would be a cold and lonely place without her company. She wanted Miriam to know that she was needed. But soon, in addition to Darling's encouragement, Miriam was experiencing one of the everyday miracles of life. She was evolving with each passing day into a mother. The money would go for pre-natal care, hospital bills, and baby clothes.

Darling and David saw that their troubles were nothing compared to those of Miriam and Dieter. They gathered a greater strength than either of them had ever thought possible by helping their friends get through their troubles. This new stamina helped greatly in amelioration of the ever-present colossal issue of Darling and David having to put up with one another.

Darling felt responsible for Miriam's welfare because she loved her. David felt responsible for Miriam's welfare because she was his best friend's girl. She also happened to be pregnant with his best friend's baby. David couldn't do much to help Tina except to send a little money now and then, and to spend more time with Tommy. But he could do whatever he could to help around the Randolph house. Now that David knew the score about Paul Randolph, he felt a new sense of a responsibility toward Darling. It was no longer just that urgent need to get at her, it was something stronger than that, something that had started during those three long days and nights while he and Darling sat together, helplessly waiting for Miriam to live or die.


Paul Randolph had gone from being "Hoo-rah!" to being in a world of shit. Paul's recruiter had made good on his promise that if Paul could survive Basic and AIT he would get to train with the Army's 82nd Airborne Division.

> I wanna be an Airborne Ranger
> I wanna live the life of danger…

The only trouble with that was that much as Paul wished to be among the elite forces, to be one of the famous "All Americans," he had only succeeded in proving himself, again, to be an All-American doofus. His unit was in their final week of training. Paul was going to be a paratrooper and a rifleman. He was doing something that would make his sister proud of him and he proud of himself. The only trouble was that Paul messed up during a night-drop. Instead of making the pre-arranged rendezvous with his fellow trainees, Paul let his parachute drag him right into a tree. A parachute weighs about forty-five pounds. The average pack of soldiering equipment weighs about sixty pounds. Paul kissed that tree hard enough to knock himself out. He stayed that way as a dust-off came in to retrieve him. He stayed that way for about an hour while his head swelled so big that the corpsmen thought they might have to drill a few holes in his skull to relieve the pressure on his brain. One bad jump has killed a lot of men over the years. Paul Randolph did not die but he sure washed out of Ranger training.

# CHAPTER 32

Miriam was no longer getting dizzy when she went up or down the stairs to her new room, but she was still deathly afraid of herself. She was always afraid she might go out of control again at any time. She was afraid of the something inside her that wanted her to die. The idea that Miriam came up with stunned even her psychologist. Miriam decided that the only way she would ever be free of that something inside her was to kill it. She named that suicidal side of her nature Benedict Arnold, a traitor to her character. In her mind, Miriam had that traitor hung, drawn-and-quartered and shot at sunrise countless times. Her psychologist saw no harm in Miriam's philosophy of self-control so long as she agreed to continue with conventional therapy.

Dieter did not know of Miriam's recent crisis. He was only aware of her pregnancy, which was now very likely in danger, also unknown to Dieter. He knew too that Miriam had been disowned so he wrote his letters to Miriam in care of Darling Randolph.

Dieter followed up that garbled Holiday radio transmission with a letter to let Miriam know he had applied for a Compassionate Leave. There was an outside chance he might just be able to come home for a few days so that they could be married. It was this knowledge that kept Miriam, who was doing her knitting in pink and blue now, from going completely to pieces. Miriam convinced herself that Dieter would somehow get home. Miriam's hope was contagious.

The fifteenth of January brought the first serious snowstorm of that winter. The Randolph house became especially quiet. It seemed as if Miriam was always napping. David packed up his overnight kit and moved back to his apartment atop the Hilltop Garage as soon as he heard about the approaching storm because he feared being snowed-in all the way out in the country and therefore unable to report for work. David's job at the ammunition plant generated his deferment. At that time, many defense workers were immune from the draft even though civil defense workers, such as firemen and policemen, were not. But that situation was soon to change. For, very soon now, *no one* would be immune from the draft unless they were actually handicapped in some way. That ruling, in turn, would lead many young men to mutilate themselves by cutting off a finger (manual dexterity, tactile sensitivity) or a toe (balance, equilibrium). Besides, David needed the money.

Practically alone in the house for the first time in two months, Darling took advantage of the quiet. She busied herself by re-reading and responding to Christmas letters. She lingered for a long time over the letter from Aunt Maggie:

> Chevy Chase, Maryland
> December 19th, 1967
>
> Darling niece -
>
> I'm sure this Christmas is a difficult one for you and Paul.
>
> I miss them too, especially your mother, my dear baby sister.
>
> I do hope you and Paul are staying close and that you are taking in some of the Christmas pageants, seems like everyone's gone all out this year. So many boys overseas.
>
> We haven't a tree this year. Uncle George is off on some kind of a mission to Laos. T.S. Things are very busy at the Pentagon and I stay mostly at the Georgetown apartment. I've just returned for the weekend, I've owed letters to so many for some time.
>
> About your schooling dear, I do think you should be full time at university. Perhaps you'll let me know more of your reasons for not complying with your parents' wishes? We were rather looking forward to having you nearby.
>
> At any rate - we won't be going to Boar's Head this year.
>
> Uncle George is planning to return in July and has taken a small island, Pockseken, in Maine. I'll be heading up

that way in early June. It's no trouble to
stop by – why don't you think about
coming along? It would be most pleasant
to have your company. And I'm sure you
could help me make this so-called cabin
into something we can live with for the
summer.

Do think about it Darling. We're sure
to have some fun.

As ever, your Aunt Maggie

Darling was reminded again with a little leap of her heart of how terrific
Aunt Maggie's company could be. She knew Maggie would pick her up in
the twin-engine Beechcraft and that they'd probably stop in Boston for tea
and cakes along the way, what a lot of fun! Darling walked blindly around in
a circle. "What do you think, 'Zac? Would you like to go to Maine? I'll bet
there'll be fish in that lake! Okay, we'll go." She sat down. "But I know Aunt
Maggie'll grill me." She stood up. "I don't care. We're goin' 'Zac, and that's
all there is to it." Then her mind began to race through the preparations.
She paced the Aubusson in the living room. She looked out onto the snow-
covered landscape. The snow was falling on Uncle Hank's tree, each warm
glowing light making a little melted place of deep moist green. As she sat
down again to compose her response, Darling began to wonder, how the
hell am I ever gonna tell her what's going on? She thinks Paul's still here.
She thinks I'm blowing off the school thing. How am I going to tell her this
stuff? And it's Aunt Maggie. And Uncle George is Over There and Chance
(Maggie's son) is at West Point. And Paul's run away. And Mim's preggers.
But, it doesn't sound like Aunt Maggie had much of a Christmas either.
And it's all in a day's work, isn't it? Carry on. Oh, damn, I'll just have to
wing it. Darling settled for a hastily scribbled note:

Thanks so much for the hundred
bucks, Auntie. It'll sure come in handy.
I'm getting the school thing straightened
out, I promise. Would just love to see
you, please come. Perhaps we can both go
on to Maine. Sorry this is so short.
There's just a lot going on right now and
it's so hard to talk about. Please write
soon, I promise to write back, your
adoring niece, Darling.

On to the next letter. Oh, shit. It's the New Year's card from Alain: *Voici l'An neuf! ... qu'il soit le plus heureux!* (Here is the New Year! It is the happiest!) It might as well have been a letter bomb. Darling buried her face in her hands and growled like an animal.

Had it really only been a year ago that she had walked with him along the quiet streets of Paris, taking refuge against the damp cold in small crowded steaming cafes, or at the place of his heart, *Sacré-Cœur*, or at the Louvre where it was free to get in on Sundays? Mother was being so famous again, so happy when she was not so very tired, and glad to send Darling off with the handsome young son of her old colleague, Brod. So much had changed in just one year. So much had ended.

To read Alain writing his thoughts of Darling, telling her how she sparkled far more than the thousands of holiday lights along the Champs Elysees was too much. She cried until long after her coffee went cold.

Balzac tried to cheer her. He purred and called as he sat up on his hind quarters like a little squirrel with his small intelligent catliness looking curiously up at Darling and his front paws on the seat of the chair as he waited for Darling to take him into her lap.

Then Darling thought of how glad she had been when they had finally reached New York again, and how she had been asking people in the airport, trying to find someone, anyone, who could tell her who had won the Rose Bowl game. Any minute now she would be all right. Maybe. She hoped. She took Balzac and put him on her shoulder like the baby he loved to be. She stroked him with her face and put him down on the patchwork quilt now folded on the sofa beneath the windows at the front of the house.

Darling sat with one leg thrown over the arm of the wing-backed chair, alternately gazing deep into the fire, deep within the flames. Then a flame flickered just so. Darling Randolph turned her attention to the view from those wide hand-rubbed front windows, all dressed by her mother in raw silk. Wondering, she watched the huge heavy snowflakes amass themselves on the lawns of Arrowhead causing the long draping fronds of the giant fir trees to bow more deeply. She gazed upon the Christmas tree. Locally famous, Uncle Hank's tree glowed most precious through the blinding snowfall. The lights always burned day and night, from the Advent through the Epiphany, the Twelfth Day of Christmas. The lights should have been taken down by now. Hannah's husband, Maury Sarn, had decorated the tree for Darling this year. He would be back on the weekend to help out again.

There they were, before her now, all tumbled out like apples from an autumn basket. Years gone by, when Grandmother Littleton would meet Darling's train at Trenton Station, the warm happy ride home for the holidays, and helping her grandfather put all the lights on that very tree. How old was she then, maybe eight? That year in particular, when the old Colonel said, "Hand me that female end." And the shy chubby girl with the thick fringes of a little dyke haircut handed her grandfather a plug and he said, "No, Darling, that's a male end. I need a female end." The child looked down, confused, fearful that she had disappointed the tallest, handsomest, greatest, most powerful man she had ever known. Then the old man crouched and pulled the little girl into his arms. "Don't you know the difference?" And she poutingly admitted, "No, Granddaddy," afraid she had done something very wrong. But, he cheerfully said, "Well, then, it's time you learned. Let me show you." Then the great man demonstrated a simple and inarguable principal of engineering that Darling would never forget as long as she lived. He took a plug from one string of Christmas lights and said, "This is a male end. Can you see it?" Darling shook her head, yes, although she could not "see" it. Then he took a socket from another string of Christmas lights in the other hand, and he said, "And this is a female end. All right?" And she had nodded her head, okay, still waiting for something to become clear to her. Then the old man plugged the male end into the female end and all the lights lit up. The grandfather said, "Now they are connected. Now the energy can flow. And see how beautiful it is?" Darling thought she understood, maybe. Then he added, "Anything that God did not put on this Earth in one piece, goes together, one way or another, just like this."

Darling listened to the hushshsh of the heavy wet snow as it came straight down to cover the earth, to cover the house, to cover her, directly from the sky. A message? At first it was a good feeling, a feeling of privacy re-visited, an opportunity to allow her drug-subdued consciousness to emerge from its hiding places.

But then, once her consciousness achieved the open, it seemed as if the burdens came upon her right away, *The Weight*. The burden of the guilt she bore for her misunderstanding of her brother, a misunderstanding that had caused him to run away from her. The burden of loneliness, which no matter how hard she tried to ignore she could not deny. The burden of Arrowhead and the family legacy which she tried so hard to think of as a gift but, passed to her like the gift of a child, it came with a great deal of responsibility. The burden of knowing she had helped put her very dearest friend into just about the same position, and of knowing that child's life was continually threatened by the trauma it had experienced at its mother's hand. Something else for her to worry over until the time came for it to be born. Only praying that time would not be until its term was up, and that it would be all right, have all its fingers and toes, two eyes and a nose, and a brain to help it to cope with the terrifying world it would be born into. Now a tear rolled down her cheek. Ah, ah, ah...It's feeling sorry for itself again. "Yeah, well, what can you expect from yourself, after all…" In her mind Darling could clearly hear her brother's voice harping on her, "Knock it off, Darling! Jesus!"

Darling took the poker and rearranged the fire's embers into a firm glowing bed. Then she hefted the biggest log she could manage without dirtying her brand new navy-blue wool pants and that gorgeous red cowl-necked lamb's wool sweater she had been waiting for just such an occasion as a quiet day in a blinding snowstorm to wear. She gazed into the fireplace for a minute or two, waiting to make sure the new log was going to catch, it was. She absentmindedly returned the poker to its usual position and went back to the wing-backed chair, this time to sit somewhat-upright yet somewhat-slumped with her legs crossed and her arms enfolding one another across her chest, completely unaware that she was embracing her own breasts.

"It has to end, Paul. It's just got to. Like, I just don't want to keep going on this way. And, well, like, I keep getting busted all the time. I'm sure I've got twelve points by now. Mustang's a good little go-cart. Aunt Maggie wrote a note in her Christmas card. She was pretty disappointed that I'm not in school for real. But we all get by pretty well on what you've left me. Dieter's coming home, and he and Mim are gonna get married. That'll be fun. And, like, then, I won't have to be this kind of a babysitter I've somehow turned out to be, and like, David will finally clear outta here, I hope. But, I'm gonna have to tell Mark Cymrot about all this stuff, Paul. I just don't see any way around it now. You need a lawyer. The cops were out here again the other day, and they were none too happy 'cause they found out I lied to 'em. This time I told them the truth, Paul. I told them I didn't know where the fuck you are, or even if you're still alive. I don't think they believed me, guess it's 'cause I lied last time. And who the fuck is this Bernadette Carlani anyhow? You know what? You've never even been drafted. I think you must still be 2-S or something if that's what it is you're running from. You didn't kill her did you? Nah, I didn't think you could do something like that. You didn't run away with her, did you? Oh, cut me a break, not for some broad, you wouldn't, would you? Look, anyway, Paul, there's just no way I can handle your problems any more. Got enough of my own. Mark's gotta at least know about this other kid thing. I want to know who it is, don't you? Well..." She rose from the chair in one smooth swift motion and poked the new log again, "Fuck it. So, I'm copping out. So what?" The poker fell to the slate of the hearth with a clang.

# CHAPTER 33

One night shortly after the big storm, while piles and piles of snow-plowed cinder-gray partially melted then frozen-over snow occluded two thirds of all the parking spaces anywhere and made attempting to cross an intersection into a slush-splashing nightmare in galoshes, David just happened to ride along with Darling when she took Miriam to her group therapy session. He kept Darling company inside the hospital's Holly Shop coffee bar while they waited out what had become Miriam's routine twice-a-week hour-long session. David and Darling came up with the brainstorm of paying Mr. and Mrs. Bolton a visit and trying to talk them into at least seeing Miriam, maybe even tell them she was getting married, that might help. And, even if Miriam's parents wouldn't see her, David and Darling thought they might be able to bring Miriam some of her things. Miriam would at least like to have her handbag.

The two conspired to stop by the Bolton's next chance they got. That turned out to be Miriam's four-month check-up. Miriam would be hung up for at least a couple of hours, waiting to see Dr. Ralosa.

Mr. Bolton was not at home. He was at some deacon's meeting. Mrs. Bolton did let them in the door, which led Darling and David to think there might just be a chance. Mrs. Bolton instructed David to have a seat in the living room. She led Darling down the hall to Miriam's room. She turned the knob and let the door swing open into the room. What had been Miriam's little white bedroom had already been converted to a brightly decorated sewing room. Darling was flabbergasted. She inhaled deeply, "But where are all her things?"

"We've given everything to the mission."

"Everything?"

"All but the cedar chest. It's in the attic. You can go up."

150

David agreed to wait in the living room for a little while longer but he really wanted to get out of there. What kind of people were these?

At the top of the attic stairs sat the Lane cedar chest already accumulating its very first layer of dust. Darling could well remember the day Miriam received that chest. It had been her sixteenth birthday. It was the nicest present Miriam was ever given and now it was all Miriam had left in the world. Darling was not sure for a moment that she should even open it, invade Miriam's private space, but this was it, her only chance. Maybe Darling could sneak something out under cover of that big old mouton lamb coat with the heavy gold satin lining. The coat had been Darling's mother's, now it was hers, and at this moment Darling was glad for all its bulk and secret pockets. She decided that this was not the time to fret over protocol. What might there be inside the cedar chest that Miriam would want or need? Just about anything.

Darling sat on the gritty plywood floorboards and let her hands slip lovingly over the chest. She felt a strong urge to drag her newfound treasure down the stairs and out the door but she knew she would never get away with it. No, she thought, we can only look, and somewhat quickly. David is trapped down there with *her*.

There was a small pile of Dieter's letters all neatly returned to their proper envelopes and tied with half a yard of lavender ribbon. She slipped those into a pocket. Miriam's driver's license and savings passbook went into the same pocket. There were costume jewelry and whatnots piled in the numerous little square trays of the hinged top piece. From this assortment of precious junk, Darling selected a green paper leprechaun dancing on top of a stick, and the day came right back, that day she had presented it to Miriam. The leprechaun had been stuck in the middle of a green-frosted cupcake and it had been Darling's seven-year-old way of saying, "I hope you get better real soon." It had been, now that Darling thought about it, kind of a dumb gift considering the occasion. Miriam had had her tonsils removed and could not eat the cupcake. But it was for Saint Patrick's Day and Darling had begged and cajoled until she persuaded her father to take her to visit Miriam. There had been a March blizzard blowing hard that evening, threatening to cut everyone off by morning, and neither Darling nor Miriam had more than a couple of drops of Irish, but that wasn't the point. The cupcake was yellow cake with green frosting and little Darling had bought it with her own money. Nobody minded that Miriam couldn't eat the cupcake and everyone smiled. Professor Randolph waited patiently on a straight-backed wooden chair in the hallway, twirling his hat in his hands and thinking about the weather and hoping Darling would not be long. The snow always drifted so badly across the road up the mount and it was getting deep fast.

There was a battered one-eyed Teddy bear in the bottom of the chest that Darling could not remember ever seeing before. There was a Christening gown carefully folded in tissue, the lace all gone that fascinating ecru of old lace; a silk scarf, brand new and a pretty gold color; and a white satin re-embroidered wedding purse, very old.

The white satin wedding purse was heavy, full. Darling pulled the drawstrings open and dumped several legal sized documents onto the floor. "Adoption papers." Darling's hand covered her mouth as if to shut herself up then slipped on down to grasp her throat. Quickly, instinctively, she gathered up the paperwork, the wedding purse and the green paper leprechaun and hurried down the narrow staircase. She was almost running as she entered the kitchen and bumped right into Mrs. Bolton. "Mrs. Bolton! These adoption papers, these are for Mim?"

Mrs. Bolton continued drying dishes. "You can read."

"Well, I mean, can I take them, and, like, read them over?"

"Do what you like. It's of little consequence to me."

"Well, then can I take the cedar chest?"

"No."

"Okay. Well then thank you. But, Mrs. Bolton, I didn't come across Mim's handbag, like, her wallet and things."

"I told you, everything was given to the mission."

"I see. I guess this is it, then."

"It'll have to be. It's time I got on with my Bible study. I have a Sunday school lesson to prepare."

"Yes, ma'am.

"Uhm, Mrs. Bolton, before we go. Mim's going to be getting married here pretty soon. We thought you and Mr. Bolton might like to come."

"Certainly not."

"Not even to your only daughter's wedding?"

"I have no daughter. My daughter is dead."

Darling Randolph's hand was unconsciously playing about her face, stroking her forehead, rubbing her eyelids, squeezing the bridge of her nose, a little huff of air was emitted from that nose as the hand fell away and Darling's shoulders slumped in defeat. But she soon thought of what she did have and hurried with David to leave.

Once David and Darling were safe within the privacy of David's car, Darling came out with it. "Dave. This is fucking incredible! I can hardly believe she's let me have this stuff."

"What're you so damned excited about? The woman's like something out of a Boris Karloff movie."

"David, David, just look at these!" David drove along trying to peek at the paperwork as Darling shuffled through all the copies too fast for him to really get a look without driving the Dart into a telephone pole on High Street. "Yeah. But what is it?"

"It's adoption papers, Dave! Real live adoption papers, and they've got Dad's name all over 'em. God. I'm gonna have to double check everything," and her eyes filled with tears, "but it sure looks, like, Mim, oh God." Darling lost control, sniffled hard, and turned her head away, crying silently at her own reflection in the car window, resting her chin against the fingers of her hand and her elbow against the bottom of the window. When she finally took her knuckles away from her teeth, she pushed the words out through a red stuffed up nose and a face deformed by her own hand wiping hard at the streaming tears. "She's my sister, Dave. Mim is. She's the one. I'm sure of it. Shit. I forgot to ask the old witch if Mim knows."

It was two o'clock in the morning when Darling made her way by starlight down to the study. She wrapped the long flannel robe more closely around her and pulled its sash tight then pulled the lamp chain and brought the DAD file out of the top right-hand drawer. The mouton lamb coat lay thrown over the arm of the sofa in the study. She pulled the white satin wedding purse from the coat's deep soft pocket and laid five documents side by side across the green blotter. She let her fingers trace the intricate beadwork of the wedding purse for a moment and laid it to one side. Mrs. Bolton's?

Darling examined the names and dates on the faces of all the documents as she rolled the creases out with her fingers. First, she determined there were two sets of duplicates. She placed the better of each of those copies on top of its inferior, now she had three eight-and-a-half-by-fourteen-inch blue-covered pleadings before her eyes:

**PETITIONER: P. Malcolm Randolph, et ux,**
**RESPONDENT: Arthur Meadows Bolton, et ux.**
**IN THE MATTER OF: Infant Adoption**
**FAMILY COURT, COUNTY OF _____, etc.**

The Petition was dated April 17th, 1946. It was to the effect that an agreement had been reached among the parties concerned. The Petitioner, Darling's father, and wife, wished to have made an order of the court that his child, unnamed, born to one Lauralie Pauline Walters, should be awarded to the Respondent, Arthur Meadows Bolton, and wife, and so forth and so on. Said child, born at McKinley Memorial Hospital, Trenton, New Jersey, on the Fourth Day of April, in the Year of Our Lord Nineteen Hundred and Forty-Six is there in residence, therefore all parties are anxious to conclude the matter so that the child may begin a normal family existence.

"A normal family existence. Dear God. God, they must have been two little babies in the very same nursery for a while. Mom. Poor Mom." Darling could not know that the infants for adoption were kept separately from the infants with two legitimate parents.

All arrangements for expenses were scheduled on the attached sheet. Darling only needed a quick glance at the second sheet. It was. Yes. It was. Nowhere could she find a name, but her index fingers went running down itemized entries and she was nodding and saying out loud to no one, "It is."

After sitting in a daze for a couple of minutes, Darling went to the remaining two documents. Here was what she needed to know. Name given to Miriam Anna Bolton, April 30th, 1946; and Consent Order, revision of the same Petition, only this time made into an Order of the Court, complete with the signatures of all parties, she noted, including the wives, and Mrs. Walters, Miriam's real-life mother, Miss Walters? Darling wondered if that meant they had all been together at one time in the same room. What a thought!

Then Darling thought of Miriam. Her sister. Did she know? Her sister in Christ she had always been, and a wonderful human being. She had preceded even Paul. She was the first born of our father. Darling corrected herself; she was the first born that we know of. May there be others for whom he did not pay? Within three days of Paul. Oh. Darling wondered what her mother had thought. What were her feelings? Paul could only have been an infant, her brand-new son, when all this was finalized. How long had she known? What had she thought, or wanted? Somehow Darling thought she understood her mother ever more, the separate sleeping arrangements, and that continuing sense of frustration inherent in her every activity.

Darling could never know that her mother had been emotionally crushed during her eighth month of pregnancy by the then associate professor's confession. She could never know that her mother had magnanimously offered to adopt the infant herself, "And raise the children as twins." Or that Miss Walters had been one of her father's students, and one of his many affairs over the years, and that she would not give the child over to, "that lying bastard," Malcolm Randolph, who had, of course, told her he was going to leave his wife for her. There were so many things that Darling would never know. "But why did Mr. and Mrs. Bolton adopt the baby? And so late in life?"

It had been Darling's grandmother who had gone to the pastor of the Presbyterian Church seeking a couple to adopt the child. Grandma Littleton was doing what she could to spare her youngest daughter any more pain. The self-righteous pastor of the Presbyterian Church had rejected Mrs. Littleton's effort saying such was not a matter of church policy. He declared the "young woman" a common harlot and told Grandma Littleton that Malcolm Randolph and his pretty wife need not show their faces again in his congregation. They need not dare to come to his church to have their child christened (the child of their marriage, Paul). That was why Paul and Darling had been christened in the Methodist Church, the second break in a longstanding Presbyterian family. (The first break had been when Grandma Littleton's second daughter, Darling's Aunt Agnes, had converted to Catholicism in order to marry her Polish lover, a family scandal back in the Thirties.)

Grandma Littleton had managed to get Paul and Darling's parents expelled from the Presbyterian congregation. But that was only a matter of a single family argument, Darling's father haranguing about Darling's mother's family always butting into their lives. It was an opportunity for him to lash out at someone else in his time of persecution. But it did not turn out so badly. Although the Presbyterian minister would not help them, he complained to the pastor of the Methodist Church about the audacity of it all whence the pastor of the Methodist Church confided in the Deacons who quietly solicited for some childless young couple to come forth and inquire.

When word finally reached the Baptist Church, Mrs. Bolton, then forty-nine years old and several times a grandmother, that the child was a girl child, Mrs. Bolton engaged her husband in a discussion. Mrs. Bolton pleaded with Mr. Bolton to let her have the baby girl. She reasoned that she had given him three fine sons and had raised them all in the Word of God. And, well, basically, that he owed her at least this much. He would not have to do anything else for her. He would not even have to be a father if he wasn't of a mind.

Mrs. Bolton had always prayed for a daughter and she was convinced that the birth of this child, finding her way to Mrs. Bolton in this round-about way, simply must be the answer to her prayers and she said, "Arthur. Remember? ...My son is my son till he gets him a wife, But my daughter's my daughter all her life."

Mr. Bolton had only grunted. Yet, when Arthur Bolton finally realized that Mrs. Bolton wasn't even going to speak to him, possibly forever, he had to make up his mind. He either had to let Anna have the child or else he had to find himself another wife, and he was too old and too tired for that. Mrs. Bolton named her Miriam. Miriam, the prophetess, the sister of Aaron; Aaron, the prophet, the brother of Moses; Moses, the man of God who was found in a reed basket floating on the Nile.

If Darling had ever known how hard Mrs. Bolton had fought for Miriam, then she really would have been confused. Mrs. Bolton was content to know that the Lord giveth and the Lord taketh away. It was just Mrs. Bolton's old-fashioned ideas that clashed. Perhaps there is a cosmic reason why it is unusual, almost unnatural, for a woman of forty-nine to give birth.

"No wonder Mrs. Bolton hated me. How could she ever have stood the sight of me, the spoiled one?" For a moment, Darling wondered if the stern old woman was not some kind of a saint. "But would a saint turn her back on a child in need? Would she have allowed this to happen to another? *Any* other?"

Mrs. Bolton really did think she had been doing Miriam a favor by being her mother. Mrs. Bolton had raised her three sons; she had made them missionaries of the Word of God, every one of them. When she had lost a daughter-in-law in Venezuela, during childbirth, and that fifth child lived, Mrs. Bolton encouraged her son to re-marry quickly for he must not be impaired in the continuation of his work. Mrs. Bolton was tough. How tough was she on herself? She had a comfortable home in the freedom and excess of the United States. She rarely lifted a finger in her own house except for some project for the church. Her husband was either never around or else he never knew that anyone was around him.

Yet she took this child. Darling doubted it had been for financial advantages because, according to the ledger pages, once the adoption settlement and birth expenses were paid in full, there was really very little allotted each year for the maintenance and support of the child, Miriam. There was no provision for a college education. "Tightwad!"

Darling carefully re-folded all the documents and returned them to the wedding purse and put the wedding purse into the DAD file and locked the desk drawers. She put the light out and leaned with her elbows on the back of the sofa, trying to keep her bare feet tucked up under the robe and stared through the windowpanes of the study into the starry night sky. David should be back anytime now.

Darling knew that Miriam had always attended the public schools. Darling had been shuffled from public schools to private schools and back, beginning with public school, then a Catholic girls' school in Washington, at the suggestion of Aunt Agnes, where Darling complained of the uniforms, the nuns, the distance from home. She only succeeded in getting herself transferred to Saint Anne's in the Pines, nearer to home but more uniforms and more nuns. This went on for several years before Darling finally wised up and at age eleven complained that she wasn't even a Catholic and that the only times she ever learned anything about her own religion were the summertimes at Vacation Bible School and that she didn't know what to believe anymore, and that she wondered if she believed in anything at all.

That complaint had caused sufficient panic and alarm to get her back into the public schools at Littleton where Darling was very happy. She did well in her studies and attended the Methodist church where she sang in the choir. But that only lasted for a few years. When her freshman year at high school rolled around and her interest in the opposite sex finally proved piquant, Darling found herself on her way to the last three years of high school at Foxcroft School for Young Ladies among the blue foothills of the Allegheny Mountains at Chesterton, Virginia. After her bad experience with Buzz, which she kept entirely secret except from Miriam, Darling did not mind getting away at all. But she would once again miss Miriam.

At Foxcroft, Darling kept submitting to and then running away from her homosexual tendencies. After the third time her parents sent her back to Foxcroft, there began her long series of attention-getting tactics. It seemed that the "young lady" could never hold still. When made to stand for correction she fainted dead away and went into convulsions. This was something all the adults had to admit could not be faked. Neurological findings were relatively inconclusive, no real diagnosis, just a need to remain active. A way had to be found to direct the otherwise quite healthy young woman's energies into constructive rather than destructive pastimes such as swimming and traveling, horse riding, more music lessons, and her brother and the cars. Hard as the adults might try to encourage her otherwise, Darling's favorite sounds turned out to be smashing glass and squealing tires.

The relationship with Miriam had been just as sporadic as her schooling. The youngsters always delighted in bumping into one another again, one day at school, or in summer at Vacation Bible school, even at camp. Darling showed up and Miriam was already there. For as long as either of them could remember. Now Darling wondered if it had all been arranged. If so, why?

Darling felt strong resentment as she thought about Miriam's upbringing and what it must have been like. How hard Miriam had worked to earn a college degree and she had made herself a nice little career in textiles in the meantime. What a waste. Damn. Darling pulled her robe more tightly around her. She stared harder into the darkness between the trees. She was certain she had caught a glimpse of moonlight on chrome. "He's done it!" She ran to greet David on the cold flagstone of the back-porch steps.

David cut the Volkswagen's engine right before pulling around the last curve and let it coast into a spot beneath the poplar trees where Darling had told him to park it. Darling was jumping up and down and clapping her hands together and laughing like a child. When David approached the porch, Darling threw her arms around his neck in an excited hug and gave him the big kiss of a hero's welcome. David's smile changed to smug, "They made it easy for me. Keys were in the ignition!"

"Boss, Dave! It was meant to be! Oh, I'll bet she'll be so thrilled!"

Their voices grew lower and quieter as the two entered the kitchen. David said, "Title's in Mim's name. Don't know how they thought they were ever gonna sell it."

Darling warmed the milk for hot cocoa. "Well, they're not gonna sell it now. Cool, Dave."

David pulled up a chair, "So now I'm a car thief on top of everything else." Darling brought two mugs of cocoa to the table. "Nuh-uh. The V-Dub is Mim's, she bought it, she paid for it, she holds the title, it's registered to her. And in the morning I'll call the old bag and let her know where it is."

"Oh, I'm sure she'll know."

"Yeah, but I don't need the cops snooping around out here again."

"Fuckin-A." David rose from his chair. "Great cocoa, but I gotta turn in. Early start."

"Me too. Thanks Dave." She kissed him again. This time it was a more sisterly, cheeky kind of a kiss. But then she kissed David's ear in the same kind of a way, taking in the aroma of his skin. As Darling's lips trembled toward David's throat she wriggled her shoulders ever so cleverly until the long warm flannel robe fell loosely about those broad buttery-soft shoulders. When she raised her arms to David's waist, the bathrobe merely hung from her arms and a pair of nipples ruched by the sudden cold pressed hard against David's chest while his face buried itself deep within mounds of soft curls and his hands found their way into discovering her.

David carried her, his smile huge and triumphant, down the hall and into Paul's room, dumping her onto Paul's big old bed. He was in such a hurry to get out of his jeans that he nearly caught his huge penis in the zipper and tripped first out of one leg, then out of the other, as Darling waited for him, laying in the dark, just glowing.

That was how it began. The rest revealed a dark warm melody. Even after he'd come David couldn't get himself to budge, neither in nor out. He was stuck there like a helpless animal, then giving in to the image and coming again, only harder this time.

Darling let him have her with that same joyful recklessness with which she drove a car or worried over life from day to day. At that moment Darling did not love David any more than she ever had, but she wanted him to have her, encouraged him, she, there, a writhing slithering hot wet sinking depth charge, she encouraged him to enjoy. This was David's reward and she wanted him to have it, he had earned it. She wanted him to have her, she wanted the sucking, biting hardness of his merciless fucking as she arched her back, rolled over onto her knees, sat astride him with wet loops of curls brushing against his face, his smiling face, his smiling sleeping contentedly happy face. And then she left him, so stealthily. She wrapped herself up in the long flannel robe and tiptoed down the hall with the last of him dribbling down her leg.

# CHAPTER 34

The air was bright and clear and very cold by the 21st of January. The facts may have been cold, but they were far from clear. One of our B-52s loaded with hydrogen bombs plunged into the Arctic ice near Greenland. There was immediate panic over the possible disbursement of radioactive materials. Additionally, the incident caused many people to ask themselves, what was a B-52 carrying H-bombs doing out there anyway? Not quite forty-eight hours later, the news of leaking radiation fell into silence. It was superseded when North Korean patrol boats seized the U.S. Naval Intelligence ship *USS Pueblo* and declared the ship and her 83-man crew captive.

Diplomatic efforts to negotiate the release of the *Pueblo* and her crew failed on day one. President Johnson, constantly reminding himself that he wasn't allowed to smoke cigarettes anymore, called up 14,787 U.S. Reservists to prepare for immediate action in North Korea. The *USS Enterprise* was ordered into strategic position in the Sea of Japan. President Johnson also sought urgent assistance from the United Nations Security Council.

On Saturday, January 27th, 1968 the North Vietnamese proclaimed a cease-fire in observance of the lunar New Year, Tet. During the first half-hour of the cease-fire, while U.S. forces scrambled to actually cease fire, Vietcong guerrillas attacked a South Vietnamese militia post near Saigon and North Vietnamese gunners fired rockets into a U.S. airfield in the Northern War Zone. The American Naval hospital in the Central Highlands was also bombed. The North Vietnamese government pretended to know nothing about the attacks, magnanimously announcing the release of three downed American pilots in observance of Tet. None of them was Billy Doyle.

The U.S. Army was shifting 15,000 paratroopers into the northernmost areas of South Vietnam to help the Marines who were virtually stranded there. The 3rd Brigade of the 82nd Airborne Division was on its way to Chu Lai (without Paul Randolph). The Tet Offensive had begun.

With events being reported in

# TWENTY-FOUR POINT HEADLINES

EVERY SINGLE DAY, the United States stood at the brink of decisions which could well have erupted into World War III, the nuclear mega-death, not of the Earth but very likely of the human race, for in one form or another, the Earth would abide forever.

By Monday, the North Vietnamese had attacked seven South Vietnamese cities and several American bases, inflicting heavy casualties. "Heavy casualties" was the sanitized way of saying, "More dead soldiers." Reports arrived sporadically or poured in all at once about scores of raids on smaller military and civilian centers. Observers' communiqués were indicating a continued massive build-up of North Vietnamese troops along the borders of the five Northern provinces.


Darling was as usual mostly uncomfortable in Mark Cymrot's office, but this time she was feeling a little less so. She was wearing skin-tight blue jeans tucked into soft worn brown leather riding boots worn over thick white cotton socks and topped by the baggy rust colored cashmere sweater she had earned so long ago. Paul had never seen the sweater on her and Darling somehow felt it would be appropriate to wear that sweater now. For Paul. Besides, the thermometer had refused to budge above 30 degrees Fahrenheit even though it was after two o'clock in the afternoon.

Darling danced around the issues for a while, complimenting Mark on the great job he had done so far, asking him to thank Jim Mariner for the checks, which had been coming regularly now, $3,250.00 every three months. "They're way more than I need. But I'm putting some of the money aside for my schooling. I'm keeping Arrowhead running pretty well." She complained to Mark that the price of fuel oil had become almost prohibitive, having jumped from 17.9 cents per gallon to 23.9. "It's the war," Mark told her, "and the new surcharge, which is really also the war."

"Speaking of the war," she broke in, "I think my brother's running from it." This definitely got Mark's attention. "What do you mean running from it?" Darling was tempted to use her brother's old trick of "which word didn't you understand?" but gave it a miss. "What I mean is, I don't know where he is. He disappeared last summer, last July, and he hasn't come home and I don't know where he is."

"Disappeared! Why haven't you informed me of any of this? Does your Aunt know?"

"No one knows. Except for me, and a couple of my friends. And the police. They know now."

"What have the police got to do with it? Draft evasion?"

"No. I almost wish it was. Nobody's asked me anything about that. According to these two investigators who've been out to the house twice now, they want to question Paul about some woman I've never heard of."

"What woman?"

"I just told you, Mark. I don't know. Her name is Bernadette, uhm, Carrino? Carrini? No, it's Carlani. That's it. Bernadette Carlani. They seem to think Paul was the last person she was seen with and no one can find her. Since all the way last summer."

"When Paul disappeared."

"Right."

"Oh, boy."

"Right. So anyway, the first time they came I tried to stall them. I told them Paul was away at school. Now they know he isn't at school because they checked. And they're kind of, well, like, mad at me for lying about it so I'm not too sure they believe me that I don't know where he is."

"Why did you lie?"

"Because I didn't know what else to do, that's why. And, I guess because I kept thinking he would be coming home, like, any minute."

"And he hasn't. Have you told him about this Carlani business?"

"How could I tell him? I really don't know where he is. I mean I got a couple of notes from him when he first left but since then I haven't heard a word. I've no idea where he is, Mark."

Mark Cymrot let his elbow swing open so that his hand fell from supporting his chin to slapping down flat against the desk blotter, "Damn. I knew things were just too quiet with you two." He was thinking, why the hell didn't I go out there to see for myself?

"So, listen, Mark. That's only part of it." Mark's ears perked up. "Well, the other thing is, well it's this." She removed the white satin re-embroidered wedding purse from the pocket of the big mouton lamb coat. "These are adoption papers. As it turns out my best friend also happens to be our half-sister. I only found out about this a week ago, before I called you. Anyway, we've known there was someone since last summer, you know? Paul found out first and I think that's why he booked."

"Booked?"

"Booked out. You know, like, left."

"Oh. Oh, yeah. Booked." Mark emitted a deep sigh. He rubbed his hand along his forehead and went back to leaning his chin upon his elbow, his elbow on the desk. He raised his head and let his fingers drum the blotter a few times. Darling sat up straight again and re-crossed her legs while she waited. Mark sighed again, "Oh, boy. Okay. Let me see if I've got this straight." Mark enumerated with his fingers, "One, Paul comes to me and tells me to get rid of everything. Two, he gets involved with a woman nobody's ever heard of before. Three, he disappears from the scene, more or less without notice. Four, you make matters worse by never telling me a goddamn thing about it," by this time Mark was standing up behind the desk, "And, five, you have the utter audacity to walk into my office and expect me to be able to fix everything!"

"Not quite. I really just want you to fix it so that our half-sister, and especially the baby she's expecting, gets a fair share of our inheritance, and I want you to keep the cops off my back, at least until Paul comes home."

"Is that all?"

"Just about."

"And what if Paul doesn't come home?"

"He'll come back sooner or later. Paul will come home."

"Darling, he's been gone now for, what, six months? And you've had no word. We have filed no Missing Person report. I should think you'd've been more intelligent about this. More realistic."

"I am being realistic. And I know my brother. He'll be back. If I wasn't certain of that, I would never have made it this far. Believe me. Paul will be back. I just don't know when."

"Fine. Okay. What about this Bernadette…"

"Carlani. I don't know. I'm positive though that Paul didn't have anything to do with her disappearance. But I also know those police investigator guys are not gonna be satisfied with taking my word for it, especially now that they know Paul has gone off, probably half-cocked. It doesn't make him look good. I know that. Maybe, well, you're the attorney, but I was hoping you might kind of be able to ask a few questions of your own."

"You mean without incriminating Paul."

Darling looked genuinely surprised. "Incriminating? I already told you, Mark, Paul did not have anything to do with it. He couldn't!"

"That's very nice of you to defend your brother. But circumstances seem to be pointing in his direction and, as I've said, he's not helping matters by not being around to answer some of these questions for himself."

Darling buried her face in her hands for a moment. She didn't really want to go through any more of this, but now that she had started it, it had to be finished. Mark went on, now pacing around, now touching the shoulders of Darling's chair but not Darling herself, he went on, "Okay, here's what we'll do for starters. You go back to Littleton. I'll make a few phone calls and see what I can come up with. As Paul's attorney my cooperation will represent Paul's willingness to cooperate, at least conceptually. And no one, well, let me just find out first what this investigation hopes to discover. Yes. Well. Why don't you run along now and don't worry about anything. Let me handle it. And if those investigators come around again, don't tell them anything, you hear me? Except my name and phone number, tell them they can contact your attorney if they have any questions."

In body language, Mark was already showing Darling the door. Darling turned in her chair enough to see Mark behind her. Then she turned back to her original position, facing the empty desk, crossed her legs in the opposite direction gently running her gloves through her left hand and then letting them slap upon her thigh. "What about Miriam Anna Bolton?" Mark returned to his desk as Darling's attentions demanded. "Uhm, oh, you mean these adoption papers."

"Yes. What can we do to help Mim? I mean Miriam. She won't accept any money from me. Can't you fix it so that she gets a separate allowance, even if it's out of mine? I mean we've just gotta do something. There's a baby on the way."

Mark's head withdrew tightly against his neck, "I see. Well, ah, Darling, I wouldn't try to move too quickly on this. It's, ah, well, why don't we just check all this adoption business out and see if it's genuine. You should definitely not go jumping to conclusions." Darling's head turned a little to one side. "It was Paul who jumped to all the conclusions, Mark. At least that's how it looks to me. All I know is what I have here in black and white. And I've shown it to you. And I want you to do something about it."

Mark was trying to handle this matter delicately. He said, "Darling. Not all documented evidence is relevant. You can't just cut anyone in who makes a claim to your inheritance..."

"But she hasn't made a claim..."

"Let me finish. Now. I'll have our clerks research the legitimacy of this claim. But even if she is a half-sister, she has no interest in your estate. Neither of your parents made any mention of a wish for provision but for you and Paul." Darling raised her finger and began to speak. Her mouth was barely open when Mark raised his hand and said, "Allow me to continue. Now. Secondly, you are a minor female so far as the law is concerned on this and you are unmarried, consequently you have no rights in this regard. Although technically you have now expressed to me your wishes. But without your brother's consent there is just no way you, or I, can possibly do as you have suggested." This time Darling jumped right in, "Now you listen to me, Mark Cymrot. Paul's been gone for all this time, and yes, he's seen to it that I have a little money, but that is all he's seen to.

I've had to see to everything else. That house may belong to both of us but I run it. I make sure its needs and my own are taken care of. My brother, much as I love him, hasn't had a goddamn thing to do with it. And I'm telling you this little baby is going to be our first nephew, or niece, and Mim Bolton and her baby are the only real family I have right now and I want them in. Dig?"

"Okay, now calm down, calm down." Mark emphasized with the fingers of his hands spread wide and his hands apart rather pushing down at solid air. Darling rose to go. "I am calmed down. Copy those papers for me, would you? I'd like to keep them just the way they are."

"Sure thing." Mark buzzed for Ruth and Ruth came right in. She would return some minutes later with warm gray photocopies of the pleadings. Darling gathered up her coat and bag and the wedding purse and paced the Kashmir carpet while she waited. Her thoughts were thoroughly engaged in examination of the carpet's scrolls and plumes. All wool, she thought, not a bad copy.

"And, Mark. There's this." She handed Mark a notification from the New Jersey Division of Motor Vehicles requiring that she surrender her driver's license. "Can you do something about this for me?" Marked looked briefly at the document. "Only on appeal, Darling. Why the hell did you wait so long?"

"I wasn't exactly sure it would happen. I guess I kind of figured it might. I mean, can't we beat it?"

"We might have been able to beat one or two of the tickets if you'd come to me when these incidents happened. But you've paid the fines. That's as good as an admission of guilt." Mark's finger stabbed at the document. "Look at this! Ninety-eight in a seventy? Do you know how lucky you were on this one? Over a hundred is automatic revocation."

Darling flinched as if she thought she was going to be hit. "That's what the officer told me. He said he only wrote it for ninety-eight. He said he clocked me doing one-fourteen. But I know that's a crock o' shit. The speedometer on the Mustang only goes to 110. But it could have been buried, that would be neat." Mark heaved a huge exasperated sigh. "And this one. Reckless driving? What was that about?"

"I don't know. Quit harping on me, will ya? I had a lot on my mind."

Mark opened the door again, "Ruth! Get me a copy of this."

"Listen, Darling. The appeals process is going to take a while. In the meantime, I think you'd better not drive. You'd better surrender your license, as it demands here, understand? Not requests, demands. You got that? Because if you get stopped again and they have to lift it, you're finished. You're fresh out of 'Get Out of Jail Free' cards."

"Okay, Mark."

"Give it to me. I'll do it for you. And send them a letter."

"No. Better not. I'll need it to get myself home."

Outside on the sidewalk, free again, the sun shone brightly but seemed to generate only a small concentrated spot of warmth in which Darling stood for a long moment with her face turned upward absorbing the rays. "Why, in the name of Heaven, does it take so fucking long to get anything done?" She casually strolled around the corner and was just fine until she sat behind the Mustang's frigid steering wheel. Suddenly she was back in that parking lot at Trenton Station on that hot sticky afternoon in August. She held onto the steering wheel tightly with gloved hands and let the chill sink deep into her fingers, her hands, her arms, and her heart. But she would not cry; she refused to cry. Her face was hot, hot, flushed scarlet, and her gray-blue eyes peered out at the world like cold bullets. She hated it; she hated everything, purely.

Darling growled like an animal and turned the ignition key. The Mustang started up with a healthy varroom. She pulled the lever beside her knee and sat watching the convertible top rise above her head allowing the sun to brightly inhabit the vehicle. She got out of the car and with swift determination snapped the cold stiff snaps of the cover securely into place. She tied her silk scarf very tightly over her head, wrapped it again around her neck and knotted it at the base of her skull. She repositioned the Lolita sunglasses and got back into the Mustang. She turned the radio's volume almost all the way up. Cannibal and the Headhunters were pounding out *Land of a Thousand Dances* as she put the Mustang into gear and pulled out into traffic.

On Tuesday, the U.S. and her allies called off the nonexistent truce for Tet. We finally knew we had been sucker-punched. Vietcong suicide bombers and North Vietnamese Army Regulars had taken control of the American embassy in Saigon. It was blatantly evident that we were in the midst of the NV's biggest single coordinated terrorist offensive of the Vietnam War. More Reserve troops were called up, and there were fragmented communications suggesting one of the *Pueblo*'s crewmembers might be dead.

Dieter's application for Compassionate Leave, which had yet to be approved, was immediately and automatically cancelled, as were all Leaves of any kind. David and Darling maintained their watch over Miriam with renewed vigilance. They did not know how she would react to the news.

David was thinking himself strangely victimized. His feelings were hurt and he was confused since the fuck-out with Darling. That night had evidently meant little or nothing to Darling. She behaved as if it never happened, which, to David's mind reduced the closeness that he had so hoped for to the emotional level of a wet dream.

No longer surprisingly, Miriam raised her head high and brushed off her will, that willingness of hers to wait for Dieter and to be proud of him because he was needed more right now right where he was. Miriam patted her little pregnant belly. She still had four months to go. Still, she could not help wondering where she would ever find a pastor to perform a marriage ceremony for such an obviously pregnant woman. She never admitted to David or Darling, and especially not to Dieter, how she often cried herself to sleep over the grief of her great loss. She grieved over the loss of respect by her parents and missed even their limited attentions. She grieved for the grand white gown and the great white church and the lifting of the veil of the virgin she would never be again. That was what young women of middle-class families were raised to anticipate as the high point of their lives. After the bru-ha-ha of the wedding, a woman was relegated to drudgery and subservience. All this Free Love stuff was meant for others braver than Miriam. She wanted no part of it. Miriam considered her situation to be different. Her love for Dieter was sacred. It was just the circumstances of the war that led them down this shameful and dangerous path. No one could possibly be as hard on Miriam as Miriam was on her own conscience. Miriam had renewed her faith and was sustained by one philosophy: **Follow the advice of your heart.**

# CHAPTER 35

The heavy fighting dragged on. South Korean allies lost many troops in their valiant but failed attempts to route the NV from their new stronghold in Hue. President Johnson had once claimed that the enemy would fail again and again. Now he was embarrassed and humiliated by the North Vietnamese surprise assaults. Photographs of dead American soldiers appeared on the front pages of newspapers throughout the world.

On Monday, February 5th a South Korean news agency reported that the U.S. and North Korea had reached an Agreement in Principal for the release of the *Pueblo*'s crewmembers, but not the ship. The *USS Enterprise* was to withdraw from its position off the North Korean coast. But negotiations fell through at the eleventh hour and the tension in North Korea, and indirectly with China, went right back to **HIGH**.

The Tet Offensive, with its hundreds of running battles, raged savagely on for the next ten weeks. Every day Americans at home were bombarded with the geography of the dying-places of so many of our young: Saigon, Hue, Da Nang, Quan Tri, Dak To, and Khe Sanh. Hearts were breaking all over the United States with each new day's very bad news. All America was being faced with what Senator Robert F. Kennedy described thus:

> "The history of the conflict among nations does not record another such lengthy and consistent chronicle of error as that brought about by first the French and then the United States in Vietnam... It is time for the truth. It is time to face the reality that a military victory is not in sight and that it will probably never come."

South Carolina State College erupted into violence during a protest that resulted in three dead. Governor of Alabama George Corley Wallace announced that he was in the race for president.

By February 10th, U.S. Army Infantry troops were brought in to make what was originally thought to be a final clean sweep of enemy activity in Saigon. But world attention was focused on Khe Sanh where North Vietnamese troops were building up again for another sustained assault against the Marines who were stranded there.

On Valentine's Day the airwaves were busy playing the oldie *Chantilly Lace* by The Big Bopper, the late J.P. Richardson. David walked through the kitchen door of the Randolph place carrying a dozen roses for, "each of my favorite girls." Miriam burst into tears, something that was happening quite a lot lately.

Dieter's letters had been arriving both fewer and farther between, and they were ever scarier as the fighting intensified. He was in the field for much longer each time his unit moved out of base camp. It was obvious that he was exhausted most of the time and under a tremendous strain. Miriam believed Dieter was becoming a killing-machine and it frightened her.

> Malcolm I remember...
> and remember he had Billy and Michael with him.
> KLEIN   Mr. Green   "DOG"...
> and one report on <u>Dr. Rat</u>
> Reporter's rights
> (if it's real as if it's <u>his</u> (whose?))
> phantassie butt...
> it's not in the primary interest of the
> "gildened sylvan steps"
> if y'know what i mean. Now.
> Michael wasn't here
> it's a FARHLEY triangle
> if conditions be the food of love
> and I don't think Ken would want you to move out
> if you have her ms fuzzy let it be that way
> No not my turn, 19, Kaplan, Myers
> oh, what's the use.
> "KILL MY BROTHER"

Miriam spooked every time the telephone rang. David was more worried about her than ever. "Good thing she's seeing that shrink." He and Darling wondered also about her ability to hang on to the baby. Miriam's most recent check-up revealed a startling elevation in her blood pressure. She was suffering from frequent violent nosebleeds, and was now on a very low sodium diet. Miriam and Darling were learning that sodium was to be found even in a glass of milk.

It was about this time that Miriam became completely vegetarian because she could no longer stand to look at the blood in meat, so Darling sought creative ways to induce Miriam to eat. She stumbled onto the idea of shelling salt-free whole roasted peanuts and whirring them in the old Waring blender. The result was a bland runny peanut butter that tasted dry and stuck to the roof of her mouth so bad that she had to drink water with it immediately. It did not spread easily on the very crispy almost burnt toast that Miriam liked, but the peanut butter did provide a good source of protein. Darling was also trying to get Miriam to practice a little Yoga, at least meditation now and then, to help lower her blood pressure. Eclampsia, they did not need.

General Earle G. Wheeler, Chairman of the Joint Chiefs of Staff, expressed confidence that the Marine outpost at Khe Sanh could be defended without the use of nuclear weapons. Darling bitched, "Is this supposed to be *good* news?" President Johnson ordered 10,500 more combat troops to South Vietnam to reinforce his depleted armies and to cope with yet another threat of assault.

The dead and wounded were flown home through the American gate at Clark Air Force Base, Manila, The Philippines. Body bags with positive IDs were loaded into pine box coffins. The coffins were rubber stamped with many blanks to be filled in with magic marker, all the data that was known: Name; rank; serial number, which was the same as the dead man's social security number now, in this war; branch of service; home state, if known; date and place of death, if known. The coffins were loaded into C-130s, by lots, for the last long journey home.

Three days after Valentine's Day, the Johnson Administration abolished all Graduate Draft Deferments except for medical students who were more than two years into their studies. They were permitted to continue their schooling because they might be needed for the war effort. The National Security Council also suspended indefinitely the list of critical occupations and essential activities that had generated more than half of the 339,474 different categories of Occupational Draft Deferments, including that of David Campbell Adams.

February 17th also marked the highest weekly number of casualties in all the hundreds of weeks of the Vietnam War. 543 American soldiers had been killed and 2,547 had been wounded during the past seven days. Casualties would continue to run at similarly outrageous levels for week after week after week after week.

The Tet Offensive would go down in history as a turning point. There was the Vietnam War before Tet '68, which had been hideous enough. Then there was the Vietnam War after Tet '68, which became an insane blood bath. After Tet '68, no one except for the Johnson Administration's most die-hard Hawks even tried to pretend that there was any strategic objective to be fought for, to die for, or to win.

We waited with tears in our eyes as the Marines took back Hue, 100 yards at a time, suffering horrific casualties. For no explainable reason, Hanoi released three more American pilots, but none of them was Billy Doyle. Harold Baxter, Valedictorian of the Class of '61 and one good looking son-a-gun, was added to the list of hometown boys Missing-in-Action, but Harold was also BD, Believed Dead.


Dave Adams ran up the back-porch steps of the Randolph house and found Darling and Miriam at the kitchen table. They were playing Gin Rummy and drinking cups of hot tea. The radio in Paul's room was on and a funky noise floated down the hall. Bob Dylan sounded like he was standing on his tippy-toes trying to sing *A Hard Rain's A-Gonna Fall.* David's eyes sparkled like a madman's. He went over to the stove and put both hands on the teakettle to warm them. Darling asked, "You want a cup? Water's still hot."

"Nah. Thanks." Miriam looked up from another winning hand, "If I have to beat Darling at Gin one more time I think I'll go bats. Gimbels is having a gigunda sale. Do you think you could drive me down there? I might be able to find a good deal on some things I need for the baby." David's hands were warm now. He took a couple of long strides over to the table and placed those warm hands around the back of Miriam's slender neck. "Sure kitten. Think you're feeling up to it?"

"Yeah. I think it'd be neat. I'm feeling pretty good today. And Darling shouldn't drive unless she absolutely has to."

Darling's head wobbled from side to side sarcastically. "Take the 'Stang. Use my gas."

"Well, in that case let's boogie. Jes' you and me, babe. We can grab something to eat at the mall."

Miriam laughed an odd little laughter. She was not laughing often these days, no one was. "Sounds like a winner, Dave. But I think I'd better stick to my creamed peas and carrots with peanut butter. 'Sides, I won't be good for more than an hour or two anyway."

From down the hall the DJ announced, "Look out. We're comin' atcha with somethin' brand new from an outfit called Steppenwolf. *Magic Carpet Ride.* Darling charged into Paul's room, saying, "Oh, I wanted to catch this one," and hit the RECORD switch on the reel-to-reel. Miriam grabbed a heavy woolen coat from the closet, one of Darling's mother's, and headed for the door.

David bowed low in Miriam's direction. "Your wish is my command." She asked, "What's got into you anyway? You're looking mighty sparky today."

"I joined up this morning. Marines."

"That's just what I needed to hear. Why the Marines?"

"They decided I might just be worthy."

Darling ran to the door but David and Miriam were already in the Mustang and backing out of the drive. They saw Darling standing on the back porch in her jeans and two sweaters and the bright blue fuzzy scuffies. David had a big grin on his face and he blew Darling a kiss as he pulled around the bend, away.


The *Pueblo* and her crew had still not been released and enemy shells were falling on 37 South Vietnamese cities. Saigon was hit yet again, and Tan Son Nhut Air Base came under sustained and heavy fire. The enemy held territory within easy range of William Westmoreland's headquarters for eight hours before they were driven back. Darling kind of hoped they would get him. The Soviet Embassy in Washington, D.C. was bombed and heavily damaged, but no one claimed responsibility.


Miriam's condition was hardly noticeable. She was dressed in her maternity jeans, another one of Paul's sweaters, and Mrs. Randolph's coat. David and Miriam looked every bit the happy couple as they chattered incessantly and smiled or laughed as they shopped for a handbag for Miriam and for baby clothes. Miriam selected two little drawstring sacks, one blue, one yellow, and a package of six long-sleeved wrap-and-tie undershirts.

David did a lot of bragging about himself and what his recruiter had told him about how tough it was going to be on Parris Island while Miriam was trying to talk David into implementing her brainstorm that he should marry Tina. That idea almost immediately sent David's eyeballs through the top of his head. But Miriam was not to be refused. "Dave. You know it's the only right thing to do. Just look at the predicament I'm in. God forbid, if anything happens to Dieter this baby will only have me. And, you know that's bad enough, but at least I can eventually go back to work somewhere, but you know, Tina, what can *she* do? What *would* she do? Without you around to give her the money and to take care of Tommy now and then, what will life be like for *him*? I know you don't care very much for Tina, but Dave, you can give Tommy your love and the best way you can do that right now is by letting him benefit from your military service. They'd have free medical care. He could get all his shots and stuff for free. They might even be able to do something to help his mother. But Dave, even if they can't help Tina, what's going to happen to Tommy? Especially, God forbid, if something happens to you?"

"Jesus, Mim. You really are deep. It's no wonder Darling just loves you to death."

Miriam froze. She let the package of receiving blankets fall back onto the pile. "Don't even mention that word. Please."

David took Miriam by the shoulders right in the middle of the Infants Department at Gimbels and then he took her into his arms. Her head rested so forlornly against his shoulder. "I'm sorry, Mim. I'm so sorry. It was just a figure of speech, that's all. I didn't mean anything by it."

"I know. I'm just tired. Whaddya say we go home?"

"Anything you want, sweetheart. I'll find out what I can do about the Tina thing. Okay?"

"'Kay." A thin smile.


More American troops were needed. The Joint Chiefs of Staff were drawing up a mobilization proposal calling for 40,000 to 50,000 National Guardsmen and Marine Corps Reservists on special orders in addition to 130,000 Army Reservists. 48,000 more young men were to be drafted in the month of April. Enemy battalions and South Vietnamese forces clashed again at Khe Sanh after the U.S. Marine base was hit with the heaviest bombardment so far. Richard Nixon caught up to President Johnson in the polls. And Paul Littleton Randolph walked into the study.

# CHAPTER 36

"Whose Dart is that parked in the drive?"

For a moment Darling Randolph did not look up from her reading. She lay on the sofa with Balzac curled up on top of her chest thoroughly engrossed in Harper Lee's *To Kill a Mockingbird*. It took a long moment for the gravelly voice to become more than a cherished memory, to surface as a reality before Balzac and the book hit the floor.

They met near the center of the room. Darling had an almost irresistible urge to slap her brother hard across the face. But she couldn't make herself do that, not in the condition he was in. She only asked, "What happened to your head?"

"Long story. Whose Dart is that?"

"It's Dave's." Darling's mind raced around like a rat in a maze but she could not recall any of the things she had wanted to say. *Dizzy*. Not one of those wise and shitty words would come. It was happening. That was all she knew. And she knew that her stomach had become a tight knot, and that her brother was standing before her dressed in Olive Drab fatigues. She did not comprehend the tingling sensation in the small of her back. The standoff continued.

"Dave. Same Dave?"

"Yeah, Paul. Same Dave. But what happened to you, why is your forehead all swollen up like that? Why is it green?" Paul rubbed his hand upward from the eyebrows where there was still a high ridge and let his hand brush on up, yeah, it still hurt. "It's green because it's getting better, and it's not nearly as swollen as it was. So where is 'e?"

"Dave? Ah, he's out. Oughtta be back any time now. Took Mim out to get a few things for the... ah, Gimbels is having a sale. So, like, how 'bout a nice hot cup of tea or some coffee? Cocoa?" Darling drew just that little bit closer, close enough so that her big brother could crook his elbow around

174

her neck in a kind of reverse half-Nelson and pull her head against his chest. The warmth and strength of his huge pounding heart and her warm tears streaming but making no sound. Paul said, "I probably stink. What I really need is a hot shower. There now." Paul's thumb wiped the tears from his sister's cheek. For a moment he could only look at her. Such dark circles beneath her eyes. "Coffee'd be good. It won't take me long, but I gotta get outta these clothes." Darling was reminded that David was camped out in Paul's room. "Hang on while I get things straightened up in there."

Paul followed Darling into the darkness of his room. She flipped the switch of the closet light and began pushing David's things to one side of the hanger rod. Her teeth shone skeletal white in the black light. Her fingernails had a wonderful matte lavender glow she often wished she could find in a nail polish. Well, she thought, at least there are a couple of his really good shirts left. And a beautiful ski sweater that no one dared to touch. "I don't know how much of this stuff'll still fit you, you've lost so much weight. Ah. There's a razor in the bathroom if you need it. Got a toothbrush, stuff like that?" Paul nodded over his shoulder. He was browsing through his reels of tape. Looking for something.

"All your jeans and stuff are in the bottom drawers."

Paul felt like a stranger in his own bedroom. A guest in his own house. He uncanned a tape and threaded the spools as if he'd never been gone. "Who's been in here?"

"Me. You know, I play a little music every now and then."

"That's not what I mean and you know it."

"Oh, you mean Dave. Uhm, yeah. He stays here two or three nights a week. Nights when he doesn't have to work late."

The tape that Paul was loading was the second of three that he had recorded between the 16th and the 18th of January 1967, just a little over a year ago. He had split from school for two weeks. Paul and his roommate, Peter Gorman, had bumped along, headed out to California in Peter's '63 Ford Econoline to the Monterey International Pop Festival, which had more than fulfilled its promise of being The music event of the century (Woodstock Nation was yet to be). "What's that all about?"

"Well, that's, like, kind of a long story too, Paul. But. Well..." Darling hugged Paul from behind as he fiddled with the reel-to-reel. No response. She let go. "Well, he kind of like helps me look after Mim. We kind of take turns. And, he helps keep the Mustang running. Fixes things sometimes."

"I'm beginning to get the picture. But I'm not sure I like it. Why does Mim need looking after? She here too?"

"Yeah. She's up in Mom's room. She's not due until late in July. But she's not been very well, Paul. She's having a hard time."

"Mim? Whoa."

Paul was interested but only half-heartedly so. The other half was remembering how he had been called onto the carpet when he and Peter returned from Monterey. Mmm, whole load-a trouble. But to Paul it would always be worth it because now he had these tapes. Tremendous applause. The screams and hoots of 50,000 or so young people who'd paid $3.50 to $6.50 a head for standing room for as long as they could take it while Otis Redding, The Who, The Grateful Dead, The Byrds, The Jefferson Airplane, The Association, The Electric Flag, The Paul Butterfield Blues Band, Canned Heat, The Blues Project, Laura Nyro, Hugh Masekela, Buffalo Springfield, Country Joe and the Fish, Booker T. and the MGs, The Mamas and the Papas, and Ravi Shankar were joined by a few newcomers like Janis Joplin, Jimi Hendrix, and Quicksilver Messenger Service. All the performers played for free. Thank God for Gorman's van, where Paul had sat glued to his headset and the analog instrument panels and taped the whole goddamn thing for three fucking days and nights. Why, he'd already duped those tapes half-a-dozen times and sold them for enough money to make up the expenses for the trip out to the Coast. And for the trip home he eventually made to explain to his father why he had taken several incompletes in a brand-new semester, in fact, his last semester. "But, Dad, that's what's so cool about it, I've got the whole rest of the semester to make it up!" That stunt had nearly blown getting him admitted to anybody's law school. Guess it didn't matter anymore.

Paul fast-forwarded Tape #2 until the counter reached 769 when he hit the STOP switch and the READY light lit up. Paul cranked the volume up to the third notch, which was always enough to rattle the rafters of that big old house in the country. As he did so, he flipped the PLAY switch. Big Brother and the Holding Company launched into *Down on Me*.

Darling took Paul's robe from its hook way at the back of the closet. She laid it across his bed, the bed where David had intended to sleep that night. And she was thinking, ah, man.

Paul reached down to unlace his combat boots. Applause, whistles, screams.

Darling shouted above the music, "Paul. Paul! We hafta talk!"

Paul now knew the music wasn't going to work its magic for him. Not tonight. He raised the PLAY switch and pushed the STOP switch down at the same time. Suddenly the house was dead quiet again. "So talk."

"Look, Paul, I'm gonna go and make us some coffee, okay? There's just, like, lotsa stuff that's gone down, ah, like, since you've been gone. Mim's in trouble. We're all in trouble, Paul. Why don't you have your shower? I'll get a fire going. You'll feel better. I just, well... Wouldn't you like something to eat?"

"I don't think my stomach'll take anything right now. But thanks." Paul rewound the spool. His sister was very nervous, agitated. Something was wrong. Very wrong. He put the tape back into its can and sat on the bed again and finished untying his bootlaces. "Looks like you've turned the place into a regular goddamn commune while I've been gone."

Darling fidgeted, fluffing up Paul's pillows, tidying things that were not untidy on Paul's dresser. "I'll just make a couple of pieces of cinnamon toast. You should at least try to eat something." Yet Darling walked up to Paul and stood for a moment, placed herself between his knees. She pretended to brush the oak-colored lock of hair that wasn't there anymore away from his swollen forehead. Their voices grew ever quieter, "Have you seen a doctor for this?"

"In the hospital four or five days." A heavy boot clunked onto the floor. "Nearly chopped the top of it off, ya know? Let my 'chute suck me face-first into a tree. Good thing I'm a blockhead." The other boot fell with a thud. Paul smiled that gentle upside-down smile of his. "At least I think it's a good thing," and he let his head fall forward against Darling's belly. His body emitted a little breath. Darling caressed Paul's head and put her own head down on top of his, and the long red-gold hair fell in a curtain about them, blocking out the light, blocking out the world.

There they stayed. Balzac wandered into the room and jumped up onto the bed. Paul was feeling warmer and happier than he could ever remember being and he bathed himself in that warmth. Unconditional love. There came into his aching head the image of Darling, that same image that had haunted him all the time he was in Canada. Whenever he drove that Woody along, there she was, right there by his side, riding shotgun as always, her face bursting with laughter, her laughter like music, and her hair whipping all about her by the updraft of tremendous speed. She had called to him as he made his way hitchhiking back to the States. And he thought of how she had been beside him after the fall, how she was calling him back into consciousness.

The bald-headed peach-fuzz had grown to a short rough stubble, but it would still be a couple of weeks before Paul could return to active duty. He had washed out of jump school. The next logical thing to do was to apply to Officer Candidate School to which he had been accepted. Paul's recovery period allowed enough time to go home, and to explain. If that was possible.

He tried thumbing from the Trailways terminal in Camden but no one would give him a ride, no ride for the man in uniform. "Fuck the lot of you!" Hitchhiking and not getting a ride, walking, all the way home. The lane, that old familiar tunnel of trees, naked in the dark and still and cold of a late winter afternoon. The supernatural strength that immediately began to return, penetrating up from the soles of his feet as each foot firmly hit the ground, one right after the other, the strength to make it that last half a mile.

In that communal dream state, Darling was reminded of the summer she had been beaten for bringing *The Teachings of Chairman Mao* home from the library. She had left the book on the staircase intending to take it up to her room and had gone off to run some kind of an errand for her mother. Hannah came along to clean and placed the book on the table beneath the reading light in the living room. For that evening the book had been misplaced, nearly forgotten. That is until about eleven o'clock.

The professor, who had not taught himself one single thing since the time he achieved his tenure and was already well past three-sheets-to-the-wind, noticed the book. He began to rave into the stairwell, "Rotten Communist propaganda! What the hell are you doing reading this garbage?"

Darling, who had been in her room writing a letter to last year's roommate at school and Mrs. Randolph who had been asleep met when curiosity brought them both to the lower landing of the staircase. Darling's sleepy mother stood in her nightgown and groaned, "What is it Malcolm?" Darling saw her father standing at the bottom of the stairs holding onto the banister for stability. Then she saw the book. She touched her mother's arm and said, "It's okay, Mom. It's just my library book. I'll get it." She hurried down the stairs to take the problem away.

Darling's father grabbed her by a generous handful of luxuriant mane and stuck his blood red face and blazing blue bloodshot eyes and stinking breath at her and slurred, "What the hell are you trying to prove reading this kind of garbage?"

Darling's mother watched from the top of the stairs. Darling said, "Daddy, let me go. It's just a book. I was curious about it. We were discussing a lot of things last semester at school. I just wanted to know." But drunks do not respond to reason. He threw her down hard against the stairs. "This is fucking Communist propaganda! You mean to tell me I'm sending you to school to read this kind of trash!"

Darling's mother called from the landing, "Now, Malcolm. Stop it. She's just a child."

He leered at Darling's mother. "Child? Okay. Well. You want our *child* exposed to this! What the hell did we fight for! What the hell did your brother die for?"

While her father carried on, Darling seized the opportunity to creep up a few steps with the damned book. Professor Randolph grabbed Darling by one ankle and dragged her back down the steps. "No!" he cried. "No, no. Never, never, never," as he beat her with the book and bashed her face into the oak staircase, over and over.

He beat her in the face with the book, hit her over the head again and again. His hand held her by the hair so that she could not pull away. The pages of the book flew everywhere until there was nothing left but the binding and a few leaves that clung to their stitching.

When Darling regained consciousness, she went to pull a mass of her hair away from her eyes and found that the mass was not hair at all but a mass of blood clots. Her mother and father were standing over her body arguing about who was going have to take her to the hospital. Darling had just begun to try to raise herself when Paul, then eighteen, walked through the door and reacted. Through a crimson haze Darling saw her brother pick their father up by his shirt collar and the seat of his pants, raise him high into the air and make as if to slam him but laid him down right in the middle of the dining room table. Professor Randolph would be unable to walk for the pain in his shaken spine for several days.

Darling's nose was broken. There was a small cut at her left eyebrow and a larger one at what had been and probably still was the bridge of her nose. Paul drove his sister to the hospital and stayed by her side while the cut was stitched and all during the days while plastic surgeons put Darling's face back together. They had done a pretty good job, although for a while she would have a more aquiline profile instead of the slightly turned up nose she had been born with but by the third surgery they would get it right; given time, a few of her teeth would die. The very first image Darling perceived when she came around after surgery was Paul's worried face leaning over her. Her hand was enfolded in his hands. His hands were holding her hand to his heart. They agreed to say it had happened in a car wreck.

When Dave Adams walked into Paul's room, there lay Paul and Darling sound asleep, entwined in one another's arms like a pair of old lovers. Paul raised his swollen head and his eyes squinted against the light, "What're you doin' here, dickhead?"

"Who you callin' dickhead, you pansy chickenshit."

Paul was up like a shot and had David pinned to the wall in a Ranger chokehold by the time Darling got to them. Balzac blazed out of the room. Darling bent down, protecting her face with her own body and wriggled herself in between the two men, yelling, "Quit it, you two. Knock it off!" She shoved both of her elbows out hard, getting each of them in the groin, David getting a more direct hit because he was a little shorter than Paul. But that broke it up for the moment. Darling said over her shoulder, "Better get your stuff together, Dave," as she grabbed Paul's boots and led him from the room and dragged him out of the house and into the night.

Miriam stood in the living room. She was still wearing her brand-new oversized Navy-blue pea coat. She was holding her new shoulder bag and a bag of baby clothes. With her mouth agape and her eyeglasses slipping down her nose, she tossed the new things onto the sofa and plopped there exhausted and wondering why she hadn't known all along that something like this was bound to happen.

By the time Miriam sat down, Paul and Darling were well on their way across the creek and into the trees. They wandered up to the high ground; the sandy places where the red cedars grew and where the deer always came for cracked corn in the winter and which Darling had not neglected to put out regularly, just like always. But tonight, it was too late for the deer and not late enough for the owl. It was just right for the kind of quiet meandering talk those two sooner or later had to have. It was just right for long stubborn silences and for listening to the snapping of twigs beneath their feet, or to the north branch of the creek, the one that defined the far property line, not quite frozen solid as it went laughing intimately along with all the time in the world.

David went into Paul's bathroom and splashed his face with cold water. He pulled a towel from its ring and held it to his face for a long moment. There was no blood coming from his nose but his left cheek was already beginning to shine.

David went into the kitchen to retrieve a couple of brown paper grocery bags into which he intended to throw anything that didn't fit into the overnight kit he had been dragging back and forth from Bordentown for nigh on three months now. Miriam was in the kitchen filling the teakettle. She asked David if he would like a cup of tea. "I'd rather have a good stiff drink." Miriam put the teakettle on a stove burner. "You know where the brandy is."

"Nah. I gotta get outta here before those two screwballs get back."

"But why?" She put a tea bag into an old porcelain hospital mug. "They'll be all right when they get back. Why run? If you run now, you'll only be letting Paul have the upper hand." She dunked her tea bag up and down. Her legs hurt. Her feet were very swollen from all the walking on the hardwood covered concrete floors at Gimbels. Her belly felt especially low and heavy. David just stood in the kitchen, wondering at Miriam. "He already has the upper hand, Mim. Like, I don't really belong here. This is his house. And Darling's. And yours."

Miriam splashed a little milk into her tea. "Mine? Why mine?"

"Nothin'. Never mind."

Miriam headed for the living room with her cup of tea. "You mean because I'm a Randolph?"

"Jeez, Mim. For a minute there I thought I'd really blown it. I figured Darling must've talked to you about it by now."

Miriam was gathering up her shopping and balancing the mug of tea. She put the new shoulder bag over her arm and slipped the bag of tiny little blue and yellow baby things under her arm. David, who had followed Miriam into the living room, was still holding the two brown paper grocery bags. As Miriam turned to go up the stairs she said, "Darling never mentioned to me that she knew. I do know. But then I've known since I was six or seven years old. And it doesn't make any difference, Dave. My parents are still my parents. And Darling's parents are both dead. Paul's parents."

David felt like a world class shit. He sat down heavily on the sofa. He knew he had blown it completely. "Damn. But how can you stand it? Knowing all this could be yours, should be yours?"

Miriam paused on the stairs. "Not so, Dave. What belongs to Paul and Darling would never have belonged to me anyhow. Professor Randolph was a nothing. He made the luckiest move of his life when he married Mrs. R. It's their mother, their *mother* Dave, who gave them 'all this' as you call it. It was hers, not his. The cars, the horses, the barns, this house, the furs, the travel, the place at the shore, the connections, the educations, even old man Randolph's education, though he worked, was funded by the Littletons, not the Randolphs, Dave. I s'pose that must be why he never left her."

"You mean your father."

"No, Dave. My father lives on Second Avenue in Littleton, with my mother. And I'm here because Darling is my best friend and because I let myself forget about God. And so did Paul. I'm not sure this place is even his place anymore. This is Darling's house. I simply can't imagine it any other way now. She loves this place. Loves it in the strangest way, like it was alive or something. Oh, I'm sorry, Davie boy, but I've just got to get my feet up. You goin' or stayin'?"

David fumbled with the folded grocery bags. He drifted away from Miriam, flipped a bag out and open. "I think I'd better just go."

"Suit yourself. But. Thanks Dave. You know. For everything." She was tired.

"No sweat. I'll call ya, okay?"

Miriam smiled her sweetest warmest smile. "You better. Else I'll tell Dieter you ran out on me." Miriam trudged up the stairs. Balzac remained quite still, peering cautiously from his observation deck, his favorite eighth stair.


David had just started his car and from the Dart's AM radio, Dusty Springfield was belting out the last strains of *I Only Want To Be With You* when he saw a pair of holy terrors emerge from behind the barn. Like straight tall shadows they were taking great long comfortable strides, and they were walking hand in hand. David rolled the window down and turned the radio's volume all the way down and quietly called, "I've told Mim I'll call her."

Darling let go of Paul's hand and ran up to David's car. She leaned against the car door and spoke with her face so near to David's mouth that he could almost reach her lips. "I'm sorry Dave. Don't go. Please? You don't have to go. Honest." Paul walked silently past them up the back-porch steps and into the house.

"Yeah, well I've about had it, and I've got nothin' to say to *him*."

"Dave, Dave, don't be silly. It was a temper, you know. Paul won't hurt you. Promise."

"You still don't get it, do ya? It's you, Darling. *You* hurt me. Better get back." David cranked the volume on the radio almost all the way up. The Troggs were right in the middle of singing *Wild Thing*. Darling jumped back so as not to be dragged along by the Dart as David slammed the gearshift into reverse and tromped on the accelerator. River rock nearly buried the toes of her shoes. She heaved a sigh and let her arms flop to her sides and then she felt the cold passing through her. She turned, taking one last look up, glancing into eons of dark stars, and went into the house.

# CHAPTER 37

By the end of February '68, the devastation that began with the Tet Offensive had its claws sunk deep within the flesh of daily life in the United States, and in many corners of the world. As enemy forces attacked ever deeper into South Vietnam, Senator J.W. Fulbright called for a congressional investigation of the Johnson Administration's policy on the Vietnam War. General Westmoreland claimed the North Vietnamese could not stand a long war (it had only been 13 years already) even as he compared the enemy's continuing offensive with World War II's Battle of the Bulge. A Marine patrol was being mauled by Vietcong guerrillas just 800 yards outside their base at Khe Sanh and Westmoreland was requesting 100,000 to 200,000 more troops.

Dave Adams was now a "maggot" at the Marine Corps Recruit Depot at Parris Island. It had only been a week since Darling drove down to Elkton, Maryland with Miriam to witness the front parlor marriage of David Campbell Adams to Christina Denise Moffett. Miriam was very proud of David for doing what she was certain was the right thing.

Darling stood close to Miriam's chair with pudgy Tommy balanced on her hip, swaying gently as she shifted her weight from one foot to the other, more like a glider than a rocking chair. It took only seven minutes for a stubby non-sectarian minister to perform the nuptials.

David would never be sorry he had stolen one last selfish glance at Darling Randolph during that seven minutes that seemed like an eternity. He wanted to remember her standing there as she was, holding Tommy. David was not feeling sorry for himself. He was only thinking of something that might have been, once upon a time. He was thinking that indeed it had never been because of the smile. It was because of the way she could shine. Darling simply radiated energy. She had the glow. At least he finally knew the answer to something he had been wondering about for such a long time. Now he could peacefully focus his attention on the pretty little junkie at his side. Darling and Miriam signed at the **X** and threw rice.

The wedding party drove back to Bordentown where they had a late afternoon dinner at Mastori's, to celebrate more or less. Tina was not much interested in her food, which was a shame, but she appeared to be quite happy and she did look pretty in her little blue mohair shift. David married his bride with a narrow platinum band from Tiffany and a nosegay of a dozen pink miniature rosebuds surrounded by dense ruffles of baby's breath and lace. It was the first time any of the three women had seen David in a suit. He wore a blue carnation with a sprig of baby's breath on the lapel, very handsome.

Strained at first, the conversation loosened up as Tommy grew more and more impatient with having to be a good boy and went from adult to adult to be held and coddled or to demolish a table setting or two. The newly united family spent that Saturday night at the Sandpiper motel in Bordentown where the marriage was, presumably, consummated. On Sunday, David moved Tina and Tommy into his old room at his parents' home on Delaware Avenue. Tommy's new playroom faced right onto the river. It was going to be difficult for Tina. She had a monkey on her back and David's father was a physician. But David had the comfort of knowing that whatever Tina did, Tommy would be all right. And maybe, just maybe, she would get well. Marriage had, after all, been what Tina wanted all along. Miriam had worked another of her little miracles. For David had regained his family's respect, if not their understanding, but more importantly, he had their assurances that Dave's Hilltop Garage and Tommy Moffett would be waiting for him when he got back from Over There. No matter what.


President Johnson received an "open letter" purported to be from the crewmembers of the USS *Pueblo*, still captive, asking the President to assist in their rescue by making a public apology to North Korea. *Bull. Shit.* As North Vietnamese Regulars and Vietcong guerrillas stormed into Vietnam's southernmost provinces, Richard M. Nixon vowed to end the Vietnam War if elected. Another transport helicopter was shot down near the Marine outpost at Khe Sanh, no sign of life in the wreckage, 44 passengers, three crew, all dead.


Paul Randolph returned to active duty with his transfer to Fort Sill. Even though the Army had given Paul a clean bill of health, Darling worried that his body had not completely recovered from the accident, but Paul was determined to go. Paul had gone from running away from his obligations to becoming certain he could find something in the Army that he could do well. He wrote letters now and then. Sometimes he sent albums from the PX for Darling to save for him. The Post Exchange had a great selection of some of the most progressive groups of the day. *In-A-Gadda-Da-Vida* (In the Garden of Eden?) was the seventeen-minute title track featuring a two-and-one-half minute drum solo by a strange bunch of guys who called themselves Iron Butterfly.

Darling knew where Paul was now. Although she secretly wished he had stayed in Canada where he would be safe, she cared deeply about his progress. She was relieved of many of her old worries. Now she could concentrate on the more immediate worries.

Bro –

Believe it or not, I've been accepted to Penn for September.

I'm trying to find a way to explain to Aunt Maggie what all has happened around here and that I can't leave Mim here pregnant and run off to Pockseken. Miriam simply can't be left alone.

Her time will be very close by then. I could use that time to knock off a lot of the books on the Penn Summer Reading List.

I'm planning to get to Ft. Sill to see you receive your commission.

If Miriam isn't well enough for me to take the time to drive down, I can take a flight down from Philly and only stay for the day.

I'm sure I'll be there for the ceremony somehow.

Only trouble is that I haven't found anything yet that would be just the right thing to wear, but I'm still looking.

Mim and I made cookies. You should be getting yours in the next few days. Dieter's will probably be crumbs. xoxo me.

On March 8th, the number of Americans killed during a single week's fighting came to 542, one short of the record set on January 17th. The next day, Westmoreland requested 206,000 more men. The force of living

American men and women in Vietnam was still hanging around 510,000. Westmoreland's continuing requests for more fresh blood to be spilled was finally instigating a major uproar. Students were getting out again, to march, to protest, and to demonstrate in greater numbers than ever before. March of 1968 wasn't that cold.

On March 12th, a day which might have been more heralded if not for all the dying young people, the United States Senate passed President Johnson's long-awaited Civil Rights Bill with only three southern Senators casting nay votes. But in spite of this victory for President Johnson and for humankind, Eugene McCarthy pulled almost half of the Democratic vote in the New Hampshire primary. McCarthy's showing in New Hampshire provided sufficient evidence of a split in the Democratic Party. It was now safe for Robert Kennedy, who had not wished to appear responsible for such a split, to announce that he too might run for the Democratic presidential nomination. Even though New York Governor Nelson Rockefeller had decided to run for the Republican nomination, Richard Nixon confidently predicted his own victory. Khe Sanh was hit with another barrage of rocket and mortar fire and a big bomb blast.

Miriam's pregnancy was on its way into its sixth month and she had moved up to two naps a day. Darling was in the basement, listening to her transistor radio. She had two feather pillows stuffed into the end of the clothes chute so that the music would not carry up the chute to the bathroom just off her mother's room. The Moody Blues were doing *Go Now.*

Darling was thinking about the meeting that took place between Paul and Mark Cymrot just before Paul went back on active duty. She was wondering how that end of things was going. She sanded and sanded. Each time she sanded, she changed the sandpaper to a finer grade. At last, she was sanding with the ruby extra fine. She wanted the softest smoothest possible finish for the old rock maple chest of drawers that she had commandeered after ransacking the attic. Darling wondered if her brother would truly be all right. Having this Carlani thing hanging over his head was sure to be a distraction.

Try as he had, Mark Cymrot had been completely unsuccessful at wrenching anything from Paul that Mark might be able to construe as an alibi. Paul confessed to his debauched evening with Bernadette Carlani and he told Cymrot of their trip to New Hope and their afternoon at Allison's Clown Ally, and of that evening when Bernadette disappeared from the dance floor. Paul was genuinely sorry that something, probably bad, had happened to Bernadette, "But I just can't tell you anything else."

"You have got to tell me where you were for the rest of that night."

"No. I don't."

"Now listen Paul. This woman, this Bernadette Carlani, has not been found. And, lucky for you, that means that without a body they have no reason to press charges against you. No crime. But sooner or later she *will* be found, and we're going to have to turn this whole thing over to Bean who handles criminal and you're not helping your own defense by refusing to cooperate."

"I am cooperating. I've told you everything I can about Bernadette Carlani. And that's all there is to tell."

"You're lying."

"I am not lying."

"Then you're not telling me everything."

"I'm telling you everything you need to know."

"That's for me to decide. And what you're telling me is that she just disappeared from the dance floor. You're telling me you were never even curious about where she'd gone or who she'd gone off with or how she was going to get home that night when you were the one who took her to New Hope in the first instance. And to top it off, Paul, you took her across the state line. That's federal, FBI."

"Mark. How can you make a federal case out of this? I took the woman out for a late lunch. It just snowballed, that's all."

"I'm not making a federal case out of it. That's just the way it is. It's the law. If you take someone, anyone, across a state line, for any reason, and a crime is committed, you have opened yourself up for federal prosecution. In fact, I'm surprised your sister has only heard from local authorities."

"I didn't commit a crime, Mark. You just don't know what she was like. I mean she was okay and everything but Bernadette did what Bernadette wanted to do. There was no stopping her. You know what I mean?"

"Explain it to me."

"Well, let's just say that Bernadette was a big girl, okay? Can we leave it at that?"

Mark pounded his fist on his desk. "No, we cannot!" Paul rose straight out of his chair and stood at-ease. "All right. She was a cunt. Okay? You couldn't figure that out for yourself?"

Mark was almost as embarrassed as Paul had intended him to be, but he persevered. "Okay. Now we're getting somewhere. Sit down, Paul. You've got to realize that I'm on your side in this. But the questions I'm asking you now are nothing compared to what the FBI will be asking when this woman's body turns up somewhere. And eventually it will. I promise you."

Paul returned to his seat, "Well, when it does, I hope it's alive. But even if it isn't, Mark, there's not a whole lot more I can tell you."

"Paul. You could be looking at a murder indictment. I mean, the best we could possibly hope for would be involuntary manslaughter. That is, unless you tell me where you went and who you were with. Because it's a lead-pipe cinch you didn't go back to Arrowhead, unless you want your sister to go on lying for you."

"No. I don't want that. And I don't give a damn what they do to me. I did not do anything to hurt Bernadette Carlani. I've already told you. I found an angel. I left the country. And that's all there is to it. I have no idea what became of Bernadette. She was a big girl. She had her own money. She could take care of herself. And it's a twenty-minute cab ride from New Hope to Trenton where she lived and she was seen walking off the dance floor with some other guy. That was all I needed to know."

"Some other guy? Who?"

"I can't tell you that."

"You mean you won't tell me that."

"That's what I mean."

"And you won't tell me who it is you picked up with after that?"

"I did tell you. I picked up with an angel. We had dinner together. We spent that night together and we spent the next two weeks together."

"In New Hope."

"Yup."

"And then you came to see me and you cashed your check for seventy-five hundred dollars and you left the country."

"Something like that."

"What does that mean?'

"Well, it wasn't that simple but that's how it turned out."

"Well, then, what else did you do?"

"I told you, I can't tell you that!"

Their voices had grown so loud that they could be overheard in the reception area. Part of Ruth's job was to ignore such outbursts and to smile reassuringly or to ignore them altogether, giving any waiting clients the impression that they were imagining things. Darling Randolph, who waited in reception for her brother, simply re-crossed her legs and sighed, "Holy Toledo," but did not let on that she had heard anything either. She turned another page of her *Harper's Bazaar* and rearranged herself only slightly. The hour passed very slowly for Darling, and she was greatly relieved when Paul and Mark walked out of Mark's office and they were shaking hands in front of Ruth's desk. Paul collected his sister, helped her with her coat, and they were outside in the fresh air again.

In spite of Darling's best efforts to pry, Paul would not yield. All he said to Darling was "I'm sorry. I really am. I had no idea in hell that besides having to put up with me being gone, like, off my head, that you'd been putting up with this Carlani crap. But you don't have to put up with it any more. I'm back now. All the way back. And I'll face the music if it comes to that." He put his arm around his sister. "I'm sorry you had to take all the heat. It'll be okay now."

Darling smiled as she looked at her walking feet, strolling along beside her brother, arm in arm. "Will you take me to see *Candy* before you go back?"

"*Candy*? You have to be twenty-one just to get in!" Paul grinned. He knew he was going to have to do it anyway.

"Oh, come on. You know I can pass! Besides, it's got Ringo in it. He's a Mexican gardener or something."

Paul walked on and held the Mustang's door open for his sister. *Candy* she wanted. *Candy* it would be. It was very naughty movie for the times.

# PART IV

# CHAPTER 38

Purple and white crocuses dotted Mrs. Randolph's rock garden and grape hyacinths were struggling hard to break through the cold moist Earth. The solid February ice on the skating pond had given way to a frozen slush. Chilly March winds still played hard among the tall treetops making the cold fingers of branches clack against one another in a frigid staccato sound that was not unlike that of an old Underwood just put to use or the cracking of knuckle bones.

The baby's maple chest of drawers now had its first coat of antique white paint and stood drying in the warmth of the basement. Darling watched the thick white frost of early morning from her bedroom window-seat. She sipped at a cup of very hot tea as she stroked Balzac's expressive face with the very tips of her fingers. While he purred, Darling watched the frost melt with the sunrise. Darling could go to sleep now if she wanted to. She had been up all night yet again working on that chest of drawers and Miriam would sleep until way past ten. But Darling could not sleep. There was something gnawing at her insides, something that would not let her rest.

David was at Parris Island, Paul was at Fort Sill, and Dieter was Over There. Miriam and Darling both grew uneasy now that all the men were away. Dieter's letters to Miriam were not coming as often as they used to. And the latest was even more disturbingly farther out.

> Now you see the mottled sky. Our-Sun
> like icey vineyards crowned in hay
> a measure caps or taps the
> song.
> A little like confusion like
> a complex thing, a little

like a paradigm of
posies, lit like caption
upon the electrick street
upon the nozzling tapping
    drip, drip, drip
Song immutable soars onto
the versicle of
averages poorly embowering
this is faltering here:
gild a
loathsome stage
can't bend     aahhhg!


In spite of the enervating quality of Dieter's letters, Miriam's blood pressure was beginning to stabilize and the nosebleeds had ceased completely. So what was Darling's problem? Why did the atmosphere that surrounded her seem so tense, so anxious all the time? Mrs. Killian had asked, "What is wrong with you child? Why can't you ever settle down?"

Darling sneaked another half-a-Phenobarb, did fifty sit-ups and a few asanas, and went to the kitchen for some toast and marmalade. She detested the month of March. She did not like the sharp winds that burned her cheeks and made her nose run and her eyes water. She bundled up in the mouton coat. The Mustang disliked crunching over the morning-frozen mud of the lane so it grabbed rubber hard as Darling turned onto the road to the mount and headed into Littleton. Today was a Mrs. Killian day.


A number of civilian officials at the Department of Defense and some senior officials at the State Department were arguing against Westmoreland's request for a forty-percent increase in American forces in Vietnam. Westmoreland claimed the increase was necessary in order to regain the initiative from the enemy. The Battle at Khe Sanh was now being compared to the 1953 Battle of Dien Ben Phu which had, after more than 10 years of battle, caused the French to abandon their efforts in Vietnam, known as Indo-China at that time. Meanwhile, President Johnson created the Anti-Poverty Agency, the final spanning arch of his dream for The Great Society.

On Saint Patrick's Day, Senator Robert F. Kennedy of New York formally announced his candidacy for the Democratic presidential nomination. Kennedy said that it was necessary for him to run because only by changing the men who were making the nation's **"disastrous divisive policies"** on Vietnam and at home would we change the situation. In response to Kennedy's announcement, Gene McCarthy declared that he was prepared to carry his candidacy right through to the California primary on June 4th.

Our GIs were reported to be attempting a World War II-style pincer move during yet another daylong battle near Saigon. In London, some two hundred youths were arrested during a huge protest against the Vietnam War during which thousands of students tried to storm the American embassy. At home, President Johnson asked for austerity to end the war. Students everywhere were cheering Kennedy onward.

Like a hibernating animal, Miriam snored away the time just before the thaw. The Randolph house was so empty and so quiet. Music could only be played in the basement while Miriam slept. During the long dark hours of Darling's sleepless nights, she began to recognize how much she had enjoyed having David around as a sparring partner. But she cured those thoughts with thoughts of approaching springtime. Every morning she watched with delight as the sun broke over the tree line another moment earlier. It would soon be April again. April. Yes, it would come again, with its long rains and new leaves, and the first anniversary of her mother's death.

Meanwhile, the CIA re-stated the obvious when it announced its conclusion that the enemy's strength in South Vietnam at the beginning of the Tet Offensive was significantly greater than U.S. officials had thought at the time. The fighting continued. New York's Mayor Lindsey called upon 3,000 college students to aid in the draft resistance movement and to push for a Republican president. A huge cache of enemy arms and munitions was discovered near Saigon within easy range of the Americans at Tan Son Nhut Air Base.

On March 23$^{rd}$, it seemed that spring had arrived at last. A bright sun broke through the damp clouds and the winds died down to breezes. The air seemed almost balmy. "Good pneumonia weather," Mrs. Killian said, for it would be bitter cold again that night. The Johnson Administration was formulating a plan to send 30,000 more fighting men to Vietnam over the balance of the year. That number was in addition to the 525,000 troops already approved to go to Vietnam plus the 10,500 paratroopers and Marines who had been rushed to Vietnam as reinforcements during the January and February crisis of Tet. (Paul Randolph might have been one among their number had he not smashed into a tree.) The increase would bring the force level to an all-time high of about 565,500 men. On that same day, however, President Johnson announced that he would bring William C. Westmoreland back to Washington as Army Chief of Staff, effectively relieving Westmoreland of his duties as Commander of

American Forces in Vietnam. The President's decision to replace Westmoreland was evidence that at least some justice and some sanity existed somewhere within the Johnson Administration. But, even as the announcement was made, Khe Sanh was again in the midst of sustained and heavy shelling.

In the eyes of many American citizens, Westmoreland had received a mere slap on the wrist in exchange for what amounted to either willful or criminal negligence or ignorance or both. It was evident that the death and destruction incurred against American forces, particularly during the 11-week siege of the Tet Offensive, should have been anticipated and therefore turned back by an informed and responsible commander. Westmoreland's ineffectiveness as a leader had cost many thousands of young American lives. U.S. planes were bombing heavily and a full 70 miles north of Hanoi, merely 18 miles from North Vietnam's border with China. At home, the Reverend Dr. Martin Luther King, Jr. led a massive protest march in support of striking sanitation workers in Memphis.

Yes, it was definitely spring. The marchers and protesters, off to a very early start this year, were already wreaking havoc. President Johnson once again offered federal aid to U.S. cities in an effort to curb the rioting that was breaking out anew almost daily. The White House press agency announced that the president would address the nation on the following evening, March 31st. It was promised that President Johnson would deal fully with the situation in Vietnam.

Private David Adams had been at the United States Marine Recruit Depot at Parris Island for three weeks. Paul Randolph was an E-5 OCS grunt at Fort Sill. Specialist Fourth-Class Dieter McKenzie's letters had ceased to arrive. Miriam and Darling were anxious to hear what President Johnson had to say.

Miriam set the ironing board in front of the television. She was thinking of herself and Dieter as they had been when they were last together. That was so long ago now, walking along the beach hand in hand and so in love. She could still hear the noisy keening of the gulls and terns as they rolled and fluttered and sailed along the angry ocean. She was thinking of how they had laughed as they watched the little sandpipers run after a receding wave with their beaks quickly poking into the sand for sand crabs then skitter back as a new wave broke powerfully and slammed itself upon the wet gray-white sand. Miriam was fully engaged in her memories and in the mindless process of ironing and folding and stacking three dozen brand new and freshly laundered in Ivory Snow diapers.

Darling was holding a cup of tea in one hand and was fiddling with the television's rabbit ears with the other. She was still trying to get the best reception when *Hail to the Chief* faded into the background and President Johnson, wearing his eyeglasses and looking very grave and very old, faded into view. A few minutes later, just as the two young women were beginning to think they were being told again what they already knew, they just looked at one another in stunned silence. Lyndon Baines Johnson, tired and heartbroken, a sweet gentle old man at last, spoke to his nation... "**I shall not seek and I will not accept the nomination of my party as your president**." President Johnson said that his decision was completely irrevocable and that he was withdrawing in the name of national unity.

"Jesus!"

"I'll say."

President Johnson concluded his speech by adding that he had ordered a halt to all air and naval bombing of most of North Vietnam and he once again invited the Hanoi government to, "...**join me in a series of mutual moves toward peace**..." Darling jumped up from the sofa and threw her arms around Miriam. "We're getting out! He's comin' home!"

It sounded so like Johnson was going to end the war that neither Darling nor Miriam knew why he was declining to run. He would surely be re-elected. In those few moments their hopes ran away with them... Dieter would be home soon... David wouldn't have to go at all... Paul...

# CHAPTER 39

On April 2nd, two days after President Johnson's historic announcement, Eugene McCarthy defeated the President of the United States and leader of the Democratic Party, Lyndon Baines Johnson, to win the Democratic presidential nomination in the Wisconsin Primary. Richard Nixon swept up more than eighty-percent of the Republican vote. President Johnson was now completely free from political considerations. He did not have an election to win so he could ride roughshod over the nation. The bombing halt, which had sounded so promising only two days earlier, was now exposed as a hoax when reports came in that U.S. jets were striking a full 205 miles north of the Demilitarized Zone, 81 miles from Hanoi.

Americans were standing around with their mouths agape. It was like a giant communal banging of the national head against the proverbial wall. What happened to the bombing halt? Certainly, the North Vietnamese had used the cease-fire and bombing halt ruse to their advantage in duping the Americans. The result of that had been Tet '68. Darling Randolph complained to Mrs. Killian, "He let us think he was ending the war! This isn't fair!"

"Whoever told you life was fair little girl?"

On that same day, a major offensive force estimated to be between 20,000 and 30,000 combined American and South Vietnamese troops was winding its way north toward Khe Sanh determined this time to give relief to the beleaguered Marines.

Martin Luther King, Jr. The Reverend Martin Luther King, Jr. The Reverend Doctor Martin Luther King, Jr., winner of the Nobel Prize for Peace, was dead. The 39-year-old Dr. King had been conferring in the evening air on an open balcony at the Lorraine Motel in Memphis. On that

Thursday evening, the fourth of April, someone was seen speeding away in a white Mustang. A discarded 30-ought-6 shotgun was discovered about a block away. Escaped convict James Earle Ray, also known as Eric Starvo Galt, would succeed in evading authorities for two full months, though the search for King's killer was intensive.

Within the first hour of that tragic certainty, Newark exploded into riots as did Boston, Atlanta, Cincinnati, Pittsburgh, Los Angeles, Hartford, Detroit, Chicago, St. Louis, Trenton, New York City, and Washington, D.C. Dr. King, the basis of whose life's work had been non-violence...

Lyndon Johnson called an immediate joint session of Congress. He issued a proclamation and Executive Order mobilizing United States military combat troops, "...because a condition of domestic violence and disorder exists." Armed troops guarded the steps of the Capitol and the White House. The president implored, "Deny violence its victory," to no avail. On Saturday, April 6th, The Siege of Khe Sanh was declared lifted, after 76 days.

In spite of the national upheaval and the dark cloud of ash and gloom that enveloped everyone with the death of Dr. King, and in spite of Dieter's absent correspondence, Miriam's energies perked up. It was as if her gears had changed. Her appetite became voracious. She began to rise early and to prepare a huge omelet or scrambled eggs for herself and Darling with sliced tomatoes on the side and tall glasses of orange juice. If the food supplies ran low before shopping day, Miriam got herself dressed and ventured forth in the little blue Volkswagen for a trip to the grocery store, albeit to a grocery store in some nearby town where no one knew her. Then one day, Miriam asked Darling if she would mind if she rearranged the furniture in Mrs. Randolph's room.

"It's your room now. You can do anything you want. But I think I'd better help. I should be getting rid of Mom's things anyway."

Miriam stacked Darling's 45s two inches high on the little record player and set to work. As she dusted the tops of the window frames and closet doors the little record player spun singles one right after the other: Jackie Wilson, *Your Love Keeps Lifting Me (Higher)*; Wilson Pickett, *In The Midnight Hour*; Jan and Dean, *Dead Man's Curve*; The Ramsey Lewis Trio, *The 'In' Crowd*; The Zombies, *She's Not There*; Percy Sledge, *When a Man Loves a Woman*; The Four Seasons, *Working My Way Back To You (Girl)*; The Walker Brothers, *Make It Easy On Yourself*; The Fifth Dimension doing *Stoned Soul Picnic* and Laura Nyro's *Sweet Blindness*; Don and Phil Everly, *Bye Bye Love*.

Miriam used a mop to wash the pink tile ceiling in her bathroom with vinegar and water. She polished all the mirrors and brass. Darling dragged everything out of her mother's closets and linen cupboards and put new lining paper on the shelves and vacuumed every nook and cranny and all the draperies. She sorted Mrs. Randolph's things into boxes. There were boxes for Mrs. Killian and bigger boxes for the Salvation Army, and there were a few boxes and hangers in bags that went into the attic. "What now?"

"I've got a diaper pail and a rubber ducky. The top three drawers of your Mom's dresser can be for baby clothes even though I haven't got much yet." Darling smiled a secret smile for she would be putting the finishing touches on the baby's new chest of drawers later that night. "But what am I gonna do for a crib? I'm afraid to let him sleep with me. I might roll over and squash him, you know? I was thinking of using a laundry basket. That's what Lois Guy did when she and Matt were hiding little Matt in his room at Yale, remember?"

"I remember. I also remember that the Black Panthers had their headquarters in the launderette down the corner. I think that whole business was pretty rough on Lois. We oughtta be able to do a little better than that, don't you think?"

"But cribs are so expensive."

"Don't I get to, like, do just a little something for this baby? I mean, it is going to be my first nephew, or niece." Darling let herself smile a big knowing smile. And bright rays of sunshine entered the not very well heated room. Now it was all out in the open. Miriam and Darling hugged one another and they were both in a hurry to go crib shopping tomorrow evening for certain, if Miriam was up to it.

Thousands of demonstrators marched down Broadway after attending a Martin Luther King memorial service in Central Park. Europe was coming to grips with its own horror of the King assassination. There was fear for the stability of American society that was genuine and global. Martin Luther King had been deeply admired in Europe and had been thought of as a bright light of hope for what Europeans saw as a hopelessly degenerate America. 6,000 more National Guard troops were called up in Chicago. The District of Columbia was put under a 4 PM curfew.

Paul's platoon had no trouble devouring the two dozen cupcakes Darling sent and which had arrived in a fairly well mushed condition. No matter, in ten minutes they were all gone and the box and the frosting-covered birthday card were tossed into the dumpster. On every street, highway and thoroughfare throughout the United States, automobile headlights burned day and night in remembrance of Martin Luther King. Sporting events were postponed and schools were closed. Coretta Scott King, the Reverend's widow, urged that her husband's followers carry on with his dream and stop the violence. **"He gave his life for the poor of the world, the garbage workers in Memphis, and the peasants in Vietnam**."

The violence eased off in Pittsburgh but more U.S. combat troops were sent into Baltimore. Word came that Mrs. Martin Luther King, Jr. would march in her husband's place during the massive civil rights demonstration which he had been planning long before his death, right there in Memphis where he died, right there in Memphis. The man had not even been buried yet.

That same Sunday, for the first time in months, Darling Randolph began to cry. Jim Clark, twice World Auto Racing Champion and winner of the Indianapolis 500, had been killed when his Lotus 48 went out of control at 175 miles per hour, somersaulted off the track at Hockenheim, West Germany, and smashed into the trees. Clark died of a broken neck and multiple skull fractures, aged thirty-two years. Darling would always remember that famous smile, so gorgeous, a go-to-hell kind of a smile like the one her brother Paul used to smile. Used to smile.

Still spouting the same old same-old, General William C. Westmoreland was declaring that, "...**militarily we have never been in a better relative position in Vietnam**." What a lot of horse hockey. Perhaps he was trying to save face. After all he had been relieved of his command, and there is no greater insult.

April 8th, a Monday with fresh damp spring air and a new green haze among the willows, became the official day of national mourning for the Reverend Dr. Martin Luther King, Jr. Mrs. King asked for a peaceful society and 1900 more federal troops were ordered into Baltimore. Cincinnati and Pittsburgh were still burning. President Johnson received a private message from Hanoi, trying to work out a time and a place for talks. *Hmmph!* Newark was having a rash of fires. In Trenton, a black youth was shot dead amidst the burning and looting while a mule-drawn farm wagon bore the coffin of Martin Luther King, Jr. through the streets of Atlanta. More than 50,000 mourners followed the funeral wagon. Five people died in the riots in Kansas City.

Miriam's newly found energy proved to be contagious. Hannah would be amazed. By the time Tuesday rolled around, the next Hannah-day, the two young women had given the whole house a thorough spring-cleaning. "Darling's Selections", rumbled from Paul's speakers while Miriam and Darling were fully occupied in doing all the windows they could possibly reach on that very first warm sunny day of spring: Gene Vincent, *Be-Bop-A-Lula*; Bobby Darin, *Mack the Knife*; The Four Tops, *I Can't Help Myself (Sugar*

*Pie, Honey Bunch)*; The Rolling Stones, *Here Comes My 19th Nervous Breakdown*; Aretha Franklin, *Respect*; (Little) Stevie Wonder, *I Was Made To Love Her* and *Fingertips (Part 2)*; The Tremeloes, *Do You Love Me?*; The Kinks, *You Really Got Me*; Procol Harum, *Whiter Shade of Pale*; Dion and The Belmonts, *Donna, The Prima Donna*; Lennon and McCartney's, *Michelle*; The Spencer Davis Group, *Gimme Some Lovin'*; Marvin Gaye, *How Sweet It Is To Be Loved By You*; Sam the Sham and the Pharaohs, *Hey There L'il Red Riding Hood*; Little Anthony and The Imperials, *Goin' Out of My Head* and *Hurt So Bad*; The Isley Brothers, *Twist and Shout*; Johnny Rivers, *Baby I Need Your Lovin'*; Lulu, *To Sir With Love*; and Norman Greenbaum, *The Eggplant That Ate Chicago*.

The crib that Miriam and Darling selected was antique white with pastel colored wooden balls that could whirl around on their spindles. The headboard and footboard were softened by images of fat auburn teddy bears playing with baby blue and pink ABC building blocks. It would be delivered in three weeks. Darling asked Maury Sarn to bring the maple dresser up from the basement. Darling had dragged it all the way down from the attic herself, one step at a time. But now that it was finished, it was not to be scratched or banged whatsoever. When Miriam saw it her bottle-green eyes pooled with tears behind her eyeglasses. "Is this what you've been up to every night while I've been stacking Zs?"

"Pretty much. Well, like, I had to have something to keep me out of trouble."

A warm, soft happy mood of anticipation descended upon the Randolph house. It felt rather like the soft pink and blue and yellow, mint green and cream-colored crib blanket that Miriam had nearly completed with its three rows of crocheted ruffled edging.

Soon after, Miriam proclaimed herself too big in the belly to hide beneath Paul's flannel shirts anymore. Darling got the hint and she and Miriam spent the entire afternoon searching the attic again, this time for Grandma Littleton's old Singer *Featherweight*. Miriam was beside herself with happiness.

Ever practical, Miriam purchased inexpensive remnant fabric in lengths of two-and-a-quarter yards or so and one pattern. She was about to create several pretty smock dresses without collars or sleeves and beneath which she planned to wear one of the lamb's wool turtlenecks donated by Darling. With black tights and Hush Puppies, Miriam looked more adorable with each passing day. "When the weather warms up, I can exchange the sweaters for blouses. And when summer gets hot I can just wear the smocks as sundresses with sandals."

Neat piles of soft cotton baby things accumulated inside the drawers of the old maple chest: receiving blankets; little drawstring nightdresses; and sacque outfits which consisted of a kind of bed-jacket that tied at the neck with satin ribbons and had matching rubber-lined pants. One drawer contained three neat stacks of the diapers Miriam had so carefully washed and ironed and folded, all ready and waiting. The top of the chest would soon become cluttered with baby powder, ointments, and lotions. To keep them sharp, Miriam stuck the diaper pins in a bar of soap. The bar of soap rested in a seashell, a souvenir of her day at the beach with Dieter. The future was looking ever brighter in spite of the darkness of the times.

# CHAPTER 40

When General Creighton W. Abrams finally took over for Westmoreland more than 100,000 troops immediately fanned out to scour any remaining enemy activity from the northern provinces of South Vietnam. The United States called on 24,500 more Reservists for active duty in Vietnam. West German students went on a violent rampage after one of their number was shot during an otherwise peaceful demonstration at The Berlin Wall. Many more would die that day. Rumors of a secret meeting between American and North Vietnamese Ambassadors were accompanied by news of stepped up B-52 raids against North Vietnam. This was followed by another breakdown in communications when Hanoi rejected all possible proposed sites for talks. That scenario was becoming routine and predictable.

Senator Eugene McCarthy suggested to the Johnson Administration that the United States consider paying ransom for the *Pueblo* and her crew who had been held captive in North Korea since January 27th. *No. Way.* The Marine base at Khe Sanh was shelled again, 19 Marines were killed and 56 were wounded.

Draft calls finally exceeded their limit. By the end of April, the Army was scheduled to draft 346,900 men, 61,900 more than originally planned. The Johnson Administration claimed that the additional men were needed, "as a result of a decline in enlistments, more discharges and other unforeseen factors..." Most of the discharges were resulting from severe wounds. The "unforeseen factors" were the deaths of so many soldiers during the past five months. Many newspapers had long ago (around Thanksgiving of '67) ceased to publish the death lists because there were so depressingly many. Since that time, the kill numbers were being displayed as a backdrop to the nightly news, every night, as if it were a football scoreboard. No names, no ranks, no identification whatsoever, just numbers.

United Nations Secretary General U Thant accurately predicted that the United States and North Vietnam would begin negotiations in Paris. On a gorgeous sunny Sunday at the end of April, 87,000 human beings gathered at New York's Central Park to march in protest of the Vietnam War. Hubert Horatio Humphrey split the Democratic Party yet again when he announced his candidacy for president of the United States. A portrait of a black American soldier made the front page of the *New York Times*.

May Day...May Day... One thousand New York City police officers were brought in to remove campus protestors from the halls of Columbia University, and Tina Moffett Adams telephoned the Randolph place. Darling caught the phone on the first ring because Miriam was having a nap.

"No, no. Not Davie. It's Dieter. I don't know what we're gonna do, but..."

"Jesus, Tina. Spit it out! Is he okay?" Darling's blood pressure surged violently just beneath her earlobes.

"I guess he's okay. But they're flyin' 'im home. They're sending 'im to some place called Reynolds Army Hospital at Fort Sill. Know where that is?"

"Yes, I do know where that is. Oh, God. God." Darling looked up through the ceiling. "Oh, oh, I can't think right now. Uh, oh damn, give me a minute. I'll call you back."

Darling hung up the phone and flopped into the wing-backed chair. She stared blankly across the lawns. The scenery was beginning to green up now with the warm rain. It was the first of May, the first rainy day of May. "What the hell am I gonna do?" She leaned over with her elbows on her knees and her head in her hands. "Oh, Jesus. Jesus. This is awful." She sat up again. "All right. All right. Pull yourself together." She took a deep breath. Nothing. She took another one and stood up. Her knees felt like they were made out of *Jell-O*. "Okay. Okay now. Call Special Services. Oh, what the hell is Dieter's number?" Darling crept up the stairs as quietly as possible. She went to her room and whipped a black leather address book from the middle drawer of the secretary. Flipping through the pages in a panic she found Dieter's APO address and wrote his serial number down on a piece of notebook paper. She fumbled through the 'M's looking frantically for Mrs. McKenzie's phone number. "There's the address. Oh shit, that's right, she doesn't have a phone. Dammit."

Darling grabbed the address book, the piece of notebook paper, the pencil, and dragged the extension phone from her night table into the bathroom. She flipped pages quickly and dialed Mr. and Mrs. Adams' number. "Oh, Tina. Sorry about that. I really lost it there for a minute."

Tina was surprised that Darling had called back at all. "It's okay. But what're you gonna do?"

"I'm not sure yet. Do you know anything else? Like, what happened? When they're bringin' him in?"

"Mrs. McKenzie came over. Half an hour ago I guess. She had a telegram. She wanted me to call Davie and get him to take care of things. But, you know, I can't fuckin' call 'im about this. I mean, like what's he gonna do about it anyway? He can't get out. He can't even use the goddamn telephone. I mean if it was like, Tommy, or something, or his parents, but I can't call 'im about this!"

"I know, I know. I guess she doesn't know what else to do. I don't know. Shit. Did she say anything else?"

"She gave me this number. She wanted Davie to call. She got a telegram. You know, she doesn't have a phone."

"Did you call it?"

"Nuh-uh. I'm afraid to. I mean, like, what would I say?"

"Give me the number." Darling scribbled. "Okay, that's the same number I have, yeah, Special Services. Yeah. Washington. Okay. I'll let you know what I find out. I gotta go. No. Mim doesn't know yet. Thanks Tina. Tommy okay? Good. Oh, good. Bye."

What Darling found out from Special Services was that Dieter had been wounded in action and that he would be arriving at Reynolds Army Hospital on Thursday. Thursday. That's day after tomorrow. And that the Red Cross might be able to tell her more.

The Red Cross would not tell Darling a whole lot more. She was not next of kin. But she did find out that Dieter had been alive as of four o'clock that afternoon, California Time, when he was transferred onto a flight from Fort Ord, and that he was scheduled to arrive at Fort Sill at 22:00 hours (Central Daylight Time) tonight. "Tonight? I thought Special Services said Thursday?'

No. It was tonight. Apparently, he'd been processed straight through. "Is that good news or bad news?"

"I can't tell you that, Ma'am. I've just told you everything we're authorized to say."

"Thanks." Darling depressed the disconnect button and held it for an instant, then she dialed the operator and asked for directory assistance. She wanted the number of the Post Locator at Fort Sill, Oklahoma. She waited. She scribbled the number and said, "Thank you very much, operator." She dialed the number of the Post Locator at Fort Sill. She asked for the number of Reynolds Army Hospital. She waited. She scribbled the number and said, "Thank you very much, operator," and hung up the phone. Darling now had a piece of notebook paper that was scribbled all over with telephone numbers and cryptic messages, and a pregnant potential suicide napping peacefully in her mother's bedroom.

Five o'clock. Darling stood at the kitchen sink filling the teakettle and staring out upon the deep greens and gentle browns of Arrowhead. God, would it never quit raining? Darling's thoughts went away to Gracie Annabelle Littleton Randolph. Darling's mother had been cremated. That had been her oft-expressed wish in life and so at death her children had complied. But protocol demanded that there had to be a closed casket "viewing" and it was a monster. For three days Paul and Darling shook hands with and received hugs from about eight hundred people, friends and relatives from far and near. Their Aunt Maggie stood with them for the entire three days. Aunt Maggie had been crying at the controls of the Beechcraft. Paul was carrying the mother-of-pearl box; he was not crying but morose. Darling waited and watched from the living room windows as their mother's ashes drifted down from the sky and came to rest across the lawns, the trees, in the pool, on the roof of the place where she, Darling's mother, had been born. Aunt Maggie made one final pass over the house and dipped the Beechcraft's wing in salute.

Darling and Paul both waited. Neither of them could sleep. They tossed and turned every night. Every day they watched and waited with darkly encircled bloodshot eyes. They survived on cups of tea and cigarettes. They shared a joint now and then. They had each other to sustain them. No food, no appetite, and no rest until on the ninth day came the first rainy day of May. That rain had been a good hard, steady rain just like this one. It began just before dawn and continued deep and steady all the long day. All that day Darling and Paul watched. They waited. They said little. But that night they both slept like the dead. Finally, it was done.

The night after that long rainy day had been the first night Darling dreamt the dream, the dream of waiting at the train station. It was a progressive dream and each night thereafter the train moved closer to the platform. But Darling would never discover who it was that she was waiting for, she just knew that something was going to happen when the train finally arrived and that it was something horrible. Darling always woke from that dream with a pain in her chest, not unlike the pain she had now. Anxiety. She would awaken frightened out of her wits. She would hurry down the stairs and into Paul's room and into Paul's big old bed and snuggle deep down into the warm bedcovers and sleep. There the dream did not find her.

When Miriam came down the last few stairs and into the living room, she found Darling standing with her arms folded across her chest. She had a cigarette in her hand and was staring out across the lawns watching the rain. Miriam stretched and checked to see if Darling actually saw anything in particular. No. "Mmmm," she stretched, "Could sleep all day on a day like this." Absentmindedly, Darling replied, "Tea's ready." She took the cigarette to the kitchen sink, ran it under cold water and tossed it into the trashcan. She washed her hands. "How're you feeling?" Darling already wanted to light another cigarette. No.

"My back's a little sore. But it's not all that bad." Miriam nibbled a fat buttery Pecan Sandy. "I was going to ask you to take those books back to the library for me, but not on a day like today."

"You finished all of them already? Heavy. Find out everything you needed to know?"

"Not exactly. But they do have some great pictures of what the baby looks like. And I've got a pretty good idea of what's gonna happen to me."

Darling wanted another cigarette. No! You'll make her sick.

"They're not due back until tomorrow."

Darling offered, "I can check them out again for you if you want." Small talk.

"I think I can get by now with Dr. Spock." Miriam smiled softly. She leaned back in her chair with her mug of tea in her hands and her hands resting across the small mounded top of her belly.

Darling shifted in her chair. She tucked one leg under her rump. "You sure you're feeling okay?"

"Fine. Just sleepy. It's the rain."

"You look a little pale."

"Mmm. No makeup. Don't worry about it. I'm fine." Miriam looked around the table. "Any good mail?"

Darling knew this meant any mail from one of their guys. "No, no. Just bills." Darling pushed the words out, "But there was a phone call."

Miriam sat up a little closer to the table.

"Tina of all people." Darling did not look at Miriam's face. She could only gaze upon Miriam's hands, those long slender fingers so much more perfectly formed for the piano than Darling's. Darling's memory was jarred back to all the demands and the knuckle rapping. She would never learn to play well, even now that her mother was gone. "It's Dieter; they're flying him home tonight. He's been wounded."

Miriam fumbled with her warm mug. She did not look at Darling. "How bad?"

"I don't know. But I've got the number of the hospital where they're taking him. Maybe after he gets in we can find out."

Big fat hot tears rolled down Miriam's cheeks. She wiped her face hard and pulled her glasses from her face and let them drop onto the table and put her face in her hands to muffle her deep sobs.

Darling went to the box of tissues that always sat tucked in a countertop corner by the refrigerator. She fluffed out five or six and brought them to Miriam then sat back down in her chair. Miriam took all the tissues and held them over her face. She wiped softly and blew her nose hard. With a very stuffy nose, she said, "But, he's still alive. Right?"

"That much we know for sure."

The tears would not stop. "Okay. Okay. Uhm. What do we do now, you think?"

Darling wandered around in a circle taking in the views beyond any window her eye fell upon. "Wait, I guess. Much as I hate it. Seems like that's all we can do. Until he gets in anyway. Then maybe we can find out something more." Darling made to hug Miriam's shoulders. She whispered. "I'm so sorry." Strangely, Miriam pulled her shoulders away. Darling let her go. As she sat up straighter and rearranged the handful of tissues, looking for a dry patch, Miriam said, "No. Don't be sorry. It's over now. It's all over. He's home. He's on his way back home. And he's alive, no matter what they've done to him." She couldn't help it now; the serious blubbering started up again. This time Darling brought the tissue box to the table.

The wait was long, agonizingly so. Oklahoma was on Central Time, 22:00 hours there would be 23:00 hours in New Jersey. It would be well past three in the morning before anyone at Reynolds Army Hospital would even tell Darling that Dieter had been admitted. But by four a.m., and by plugging one nostril and claiming she was Mrs. McKenzie, Dieter's mother, Darling was able to get through to a nursing Lieutenant on Dieter's floor who would only say he was doing well, "under the circumstances." Darling asked the Lieutenant to be kind enough to convey a message to Dieter, "Would you please tell him that we love him?" Yes. She would do that. But she was not permitted to tell "Mrs. McKenzie" what Dieter's *circumstances* were. At that point, Miriam announced, "I have to go." She sat propped on the sofa with her legs up and her arms folded across the top of her belly, gazing at her slippered feet.

"Where? There?" Darling began to pace.

"Yeah."

"Oh, Mim. Not in your condition, please. I know your upset, but..."

"Don't even waste your breath. I'm going. And that's all there is to it."

Darling stopped pacing. "Okay. I understand. But how?"

"Drive."

"Drive? Are you crazy? It'll take at least two, maybe three days to get there? You can't do that!" Again, Darling paced.

"Yes, I can. And, besides. I don't have any choice."

"Maybe. But why drive? I mean, like we could fly out. It wouldn't be nearly so hard on you."

"I'm gonna need my car."

Darling could tell that Miriam's mind had been fast at work. She already had some kind of a plan in her head. "Okay. Okay. I can drive you out. But we'll have to take our time, Mim. You know you need your rest. You've got to be all right. You don't want something bad to happen now."

"Nope. I'm going by myself."

"But, you're..."

"Darling. *Something bad* has already happened. There's nothing bad's gonna happen to me. Nothing that could be as bad as this. Not now that I know he's alive."

"What about the baby, Mim? I mean, maybe Dieter's not hurt so bad, you know?"

"No. It's bad. They never would've brought him home if it wasn't bad. They would've patched him up and shipped him back out to the field if it wasn't really bad."

Darling's head nearly rolled off her shoulders. "Jesus."

"Yeah."

Dieter had fought for his life for nine days after the explosion and had been patched up like a leaky lifeboat, quickly and sometimes sloppily, anything to stop the bleeding holes, for instance, two huge stitches to close a gap six inches long and just as deep. For nine days the doctors and nurses of the U.S. Medical Corps in Saigon waited to be sure his body would accept all the whole blood he was sucking up, and to see if he would be strong enough for the trip back to the States and better medical facilities. Maybe someone stateside would be able to save the legs, but it was very unlikely, not after being thrown 250 feet and having most of a howitzer land on them. Both femurs, the largest bones in the body, had been comminuted, reduced to dust. Dieter's own red blood cells could not reproduce fast enough to replenish his blood supply. There were many gash and laceration wounds, and he was pockmarked with small-to-medium-sized holes where shrapnel had been removed. Dieter was knocked down on morphine as soon as he had been found. Fortunately, that was immediately and by DogFace Smolinsky, the radioman who called in the dustoff.

After two days and a night on the road without sleep, Miriam reached Lawton, Oklahoma around five-thirty in the morning. She was hungry but she knew she was not starving. There would be a snack shop at the hospital she was sure. There is a snack shop in every hospital. Miriam had sustained her determination during the long road-trip with thoughts of urgency and fears of what she would find. Miriam ignored her own discomfort, knowing that Dieter's pain must be gruesome and several orders of magnitude greater than anything she could possibly imagine.

At first, the Military Police turned Miriam away at the gate, but Miriam began to cry. She sputtered out to the guard about herself and about her Dieter. The guard said, "Wait here a minute," and went into the gatehouse. He rang the hospital and found that Spec4 McKenzie was indeed a patient and that his condition was listed as FAIR. The guard emerged from the gatehouse, handed Miriam a four-hour pass, and raised the gate. Miriam did not look back.

As it had happened, Miriam's route down the main thoroughfare took her straight past the runway at Wiley Post Army Airfield. Even though it was barely dawn, the huge MedEvac carriers were one after the other greeted by white-uniformed Medics who reverently transferred the stretchered heroes to Olive Drab ambulances. The ambulances carried the wounded one-quarter of a mile, a very short walk if one could have walked the distance, to Reynolds Army Hospital, Miriam's destination.

By this time Miriam felt as if her heart was in her throat. It was obvious that this was a place that knew no terms of day or night. The twenty-four-hour clock of military time was very real. A little further down the road, Miriam's ears were invaded by the stampede of footfall as thousands of troops assembled on the drill fields outside their barracks in preparation for morning calisthenics before breakfast, which she knew was called mess, but she still did not understand why.

Reynolds Army Hospital was an immaculate honeycomb of psychologically comforting military-pale-green walls of semi-gloss cleanliness. It was a place where plasma and urine and disinfectant all blended to affect a pleasant contrast to the smell of sulfur, napalm, and the color of smoke on skin.

Miriam was no longer hungry. One could not feel hunger pangs here. Such minor discomfort was immediately disqualified by the suffering that lay in every corridor, waiting for a bed or waiting for one of the surgeries to open up for the next one's turn. Dear Father in Heaven. Why isn't any of *this* making it into the headlines or onto the evening news? No one ever even mentions these guys. You'd think that these men just "went over," they never "came back," especially not in pieces. *This* is war.

Miriam made her way to the wards and she wondered, are these guys the "bad off" or are they the "lucky ones"? These men have been hit so badly they could not be given any but the most necessary care that could be had Over There. Yet they have survived for long enough to be flown more than eleven thousand miles to be brought here for further care. Most of them made it, although some did not. Every now and then Miriam would pass a sheet-covered lump of about six feet in length that was still emanating a warmth that had only moments or hours ago been a life.

On the fifth floor, all the way at the back of a newly arranged ward of thirty-two beds, in the fourth bed on the right, rested Specialist Fourth Class Dieter McKenzie. Miriam stood for a long time quietly watching the irregular rise and fall of Dieter's breathing. She gazed from the foot of the bed upon his beautiful face and whispered, "Thank God you're alive. Do you know you nearly made me a widow before I was even a wife? Now how would that have been?"

Dieter's lips were purple and swollen. His eyes were blackened perfectly matched. There was a deep laceration that ran from his right temple across his forehead almost following the hairline then down the other side to where it stopped centimeters from his carotid artery. The lower third of his left earlobe was gone. But it was Dieter all right. Beneath the intravenous tubing and a lot of gauze and the ominous tent that made unrecognizable the lower portion of his body, it was her Dieter. Miriam was especially comforted by the fact that dangling from the very end of the bed was a matched pair of twenty-pound lead weights. They *had* to be attached to legs.

Bloodshot bulbs of pale blue eyes opened to slits. As they saw Miriam, they opened to saucers then closed. There came a faint but definite, "Oh."

"Sshh," Miriam whispered, "Where can I kiss you?'

"Oh. Lips. On the lips."

"I don't want to hurt you."

"I don't care. Oh."

A voice said, "Visiting hours aren't until sixteen hundred. How did you get in here?" Miriam turned and stood straight, her belly announcing her condition. "I walked in." David was zonked again.

The doctor, a handsome young Captain, examined Dieter's chart. "You his wife?"

"Ah, no, I'm not."

"Let me see your ID card."

"ID card?"

"Military ID, lady."

"I'm sorry, doctor, I don't have one of those. But I do have a pass."

"I don't know how you managed to get this far, but you're going to have to leave. Now."

Miriam started toward the doctor but hesitated, remaining at Dieter's side, "But, please, I only just got here, and...."

"I don't wanna hear it, Ma'am. I can have you arrested right now for trespassing on federal property. But if you'll leave right this minute and let me get on with my work, I won't report the incident."

Miriam was devastated; she began to plead, "But..." The Captain cut her off, "I'm sorry," and walked on toward the next bed.

# CHAPTER 41

The Poor Peoples' March began during the first week of May. The late Reverend Dr. Martin Luther King, Jr. had planned it the previous autumn. The Reverend Ralph Abernathy chose to lead a march that had been patterned after Mohandas (Mahatma) Gandhi's great march to the sea. The participants intended to march, as Gandhi had, on foot, all the way from Memphis to the steps of the Capitol building in Washington.

The United States and North Vietnamese governments finally agreed to Peace Talks that were set to begin in Paris in about a week. At the same time, more than 500 students were arrested and scores injured when armed riot police stormed the Quad at the Sorbonne in an effort to disperse what were referred to as left wing demonstrators. Saigon was once again under mortar and rocket attack, and four newsmen were killed when booby-trapped bodies exploded into a mist of shrapnel and gore. An official of East Germany's Saigon Embassy was found murdered execution-style with a bullet in the back of his head and a blindfold over his eyes. Robert F. Kennedy won the Indiana primary, putting hope and joy into the hearts of so many young people both at home and abroad.

Darling Randolph returned very tired from a long day of getting out bumper stickers. Democratic Headquarters had been split into three local chapters: McCarthy, Kennedy, and Humphrey. Although Kennedy had just won Indiana, Darling felt that her allegiance had begun with Eugene McCarthy and that it should remain there until McCarthy pulled out of the race or until Kennedy won his party's nomination. The energy generated by the Kennedy workers seemed like more of a brotherhood, but that was just the way it was. She knew that if McCarthy pulled out or didn't get the nomination, those voters would in all probability be going over to Kennedy and she would eventually wind up working in the Kennedy camp anyway.

Even though it had only been three days since Miriam left for Oklahoma, the Randolph place was once again a big old empty house. Darling blew a speck of dust from Side One of her brand-new album while she bent over with her eyes level with the platter delicately aligning the needle to the record. As Quicksilver Messenger Service sang to her, Darling wandered about the house dressed in her flannel robe and sweat socks. From room to room she went, thinking, wondering, with Balzac peering over her shoulder like a baby. Miriam's room, always so quiet and neat, was quieter still, and there is nothing so lonely as an empty baby bed or an abandoned chest of drawers.

Balzac jumped from Darling's arms and took advantage of his first opportunity to sniff around and investigate what had become Miriam's room. Darling went with clear intention through the room to the rather short double-paneled doors that opened onto Mrs. Randolph's music library. She pushed the heavy doors open releasing a cold blast of stuffy air and revealing three sides of a small room filled from floor to ceiling with sheet music and recordings. "Oh, Mother. Sometimes it seems like you've been gone forever. Other times it was only yesterday."

It was difficult to stay there. The little room was very cold. Shelf upon shelf. *Gracie Littleton Plays Grieg.* Liszt. Chopin. Debussy. Mozart. Rachmaninoff. They were all there. *Gracie Littleton Plays Beethoven* was the last of her mother's nine recordings. From this very album, Mrs. Randolph's own rendition of *The Moonlight Sonata* had been played at her memorial service.

Darling was having another one of those moments, those moments when the reality of her mother's death was undeniable. For much of the time, Darling managed to make herself believe that her mother was still on this Earth somewhere, not dead but merely busy, not able to be with Darling. Those times when her mother was traveling or was too busy happened often in the past. Darling let her mind trick herself into believing in this way. Some comfort.

Darling's eyes pierced through the thin spines of album covers. She could hear the music that was protected within each sleeve. It was a certain Van Cliburn she was looking for now. Tchaikovsky. *Concerto No. 1 in B Flat Minor, Opus 23.*

Darling stood still in the middle of the room, holding the album to her breast. She stood thinking of the day when her mother took her out of school and to New York City to hear the twenty-three-year-old winner of the first International Tchaikovsky Competition recreate his spellbinding performance in concert at Carnegie Hall. How could that possibly have been ten years ago? But it was. Darling had only been eight years old. She remembered wanting so badly to let her eyes go crossed while focusing on the magnificent ceiling of the place. But her attention was always drawn back to the tall skinny handsome young Texan whose huge hands ruled the keyboard and whose music demanded the attention of the listener. His performance sent a strange electrical impulse that shot through Darling's whole skeleton. That electric shock went straight from Van Cliburn's fingertips into each and every one of the listeners who were then no longer merely listeners but participants in what each knew was a great moment in music. "Once in a century, if you're lucky," Mrs. Randolph said. At the time Darling only thought she understood what her mother had meant by those words.

She closed the doors securely against the dust and heat and moisture that could make the sheet music turn yellow and warp the records. For how many generations would they remain in that room, unappreciated? Perhaps until someone else came along, someone as yet unborn, who could bring to that room the special blessing of a One Who Could Really Play. Once again please, from the top, with feeling.

Darling left the album in Paul's room and headed for the kitchen. It was time for Balzac's dinner. Once that essential chore was completed, however, Darling found that she was not quite ready to make herself go back into Paul's room. She found herself not quite strong enough to go and play that music, to re-live that moment, as she had intended to. She was not ready yet.

It was still fairly early morning when Miriam telephoned. She was in serious distress. Unless Miriam was a relative, she would not be permitted back on the base again, much less to see Dieter. Between choking sobs, "This just can't be happening! I don't know what to do." Darling said, "Listen to me Miriam. Where are you?"

"Downstairs, at the hospital, in the lobby. I'm afraid if I go off base I won't get back in."

"Where're you staying?"

"I was going check in at the Holiday Inn in town, Lawton, but I came straight here first. Why?"

"Because I want you to go there now and rest up. I'll call you there in a little while."

"What're you going to do?"

"I'm not sure yet. But there must be something."

Miriam had not mentioned that she was exhausted and in a lot of pain, yet Darling seemed to know that. The baby was becoming very active all of a sudden. Miriam thought that it was probably from the long days and the even longer nights, the monotonous hours and hours and hours of sitting in the car. And hunger. She agreed with Darling that she could do with a bit of a rest.

When Darling hung up the phone, she apologized to Balzac for having to put him gently on the sofa. Balzac immediately jumped down from the sofa and headed for the comfort of his bowl of crunchies and Darling went up to her room, again retrieving the black leather address book. She sat on her bed lotus fashion and flipped the book open to the 'D's. Aunt Maggie DeLamar's entry carried a list of seven different locations and telephone numbers. Darling dialed Maggie's number at the Pentagon.

Margaret Littleton DeLamar was a very busy woman. She served as a civil attorney attached to the offices of the Army Chief of Staff. The offices were in the process of changing over to a new chief of staff, William C. Westmoreland. Everything was more than a bit of topsy-turvy. But Maggie's no-nonsense feminine voice gave Darling undivided attention as if Maggie had not another care in the world. "Hello, Darling."

"Sorry Aunt Maggie. I know you're busy but it's pretty important."

"Shoot."

"It's kind of like a long story, but anyway, it's like my friend, Mim, Miriam…"

"The Christmas call."

"Right. She's in a world of hurt, Auntie. She's out at Fort Sill and she's trying to get in to see Dieter. Dieter's, like, just got back and he's hurt pretty bad and they won't let Mim in to see him. It's because she's not a relative, Aunt Maggie, and she's just driven all the way out there, and she's like, having a baby with the guy."

"How can I help?"

"I don't know, Auntie. I just didn't know what else to do, I mean, like, Mim's beside herself. Can they really do this to her? I mean she's been waiting for Dieter and trying so hard to hold herself together and she's supposed to be having this baby in July, if she makes it, but an awful lot's happened and she's just not, like, very together, you know what I mean? I'm scared for her."

"Darling, this doesn't sound like a problem I can do anything about. It's just not up my alley. But I really do think you should have your friend telephone the Chaplain's office and explain her situation. I'm sure this isn't the first baby the Army's had to usher in for a wounded daddy."

"Jeez. That's exactly what she needs to do. I just knew you'd think of something. You're the best!"

"Only sometimes, Darling. But I do wish your friends a lot of luck. Now I've got to carry on. But tell me, does this mean you're out there all by yourself again?"

"Well, yeah. I mean, well, it's all right and everything."

"And Paul's doing all right?"

"Yeah, I guess so. I haven't had a letter from him for a few weeks now, but I guess he must be pretty busy. There really were a couple of things I wanted him to answer, like, from my letters. I think he's probably working pretty hard."

"And you?"

"I'm keeping up with my homework," she lied, "take the final in about three weeks. Then I'll be ready for Penn. So it's not too bad. And 'Zac's here. And, you know, Hannah's around two or three days a week. I have Mrs. Killian and my volunteer work."

"Good. Darling, why don't you think about coming up to the lake?"

"But Auntie. I couldn't just leave Mim all alone in her condition. And, I mean, I guess she's gonna be back. She's gonna need to see her doctor and stuff."

"I wouldn't be too sure about that. Things just may work out for those two. The Army has a way of taking care of its own. Why don't you think about going up to Pockseken? You don't really want to be alone on your birthday, do you? And you might just have some fun."

Fun. What a hell of an idea. "You really think Mim'll stay out there?"

"Let's just put it this way. I'm sure that if she wants to she'll be able to."

"Okay." A big smile. "Let's do it!"

"You got a date, kitten."

"Oh, Auntie, you're just the greatest."

"Thanks, baby. Gotta run. Love you."


Fifteen hundred miles away, Dieter woke up thinking, must be time for a shot. All Dieter was certain of was that he had been in the midst of a marvelous fantasy. He was romping naked through a tropical wonderland, in the vast company of exotic creatures and giant blooming flowers, sheltered from the humid rains by the lush triple canopy of the jungle. Someone was calling his name. How could anyone know he was there? Dieter watched himself as he kneeled among the sansevieria and waited for the hunting voice to meander off in another direction. There came the sound of footfall very close to where he was hiding. Curiosity urged him to peek between two juicy leaves. There stood his beloved Miriam. Is she here? How much of this is a dream? Then Miriam's image disappeared and a warm tingle went through him as he dreamed of his next injection. He tried to find his way back into the dream and its sweet relief. It was so unlike past times when he'd had to sweat it out, moaning, unable to even move his head from side to side. A nurse jammed a hypodermic needle into the top of Dieter's right thigh. He did not notice that anyone was near him but he found himself drifting away on a soft cloud. *Tales of Brave Ulysses* came softly down the hall from a bedside radio that was far away from Dieter's bed in the ward.

Back east, on Parris Island and still very far away from the facts, David Campbell Adams was sitting on his footlocker. He was working beneath the bright lights of the barracks, spit-shining yet another pair of boots. As usual at this very tired time of night, he was wondering why he ever decided to do a thing like this.

Paul Randolph was up late that night too. He had no idea that Dieter and Miriam were so close by. He was engaged in very important Army business, using several *Q-Tips* to polish the inside of a brass belt buckle. Earlier that day, Paul had received a whole pile of documents from Mark Cymrot that needed signing. Mark had prepared a statement for Paul, which Paul would have to take over to the Judge Advocate's offices in order to have his signature notarized. "Christ. You can sure tell Cymrot knows absolutely zilch about the Army. I don't even have time to read the fucking things."

Paul was saddened to hear that Bernadette had turned up dead. But, at the same time, it was a relief to know that because of the circumstances, heroin overdose, and because of the timing, seemed as if she had been dead for about two months, Paul would be exonerated from any guilt although he would have to give a written deposition for the inquest. Paul was in the most supervised place he could possibly be short of a psycho ward. Still, he could not help remembering Bernadette and how she had made him come like ten men. Wonder why she had to go off with Fred. Man. She'd hung in there with him for an awfully long time. Guess he had what she needed. A big dick. And good horse; you can get to need that pretty damned bad.

Bernadette had taught Paul a great deal about life, lessons he would never, never be able to forget. Alice. Sweet Alice Angel. Wonder where she is tonight. Or who she's with. Well. There was nothing he could do about it now.

# CHAPTER 42

On Sunday, May 12th the French Labor Movement called for a nationwide twenty-four-hour strike, beginning on Monday, to protest police tactics in suppressing the recent student anti-government demonstrations. That same day the first 5,000 members of The Poor People's March arrived in Washington and set up camp at the base of the Capitol Building.

By mid-week the French workers were still on strike in what was quickly becoming an extraordinary protest against police repression and the de Gaulle regime. The strike threatened to paralyze all of France and was considered the most massive outpouring in the recent international wave of student-led demonstrations. *Les evenements de mai.* The Paris Peace Talks began in what would be a years-long display of posturing and aggrandizement.


The Chaplain's office had been most helpful and very kind. Arrangements were made for a special ID card for Miriam who discovered that without an ID card one did not exist as far as the military was concerned although she also discovered that sometimes allowances would be made. Miriam's ID card, though temporary, could be used to obtain hot meals at the Post Exchange cafeteria for thirty-five cents each. She was also entitled to a free room in one of the guest cottages, which she was to share with another young woman about her own age.

Miriam's new roommates were Dotty Lake and her son Little Buddy. Dotty would be going home soon, back to Colorado where she and Little Buddy lived with her parents. The commonality of their situations made their friendship immediate and intimate.

Dotty went to Oklahoma, intending to stay only for the week. She had saved up some vacation time to make the trip. Dotty's husband, Big Buddy,

would soon to be moving on to the Veteran's Rehabilitation facility in Minnesota. He was going to be away from home for a long time yet, at least until he had been fitted with his new prosthesis and learned how to use it. Big Buddy's resentment and bitterness were inhibiting his progress and doing a very good job of destroying his relationship with his nineteen-year-old wife and with Little Buddy.

One afternoon, after another blow-up with Big Buddy, Dotty went for a long drive and found herself crying her way through the winding turns of the nearby Wichita Mountain Wildlife Refuge. Half-blinded by tears, Dotty rammed her Chevy Nova right smack into a buffalo. The buffalo had the right of way. The State of Oklahoma was fining Dotty two hundred dollars for killing the buffalo and the Nova was in the shop where the entire front end was being replaced. So, by the time Miriam met Dotty and Little Buddy, in their room at the guesthouse, Dotty was without wheels. Miriam was happy to have someone to chat with and give aid to. This greatly helped Miriam to while away the long hours between visits to Dieter's bedside.

On the day Miriam drove Dotty to collect her car from the repair shop, Miriam went out of curiosity into the Post Nursery along with Dotty while she dropped off Little Buddy. In yet another way, Miriam was hit hard with the far-reaching reality of the heartbreak of this war. The young widows who organized and operated the nursery for infants were there because they had already lived what Miriam was living now and had lost their battles anyway. These women felt themselves and their children were better off, at least for the time being, in the company of other young wives and with the babies of other young men who had been very much like their own. Dotty and Little Buddy went home to Colorado the next day. But Dotty's company was soon replaced by that of another young woman with a different name and from a different place, but with a very similar story.

The first thing that Miriam had to learn and accept was that Dieter was not by a long shot out of the woods yet. The second thing she had to learn and accept was that he was addicted to morphine. This second fact made for an abominable situation, for Miriam did not want to see Dieter in the kind of pain his injuries created, but he could not have his injections more often than once every four hours.

The effects of an injection gave Dieter the benefit of almost immediate and most blessed deep sleep, which would be the only rest he could obtain. After the hour of deep sleep, Dieter experienced approximately one-half hour during which time he was semi-conscious, almost coherent. Sometimes he would only mumble but once in a while he would smile. During that half-hour Dieter knew that Miriam was there.

Then, for the remaining two-and-one-half hours, until it was time for his next fix, Dieter often went out of his mind in indescribable agony. The most horrible part was when the muscles of his spine began to twitch. The twitching could be started by a sniff or a sneeze, or by a person walking too heavily near the bed. Once the twitching began there seemed to be an endless cycle. It began with the twitching spine, which would cause the torso to convulse. The convulsions pulled Dieter's legs up suddenly. The sudden pull lifted the forty pounds of lead weights attached by spikes through his knees and then just as suddenly, the twitching slammed his torso down sending the weights crashing back to their original position. The crash in turn made the lead weights yank madly at Dieter's crushed femurs and caused such pain that Dieter became completely hysterical, screaming sometimes until the grace of God removed him from consciousness. But even then the twitching did not stop, it did not stop until the next injection of morphine came along to make a dead man out of his senses for another hour and let him rest.

This kind of exhaustion was what was really killing him. There was so little time for his battered body to recuperate energies that were burned to a frazzle during those twitching seizures. The violence of the seizures often re-opened one or two of the large-and-closed-hastily-by-a-stitch-or-two wounds. Sometimes those wounds bled profusely. Since the two largest bones in Dieter's body were essentially reduced to dust, Dieter could not manufacture enough red blood cells to keep him alive. So, there was often a pint of red life dripping into Dieter's arm. The bleeding wounds soaked the bandages and the bed sheets. Then Dieter had to be cleaned up. The clean-up process was another madness because every movement caused him screaming pain. Dieter often begged to die.

There were good hours, when Dieter could actually get from fix to fix without any of the seizures. The good hours required only two-and-a-half hours of waiting, sweats, delirium, groans, cold compresses, and a lot of stroking of the one hand that was exposed but on which the thumb had been almost entirely severed and had been stitched back on with about a hundred tiny stitches. Miriam often wondered who it was, which one of the corpsmen had the talent and had taken the time to do such a fine job. After all, the entire front portion of Dieter's left leg below the knee had been sewn back on, dirt and all, with four huge stitches. Once in a while Miriam grieved about how addicted Dieter was, and she wondered how Tina could do this to herself intentionally.


France's social revolt continued to spread and to change rapidly in nature as 100,000 strikers occupied dozens of factories in all parts of the country. In Paris, the Latin Quarter was like a war zone. The Peace Talks continued in ruffles and flourishes of hope and disappointment while Charles de Gaulle held his own talks on unrest. Who was it he thought he was speaking to? The strikes in his country continued to widen.

By Tuesday, May 21st, France was lost deep in the action of inaction as millions of people joined the strike. A state of panic and confusion took a firm grip on French society; money, food, and gasoline disappeared. Telephone lines were dead. Alain could not be reached; no matter how often Darling might try.

The task had fallen to Darling Randolph to write to David about Dieter's injuries. Darling procrastinated for a few days, until Miriam had seen Dieter and was settled in for the long haul. After Miriam's initial problems were taken care of, Darling reported the situation to David from the most positive viewpoint she could muster.

David telephoned Darling collect from Parris Island as soon as he received permission through proper channels. Darling was so glad to hear his voice. "I called Tina real quick. She's having a rough time herself right now, withdrawal and all. But Dad's looking out for her and Mom's just about taken over with Tommy. They're pretty happy."

"Oh, Dave. That's really good news. Has anyone heard anything more from Mrs. McKenzie?"

"Nah. Mrs. McKenzie doesn't give a damn about Dieter. I don't know why she's like she is, but she's just always been that way. She prob'ly cries the blues to all her gossipy soap-opera friends, but she's not gonna get on a bus and go down there and see 'im or anything."

"Guess I should be glad Mim's there for him."

"I can't believe she drove the whole way by herself."

"She did it. Like, I know she's not a Littleton but she sure could've fooled me when she pulled that stunt."

"She doin' okay?"

"Guess so. I think she's planning to stay down there. You know, 'til he's well."

"This sure is some bunch of Mickey Mouse shit we got ourselves in. You okay?"

"Yeah. I'm okay. Kinda got used to having everybody around though. It's so quiet here again. When are you gonna get a Leave?"

"Prob'ly get a few days when I finish up here. But I won't be sure about anything until it happens. God, Darling, there's guys that were graduating when I first started out here and they're dead already."

"I don't want you to go. You know that. We love you, Dave. You do know that, don't you?"

"It's good to know. Guys're waitin' t'use the phone. You take care of yourself, okay? And keep me posted on what's going on with the Dieter."

"You take care too. Let me know if you're gonna get home. We'll try and get together somehow."

"Outstanding. When you talk to Mim, be sure to tell her I love her, Dieter too."

"You got it. Bye..."

The toughening process of Marine Recruit training was definitely having its effect on David. David was there and he cared. But news such as Dieter's was something that fighting men were trained to accept as a part of their day to day duties.

David walked across the parade grounds. He was very glad to know that Dieter still had his legs. Silently, he prayed that his best friend would walk again someday. "God, for the days when we was driving buddies."

# CHAPTER 43

The French strike continued to expand until all of Europe was becoming uneasy. Federal troops invaded Columbia Hall after the New York police requested help in containing the mobs. The international search for Martin Luther King's killer carried on. President Johnson refused the diagnosis of a fatal sickness in our society.

'On Thursday, May 23rd Charles de Gaulle's regime was upheld and the vote of censure had failed. By that time, there were ten million people on strike. Some kind of a final warning was bull-horned to Columbia's rebelling students after 65 of their number were hurt during campus chaos. Students and police clashed again in the Latin Quarter of Paris. At the City of the Poor in Washington, the Reverend Ralph Abernathy began to urge whites to prod Congress to act. Blacks needed jobs and education and they were entitled to a life.

Darling Randolph worked hard at her studies. She had not paid much attention all semester. She continued to work for Gene McCarthy, but it was looking more and more like Bobby Kennedy was going to push anyone else right out of the running. Darling wrote to Paul that she had found a lovely dress to wear to his graduation, a sleeveless navy blue linen A-line with red and white trim and brass buttons. Aunt Maggie said she would be glad to take Darling from Pockseken as far as Bangor and put her on a commercial flight and maybe even fly out to Fort Sill herself. They would see how things went when the time drew nearer.

Miriam did not ask for medication for her nerves. She did not know that had she asked, it would gladly have been prescribed. But she did spend a considerable amount of time alone in the Post Chapel. She often spent entire nights sitting up staring at the wall of her little cottage. Her eyes never closed. In the morning she would be hard pressed to try to recount anything that passed before those glaring pupils. All she could remember was "the mottled sky" and "our-sun" and she wondered where within that helpless figure lay Dieter, the person, the poet.

Darling petted her cat and read incredible letters from Miriam in which Miriam poured out her adventure in great detail. Miriam felt that the morphine addiction was the least of their problems, and that when Dieter was well again they could attend to the business of getting over that hump. Miriam considered Dieter to be one of the "lucky ones" even though his weight had dropped to 95 pounds.

Prior to that time, and in many places at that time, the only solution to the problem with Dieter's legs was amputation. But that was why Dieter had been sent to Reynolds. At Reynolds, surgeons were attempting a new kind of surgical technique which would very soon be making a man named Evel Knievel famous (not for inventing it but for using it). It did not make any soldiers famous, but it did send some of them home walking on their own legs.

Well, at least they were mostly their own legs. The technique required surgeons to open up the legs, remove all the splinters and bone fragments from the muscle tissue into which they had become embedded and to line up the larger remaining fragments into something that vaguely resembled a femur. Then stainless-steel plates were implemented, each plate fourteen inches long, one-inch wide and one-quarter inch in thickness. The pieces of femur were attached to the steel plates by means of two-inch stainless-steel carpenter's screws, eleven screws for each femur. The completed procedure added one pound and seven ounces to Dieter's natural body weight, and reduced his natural height by just a hair short of an inch. No one minded at all. Dieter, if he was determined enough, would eventually walk.

Miriam was surprised to learn of Mrs. McKenzie's lack of concern for Dieter. Mrs. McKenzie never did write to her son. There was no telephone message from her. When Miriam asked Dieter about it he only responded, "She has other children."

The Esther Williams crew had done a good job. Darling stood at the diving board and gazed out across the vast green springtime of Arrowhead. The plunge. Naked breasts. Nipples ruched by the cold of sixty-degree water. Bright ripples of a clean dive, barely a splash. Laps. How many do you think you can do? Forty? Eighty? Eighty is a mile, give or take. Well, five, try five for starters. See if you can do five. Ugh. Too many cigarettes. Roll over onto your back and kick along. Relaxed. Remember when Mother used to swim with you on her back? Remember how the willows drooped all the way down until their fronds touched the water and how Mother swam and swam and you just hung on and felt the willows and the waters of the Rancocas go drifting by? How beautiful she was. That was before.

Before we moved into the big house. Before I was two, back when Mom and Dad were still so happy together. At least they seemed to be. But I don't remember Dad ever being there really. But Mother was happy. And she was very beautiful. Very beautiful.

Paul says he can remember when Dad used to tell him stories, read to him. Wish I could remember something like that. I just remember the arguments. No. Fights. They were fights, bad ones. But there was that time, that rainy old night when Dad came home so late and we were all so worried about him and he was so drunk, but he was in such a good mood that nobody minded, and he took that tiny puppy out of the inside of his raincoat and said, "What do you think we should name her?" We named her Lady and she was our partner in crime for seven years, Paul's and mine, for our very own, until she was shot by a trespassing hunter who thought our German Shepherd was a deer. Idiots. Why does it seem like there's a whole world full of them sometimes? Nine laps. God. That's awful.


One day, not too long after Dieter's big surgery (there would be many smaller ones), Miriam popped in to see Dieter and came upon two nurses engaged in the effort of rolling Dieter over a bit in order to get a clean draw-sheet under him. Miriam was in terrible pain just witnessing the ordeal. Dieter saw his girl and gratefully outstretched his hand to Miriam. His voice was straining and was barely more than a whisper. "Oh. I'm so glad you're here."

One by one Dieter's body functions came back to life. The surgery was successful in that each twenty-pound lead weight could be reduced to a six-pound lead weight attached by ace bandages instead of spikes through the knees. The bone fragments finally did begin to mend. Dieter began to make his own red blood cells. It was almost four full weeks after his arrival at Reynolds, but Dieter started taking clear chicken broth, one teaspoonful every hour or so. Amazingly, after that moment, progress was made in something that resembled giant steps compared to the way things had started out.

Miriam had presumed that as Dieter began to recover, the pain he was in would begin to subside. What she had not understood was that the scale of the pain was open-ended and of immeasurable magnitude. Dieter often lost his mind during the weeks that he lay in that bed, never to be fully recovered. The pain he was experiencing now was minor in comparison to the way he started out, but it was still far beyond anything that could be termed tolerable. His surgeon told Miriam that Dieter would become inured to the pain. Was that surgeon even human? Dieter was no longer getting that hour of sublime relief. His injections now only brought at best fifteen minutes of rest. The remainder of the time was only an interminable period of waiting.

When the day came to crank the bed up so that Dieter could be positioned at a forty-five-degree angle, Miriam got up the nerve to ask the doctor about the morphine. Together they asked Dieter if he thought he was ready to back off to Demerol. Dieter's response was, "Only if she'll marry me."

To Paul Randolph, his failure at jump school meant that he absolutely *had* to succeed at OCS. It was his last chance to prove himself to himself. David was definitely cutting the mustard, hacking it at Parris Island, shouting in unison with his platoon, "Semper Fi! Do or Die! Gung-ho! Gung-ho! Gung-ho!" Dieter expected to be shipped up to Minnesota, following in the path of Big Buddy Lake, or to one of the Army's several places of a similar nature, for psychological counseling, therapy for his drug dependency, and physiotherapy to help Dieter bend those knees that would not yet bend at all.

Miriam wrote that she was uncertain whether or not she would be going on to Minnesota, or wherever it turned out to be, with Dieter. She was very confused. Her temporary ID card would be expiring soon and unless she and Dieter actually did get married she would have no choice but to come home. But Miriam was also frightened. Dieter was having such an awful time weaning from the morphine. It often looked so hopeless. Still, there were only six weeks or so to go before the baby was due. If she married that baby's father, the Army would ensure she received the best care available.

Darling wrote to Miriam, "Do it. Do it now. Worry about the rest later." She did love him, didn't she? He was, underneath it all somewhere, still Dieter, wasn't he? And on the telephone, "Listen, Mim, I'll come out there for the ceremony if you want." Miriam smiled to herself, saying, "I want. I'm just not sure when I can do it. Somehow, I think I'll know when the time is right. He needs this waiting, though. Don't you see? It gives me something to, well, you know, threaten him with when he's acting up for his drugs. Maybe when we get away from here it'll be different. You know, different atmosphere and all."

Oh, jeez, thought Darling, she's gonna fool around until she gets sent home and that'll be the end of it. Oh, well, maybe she *will* come back and need the crib. Maybe she'll need *me*. "You know what's best, Mim. Just be careful will ya?"

# CHAPTER 44

McCarthy beat Kennedy in the Oregon primary. Bobby Kennedy announced that he would drop out of the race for the Democratic nomination if he did not garner a victory in the upcoming California primary. The Fast Attack Nuclear Submarine *USS Scorpion* with her 99-man crew was lost-at-sea 400 miles southwest of the Azores. A weak signal emanated for a time as she drifted toward the bottom, which was 10,000 feet deep. The nation waited and prayed. 99 stranded seamen waited and prayed. The sailors knew they were either going to suffocate or be crushed to death by the deep-sea water pressure. Most Americans only knew that we did not have the technology to save them.

The United States Senate finally released its hold on funds for the poor, which had long ago been requested by President Johnson. Perhaps the Senators had grown weary of trying to ignore the poverty and the squalor that continued to represent itself right before their eyes as the City of the Poor in Washington. The United States had much to be ashamed of.

Darling Randolph received an early birthday gift from Dieter and Miriam. With PX watercolors and some pieces of white hardboard, Dieter had created a world with two suns. It was a disturbing work showing a bamboo shed on stilts. Many high-fronded trees dominated the background. In the foreground there appeared the head of a soldier with earlobe-length hair beneath a camouflage baseball cap. The face in profile was breathing flames.

Tanks roamed the streets of Paris and French Labor chiefs sought new ways to end the strike. Then, suddenly, miraculously, on June 2nd the crowds began to disperse as all of Paris, all of a morning, drifted away into the tolling bells of the grand cathedrals and little churches. It was Pentecost.

Tuesday, June 4th 1968. A Tuesday not as costly as the human mind.

Voter turnout in the California and South Dakota primaries was expected to be heavy. Andy Warhol lay gravely wounded, shot in the chest by a woman scorned while working in his "Factory" at 33 Union Square West. Bloody riots erupted near Belgrade, Yugoslavia where students seized a building at Belgrade University and were shouting down Tito's communist presidency.

It was almost 3 a.m. on Wednesday in New Jersey when the results of the California primary declared victory for Bobby Kennedy. Darling Randolph started jumping up and down and laughing out loud. Balzac was unimpressed. His dinner was late. "Okay, okay. Just wait a minute." Darling watched with happy excited tears in her eyes and her car keys flopping back and forth over the top of her hand as a beaming triumphant Robert Francis Kennedy left the podium in the ballroom of the Ambassador Hotel in Los Angeles just after midnight California time.

Darling jumped down the back-porch steps and threw the Mustang into reverse for a quick trip to get a can of tuna for poor old patient Balzac. She was out-of-her-mind excited as she drove down the lane. Kennedy was going to make it. Surely, we were on our way to having free milk for hungry children everywhere, and to getting the hell out of Vietnam. She peeled out at the end of the lane and barreled up to the top of the mount with the bright image of that rowdy rumple-haired good-looking son-of-a-bitch as he smiled and grinned and waved. Life hadn't looked this good in as long as she could remember. "...**So my thanks to all of you and on to Chicago and let's win there.**"

Aunt Maggie was due to arrive at 7:30 in the morning. In just a few hours Darling would be winging away to Pockseken with Balzac and Aunt Maggie in the Beechcraft. Darling would be filling Aunt Maggie in on so many things. Her stomach churned to think of it all. Penn and her plans for the future. Miriam and Dieter were to be married in the Post Chapel at Fort Sill. Dieter would still be in a wheel chair with his legs sticking straight out in front of him but nobody minded, and then the newlyweds would fly to the Veteran's Rehabilitation Center at Menlo Park, California where Miriam planned to lease an apartment for them. The situation sounded just as close to ideal as it could possibly be under their exceptional circumstances. Darling thought she might wear the pink cotton gauze sundress for that ceremony. Well, maybe the yellow one. "Yes, the yellow one."

Darling glanced quickly left-right-left at the top of the mount, out of habit really for there was not another soul in sight. She hung a left at the old oak tree then sped into the mists of the wee hours. She accelerated as she anticipated that little rise where she would fly across with all four wheels off the ground, the Mustang airborne, and lose her stomach just like always. The speed made a warm summer wind that whipped her hair far out behind her, red-gold against the night. She laughed and shouted, "God we won!" as she banged the steering wheel with the flat of her hand. "God, how great this is gonna be!"

As the Mustang approached the magic speed of 87 mph, the steering began to jiggle. Darling suspected it might be either a low tire or the alignment, seemed like driver's front might be pulling. It couldn't be a flat because there was no hard pull, but she passed up her chance to go flying over the little rise and coasted to a stop in the dip just after it. She stepped out of the Mustang and walked around examining all the tires. "Nothin'. Must be the steering. Not good." The night air felt so cool and moist, and the moonlight was so fine and the stars looked so far away. Darling slid back into the driver's seat. "Who am I gonna get to fix it?" She closed the door and slipped the gearshift out of park and took her foot off the brake. Her foot had not yet touched the accelerator when a speeding Cadillac loaded with laughing GIs appeared at the top of the little rise.

Darling barely had time to see the headlights in her rear-view mirror; barely time for a thought when time stood perfectly still. The impact sent her head up nearly yanking her body completely out of the seat so that the articulated convertible top sliced off a substantial part of her scalp leaving the red-gold hair behind as the crumpling rear of the Mustang pinned her fast behind the wheel. The Cadillac veered off to the right, hit a pole and caught fire. By the time the young soldiers got out of their burning car, Darling's body had been whipped back and forth, back and forth, back and forth so that the sun visor gashed the top of her forehead, so that her face smashed right straight through the windshield then was pulled back through as her body was thrown back again and a bit of crumpled metal punctured her left kidney. A spring from the seat lacerated her right shoulder down to the bone. Back and forth, back and forth. And again, as her face broke the steering wheel in half shoving the mandible of her left jaw into her brain. The ongoing momentum of the impact projected the Mustang across the road and straight into the roadside berm of a cornfield. That second impact ejected Darling over the hood of the Mustang and slammed what was left of her into the warm soft Earth where it landed with a dull thud. Darling was already gone, but that thing that had been her Earthly host lay amidst the cornstalks enshrouded by drifting mists. The gray-blue eyes were fixed and seemed to be gazing upon the stars. The soldiers fled on foot across the fields and toward the highway. They evaded arrest for almost fifteen hours before the MPs knocked on a door of the Sandpiper Motel in Bordentown and led them all away to the stockade.

A small transistor radio is blaring. The vigil for Robert Kennedy's life has begun. An emergency room physician lightly lifts the edge of a bloody sheet then drops it. "I'm pretty sure it's a Randolph. It's Darling Randolph." The staff hesitates for only a moment then returns their attention to their duties. There are more important matters to attend to, the living.

Darling's body went cold in the morgue for five hours by the time the New Jersey State Troopers finally reached someone, anyone, who could come. Mark Cymrot showered and shaved and drove from his home in Princeton to Memorial Hospital to make the positive identification. It was, and was not, a difficult task.

The well-turned ankles were undoubtedly those of Darling Randolph. The red-gold hair that spilled over the edge of the slab, tangled and matted with dirt and dried blood though it was, could only belong to Darling Randolph. Mark Cymrot knew, and even as he did not wish to know anymore, the magnificent head of a lioness lay unrecognizable. Cause of Death... Massive Cerebral Hemorrhage... They said she never knew what hit her, but Mark would always wonder. He telephoned Margaret DeLamar who gave him instructions for disposition of the remains.

# CHAPTER 45

A mile of limousines, Hot Rods, Harleys, Triumphs, and BSAs created a stream of silver-studded ribbon candy as the funeral wound its way from Martingale Chapels to the ancient cemetery at the top of the mount. After the flowers and the final words and after everyone who was going to had repaired to Arrowhead for refreshments, Paul stood alone at the graveside. He stood waiting for the crane to come along and lower the lid onto the vault. He stood alone beneath the lacework fingers and heart-shaped leaves of a very old silver birch tree.

Paul removed a rose from a spray without a card, only he and Darling knew who had arranged for the white spider mums and red roses. He stooped down and leaned far into the grave. The sleeve of his uniform brushed against the broken and exposed roots of the birch tree. Paul prayed that the beautiful tree would recover from the shock. Darling would have liked that tree. Paul placed the rose on the vault and waited there for a long time. He reminded himself of what Darling had said to him only the day before. Paul had awakened, startled out of his anguish. He was strapped into his seat on the airplane but his mind was desperately engaged in images of fleshless bone and gaping jagged wounds, the horror of what must have been left of her face. They would not let him see her. He would never be able to touch her again. The funeral director had told Paul on the telephone, "We will try to close the eyes. We will try to close the mouth."

Paul wrenched in his seat in agony. The voice of his mind was crying out, "Poor Darling. Poor Darling." It was at that moment that she came to him, or more rightly took him to her. Darling's unmistakable presence settled over him. It was light and warm and billowing and almost smothering and it brought Paul into a place of indescribable quietude, yearning and erotic. "Don't think of me that way, Paul. Think of me as I am now." It was *she* who felt sorry for *him*. The ear of Paul's mind listened obediently and the image of his mind's eye did change. It changed immediately to the way she was now, soft, floating, drifting free along dense waves of a deep mist, busy in the absorption of the hereafter. Bravely, hesitantly, and fearfully his mind's voice asked, "How is it?"

A frightening silence. Loss of contact? Then. "It's all right. It takes a little getting used to, but it's all right." And then she let him go. He woke up. He was still on a plane. He gazed through the window and into the clouds. Nothing. It was over. She was gone.

Finally, it was time to leave her there. Alone. The truck would not be along to fill the dirt in for an hour or so. There was nothing else he could do. Nothing was ever going to bring her back to him. Nothing. And if he stayed there for another hour, he might not ever go back. Surely, he did not want to. Paul wanted never to go back into the world of the living, the damned. Paul knew that if he stayed there much longer he would most probably sink deeper and deeper into the realm of the living dead. Insanity. The insanity of it all.


Parties at Arrowhead always separated into two groups. The young people hung around by the garages and the barns while the older generations stayed comfortably indoors. Paul wandered aimlessly through a magnificent parking jumble of antique and classic cars, hogs, choppers, and limos toward the crowds of young people who were drinking beer, smoking cigarettes and passing joints. The blow-by-blow of the Kennedy funeral was coming from one of the car radios.

Paul had never met Rita but he was pretty sure she was the one in the black silk shirtwaist and the thick black wings on her eyelids. Paul remembered Darling's eyelids, how they were naturally lavender-blue. He guessed the half-dozen slender pairs of legs belonged to Rita's models since they all seemed to hover near Rita like chicks around their mother hen. Once in a while one of the bikers would make a clumsy but endearing attempt to enter their circle. But the girls were only interested in hanging out with one another and with exchanging glances with the clean-cuts, each of whom hung out near his own Rod with his racing buddy. Paul knew that attitudes would improve and that everybody would get loose once they were properly lubricated.

Paul turned his attention to a young woman who carried a little boy who looked to be eight or ten months old on her hip and who introduced herself as Karen Doyle. Karen burst into tears. "I'm so sorry. You just don't know. Darling helped me write so many letters to try to find out what's happened to Billy. Congressmen. Senators. The President. Anything to try and get him out. This is little Billy, Paul." Paul smiled and put his hand out to shake but little Billy looked shyly down with his big brown eyes. Karen Doyle smiled softly, wiping her tears, saying, "I'm so sorry," and returned to the company of Tina Adams and little Tommy Moffett who sat on the soft green grass laughing together and playing with a big red ball. They were sitting at the feet of an Army Sergeant who had a pair of crutches resting against an oddly positioned wheelchair. Paul was trying to place the man in uniform when from over his shoulder Paul heard a jolly voice. "Hi. You must be Paul." Paul turned to see a big-boned woman with green eyes and long glossy black hair. "And I'll bet you're Lois Guy." Paul glanced in the direction of a naked eighteen-month old boy who was peeing up against the barn. "And his little self over there must be Matthew Broward Guy the Fourth. You came down from New Haven?"

"Oh. Had to."

"Thanks. It's really comforting to know Darling had so many people who loved her. I noticed your flowers. Gorgeous. All purple. So passionate. So like my sister. It was very kind of all of you. Listen, have you had anything to drink yet? You can help yourself here, or there's another party going on inside, a bit more refined libation."

"Thanks. We're not gonna hang around. But we did want to offer our condolences."

"I appreciate that. I know your friendship meant a great deal to my sister."

Dieter didn't give Paul time to get caught up again in the crowd. Between the heat and the pain, Dieter was struggling to hang in there as it was. So, slowly, painfully, and with enormous determination, Dieter maneuvered himself from his chair up onto his crutches and approached Paul. Dieter's crutches crunched deeply through the gravel as he moved with firm intention toward Paul in his newly mastered swing-to and swing-through gait. He carefully balanced himself and held his hand out to the man he had never met. Paul took the proffered hand. It was so frail and yet so strong. "Dieter McKenzie."

"Ah, finally I meet Mim's famous Dieter. Goddammit. How'arya buddy?"

"Pissed, you know?"

Together Paul and Dieter shared the sky that was clear and blue now with just a hint of the humid haze that would thicken as the afternoon wore on. "I left a message for ol' Davie. Hope the news doesn't kill 'im. It really has me worried. My God, he was in love with that woman." Paul stuffed his hands deep into his pockets. He shuffled his toes along the river rock and stared into it as if it mattered. How many times had they walked across that drive together, heard its crunching as the only noise on a deep dark night of working on the Merc, laughing and speaking in low tones, keeping the radio at low volume, not to disturb Mom and Dad? "Ouch! Another knuckle with no skin on it."

"Is it bleeding?"

Paul regained himself and said, "That's for sure. But then, just about everybody was. Me too. Mmm. Me first, I guess." He stopped it. He smiled faintly. He changed the subject, "Like your button. When'd you get that?"

Dieter pulled his lapel up and brushed his cheek gently with the pink button that announced **IT'S A GIRL!** "Out of uniform, right?" He chuckled warmly, "Oh, man, just as soon as we heard the news. WHAM! Mim went right into labor, hard. It was a big mad scramble there for a while. We thought we had at least another month. Said, 'I Do' in the labor room." Paul smiled softly, painfully, "Congratulations! Twice! Everybody okay?"

Dieter felt almost uncomfortable with his happiness, but he could not help smiling proudly, "Yeah, yeah, they're okay. They're gonna be all right, just fine. Mim's pretty down about this, but then she gets happy when they bring the baby to her. Her name is Faith."

"Yeah? Darling would like that. I know she was really looking forward to the wedding."

"Such a day for a little child to come into the world. But it was happy, Paul. Maybe it doesn't sound right, but it was. And she *was* there. We both just knew she was there. And we were happy in knowing that. Yeah. Faith Darling Randolph McKenzie."

Paul looked at Dieter with his eyebrows thoroughly knitted together, hurt and confused, proud and questioning. He knew, in fact he intended to make certain, that innocent baby Faith would receive the benefits of that title. Dieter's feet were turning purple inside his shoes. He knew he should be back in his chair but he did not complain. As he began his painful return, slowly swinging-to and then swinging-through, Dieter simply said, "Your sister went to Heaven so fast that she prob'ly crashed the gates."

Paul smiled that gentle upside-down smile of his, and paced himself alongside Dieter as he struggled without complaint. "I know it isn't easy for you, man. I'm so sorry this had to happen. I really am. But I am more grateful than you will ever know that you could be here."

"Hey. I'm trying to be standin' on my own two feet, you know? And I got to hold my newborn daughter yesterday. A lotta guys didn't make it, you know? Besides, I've got my Miriam now. And that's all I ever really wanted. And now we have our little Faith. She's mighty pretty too."

"I'll bet she is. I'm gonna have to get to know her, when I get back and all. Right now, I'm just really glad you could be here, and I hate like hell to do it, but I've gotta go in there for a while. Have a beer for me, will ya? I won't be gone long, I promise."

"No sweat. Besides, looks to me like we got reinforcements. Marines." Dieter gestured with his eyes toward the poplar trees. Paul turned to see the cherry red 1953 Mercury pulling into Darling's empty parking spot. Private

David Campbell Adams jumped out of the car and headed straight toward Dieter and Paul. His Service Utility Browns blended nicely with their green Class-As. "Sorry I couldn't get here earlier. Goddamned train sure took its fuckin' time."

The men shook hands. "Well, you're here now buddy. Good to see you."

Dieter looked at both men. Neither of them knew yet what they were on their way to. Dieter knew. And he knew that if he did not get off his legs right now, he would collapse. Not strack.

David grinned as Tommy Moffett came bounding over to him. He picked his son up from the ground with a strong hug. Dieter hoped he would be able to do that someday; lift his child into his arms. Maybe. "Hey Davie. Paul's got to go in there, do his thing and all. How 'bout a beer."

"Don't mind if I do." The two men and a boy headed slowly and painfully back toward the intimate circle with its wheelchair. Tina had already popped the caps off two cold bottles of *Miller High Life*. She and David were positioning Dieter in his chair with his reconstructed legs sticking straight out in front of him, David saying, "We should move him into the shade." Paul took a deep breath and a quick look at the Merc. "How the hell did he do that?" He opened the door.

Inside the house, familiar faces were gathered. This was family business, all of them speaking in low tones, one to the other. The television was flickering away with the monochromatic portraits of a devastated family, flashbacks of a slow-moving train and swarms of people pouring onto the tracks. A news flash broke into the televised funeral. Scotland Yard had just apprehended one James Earle Ray, the alleged assassin of the Reverend Dr. Martin Luther King, Jr., at London's Heathrow Airport. The screen flashed back to Robert Kennedy's funeral, to pregnant Ethel and all 10 of his little children.

Aunt Maggie was circulating among the Randolphs and the Littletons, family members who rarely saw one another except at weddings and funerals. Maggie was dressed tastefully as usual. She had been very fond of her niece and attended in a black linen dress with a wide white linen collar. The dress's generous skirt reached almost to her ankles, perfect for mourning in all this June heat. Hannah wore a tight black suit and sniffled as she made her way about the rooms with a silver tray dutifully offering everyone some refreshment. Aunt Maggie was softly saying over and over again, "Thank you for coming. Good to see you. Oh, Tyndal, I didn't see you at the cemetery, so glad you could make it."

Maggie was glad to see Paul. She hugged him not so hard as she might have liked, but they were in public. She told Paul she had not recognized any of the young people who hung around outside and that she was counting on him to take care of all that. "I'm so glad you managed to get away."

"Got 'til reveille tomorrow morning."

Maggie raised a finger in the air slightly as if she had just remembered something. "The cat, Paul. Do you think you can help? He simply will not come out of the bottom of Darling's closet. I've tried everything. And he won't eat. He's just sitting in there looking so frightened."

"'Zac? Sure thing Auntie."

Then Maggie handed Darling's black leather address book to Paul. "And you'd better hang on to this. I've used it to contact everyone. But I think that from now on it should be for your eyes only. Most of the names are in the funeral registry. I'll send the Thank-You notes from the registry."

The pages of the book were well thumbed and thickened with scribbles. Paul flipped through those pages, quickly, randomly, glancing at names. Darling's handwriting. Oh, man. This hurts. Then Paul came upon a page, a page somewhere near the middle of the book. He had to stop there and read it again, and then he laughed with tears into his sleeve. "Why, that little shit-head!" He had to stop when he came upon the page that read:

## FUCK YOU FOR READING THIS

Paul tucked the address book into his inside breast pocket. "I see what you mean." Then he approached the staircase. Yes. It was a long climb to the top of those stairs.

Paul lifted the cat out of the closet, "Come on, 'Zac." Balzac didn't hiss at Paul as he had at Hannah and Maggie nor did he attempt to scratch Paul as he had done to Hannah and to Maggie. "Darling's gone away for a while. You're gonna have to go home with Aunt Maggie. But for now, you can come with me. It'll be all right. You'll see. These people will all be gone in a little while." Paul closed the door behind him as he went back downstairs with the cat in his arms.

As Paul made his way through the living room he noticed a frail little brown woman seated alone in one corner of the room. Paul didn't recognize her. He introduced himself. "Hello, Ma'am. I'm Paul Randolph, Darling's brother. Were you a friend of my sister's?"

Mrs. Killian's milky eyes looked up to Paul. "Oh, yes, yes. Elizabeth Killian. And you look just like her too. Yes. Darling was a good friend to me. She's been driving me to my physical therapy sessions. Twice a week since I had my stroke. I'm much improved. We had the loveliest chats. Darling always enjoyed hearing about the old days when I was a girl."

"I'm very glad you could be here, Mrs. Killian. I'm sure you must've had some whoppers to keep the attention of that sister o' mine."

Mrs. Killian's eyes drooped. "I'll miss her." Paul continued to pet the cat, getting long tabby cat hairs all over his jacket. He said, "We'll all miss her, Mrs. Killian. We'll miss her very much. Funny. I keep expecting her to come bouncing through that door. If I didn't know better. If you'll just excuse me. I've got to attend to our 'Zac, here. He's not taking it very well either. I'll get Hannah to bring you something cool to drink. If you'll excuse me."

"Certainly. You are a nice young man."

Paul thought again, "Have you a ride home?"

"Oh, yes. Pastor Wagstaff's son is going to take me home. He's out there with the young people. He told me he was always sweet on Darling even though she was a year or so older."

"Yes," Paul smirked, "There were a few of those."

Mrs. Killian turned her attention back to the TV. "Isn't it awful about our poor Mr. Kennedy? And Darling was so hoping he would win the election. Do you think she knew, well, of course, not that he died, but that he was shot?"

Paul absentmindedly said, "I hope not." He bowed a little in Mrs. Killian's direction and carried Balzac into the kitchen where he retrieved a can of shredded tuna, a spoon, and a clean china plate. Then he took Balzac and his dinner into his room and closed the door.

Paul turned on the black light in his closet and spooned Balzac's dinner onto the plate. "God, this stuff stinks!" Balzac sniffed at the food, which was a start, but turned away and jumped up onto Paul's big old bed and curled himself up in the center of the covers. What he wanted was Darling and he could wait.

Paul removed his jacket, loosened his tie, and rolled up his sleeves. He set to work opening the windows of his room and putting one speaker in front of each window. Then he went about loading up the spool of *Darling's Selections*. Just as he was about to hit the PLAY switch, Paul noticed a record album lying on top of the turntable cover. He picked it up and looked at it. "Tchaikovsky? Wonder when she was playing this." It was only a moment before something greater than Paul removed the record from its sleeve and set the needle gently in its groove and let the music play: *Allegro con spirito*.

# EPILOGUE

The troop strength in Vietnam continued to hover around 543,000 until January of 1969, just before Richard Milhous Nixon received the Oath of Office as the thirty-seventh president of the United States. Three months later the numbers began to decline and by January of 1972 the number of American Soldiers in Vietnam was down to 139,000. The year after Nixon's re-election in November of '72, the last of the living finally arrived home, not to cheering crowds of welcome but to a miasma of painful recollection, just in time for the holidays. None of them was Billy Doyle.

On January 22nd, 1977 President Jimmy Carter issued an Executive Order granting pardons to all deserters and draft evaders of the Vietnam War Era.

Negotiations continue to this day in an effort to learn the whereabouts of Americans who are still listed as Missing-in-Action or Prisoners of War.

# ABOUT THE AUTHOR

Miriam Katherine MacFarland was born in Trenton and raised in South Jersey and Washington D.C. with a generous San Antonio influence. An unmarried mother much too young, Mimi applied her writing and mathematical skills to succeed, ultimately at the highest levels of the computer sciences, including a stint with NASA, while writing poetry and fiction and fulfilling the responsibilities of a single parent. In 1981, she combined those skills to become the Founder & CEO of Mimi MacFarland LLC, which has long been among the most trusted names in technical writing.

In addition to her published contributions to multiple agencies of the United States federal government, the United Nations, the World Bank, and many Fortune 500 companies, Mimi MacFarland's byline publications have continued to appear in print and on-air by fits and starts for many years.

*CONTACT/II*, *The Bloomsbury Review*, *Another Chicago Magazine*, and *Renovated Lighthouse* are among the literary magazines to have published poetry, essays, stories, and literary and theatre reviews. Mimi's articles, "Water Rights: Native America and the Bureaucrats" and "Sacred Ground: Native American Land Rights" were featured in *High Times Magazine*.

Mimi has taught English Literature and Writing at Long Island, Cameron, and Rider Universities.

www.ingramcontent.com/pod-product-compliance
Lightning Source LLC
Chambersburg PA
CBHW021028130626
46552CB00005B/1742